THE STARS OVER BITTERGATE BAY

EMILIA LEE

For Alex & Scott

1

The cab driver let out a low whistle, and Sidney opened his eyes as they pulled up to the curb in front of Sidney's residence.

Kilton House was a century old brick building, currently crawling with co-eds. Never mind that it was a frigid October night. And a Wednesday. Sidney closed his eyes again and barely managed to bite back a groan. He pressed his temple against the cool glass of the window. It had already been a rough day, and he was determined not to let it get any worse.

"Looks like a party," the cab driver observed.

"Yes." Sidney sighed as another group of students jostled their way into the house. "It certainly does."

Sidney paid the driver and then, hands tucked in the pockets of his peacoat, Sidney bowed his head and waded through the crowd into the house. He'd walked out of dinner with his father and brother before the entrees had made it to the table, so the kitchen was his destination. There was a good block of aged cheddar in the shared refrigerator with his name on it. If only he could get there without getting a beer spilled on him.

Music blared out of the Victrola, shaking the photographs of the past rosters of the Holyworth Heroes, the college's football team. That Sidney had gotten stuck as the Resident Faculty Advisor for this year's roster seemed like a cosmic joke. One his father had delighted in pointing out.

"You never had much muscle, but Leo was a great quarterback," his father had said as the breadbasket arrived at their table, clapping Sidney's brother on the shoulder. "Maybe he could show your boys a few things." Leo looked apologetic, and had opened his mouth to protest, but Sidney beat him to the punch.

"They're not 'my boys,' Dad. They're students."

And maybe it was true that because Sidney was slight and young he blended in with the students, even though he hadn't been one for several years. The other Resident Faculty Advisors who lived on campus were over-zealous, matronly dorm mothers. Or former college athletes past their prime, trying to relive their glory days by hanging around with freshmen. Sidney was neither. He'd taken the position specifically, almost explicitly, for the stipend and for the dormer room at Kilton House. The take-home pay for an Astronomy lecturer, even at an expensive school like Holyworth, was not really enough to make ends meet.

In the corner of the living room, two students, Charlie Kinsey, an amiable fullback, and Gregor Wambeck, defensive tight end, leaned toward each other whispering, eyes wide at the sight of Sidney. Clearly, the thought that their Resident Faculty Advisor might return home during the party hadn't occurred to them.

Charlie passed Gregor a lit blunt, and Gregor shoved the whole thing into his pocket with absolutely no subtlety, their eyes fixed on Sidney. Sidney turned away to hide a smirk, the first genuine spark of joy he'd had all night.

Sidney had no interest in spoiling anyone's fun, but he did

have a doctoral dissertation to work on. He didn't mind festivities, so long as the house stayed reasonably in order, and no one messed with his things.

The crowd in the kitchen he did mind, though. Sidney grit his teeth and began to wind through them, his thoughts already upstairs with his star charts.

The star cluster wouldn't be up for another hour at least, but he could do some pre-charting. He'd been following it long enough, that predicting its movements was beginning to feel easy. He was hoping to make it the centerpiece of his impending dissertation.

Sidney was of two primary thoughts about his star cluster, which he'd begun to take ownership of when he realized that no other charts or books contained any record of it. The first was that it was a unique discovery and was therefore incredibly exciting. The second was that it shouldn't exist.

It wasn't a small cluster. It wasn't massive. Sydney wasn't even sure if they were stars. But someone should have seen it, and no one else had. This made Sidney even more determined to track it. What was the damn thing? If he hadn't seen it so regularly, he might have assumed it was a hallucination brought on by stress and lack of a decent meal.

"Hey Professor!" Charlie had managed to shoulder through the crowd in record time and was standing at Sidney's side like an overgrown golden retriever. "Sorry about all this crowd. Just a little celebration. We beat Rutledge today."

"As long as no one's eaten the last of my sourdough there's not a problem," Sidney said sincerely.

"Jack and the others went down to the mess to get some more food." Charlie followed dutifully behind Sidney. Was there a tactful way to ask him to go first and clear a path like some kind of a human cowcatcher? "They'll be back soon!"

"I just need my bread and cheese and I'll be fine." Sidney's stipend was small, and he wasn't about to waste his own money on good food that would be devoured in seconds by a horde of drunk football players. He should have taken his sourdough up to his room with him; it was probably already soaking up cheap beer in someone else's stomach, when it could have been soaking up scotch in his.

"You're not going upstairs already, are you?" Charlie cajoled. Sidney paused.

Being invited to stay at the party was the most suspicious thing that had happened to him that day, and the day had started with Sidney's father's campaign manager calling to ask him to have dinner. Sidney hadn't spoken to his father since Christmas; the man had forgotten Sidney's birthday three-months ago, and when Sidney had taken the call, it was really only because he thought his father might have died. The invitation to a steak dinner was suspicious. But Charlie Kinsey asking Sidney to stay at a football party was even moreso.

Sidney narrowed his eyes, but he didn't bother looking back at Charlie. He continued forward, shooing two sophomore girls out of his way.

"The stars aren't going to chart themselves." Sidney pulled open the door to the fridge and shuffled things around until he could reach his drawer without knocking over the uncovered stockpot of week-old pasta. Relief at discovering his block of cheddar exactly where he left it was somewhat tempered by the further discovery that it was considerably lighter than it had been the day before. Sidney scowled at the cheese in his hand. When he closed the fridge Charlie was still beside him, holding out all that remained of Sidney's sourdough. Little more than a heel. Damn.

"I was thinking about taking Astronomy next semester," Charlie said. Sidney blinked at him. What on earth was going on?

"Oh?"

"Yeah, I've always been curious about space. What's up there, you know?"

"What, indeed." It was a little funny that even though it was utter nonsense, Charlie had hit on the exact same question that had been preoccupying Sidney. Sidney took the sourdough from Charlie's outstretched hand. "Well, I'll be teaching a couple of 100 level classes next semester. I'll be sure to get you on the roster if you're interested." And with that, Sidney turned and headed up to his room where he could eat in peace before he climbed up on the roof to chart his stars.

Or he would have if, just as he reached the servant's stairs in the back corner of the kitchen, a hand as heavy as a honey-baked ham hadn't landed on his shoulder.

"Wait. Professor—" Sidney whipped around and came up short. Charlie was looming, his frame twice as wide as Sidney's, his mouth a crumple of worry.

"Charlie, not to be rude, but what the fuck is going on?"

"Nothing!" Charlie said too quickly. Sidney sighed.

"You're very bad at lying."

"Stay and have a drink."

Charlie's eyes were wide and imploring and Sidney found his own narrowing again, as he pushed his hair back off his forehead and tried to understand what was happening. Was Charlie coming onto him?

Aside from the fact that Sidney was at least six years older than Charlie and they had literally nothing in common aside from the fact that they both lived in the same house, Sidney would never sleep with a student. He valued his shot at tenure too much. A research position was right around the corner, he was certain of it. And life was certainly hard enough as it was without involving anyone else.

"Where's Jack?" Sidney asked. Jack, the captain of the football team, could generally be relied upon to keep the others in line. His absence and Charlie's strange attempts at chumminess were almost certainly aligned.

"He's... around."

"I thought you said he was at the mess hall?" Sidney said, feeling triumphant and apprehensive both at once. Charlie hesitated and Sidney sighed. "Charlie..."

"He's upstairs."

"Upstairs where?"

"Your room."

Sidney shoved the bread and cheese in his coat pockets and took the back staircase two at a time. Charlie thundered up behind him without offering any further explanation.

Sidney's room was at the top of the house. The dormer sat on the fifth level, bookended by attic space on both sides, with a northeast facing window and widow's walk that pointed away from the bright lights of Bainbridge to the southwest. Aside from the Astronomy building, it was, by far, the best place for looking at stars on campus. It was quiet. Even the roaring sounds of the party down below faded away and instead Sidney could hear, from behind his own closed door, the sounds of metal and glass clacking discordantly together.

When Sidney yanked open his bedroom door, he was met with the well-muscled back of Jack Brewer, barely masked behind a straining white button-down shirt. The young man was crouched beside one of his teammates, and they were both hunched over something on Sidney's floor. Sidney cleared his throat.

"Professor!" Jack spun to face Sidney. They were of a height, though Jack's musculature made him considerably larger than Sidney. Still, Sidney crossed his arms over his chest and tried to look his most officious.

"Jack, what in the hell is going on?" Jack's gleaming white

smile slid off his face, and his eyes darted over Sidney's shoulder to Charlie.

"Ah. Well…"

"At the start of semester, I expressly stated that under no circumstances was anyone allowed in my room without my—"

Sidney pushed past him through the narrow doorway into the room, where a shattered telescope lay in the center of the floor.

"I'M SORRY, PROFESSOR!" JACK WAS EASILY KEEPING PACE WITH Sidney, which was annoying as Sidney was trying very hard to storm off.

"'Sorry' doesn't fix my telescope, Jack," Sidney snapped, doing his best to push through the crowd, which had somehow thickened in the past ten minutes. Jack managed to get in front of Sidney and began cutting a swath through the party goers.

"They've already said they'll cover the cost."

"Damn right they will." Sidney certainly didn't have the two-hundred dollars a new telescope would cost. And it wasn't as though he could ask his father for money to make up the difference.

"It's my fault. I asked them to get—"

Sidney was fuming and not listening to the explanation he'd already heard once upstairs. But also his rage didn't matter because the telescope was already broken and if he wanted to chart his stars, which was all he had wanted to do that night in the first place, he didn't have time to fix it.

Being angry or upset was useless and he didn't have time for useless things. He would just go back to the Astronomy building and get a new telescope. A cold gust of wind whipped up as Jack opened the front door for Sidney.

"Clear these people out, Jack." It was as close as Sidney could get to retribution. And really, it was what he should have done in the first place. Jack nodded grimly, as though Sidney had told him it would be pistols at dawn.

"You've got it." It was irritating that he was genuinely sorry. But then, yelling at someone was never as satisfying as Sidney wanted it to be. He was better at storming off. Twice in one night at this point. He wished he could say it was a new record.

But none of that really bore thinking about. Sidney needed to run to get across campus, get a telescope, and get back in time to chart his star cluster. And he needed to eat.

"Do you want to borrow my bike?" Jack offered. Sidney clenched his fist around the heel of sourdough in his pocket.

"Please."

2

By the time Jack had returned with his bike, Sidney had eaten the last of his sourdough and had taken several large bites of cheese straight off the block. When he got off the bike at the entrance to the astronomy building, his stomach hurt, but he didn't have enough time for the slowest elevator on campus to take him up to the third floor where faculty offices and the equipment room were located.

Panting and with a stitch in his side, Sidney heaved himself into the cluster of offices that the adjunct lecturers shared. Hanging on the wall beside the light switch was a hook. An empty hook. The key to the equipment closet was missing. It wasn't possible for his night to get any worse.

"Fuck," Sidney groaned, his eyes scanning the clipboard where people were supposed to sign the key out and in. Unsurprisingly, it had not been signed out.

"Sidney?" A head of brown curly hair poked out of one of the open office doors. Bodie Thomsen, Sidney's occasional officemate, pushed his glasses up onto his nose.

"Bodie," Sidney sighed. "Thank God. Where's the key for equipment storage?"

"Oh, Mars probably has it."

"Mars?" Sidney wrinkled his nose. "Who in the hell is Mars?" Bodie blushed.

"Mark. Professor Heaney. He goes by Mars now." Christ. Sidney had to fight the urge to gag. He had been avoiding Mark since the beginning of term, and this was exactly the sort of reason why. Sidney breathed out through his nose and blinked at Bodie, who answered in a rush. "He's with a 102 class in the observation hall. It's a practicum night."

"Thanks, Bodie," Sidney managed before he turned and walked back out into the hall. He had one flight of stairs and half the length of the building to compose himself. First his father, now Mark. Maybe Satan himself would be waiting for him at Kilton House when Sidney returned. Apparently, anything was possible, so long as it made Sidney's life horrible.

Mark was standing at the back of the observation hall, too close to a student who couldn't have possibly been more than a sophomore. Mark Heaney's dark hair was slicked to the side, tortoise shell spectacles perched on his nose, tweed jacket straining over his broad shoulders. Sidney watched as Mark leaned toward the student, brushing her arm as he pointed something out to her on the star chart. As he pointed up to the sky, Sidney could see the edge of a tattoo on his wrist and did his best to swallow down the bitterness crawling up his throat.

"Mark," Sidney said from the doorway. They were no more than four feet away, the dark classroom lit by stars from the glass roof and the small, dim lamps the students were taking notes by. Mark did not respond. Sidney sighed. "Mark!"

The student Mark was talking to looked over Mark's shoulder, arching an eyebrow at Sidney.

"Mars." She nudged Mark in the elbow, and Mark finally turned toward him.

"Oh, Sidney!" His smile was more like a smirk, one eyebrow arched up to his hairline. Mark stepped close enough that Sidney could smell the overpowering vanilla cologne he preferred. He wore his shirt without a tie, the top two buttons open at the throat, a star chart tattoo visible across the top of Mark's chest.

The tattoo was real, though it wasn't accurate, and Sidney had been more than a little disappointed to discover that it was possibly the only real thing about Mark Heaney.

"You have the key to the equipment room." Sidney held out his hand for the key in lieu of asking. Mark patted down his trouser pockets.

"It's around here somewhere," he turned back to the podium where a stack of papers sat. "How are you?" he asked as he began to shift things around with no urgency. "I haven't seen you around much."

"I've been busy."

"How was your trip? Falklands, right?"

"Menelaus," Sidney sighed. Wrong body of water. Wrong part of the planet. Another student came up to the podium and Mark immediately got distracted. Sidney bit his tongue. "Mark, I'm kind of in a rush."

"It's Mars now," Mark corrected, as he held the keys aloft and struck a triumphant pose. Two students clapped. Sidney tasted regurgitated sourdough. "I visited a shaman over the summer, and she renamed me."

"Shame she couldn't relabel your tattoos for you too," Sidney muttered.

"What?"

"Nothing," Sidney said, taking the keys from his outstretched hand. "Thanks!" he said and beat a hasty retreat.

They'd been in bed together when Sidney had noticed that the lines of the star chart on Mark's chest, and the stars and planets themselves, were in the wrong places. And labeled incorrectly.

Sidney should have noticed it sooner. He should have realized that the time Mark claimed he had spent sailing up the east coast and charting the stars, overlapped with the time that Mark had supposedly been summiting Kilimanjaro and filing his award winning dissertation.

"What chart is this from?" Sidney had asked, tentatively, barely letting his fingers brush Mark's chest. The sex hadn't been stellar either, and Sidney wasn't trying to instigate a second round until he'd had some time to figure out what or who had gone wrong. Looking at Mark's tattoos had just seemed like the simplest way to pass the time before Sidney could politely roll out of bed.

"Chart?" Mark blinked his eyes open and then stared down at his chest. "Oh, that. You like it? I drew it myself. The stars from the crest of Olympus. On my birthday." It wasn't his first clue that Mark was a hack, but it had been the most damning. The fact that Sidney had gone back to Mark's apartment a few times after that still chafed. His loneliness had gotten the better of him, that was all.

Sidney tried to shake off the lingering discontent that Mark's presence always brought, as he unlocked the equipment storage room. He was going to have to warn Bodie not to get involved. Sidney and Bodie weren't friends. Sidney didn't exactly have friends in the department, except Karolina, but she was also his advisor, so forced proximity had played a large part in the growth of their relationship. And to her credit, Karolina had tried to warn him about Mark ("an inconceivably useless blowhard.") Sidney just hadn't listened. He was reasonably accomplished at deluding himself, when he wanted to be.

Equipment storage was barren. A few telescope cases with broken latches sat high on upper shelves. Sidney hoisted himself up, one foot on the bottom shelf, stretching his neck as he peered around for a case that would at least survive the trip across campus. Behind a short stack of standard tripods was a brown leather satchel, the strap for it snaking around the other equipment.

Sidney grabbed for it, pulling it down as he stepped back off the shelf, the whole unit creaking under the shifting weight. He unbuckled the flap of the bag and paused. The pretty mahogany telescope inside was not something the university would ever have purchased.

Sidney put the bag on his shoulder and pulled out the scope, turning it over to check the lenses, which looked to be in good working order. There were the intricate etchings on the metal fixtures on the tube, but in the low light of the equipment room Sidney couldn't make them out. Three brass levers on the side, about halfway up, likely had something to do with focus or aperture. Maybe there was a way to attach a camera to it?

None of that mattered, though. What did matter was that it looked like it would work. Sidney slid the telescope back into the satchel and checked his pocket watch. He was running out of time.

He signed out the telescope and then returned the equipment storage keys to the hook. The office where Bodie had been working was dark now, and Sidney dipped inside, leaving a note on the top of Bodie's folder.

'Mars' is a gasbag. He should have named himself 'Jupiter.'

Sidney smirked to himself, and then headed back out into the night.

Kilton House was practically vacant by the time Sidney got back. The party must have moved to a different part of campus, which was perfectly fine with Sidney. He ducked into the kitchen, grabbed the first sleeve of crackers he encountered in the pantry and then made his way to his room.

Jack had at least had the decency to pick up the remains of Sidney's telescope. It was on the desk with an apology note from the students who had broken it, 'in an attempt,' it said, 'to better appreciate the finer points of campus architecture.' Which meant they were trying to look into the all-girls house across the back alley. It didn't matter, in the end. What was done was done, and Sidney had a star cluster to chart.

The scope worked beautifully; the image perhaps even crisper than what his own telescope had provided. He got the telescope set to the same angle and quickly found his purplish star cluster.

Sidney made notes for at least an hour. The star cluster moved in the ways that it had been moving, which was heartening, and Sidney took a break to climb down and fish his bottle of scotch out from beneath his bed.

Alone in the dark, under the sky, Sidney tried not to let his mind wander toward any of the horrible things that had happened in the last five hours. He was small in the vastness of the cosmos. And so were Mark Heaney and Sidney's father. And so was the fact that his research wasn't yielding results that made sense. Maybe it shouldn't bother him that he was no closer to understanding why no one else had charted this cluster than he had been six months ago when he first saw it. But it did.

And he was still lonely. Leo used to tell Sidney that if Sidney could get one piece of it right the rest would fall into place. But if this night was anything to go by, even one piece wasn't going to fall into place any time soon.

With a heavy sigh and thinking longingly of bed, Sidney leaned forward again. He held his eye to the telescope and let the cosmos come into focus. Sidney yawned, reaching for the levers he'd previously ignored, and pressed down on the first one, just to see what it did.

A lens slid into place, coloring his vision a light teal. The celestial bodies remained, hued differently, shining brightly. Sidney let it go and the lens clicked back down. Then Sidney pressed the second one. It was a blackened lens, or something like it. Sidney's vision faded almost entirely, only the brightest stars still visible. Not a particularly useful addition to a telescope. He released that one as well.

Sidney took a drink of his scotch, stretching his back before bowing over the eyepiece again. He pushed down on the final lever, holding it steady with the pad of his forefinger, seeing the sky through a bold magenta hue.

And the sky was different.

The stars were not where they should have been. Or perhaps they were different stars altogether. For a moment, he'd thought they'd reversed. But then, his purplish cluster, what he'd thought was a spiral, was suddenly bright and clear. It was a curl of celestial bodies. Seven perhaps, or eight? The center one might have even been a planet.

Sidney removed his finger, the lens clicking down, and he looked through the eyepiece again. The same stars he'd been watching for months. Cautiously, as though he was approaching a wild animal, he pressed the furthest lever down again. And everything was different.

Sidney stayed up until dawn light and exhaustion began to cloud his vision. He had to teach in the afternoon and he should have been in bed hours ago. Instead, Sidney had followed the stars for hours. Were they coming toward him? Which would mean they were moving in a different planar direction than they ought to have been, but might have explained why, after six months his star cluster hadn't dropped out of the sky yet. It was more than unusual. It was unnatural. Wasn't it? Even the flimsy veneer of predictability, of understanding, that he'd thought he'd had over the world around him, had been peeled away. Maybe he really had lost his mind.

Sidney taught that day's lessons in a daze and stumbled back to the house in the early evening, taking the telescope with him everywhere he went. He wasn't going to risk it getting broken by his housemates. Sidney slept for a couple of hours and set an alarm for eleven. There must have been football practice early because the house was largely deserted when Sidney went down to grab a bowl of cold leftover pasta. He brought the food back up, gathered the telescope and his notebook into his arms, and climbed out to the widow's walk again.

Through the magenta lens, several of his stars were more clearly defined, and were larger again. Sidney made more notes and drew pictures of what he was seeing through each of the lever-triggered lenses. He packed everything up that night, telescope and charts, putting them all in a bundle at the foot of his bed.

His advisor, Karolina, had been on a research trip, then a sabbatical, then a honeymoon. Sidney had been chomping at the bit to get an appointment to see her, and that afternoon he didn't even bother calling ahead. He saw that her light was on and bustled into her office, charts under his arms, the mysterious telescope flung on his back.

"I don't know what it is," Sidney said once all his charts, the drawings and the telescopes were laid out on Karolina's formerly clean desk. Unlike every other professor in the department, she kept her office spotless, all her documents and charts neatly filed away in a series of massive cabinets along the wall. Sidney took a secret joy in making a mess in her space.

Karolina cocked her head to the side, looking over his

sketches, her long, straight chestnut hair obscuring her expression. When she straightened up, she reached for the telescope, picking it up carefully with light brown fingers, extra tan from her trip to Bali. Then she turned it over and examined the other side, one eyebrow arched.

"Where did you get this?" she asked finally.

"It was the last one in equipment storage. I figured it was an old student's or something."

"I know who it belongs to." Karolina set the telescope down, her gaze briefly fixed on it, like it might be about to jump up and scare her. Then she sat, folding her hands in her lap and peered over Sidney's charts again. "You said you first noticed the cluster in Menelaus?"

"Yes," Sidney said. "But now... with this telescope I don't think it's a cluster at all. And no one has notes on it. There's nothing to—"

"What did you get up to in Menelaus?" Karolina interrupted. Sidney frowned.

"Nothing," he said honestly. "Just the same as here. Sleep all day and stars all night. But, Karolina, what's really interesting is that there aren't any notes on this thing anywhere and it's supposed to—"

"You didn't..." she arched an eyebrow, "meet anyone in Menelaus, did you?"

"Meet anyone?" Sidney stammered. What was she talking about? "Like the other students, or...?"

"*Meet* anyone," she emphasized again. Sidney's eyes widened.

"Oh! No!" Sidney shook his head. He'd only left student housing to walk down to the beach in the evenings, telescope in hand. He'd encountered a few locals. One a young woman who'd come around a few times, occasionally with her friends. But even still, they'd never done anything more than chatted amiably, a pleasant distraction as he watched the stars. Karolina still looked skeptical. "I didn't. I was— Wait. Why?"

"Never mind," she shook her head. "I think you need to talk to Jonas."

"Why should it matter if I met anyone? And who's Jonas?"

"Jonas Rookwood. That's his telescope," Karolina said, reaching for her desk drawer. She produced from it a small, black book. "Let me give you his address. You should take that back to him as well."

"You really don't know what this is? At all?" Sidney pointed to the chart. "Because I'm thinking it's an uncharted open cluster, semi-spiral. And it's shifting in a noticeable orbit, which is part of why it doesn't make sense for no one to know about it. And these lenses—"

"Jonas will have better answers than I would. And I'd rather not steer you wrong by making a guess." She handed him a card that she'd scrawled an address on the back of as he talked. "Also," she said with a smile, "this is all very impressive."

"Impressive enough for a dissertation?" Sidney asked, hoping she'd ignore how desperate he'd just sounded. Karolina made a noise that was not a cough or a snort, but something in between. Sidney frowned at her.

"Talk to Jonas," she said. Sidney looked over the card again.

"Elmmond House, Hindry. Where's Hindry?"

"About five hours north, if you take the train." She began to gather Sidney's charts for him. "It's on the coast. Bittergate Bay. Has a beautiful view of the night sky. You should leave today if you want to get a few more decent looks at your cluster," she added. "I don't imagine it'll be in the sky much after next week. Just following your patterns."

"Right," Sidney frowned down at his charts. This was not what he'd expected. "I don't really think I can afford a train ticket at the moment. Or housing. Maybe I'll just write Mr. Rookwood, and—"

"The department can cover expenses if it's for your dissertation." Karolina winked at him and Sidney opened his mouth to protest. Karolina shook her head. "I'll speak to the dean. And I doubt you'll have to find housing. Elmmond House is large and Mr. Rookwood is one of only two occupants. I'll write him a note. He won't turn you out."

"You know him, then?"

"Oh yes," Karolina smiled. "I've known Jonas for a very long time."

3

"There's a man knocking on the front door of Elmmond House," Delilah announced, startling Jonas out of his stupor. The calligraphed lines of ecclesiastical Latin had begun to muddle together in his head, even as he plodded through the transcription and translation. He hadn't realized how close to dropping off he was until she spoke. Delilah leaned in through the doorway, her hands clasped behind her back.

"You changed your clothes." Jonas cleared his throat, voice gruff from disuse as he straightened up and tugged off his glasses, forcing his eyes to focus on Delilah's sparkling beaded dress. Her carrot hair was pinned back in a complex chignon.

"Do you think he's here for the party?"

"How long did it take?"

"Oh this?" Delilah fluffed out some of the beaded tassels with her hands. "It's something I've done before. And besides, you've been in here a long time."

"Not so long." Jonas grunted as he got slowly to his feet. His hips were stiff. He needed to go on a walk.

"So, as I said, there's a man—"

"The party isn't for a week. No one's arrived yet, and when he realizes," Jonas stretched one elbow up over his mouth to cover a yawn, as he pushed his hand through the errant strands of hair that drifted down over his forehead. "He'll go away." Jonas closed the old, leather-bound tome. It sent up a small puff of dust that was illuminated by the waning light of the setting sun through the window. Delilah shook her head.

"I think someone ought to tell him there's no one in Elmmond House."

"You're more than welcome to," Jonas replied. He drew his other arm across his chest and cracked his shoulder. "I'm going to see to supper."

"Don't you want to know why he's come all this way?"

"Not really."

"He didn't ask the cab to stay," Delilah said. Jonas snorted at her.

"You are the nosiest woman I've ever met."

"Well, you are incredibly boring. I have to find entertainment somehow."

"The next book I'm going to be working through is in French," Jonas said. "You could start the translation for me. I know you're fluent."

"*Non, je ne suis pas*," she replied in excellent French. Then there was a knock at the door. Delilah grinned as Jonas sighed. "I forgot to mention, he was looking toward the garden cottage."

"How absentminded of you," Jonas grumbled. Visitors were irritating, and he hated having to glamour himself in his own home. He took a deep breath and tugged out what was left of his magic. It felt like wrapping himself in an extremely worn dressing gown, comfortable but thin.

Jonas's glamour covered his orange skin and his onyx horns, but little else. He'd gotten lazier with it over the years, his tattoos a bright black on his illusory peach skin. Between his size, his dark maroon hair, and his tattoos, it would have been easy to mistake him for a wayward circus attraction. His looks kept most people in Hindry from trying to get too friendly. He was other, unusual, and strange, even in his magical disguise. And that was how Jonas Rookwood preferred it.

Another knock on the door. Delilah left down the hall, likely to spy from the front parlor. Jonas buttoned his waistcoat and checked the rest of his appearance with his hands as he walked down the creaking wooden staircase. He elected to keep his sleeves cuffed to his elbows, revealing tattoos in designs ranging from the alchemical and celestial to the strictly earthbound. Hopefully they would encourage this tourist, whoever he was, not to linger.

Jonas pulled open the door midway through the third series of knocks. His first thought, a foolish one, was that Delilah had failed to mention that the man was handsome. He was shorter than Jonas by only a few inches and thinner by a far greater percentage of inches. His black hair was parted in the center and flopped down below his cheekbones. Dark, full eyebrows crowned angled, and currently narrowed, eyes. His nose was long, the tip of it shaped like an arrow and his lips were full. He was young, but then, all humans looked young to Jonas, who was not.

"Can I help you?" Jonas asked, suddenly aware of how unkempt he was.

"Uh, yes," said the young man, taking the flat cap he'd been kneading between his hands and placing it back on his head. His gaze stuttered over Jonas, and then dropped. He reached for the satchel on his arm, flustered by the intimidating personage Jonas had presented him with. "I'm looking for Jonas Rookwood," he said as he produced an envelope from a familiar set of stationery. Jonas was surprised to hear his own name come out of the man's mouth, but he shrugged and held out his hand to receive the letter.

"I'm Jonas Rookwood," he said.

"Oh." There was a pause as the man looked at him again, a pink flush coloring the tops of his cheeks as he handed Jonas the envelope. He smelled a bit like an ocean breeze in the summer, a soft tang of salt drifting off him, and not at all an unpleasant one. Jonas arched an eyebrow, scrutinizing the young man until the moment that he realized he was being scrutinized in return. Generally folks just gave him a once-over and moved on.

Unsettled, Jonas turned his attention to the letter, where his name was written on the front in Karolina's perfect script.

"How do you know Karolina?" Jonas asked. The man's eyebrow arched.

"We work together."

"You work at Holyworth?"

"I'm an adjunct there," he said. Jonas felt uniquely old as he opened the envelope.

> *Dear Jonas:*
>
> *Don't be a prig. This is Sidney Quince. He's an exceptional astronomer and a very nice man, but I think he's somehow managed to gain sight in the past four months, through apparently non-traditional methods. He's got quite a good chart going of the Ascension from the humanist perspective, though he has no idea what it is. Still, I thought you might be able to help him salvage his dissertation. You should be honest with him. I think he can handle it.*
>
> *At the very least, don't be as big of a prig as you normally are. Also, he needs to stay with you while he's in town because he doesn't have any money. Holyworth's salaries have not improved much since your permanent sabbatical.*
>
> *Much love,*

Karolina

P.S. Thank you so much for the decanter. Claire loves it and has insisted it take the place of honor on our bar cart. Perhaps you'll come by for a drink some time.

"Sidney Quince?" Jonas looked up at the young man.

"Yes?" Sidney Quince responded. Jonas sighed. He folded the letter up and stuck it in his back pocket.

"You'd better come in then."

Sidney stepped into the cottage. He set his luggage on the floor and shrugged out of his grey wool peacoat, his head on a swivel as he took in Jonas's small foyer.

"What's that?" Jonas asked, pointing at a familiar leather bag that sat atop a worn suitcase.

"Oh. Yes, sorry!" Sidney said, hanging his coat on the hook by the door and scooping up the bag by its strap. "Karolina said this was yours."

"It is." Jonas smiled, surprised, as he took the case from Sidney, the weight of it telling him that his telescope was still inside. Holding the bag in his hands was like receiving an old friend who had been gone for too long. "Where did you find it?"

"Ah, well. It was in astronomy storage, I'm afraid. Though I imagine I'm the first one who had it out in some time. It works a treat."

"Of course it does," Jonas said proudly. "I built it myself."

"Are you an engineer, then?" Sidney asked, eyebrow arched.

"I'm a lot of things." Jonas shrugged. Then he turned and started down the hall. "Karolina's note said you had questions about some charts?"

"Yes, actually. But I—"

"Come on to the library, then. Let's see them."

The garden cottage of Elmmond House was part groundkeeper's suite and part carriage house. Jonas had converted the original outbuildings after he decided the interruptions at the big house were far too numerous for his work. The carriage house he'd retrofitted over a summer into a serviceable library, plugging up drafts as they revealed themselves in winter. It was in a strange location in the cottage for a library, off the back of the kitchen, but it held books alright and was in good proximity for afternoon tea.

The kitchen had a dining area in the corner nook, and on the hob was a pot of fish stew that Jonas had put there to simmer earlier in the afternoon. Sidney's stomach let out an audible growl as they walked past. Jonas slowed, glancing at Sidney over his shoulder.

"Hungry?" he asked.

"Sorry," Sidney eyed the stovetop. "I'll just... it smells fantastic. But no. I'm fine. I'll have something when I get back to town."

"I thought you were staying here?" Jonas said. Sidney's cheeks reddened adorably. No. They just reddened.

"Ah. Well, I mean—"

"We have rooms. There's also a phone at the big house, so you can call yourself a cab if you change your mind. Fair warning, the houses are haunted," Jonas added, as he continued into the library and flicked on the light.

"You're being awfully rude," Delilah said, stepping through a bookshelf. Sidney screamed and stumbled back, grabbing for the door frame. Jonas only barely caught him by a flailing hand and yanked him upright. Then he arched an eyebrow in Delilah's direction.

"Who's being rude now?"

"Oh shit! Can he see me?"

"He's got sight, somehow," Jonas said. All the flush had gone from Sidney's cheeks and he looked rather peaky. Jonas steadied him as best he could, keeping one hand on Sidney's elbow, as Sidney tried to catch his breath.

"Sorry, what? What in the hell—?"

"Sidney Quince, please allow me to introduce Delilah Heatherington. Delilah's been dead for what is it now?"

"Fifty years," Delilah said, her hand on her chest, her mahogany eyes fixed on Sidney. "But don't lead with that! Goodness, Mr. Quince, I'm ever so sorry! Usually, Jonas is the only one who can see me. I didn't mean to scare you."

"How is—?" Sidney stammered, looking from Delilah to Jonas and then back again. The man's hands were shaking as he straightened up, and Jonas felt a wellspring of sympathy for the chap, even if he wasn't as steadfast as Karolina had intimated. "I'm very sorry. How is this happening to me?" The question seemed to be posed to the room at large. Delilah and Jonas glanced at each other.

"Have you made a deal with a demon?" Delilah asked. Sidney shook his head.

"Dined with a faerie?" Jonas asked.

"A what? I mean, no— not on purpose?"

"You would know if you had," Delilah said reassuringly. Sidney looked as though he was about to cry.

"You've been granted witch sight, Mr. Quince." Jonas let go of Sidney's elbow and walked over to the large table along the far wall to begin clearing it off. "There are only certain types of humans that can see ghosts. Either you've always had the ability and it's recently been unlocked, or something happened to you that gave you 'sight.' If we can determine how it happened, we can also determine how best to remove it."

"Remove it?" Sidney asked.

"Usually being granted sight comes with a cost. Generally, it keeps you tied to whatever being gave it to you in the first place,"

Delilah explained, wringing her hands as she looked over at Jonas. "So close to the Ascension. Do you think it's a coincidence?" Jonas shrugged.

"The Ascension?" Sidney asked.

"There are celestial events at hand, as well as earthly ones, Mr. Quince. Which would you prefer we tackle first?"

4

Sidney only ever had a head for celestial problems, so he spent the next half hour unpacking four months' worth of star charts, explaining what he'd seen in the sky, and what had happened with Rookwood's telescope. When he finished, he took a deep breath and finally dared to look up from his charts.

Jonas Rookwood sat on a stool in front of the wide table. The last rays of the setting sun set off a deep reddish hue in Rookwood's dark hair and lit his irises a shockingly bright amber. Sidney tried not to ogle him, but Rookwood was massive, standing easily eight or nine inches higher than Sidney's five foot eleven. The height would have been intriguing enough, but Rookwood was broader than two Holyworth fullbacks put together. His shoulders were an intimidating square wall, as he hunched forward over the charts, peering through a pair of small gold wire frames that sat incongruously on the wide bridge of his nose.

Rookwood had asked him no questions for the length of his tale, which Sidney appreciated. Relaying the chronological sequence of events was the only thing keeping him from falling into an absolute panic at the very idea that the young woman standing on the other side of the table from him, partially *in* the window sill, was a ghost.

She seemed perfectly nice, and only incorporeal if he squinted slightly. The edges of her, like the places where her red hair frizzed out of its updo, were differing measures of transparent. At one point during Sidney's tale telling, she moved one of his charts across the table to get a better look at it, and Sidney had to swallow a sharp gasp that left an uncomfortable bubble of air in his chest.

"When did you first see the star cluster?" Rookwood asked, shifting the charts around, looking apparently for the first one in the sequence. Sidney leaned across him and tugged the paper out from beneath several others.

"Here. That's... June fourteenth."

"But that's not the first day you were stargazing in Menelaus," Rookwood posited. Sidney frowned.

"That's true," Sidney said. He hadn't thought of that.

"So, something happened in the first two weeks you were there," Delilah said. Her elbow was propped on the table and her hand held her chin, all of which required her to have some physical structure. Or she was just very accomplished at pretending to have physical structure. Sidney would have asked, but he didn't want to be rude.

"Nothing happened while I was in Menelaus. At all," Sidney said. "I worked. I was studying. I told Karolina—"

"No dalliances in the evening? No moonlit strolls along the Aegean?"

"Menelaus isn't on the Aegean," Rookwood corrected. Delilah sniffed.

"Well, I don't know. I never went anywhere but Athens, and I only read the Iliad once for school. Still," she looked back at Sidney, her gaze piercing. "There wasn't *anyone*?"

"Is witch sight granted exclusively by sexual congress or

something?" Sidney stammered, irritated more by his embarrassment than by the concept itself. He wasn't a prude, but these were total strangers.

"Sex is the easiest way for it to occur by accident." A small smile curled at the corner of Rookwood's handsome mouth, like he might have some suspicion he was making Sidney uncomfortable. Ass. "Humans only gain sight by taking in component fluids of an entity from another realm. Blood, for example, in a blood oath or a pact. Though I imagine you'd know if you'd made one of those. Then, of course, there's the other sort of component fluid," Rookwood blinked at Sidney and then skated his eyes downward toward Sidney's hips in a way that Sidney did not appreciate. He could feel the heat stain his cheeks as he blushed again, which was also very irritating.

"I didn't have any relations with anyone between the time I got to Menelaus and June fourteenth," Sidney said. "I'm quite sure of it." Rookwood shrugged.

"Well, then it must be something else. A bit of fae trickery, perhaps?"

"Did you eat food you found on the ground? A delicious candy, or something? Turkish delight?" Delilah asked. "God, I used to love Turkish delight."

"No," Sidney shook his head. "I really didn't. And I wouldn't. And anyway, I don't feel like I'm tied to anyone, so is it really that big of a deal?"

"You don't feel like you're tied to anyone right now," Rookwood said. "But if someone comes around to collect on a bargain you've accidentally made, you're going to be bound to it, whether you remember it or not."

Sidney pursed his lips. That did not sound good. And he really had other things to be doing, and part of him felt like this was a load of nonsense and he was very eager to wash his hands of all of it. How did Karolina even know this man?

But if he walked away now he would always wonder. And he would be stuck awaiting the return of what or whoever had granted him witch sight. Possibly forever. Which sounded miserable. Sidney groaned and dropped his head into his hands, trying to think.

"Maybe we ought to stop for supper," Rookwood suggested. Sidney could feel the looks Rookwood and Delilah were exchanging over his head. Sympathy from Delilah, exasperation from Rookwood. Sidney sighed. And then something occurred to him.

"What about a kiss?" he asked, straightening up. Delilah's eyebrows shot up and Rookwood's lips remained in a thin, skeptical line. "Is saliva a component material? Sealing a deal with a kiss? That's a thing, isn't it?"

"Only with humans, I think," Delilah said.

"Merfolk," Rookwood said. Sidney's eyebrows shot up.

"Merfolk? Mermaids?"

"Any gender," Rookwood said. "Water is a component element for merfolk. So, kissing is a sort of marking for them, I think. Not a permanent one, like some of the others. Draws you to the..." he slowed, his eyes narrowing as he looked at Sidney. "Draws you to the sea. I don't suppose you swim much?"

"I never learned," Sidney said.

"You didn't go into the water at all in Menelaus?" Rookwood asked. Sidney shook his head.

"But then how would he have met a merfolk?" Delilah asked. Sidney frowned.

"The best place to see the stars was on the north shore of the island. There was a little group of locals," Sidney bit his bottom lip, trying to remember if he'd ever seen which direction they arrived from. He would be watching the stars, and he'd look up from his eyepiece and there they'd be. That was how it happened. "One of them kissed me," he said, his hand coming to the corner of his mouth, remembering her cool skin on his cheek, when she'd pressed soft lips to the corner of his smile. It hadn't been romantic, just friendly. He assumed it was a local custom of some sort and hadn't questioned that he never saw anyone else do it.

"Hoping you'd come into the water so she could drown you and eat you, most likely," Rookwood scoffed, shaking his head. "Well, that's that then."

"What do you mean, that's that?" Sidney demanded. "That's nothing. What does it mean? Do I never go into a body of water again? Should I be careful in the tub? What am I—?"

"I think we can remove it," Rookwood said, his voice calm though his mouth twisted in a smirk of amusement that lit his amber eyes. It made him even more attractive in a way Sidney deeply resented. "Marks are curses, of a sort."

"Well," Delilah interjected, and Sidney glanced at her in time to see a skeptical purse of her lips. "'Curse' is a little strong, isn't it?" Rookwood rolled his eyes, sweeping his glasses off his face before he continued.

"We just have to meet its conditions and, luckily, I think that mostly involves getting you into the water and then back out without letting merfolk kill you. We can manage that, surely."

"Can we?" Sidney asked weakly. The way his day was going, he'd be lucky if he made it two feet without stumbling headlong into a cosmic wormhole filled with interstellar creatures who wanted to eat him. "Are you sure there isn't a less wet way?" Rookwood looked at him with an arched eyebrow, and Sidney tried to be reasonable. "I can't swim," he repeated. Rookwood sighed.

"I'll do a bit of reading after dinner."

"We could go up to Bittergate Chapel in the morning, and talk to Father Michaels," Delilah said. Rookwood nodded as he stood.

"We could, though I think he'll say the same thing as me."

"I'm not opposed to a second opinion," Sidney said. Rookwood snorted.

"Fine." He started into the kitchen. "We'll go tomorrow morning. If you feel the irascible call of the sea before then, do your best to ignore it. In the meantime, we ought to eat. We can talk about your charts over dinner if you like."

With that topic of conversation proposed, Delilah excused herself, assuring Sidney that she didn't eat anyway, and so it was no trouble for her to find something to do elsewhere. Rookwood ladled them each a large earthenware bowl of stew and retrieved two bottles of beer from the icebox. He handed one to Sidney before taking a seat at the end of the table. Sidney sat opposite him and tried to swallow down a million questions.

The tattoos at the base of Rookwood's neck were visible and shifting as he swallowed. It reminded Sidney suddenly and severely of Mark Heaney. Not that Mark was even half as muscular as this man. It was a testament to Sidney's foolishness that he found Rookwood handsome even amidst all this weirdness. He blushed, taking a large bite of stew and staring down into his bowl. When he'd first opened the door, Sidney had felt his knees go a bit weak. As though he hadn't learned anything from Mark's deceptive appearance.

He needed to focus on something else. Sidney took another bite of stew and began to sift through his numerous questions. He wanted to know about the symbols tattooed along the tops of Rookwood's fingers. About this house, and its ghostly denizen, and how Rookwood had been granted his own witch sight. What other creatures that Sidney had assumed were firmly in the realm of fiction were actually real? For the first time in many years, Sidney's charts felt like the absolute least interesting thing he could talk about.

"Why don't you live up at the big house?" Sidney finally asked. Not chart related at all. "It's empty, isn't it?"

"Too large for just me," Rookwood straightened up, like he'd just remembered he wasn't eating alone.

"Can Delilah not join you?"

"She could," Rookwood said. "But she prefers the garden cottage. Besides, I've been here for a while. I'm quite settled in." The house was cozy, if a little worn around the edges. There were places where the paint had chipped, and cabinets hung slightly loose on their hinges. But it was warm and comfortable, the breeze off the water kept out by well-maintained windows and walls.

"Are you an astronomer?" Sidney asked.

"Only accidentally," Rookwood's smile curled toward mischievous again. Now that Sidney's stomach wasn't angry with hunger, it swooped at the sight of Rookwood's clever smirk. Embarrassing. Keep it together, Quince.

"How is one accidentally an astronomer?"

"It was a subject I ended up studying in pursuit of better understanding something else."

"What else?" Sidney asked. Rookwood snorted.

"My turn to ask a question." Sidney could hardly deny it. "Does it mean anything to you when I tell you that your purple star cluster is in a different celestial sky?"

"No," Sidney said. Rookwood nodded at his bowl, apparently satisfied by this. "What is a different celestial sky?"

"The creatures Delilah and I mentioned to you earlier, faeries and demons, and even some merfolk.... They don't live in this dimension. What your witch sight has allowed you to do, along with my telescope, is to see the cosmos of different dimensions. They usually call them 'realms.'" Sidney lowered his spoon into his bowl and considered the implications of this.

"So, the purple star cluster is actually a planetary cluster from a different realm, drawing close enough to this one to be seen?" Sidney asked. Rookwood nodded.

"I believe so."

"Do gravitational forces operate across realms?" Sidney asked. Rookwood chuckled, a deep, warm sound that made Sidney smile.

"And you've already struck on a topic beyond the scope of my knowledge," Rookwood said. "They could, I suppose. Inter-dimensional planetary alignments do generate other phenomena."

"Like what?" Sidney asked.

"There are literal books on the topic, Mr. Quince. I own several of them."

"Can I borrow them?" Sidney asked. Rookwood shrugged.

"Be my guest."

5

Jonas woke up to the smell of sweet honey and yeast. Someone was baking. Someone who wasn't him, obviously, as he was still tangled in his sheets, the dregs of a dream he could barely remember making his limbs and his mind sluggish.

He got up and dressed, remembering that he'd put Sidney in the guest room across the hall the night before. It was hard to think of the last time he'd had a substantive conversation with someone that wasn't Delilah, but he found, in the cool light of morning, that he'd probably enjoyed himself. Which was fine. It wasn't illegal or anything. But he shouldn't get used to it. Or the idea that his house would smell this good all the time.

Even though he'd looked at himself in the mirror, it wasn't until he put his red-orange palm on the banister that he realized his glamour had slid off sometime in the night. He stopped on the top step and took a deep breath, pulling the magic back over himself. It wouldn't do to frighten his guest. A guest who didn't need to know any of Jonas's personal business, like who or what he actually was. They were taking care of the witch sight. They were going to talk about the telescope, and then the pretty professor would be off back to Holyworth, and out of Jonas's hair forever.

With his day thus efficiently planned, Jonas settled into his glamour and continued into the kitchen.

Sidney was engulfed in a small cloud of steam, hunched over the oven, pulling out a tray of the most delicious smelling sweet buns Jonas had ever encountered. Jonas's stomach growled immediately and enthusiastically. Sidney glanced over his shoulder.

In the sunlight that came in through the window over the sink, Sidney was practically glowing. His skin shone where the light hit him and his dark hair looked fine and soft where it swept haphazardly over his forehead. The longest strands brushed his cheekbones, and Sidney swept them away before scratching absently at his throat. Jonas could see the muscle there, the pulse of his heartbeat, and where Sidney's neck met his shoulder and the skin turned paler and infinitely more biteable.

Jonas should have backed out of the kitchen slowly. He needed to have a stern talk with his libido, which had apparently chosen that moment to rise from a long dormancy and turn distinctly feral.

He wasn't going to run from an astronomy lecturer, for Christ's sake. Or from those sweet buns. Jonas took a breath and tried to force a sardonic smile.

"Made yourself at home, I see."

"I woke up early," Sidney turned away, placing the dish of buns on top of the stove, and Jonas did not notice or care about the way Sidney's white undershirt clung to the line of his ribs. "Didn't see you had much in the way of breakfast, so—" he turned suddenly, his face apologetic. "I really didn't mean to intrude in your— I just thought—I couldn't lay awake in bed anymore."

"It's fine," Jonas said, because anything that yielded him a pan full of steaming hot sweet buns was well and truly fine. "I'll put the coffee on."

"I couldn't find the grounds in the pantry."

"Ah, cause they're not in the pantry." Jonas reached up into the cabinet above the icebox to produce the can of ground coffee.

"Noted," Sidney said. Which was ridiculous, as he'd be staying here at most one night more and didn't really need to be knowing where the coffee was. But again, fine.

As Jonas waited for the percolator, he glanced into the library where the light was on. A large book was spread open, hanging off the small side table beside one the armchairs.

"Doing a bit of reading?" Jonas asked. Sidney was taking the buns off the tray and dropping them onto a cooling rack. Jonas hadn't even known he had a cooling rack.

"I was, well—I was just browsing your collection when I saw that bestiary. It looks medieval." That was because it was a medieval bestiary, written by a couple of twelfth century monks, but it would be a little hard to explain why Jonas was in owner-ship of an artifact that at least belonged in an archive if not a museum.

"It's a copy."

"Well, I assumed as much. I can barely read the text. I mostly know Greek and Latin. But I think it's talking about merfolk as prophets. Or maybe fortune tellers?"

"Some people think so," Jonas concurred. "Though they're generally not keen on handing out prophecies to humans. They mostly see people as a food source."

"Right," Sidney said slowly. Jonas smirked.

"Are you in need of a clairvoyant, then?"

"I mean," Sidney gave a sheepish smile, his gaze dropping to the sweet buns. Jonas's stomach did a small flip, that was certainly due to hunger. "There are some parts of the future I'd like to know. Wouldn't you?"

"The future is what it is," Jonas said. "And even if you knew what was going to happen, I'm not sure that I think you'd be able to do anything about it. All you could do was change your reaction to it. Prepare yourself, I suppose."

"That's a little fatalistic for my tastes," Sidney said. Jonas shrugged.

"There's very little control to be had over the whims of the universe. And even less over other people. You're better off just worrying about yourself." Sidney made a noise in the back of his throat that felt purposefully noncommittal, and Jonas thought briefly that he didn't know this man well enough to be making personal philosophy statements to him. He finished his coffee in silence before snagging a bun and retreating to the kitchen table.

HALF AN HOUR LATER, HIS STOMACH NICELY FULL OF SWEET BUNS and coffee, Sidney followed Rookwood out the kitchen door and along the back path up into the garden, stifling a yawn. He'd fallen asleep late and had woken up well before the sun, his mind abuzz. There was a Shakespeare quote that was circling in his thoughts, *'O brave new world, that has such people in 't.'* If the bard had only known.

Sidney stretched as they walked, waiting for the proper moment to begin asking the questions he'd been mentally cataloging in the wee hours of the morning. The grounds were lovely, even where the grass changed to cliffside and dropped off into the silvery bay below. Sidney strayed toward the edge as they walked along in silence, looking down at the fauna and the stones that stuck out oddly from the edge of the earth. A furry creature of some kind, small and sleek looking, scuttled along the sheer rock face, and Sidney stopped to try and catch a better look. Rookwood clicked his tongue.

"Ah ah, back away from the cliffside, Quince, if you'd be so kind." Sidney scowled.

"I promise Mr. Rookwood, I have no interest in taking a dive."

"Whether or not you personally have an interest is entirely immaterial," Rookwood replied. "That's not how marks work."

"Well, how do they work?" Sidney asked. One of his questions, perfectly lobbed. Rookwood gave Sidney a handsome scowl. He ran his hand through his hair, pushing the dark tendrils out of his face, and continued up the path without responding. Christ, but he was irritating. Still, Sidney had no choice but to jog to catch up with Rookwood's long strides. And when he finally did, Jonas Rookwood began to speak.

"A merfolk mark wouldn't necessarily make you want to throw yourself into the water. It's more like a compulsion. Your body would want to do it, even if your mind wasn't inclined to. You could try and stop it, but it would be a battle of your will against the magic of the mark."

"I think my will and I are in particular alignment on the subject."

"A mark can shift its power depending on how close or far you are from the creature who placed it. Or even creatures of a similar genotype, depending on what it's intended to do."

"Magic cares about things like genetic morphology?" Sidney arched an eyebrow. Rookwood nodded, then smirked at the expression on Sidney's face.

"Skeptical already?"

"I'm just trying to understand."

"But you don't believe me."

"I barely know you, Mr. Rookwood. I came here because

Karolina suggested it, and I trust her judgment more than my own most days." Rookwood smiled at that. A real one, brilliant and maybe a little bit proud.

"You seem like an intelligent fellow, Quince, but that's easily the smartest thing you've said to me so far."

"How do you know her?" Sidney asked. Rookwood chuckled.

"She's my younger sister. Half-sister, technically." Sidney tried not to let himself look as shocked as he felt.

"She never said."

"Well, when your brother's a mad old recluse, it's hardly worth bragging about."

"You don't seem mad."

"You just got here. Give me a day or two to really get going."

"What could be madder than telling me merfolk are real and that one of them marked me for death?" Sidney asked. Rookwood smiled.

"What indeed?"

"So, what are marks used for?" Rookwood looked heavenward, as if asking a benevolent god for strength. When he looked at Sidney again, it was with an audible sigh.

"Let's say I was a demon. Perhaps you wanted something from me—"

"Like what?" Sidney asked. Rookwood blinked at him.

"Anything you like."

"Anything?"

"Magic," Rookwood said, his tone strangely hollow, his gait stiffening, as they continued up the hill. "Say you wanted the ability to use magic. So I grant it to you, in exchange for part of your soul. That marks you. Now, later, when I've used up the portion of your soul that I had, the mark might trigger. It would draw us together, or more accurately draw you to me. A human who has consorted with a creature once, for whatever reason, is more likely to be willing to do it again. Presumably they know the benefits or have already reaped the rewards."

"But it wouldn't make me do anything," Sidney considered. "Just because you've found me again using the mark doesn't make me want to give you more of my soul."

"Not necessarily. It would draw you to me. And then between the enchantment in the mark and my own persuasive capabilities—"

"Fish stew?" Sidney teased. Rookwood narrowed his eyes, then rolled them when he got the joke.

"Amusing," he grumbled, but Sidney caught the ghost of a smile that drifted across Rookwood's face.

"I think I understand," Sidney said. "The merfolk just need the mark to get me in the water, and then they can take care of the rest."

"Precisely."

Bittergate Chapel was a compact white stucco building up on a hill about a twenty-minute walk from the house. An alcove had been cut out of the forest, just the right shape for a little graveyard, the church, and then a dainty cottage, overgrown with vines, smoke puffing merrily out of the chimney. It looked exactly like something out of a fairy tale.

Sidney followed Rookwood up the steps, pausing beside him on the porch as he knocked. It didn't take long for an older man with dark skin, a shock of white hair, and silver spectacles, to answer the door. He was dressed all in black and had a white clerical collar tucked around his throat. For a moment, the man paused, looking between the two of them. Then his gaze settled on Rookwood and he smiled.

"Jonas! It's been a minute since I've seen you like this."

"Company," Rookwood said gruffly, gesturing to Sidney. "Father Michaels, this is Sidney Quince, a lecturer who works with Karolina at Holyworth. Mr. Quince, this is Father Michaels, our local clergyman."

"Pleasure," Sidney stepped forward and held out his hand, which the priest shook with a warm dry palm and a pleasant smile.

"A teacher? The noblest of professions."

"Said the preacher," Rookwood replied dryly, clearly teasing. Sidney couldn't help but smile, as Father Michaels laughed.

"Good to see you're in pleasant spirits," he said, clapping Rookwood firmly on the shoulder. "Now, how can I be of assistance?"

SIDNEY HAD FORGOTTEN HOW NICE IT WAS TO SHARE A RESEARCH table whilst you were working. Ever since Mark, Sidney nearly always worked by himself. The company, even when spent in silence, was nicer than flipping through old tomes and charts alone. But in the basement of the vicarage where Father Michaels kept his own library of strange, old books, Sidney found he enjoyed the comfortable quiet of pages turning, Rookwood's small hums of interest. The scratch of a pencil that wasn't his own.

Father Michaels had gotten them set up and then left them to it, excusing himself to go work on that Sunday's homily.

"Do many people attend service?" Sidney asked. Rookwood shrugged.

"I couldn't say. I'm not a parishioner myself."

"You seem to know the vicar well enough."

"We have certain shared interests. And I give him my squash, and he gives me his extra tomatoes."

"A symbiotic relationship," Sidney said. Rookwood nodded.

"Exactly so."

An hour passed more quickly than Sidney'd thought possible, when Rookwood stepped back from the table, clicking his tongue.

"What is it?" Sidney asked, straightening up, ignoring the pops of protest his spine made.

"'*A complete submersion within an infested body of water, combined with the safe extraction of a marked subject after a number of minutes, dependent upon the strength of the pull,*' et cetera, et cetera." He looked up, amber eyes catching Sidney's across the table. Warmth crawled up the back of Sidney's neck with an uncomfortable speed.

"Meaning?" Sidney asked, already knowing, really, what it meant. Something in him needed to hear Rookwood say it before he could begin to come to terms with it.

"Meaning we're going to have to go for a swim."

6

"Wait until morning." Father Michaels was seated behind the desk in his office. Jonas leaned against the doorway, glancing over his shoulder at Sidney, who was putting his coat on by the front door. "You know they sleep early. It'll be easier to get past them."

Another night of company. Not that the company was bad, but the prospect of it made Jonas uneasy. He didn't exactly have prolonged engagements with visitors.

"Why the glamour?" Father Michaels' voice was low, certainly quiet enough that Sidney wouldn't have been able to hear. Jonas blinked at the old man in surprise.

"I don't know him."

"That didn't used to matter," Father Michaels said. "You looked like yourself the first time we met."

"That was a long time ago," Jonas said. His shoulders were tight at the accusation. Except it wasn't an accusation. Just a question. Father Michaels only shrugged and smiled.

"He seems nice."

"They all seem nice," Jonas replied. Father Michaels

hummed in consideration, turning his attention back down to the book in front of him.

"Well, come back any time, you know. The library is open to you. Both of you."

"Thank you again."

Jonas left, herding Sidney out into the midday gloom. The leaves were trembling in the wind off the water, and it looked as though a storm was rolling in. Par for the course this time of year. Jonas tried to breathe. Tried not to think about anything other than that he'd been right about the merfolk. Odds were good he'd be right about Sidney Quince too.

"Are we headed down to the bay, then?" Sidney asked. Jonas shook his head.

"We'll go in the morning. Early. If you can stay another day. The vicar reminded me that merfolk are quieter in the early hours of the morning. Less of them to contend with."

"Less sounds promising. Some of those illustrations were a little," he trailed off, his voice lifting as if in question. Jonas nodded.

"Toothy? A bit, unfortunately. But you know they're different everywhere. Up here you get the cold-water sort. More shark-y. I've no idea what sort of bite patterns you'd have encountered in Menelaus."

They continued past the garden, which had gone two days neglected now. A rumble of thunder meant it might end up being three. Jonas paused at the corner of the house, glancing up at the sky. It took him a moment to realize Sidney had paused with him. His hands were shoved deep in his pockets, and his mouth was crumpled into a thin line.

"What's wrong, Quince?"

"Oh, nothing." Sidney's cheeks flushed. Had Jonas ever met someone who was so easy to fluster?

"Nothing to worry about with the merfolk. Should be in and out."

"I was thinking. I mean, if it works and I'm not marked anymore, will I still be able to see? Use the witch sight, I mean?"

"You're thinking about your star charts?" Jonas almost laughed, but Sidney nodded sincerely. Good gods. "Once you've been granted witch sight, it can't really be taken away. You can't unsee something you've seen. I'm not sure that'll help you with your research any."

"What do you mean?" Sidney asked. The first rain drops began to patter down between them, and Jonas turned toward the kitchen door.

"I pulled those books for you last night about the different celestial skies. Did you take a look?"

"I hadn't yet." Sidney followed him into the kitchen, where they both shucked their coats. Jonas pursed his lips, trying to decide how much to tell him. How much to let him read for himself. He held out his hand to take Sidney's coat.

"It's a challenging area of study, anything to do with the other realms. Not because it's so vastly different from anything here, Earthside, they call it. Just because most of the human population doesn't have witch sight."

"Right," Sidney said slowly. His frown increased as he gave his coat to Jonas.

"I put the relevant texts in a pile at the corner of the desk."

"Thank you," Sidney said, turning toward the library. Jonas wavered, feeling like he ought to say something. Apologize somehow, though it wasn't his fault in the slightest. Most humans had stuck magic firmly in the 'imaginary' category of existence a long time ago. Whether that made anyone's life easier or harder didn't matter much. It was just the way it was.

Jonas watched through the library door as Sidney laid his hand on the top book in the stack Jonas had left for him. Jonas felt sorry for him, when he knew he shouldn't have felt anything at all.

THE SKY CLEARED BY THE TIME SIDNEY NEEDED TO WATCH THE cluster. But he wasn't sure why he was doing it anymore. He'd spent the length of a thunderstorm flipping through the books Rookwood had left out for him, growing more and more dejected with every turn of the page.

Each book seemed to begin with a minor treatise on how the study of other realms (sometimes called dimensions) wasn't considered serious scholarship. One of the authors spent the entire introduction of the book listing all the academic institutions that had derided him, even though Sidney thought his primary theory seemed sound. Sidney's reading highlighted a new problem that he liked to think he would have landed on before too long: what he was proposing to research was a largely invisible phenomenon. Unless he could compel the dean of the astronomy department into an accidental mermaid kiss, no one was going to take his months of charting seriously.

Still, for some reason, he was out in the cold damp, standing outside between the kitchen door and a dilapidated gazebo, staring up at the stars. Habit, he supposed. Though that didn't make it any less foolish.

He couldn't just stop, was the thing. Sidney wasn't good at giving up when there was still a chance something might work out. It was a failing of his. It was why he'd kept trying to make Mark into something he so sincerely wasn't.

Sidney's father liked to call him pigheaded, and it was probably a fair assessment. But Sidney just couldn't imagine his months of work had been for nothing. There had to be something in the movement of these stars and planets that impacted earth. Massive celestial bodies shifting around was the reason for the tides and gravity and all kinds of things, and so this had to mean something. He couldn't let it go just yet.

Learning about new realms was a bit like he'd spent six months trying to read before he'd been taught the first letter of the alphabet. It wasn't much, but he supposed it was helpful.

Sidney straightened up, tucking his notebook and chart paper between his knees, and shoving his numb fingers into his armpits. Far below, the bay churned against the bottom of the cliffs, the sound of the tide calming, despite Sidney's general frustrations.

"Alright?" Sidney yelped and turned, dropping his notebook into the damp grass. Rookwood was quiet for such a big man. "Sorry! Thought you heard the door open." He was mostly shadowed by the lights of the cottage behind him, but Sidney could see he was carrying a bowl in his hands. "You skipped dinner," he said. "Thought you might be hungry."

"Thanks." Sidney gathered up his notebook off the ground and tucked it under his arm. He stepped closer to Rookwood, taking the bowl from him. The crockery was warm against his numb fingers, and he could smell the rich creamy fish stew that they'd eaten the night before.

"It's just leftovers," Rookwood said. Sidney was already feeling for the spoon around the edge of the bowl.

"Sorry, I missed supper," he said. Steam rose from the full spoon, thawing the tip of Sidney's nose. "It's been a while since I was anyone's house guest. My manners aren't up to snuff."

"I'm not going to fault you for skipping out on a meal. God knows I forget myself often enough when I'm in the middle of a project." He stepped forward then, away from Sidney. Sidney ate several bites of stew as he watched Rookwood lean down and look through the telescope. His shoulders were so broad, Sidney found it hard to imagine this man ever skipping a meal. After a few minutes, Rookwood turned back to him.

"How did you find those books?" Rookwood asked. Sidney smirked.

"Illuminating. Frustrating."

"And yet you're still out here." Rookwood gestured over his shoulder at the telescope. "I admit, I'm a little surprised."

"There's still something to it, I think," Sidney replied. "An observable cluster of that size, moving at that speed. I find it hard to believe it's not making an impact here in some way."

Sidney could see Rookwood's face now and felt himself stiffen slightly under Rookwood's considering gaze. He looked as though he wanted to say something and was actively thinking better of it.

"What?" Sidney prompted.

"Nothing," Rookwood shook his head. "Perhaps you're right." It was a weak lie. Rookwood knew that the planets in the other sky had some impact on earth.

"Maybe something to do with solar flares?" Sidney mused, not because he really thought it was a decent guess, just to see what Rookwood would say. Rookwood only shrugged and leaned back over the telescope. Irritating. What did he know? And why wouldn't he tell Sidney?

Sidney tried to sort out the best question that would elicit a more useful response. He ate another mouthful of stew and came up with nothing. Rookwood straightened up. Confirmation that Sidney was right would have to be good enough. He sighed.

"What?" Rookwood asked. Sidney shook his head.

"Nothing."

"Well, don't stay out too late." Rookwood started past Sidney, back toward the kitchen door. "We've got an early morning ahead of us."

JONAS HADN'T REALIZED HOW ACCUSTOMED HE'D BECOME TO keeping his own hours. Delilah didn't sleep, and Jonas was an early riser by nature. Sidney Quince, it seemed was the opposite. He'd declared the prior day's sweet buns an anomaly and then proceeded to eat toast and drink coffee in slow, groggy silence. By six o'clock Jonas chomping at the bit. They should have already been out on the water.

Jonas drove them into Hindry in his old, rust-colored pick-up truck, without bothering to attempt conversation. If Sidney had any questions, he would ask them in his own time, or not at all. As far as Jonas was concerned, he'd given Sidney some research and was about to save him from a merfolk marking. That was going quite above and beyond. Even Karolina couldn't fault him for doing less.

The grey gravel in the marina crunched under the tires. They parked and Jonas climbed out, turning up the collars of his brown leather jacket against the cold. It would be bitter on the water.

Sidney pulled his wool coat tight around his narrow waist, black hair ruffling in the wind, as they boarded Jonas's fishing boat. Once they were safely on deck, Jonas handed Sidney a thermos of the last of their coffee before he went into the wheel-house, leaving Sidney to warm up on his own.

The sky was cloudy, the water equally so. And choppy, even when they got to a point far enough from shore that Elmmond House was visible high on the ridge above.

"What do you use the boat for?" Sidney had come into the shelter of the wheelhouse once they'd made it into open water. His nose and cheeks were pink, his eyes considerably brighter than they had been in the truck. Perhaps the sea air agreed with him. Or perhaps the merfolk mark was enjoying itself.

"Fishing," Jonas said. "It's nice to spend a bit of time offshore." Sidney looked at him, clearly expecting more, his eyebrow arching skeptically as the silence drew out. It wasn't untrue. More like, a half-truth. "I was doing some research a few years ago," Jonas continued as though he'd always meant to. "It required several trips to Clement's Island, one of the little coastal spits north of here. Chartering boats got tiresome, so I bought one of my own."

"What were you researching?"

"A type of moss," Jonas said, turning the boat back toward the harbor and slowing to a stop.

"So, you're a botanist too?" There was amusement in Sidney's voice, the same that he'd heard when Sidney had made the gentle jibe about Jonas's fish stew. The familiarity of it was more jarring than the teasing itself, and it made Jonas feel bizarrely exposed. "Optical engineer, botanist, fisherman?"

"You may as well add healer and babysitter to the list," Jonas depressed the lever that dropped the anchor, and Sidney's pretty smirk vanished; his cheeks reddened slightly. Jonas shook his head, unsurprised he'd gotten the tone wrong. "You can tease, and I can't?"

"It's impressive actually, your resume." Sidney sounded horribly sincere, and Jonas laughed over the ridiculous sensation of his stomach doing a flip.

"Don't try to endear yourself to me now, Quince," Jonas replied. "You're not going to like what I have you do next."

"Which would be what?"

"Strip down." Jonas took the flask from Sidney's hands. "Time for a dip in the Bittergate."

7

It was so bitingly cold that Sidney almost didn't have the capacity to be embarrassed by standing on the deck of Rookwood's boat in nothing but his shorts. He knew he looked more boy than man, arms folded around himself, shivering with every gust of wind, but he didn't care. The call of the sea was not particularly strong or compelling at the current juncture, and he couldn't imagine that a single merfolk resided in these inhospitable waters.

"Are you sure this is going to work?" Sidney asked, as Rookwood handed him a rough braided rope that was tied to the back of the boat.

"We've had confirmation from two different sources."

"This isn't just some hilarious prank?" Sidney shivered. Rookwood raised an eyebrow at him.

"Do I seem like the sort of person to inconvenience myself for a joke?" He didn't, but Sidney was not unused to being the butt of other people's jokes. Still, when Rookwood placed his hand between Sidney's shoulder blades, Sidney nearly jumped at the not unpleasant heat of Jonas's palm against his skin.

Blushing like an idiot who wasn't about to be eaten by

merfolk, Sidney followed as Rookwood led him to the back of the boat and onto the small platform that hung there.

"Swim out a little way, and then come back. Just make sure you're fully submerged."

"And all the merfolk are asleep?" Sidney tightened his grip on the rope.

"Probably," Rookwood shrugged, and before Sidney could tell him that that wasn't very comforting, the warm pressure of Rookwood's hand turned to a sharp shove.

The water felt like ice. Sidney's whole body stiffened as he dropped down below the surface, buffeting in the waves like a badly tied buoy. As he began to rise, he gripped the rope more tightly, twisting it around his wrist as he started to swim.

Sidney was not a strong swimmer. Most of his time in the water was spent on a raft in the shallow part of the creek that ran behind the town he'd grown up in. Half the time it was barely deep enough for a current.

When he broke the surface of the water, the air above him felt warm, which he knew it wasn't. He gasped in a mouthful of brackish foam and spit it out as he started to swim again, away from the boat, before Jonas could say anything snide, or make any suggestions about his form.

More than once, Sidney was knocked off his tenuous course by a rogue whitecap that had leapt out of nowhere, seemingly just to slap him in the face. He might have been embarrassed by how inept he was sure he looked, except it was too fucking cold to be anything but cold. And then Sidney felt a strong tugging on his ankle. He kicked, and something sharp and thornlike bit into the top of his foot. He opened his mouth to shout in pain and sank below the surface.

Salty water stung his eyes, as Sidney thrashed onto his back, looking for whatever fishing line or hook or idiot fish had thought him food. He was not expecting a pair of wide, yellow eyes to be looking back.

Sidney dropped the rope. His hands spread wide as he tried to swim away from the creature, the merfolk. Its webbed fingers, tipped with talons, dug furiously into Sidney's foot, leaving a stream of blood in the water. Long inky hair flowed out behind its head, its body humanoid and distinctly inhuman at once. It reached forward with its free arm, trying to grab Sidney around the calf, and Sidney managed to kick it right in the center of its face.

The creature shrieked, a strange, high-pitched gurgle. Sidney got two kicks and a half a stroke away before it grabbed him again, wrenching him backward through the water, digging its talons into his leg. Sidney opened his mouth to scream in pain and emitted a stream of bubbles, the last of the air from his lungs. The water shifted in a rush behind him. Sidney looked back over his shoulder at the same moment that his leg was released.

Jonas Rookwood had entered the fray. Jonas had one of his massive forearms around the merfolk's neck in a boxer's headlock. He bared his teeth, wrestling with the creature. In Jonas's fist was the shining, business end of a harpoon. He dug the barbed tip into the creature's chest.

Without the merfolk dragging him down, Sidney surged toward the surface, desperate for air. He managed to bob far enough up to take in two good breaths, before water crested over his chin. The line he'd been holding floated on top of the water. Jonas hadn't surfaced.

Sidney filled his mouth with as much air as he could and dove back down, leg stinging, chest aching, head throbbing. All secondary to the fact that he had to help Jonas. Before Sidney had made it deep enough that he could even open his eyes, a warm, firm body collided with him.

For the first time since he'd entered Bittergate Bay, Sidney's chest breached the surface of the water. Beneath him, muscular, tattooed forearms wrapped around his hips, and a head of dark, red-tinted hair collided with the bottom of Sidney's chin.

"Fuck," Jonas panted. His amber eyes were wide, and water streamed off his cheeks and nose and into his beard as they bobbed in the water. "Lost my harpoon."

~

JONAS TIGHTENED HIS GRIP ON SIDNEY AS HE PADDLED THEM THE fifteen yards back to the boat. He'd certainly spilled enough merfolk blood to keep the creature's fellows at bay, but it didn't hurt to be cautious, injured as they both were.

When they reached the boat, Jonas hoisted Sidney partially onto his shoulder, placing him on the edge of the narrow swim platform. The strain of heaving himself out of the water brought Jonas's attention to three angry claw marks slashed across his right shoulder.

"You're b-b-bleeding," Sidney managed through chattering teeth. Sidney's left knee was folded up to his chest, where the gashes on his leg were draining watery blood down his calf and over his foot. They were far more concerning than Jonas' injury.

"I'll be alright." Jonas got to his feet on the platform. "Come on, we need to get you inside." He reached over to pull Sidney up, but Sidney was already halfway to standing on his own. He placed a slippery, shaking hand on the back panel of the boat and supported his weight on his good leg, as Jonas watched in amazement.

"D-d-d-do you think it worked?" Sidney grabbed Jonas's outstretched arm to balance himself as he began to shift his bad leg over the back of the boat.

"I do." Jonas said, still awestruck by how Sidney wrangled

himself onto the boat without so much as a whimper of discomfort. It was an injury that would have brought plenty of heartier men to their knees, and Sidney seemed determined to grit his teeth and bare it. His hands were shaking as he steadied himself, turning to reach back and offer Jonas his arm. Jonas didn't need it, so he didn't take it, waving Sidney away gently.

"How's the leg?" Jonas asked.

"Stings." Sidney's chest heaved from the effort he'd expended. His lips were turning blue, his muscles twitching in the cold. For a moment, Jonas's mind was strangely preoccupied with the shape and angles of Sidney's body. Just for a moment.

"I've got bandages downstairs." Jonas moved to Sidney's injured side, and tucked himself under Sidney's arm, trying to take the bulk of his weight, which, judging by the way his ribs were poking out, couldn't have been more than sixty pounds. "Lean into me."

"You're hurt," Sidney protested.

"Good lord, Quince. Don't be an idiot." Sidney rolled his eyes, and Jonas ignored him, half helping, half hauling Sidney to the narrow steps that led to the small cabin below deck.

It wasn't much. A bathroom was tucked into the alcove behind the stairs, and in front of them stretched the full length of the cabin. Primarily, the space was a bed beneath a low ceiling. It was the perfect size for Jonas alone and would have been snug with two. In the narrow open space where they stood, a table was folded into the wall on their right. On the other side was small ice chest, a single stove burner, and a cabinet which held dried goods, instant coffee, tea, whiskey and the full extent of the boat's kitchenware.

Jonas made sure Sidney had a hand on a wall before he stepped forward, tugging open the storage drawers beneath the bed to produce towels and more blankets. Even Jonas, whose skin was preternaturally warm, was beginning to feel the ache of cold setting in.

"Here," he stood with three towels in his arms. "Extra blankets there," he pointed to the pile of them he'd placed on the end of the bed. "Dry off and then wrap yourself up. I'll be out in a minute with bandages." He handed Sidney two towels, tucked the other under his arm for himself, and went into the bathroom to ungracefully shuck his wet clothes. He wrestled more vigorously with his pants than he had with the merfolk, the wet fabric tightly suctioned to his thighs.

Once Jonas stripped, he recovered his first aid kit from the cabinet under the sink. He wiped the excess blood off his shoulder before dousing the wound in antiseptic. Then he gathered up all the bandages he had and the rest of the antiseptic. With a deep, fortifying breath, Jonas cinched his towel around his waist and walked back into the cabin. He hadn't done triage in a while. That was all.

Sidney sat on the foot of the bed, a towel low around his narrow hips, and the other folded neatly on the bedspread beside him, when it should have been around his head or shoulders. His hair was still far too damp and hung over his face as he leaned forward.

Sidney prodded gently with long fingers at the skin near his wound. Was there nothing about this man that could not be described as long and thin? The next thought Jonas had made his cheeks heat, and he studiously didn't look at the place where the thin towel was draped over Sidney's lap. Instead, he decided to be irritated, because Sidney apparently had something like negative survival instincts. He'd only taken one blanket from the stack Jonas had left and had draped it loosely around his shoulders.

"No." Jonas shook his head. "Scoot back and get under the blankets."

"I'll s-s-stain everything."

"I don't care." Jonas grabbed the towel from beside Sidney and held it out to him. "If you catch your death, I'll never hear the end of it from Karolina. Dry your hair."

"It is dry," Sidney said. Jonas dropped the towel over Sidney's head.

"No, it isn't." Sidney grumbled and yanked the towel down, scrubbing it over his hair, pouting like a child. Jonas ignored him, kneeling down to check Sidney's leg.

Sidney didn't whimper or hiss. Hell, he barely flinched. Jonas cleaned the gouges in his leg and the top of his foot as gently as he could, then lifted Sidney's heel, bracing it against his own knee as he wound the linen bandages around Sidney's leg and tied them off beneath the arch of his foot.

"You're quite good at that," Sidney said.

"Field medicine," Jonas responded, unhappy with how loose the bandage was at Sidney's ankle. He untied the bottom knot and began to adjust.

"You were a solider?"

"For a little while," Jonas admitted, getting the bandage to a better spot. "It didn't suit."

"Your resume truly is long and varied," Sidney said, and Jonas couldn't tell whether he was being cheeky or if his tone was actual amazement. Which would have been wildly unnecessary.

"Flatterer," Jonas accused. Sidney flushed, and Jonas felt unduly pleased by that. Which was strange. Gods. What had gotten into him? Jonas stood and cleared his throat. "Now, scoot back and lie down, so I can get you under some blankets." Sidney gave him a skeptical glance, and Jonas could see the flush on his cheeks deepen. Likely from the cold. "Please don't make me tackle you, Quince. It'll be undignified for both of us."

Sidney snorted but scooted backward. When he was far

enough on the mattress that the entirety of his bandaged leg was supported, he collapsed onto his side, pulling his arms into his chest, wrapping his sad shoulder blanket tightly around his chest. Jonas ignored how low the towel around Sidney's waist had slid.

"How l-long until we get back?" Sidney's teeth were still clicking together.

"Not long," Jonas said. "But I wouldn't worry about that now." Jonas grabbed the softest blanket from his stack, a cashmere throw; a gift from someone who far overestimated Jonas's appreciation for luxury. It covered Sidney from his shoulder to his feet but little else. Next was an old woolen camp blanket that weighed a metric ton. Jonas spread it out with a shake, before tossing it over Sidney's body and the majority of the bed, where it still had extra fabric to spare. Finally came the comforter that had been meant for the cabin bed, piled on top for good measure.

"Are you trying to c-crush me?" Sidney chattered.

"No. I'm trying to keep you from getting hypothermia." He glanced down at himself and his injured shoulder where he was feeling the cold more readily. His own clothes he'd tossed over the heater in the bathroom to dry. It wouldn't do to go up to the wheelhouse undressed, not in the wind, with his beard and hair still damp. The pile of blankets that made up Sidney Quince was shaking slightly. Jonas sighed.

"Budge." Jonas knocked Sidney's feet with his knee. Sidney lifted himself up onto one elbow, looking down at Jonas with an arched eyebrow.

"What?"

"You're still shivering. You need more heat, and I'm the closest thing to a radiator on hand." Sidney blinked at him for a moment, and then lay back down, scooting back without a word.

It was a practical solution, nothing more. It did seem far too suggestive, or perhaps just rude, to lay with his back to Sidney, so Jonas laid on his hip, leaving them face to face. Sidney's lips were slightly less blue. Jonas kept the cashmere blanket between them, both for modesty's sake, and that to have wormed between it would have put them chest to chest. As it was, there was barely six inches between them, and less between their feet.

"Alright?" Jonas asked. Sidney nodded. Jonas tugged the upper two blankets up to his chin and breathed in a sigh of relief. Laying down felt very nice indeed. Not so awkward now that they were both settled.

"What's the likelihood that that merfolk will crawl on board and k-k-kill us?"

"Low. I left it alive, primarily as a warning. They'll take the hint. They're not dumb creatures."

"And the mark is gone? You're sure."

"Fairly," Jonas said. "You don't really smell like it anymore."

"Smell like it?" Sidney's eyebrows approached his hairline. Jonas hadn't realized how odd that would sound.

"You smelled like, well, Menelaus, I suppose. The sea. Warm, salty. You don't smell like it now."

"What do I— Sorry, are you sure I don't smell like it now?" Sidney asked, tilting his chin down and inhaling deeply. Jonas chuckled.

"No, now you smell like bracken and..." Jonas leaned forward, his face arguably too close to Sidney's neck. Creatures had a good sense of smell, fae and demons alike, but the human Jonas was pretending to be would have to get closer. Though he shouldn't have. Adrenaline was clouding his judgement.

Still, there was a soft warm smell to Sidney. A dry place, likely a library, and a sharpness of pine, almost like cologne. "You smell like books and trees." Jonas said, trying to ignore the intimacy of the declaration. Sidney only cocked his head, his wet hair leaving a dark stain on the blanket below him.

"That's what I smell like?"

"Everyone has a smell," Jonas shrugged. Sidney leaned forward and inhaled.

"You smell warm," he said.

"Almost always," Jonas agreed. "Here, give me your hands." Sidney slid his hands out from beneath the cashmere, meeting Jonas's palms in the space between their chests. His fingers were practically ice shards. Jonas huffed as drew Sidney's hands toward his chest. The bulk of his body was the hottest. That was all.

"My god, you're like a furnace," Sidney breathed. "You must hate the summer."

"There's a reason I live so far north." Sidney stretched out his hands, his fingertips grazing the skin just below Jonas's sternum, pressing just enough that Jonas could feel the gentle scratch of his fingernails. It was a nice sensation, and Jonas didn't say anything as fingernails became the soft push of the pads of Sidney's fingers. Something in the back of Jonas's mind was beginning to panic, but it didn't mean anything. He was warm. Sidney was cold. Nothing more.

"You have a lot of tattoos," Sidney said. Jonas looked down to see where Sidney's fingers pushed gently against the lines of black ink. Jonas's chest was mostly taken up by a star chart that ran over the ribs on his right side. "I thought I knew all the constellations, but I don't recognize this one."

"Different skies have different constellations," Jonas said. He traced the line Sidney was examining, making the shape of stars he knew from years of looking up at them every night. "That's Peregrine, the traveler."

"From the magenta cosmos?" Sidney asked. Jonas nodded. Sidney watched him, his dark eyes bright and studious, and, for a moment, Jonas wondered if Sidney was about to expose him. To say, 'you're from there too.' And then what? Immediately the question humans always asked: 'what can you do for me?' But Sidney didn't. He dropped his gaze, eyes shadowed by long, dark lashes.

"This one I recognize," Sidney's hand trailed slightly lower, over the curve of Jonas's stomach. "Lupus, isn't it?"

"It is."

"An asterism, people used to say. Part of Centaurus. The mad dog about to be killed."

"I never liked that," Jonas said. "Who's to say the creature doesn't best the centaur?"

"That probably doesn't make for a compelling story," Sidney smiled. He had a lovely smile.

"I think that fully depends on who's telling the story."

"Or who's listening," Sidney conceded. Jonas nodded.

"True enough."

"Are all your tattoos stars, then?"

"No," Jonas replied, his hand immediately pressing against the mandala between his collarbones, at the base of his throat. Sidney looked at it, his fingers hovering a centimeter off Jonas's skin, as though he couldn't really see without touching. But he didn't touch. Jonas swallowed and closed his eyes, so he couldn't watch Sidney study him. The anticipation of sensation was doing strange things to the pit of his stomach.

Jonas took a deep breath and relaxed into the comfortable warmth of the blankets. It was both strange and not strange to have someone so close. Or perhaps it might have been stranger if it was someone else. Sidney Quince felt oddly safe. It was a fallacy to feel that way about any human, of course. Especially one so willing to be in over their head.

"Turn," Sidney's voice was quiet, his fingertips gentle as he pushed Jonas's jaw up, away from Sidney's face. Jonas moved without thinking of anything aside from how cool the tips of

Sidney's fingers still were. How nice the gentle pressure felt against his skin.

Sidney's hand drifted slowly over Jonas's neck. Jonas almost sighed, just catching the sound and turning it to a hitch in his breath, nothing more. When he opened his eyes, Sidney wasn't looking at his tattoos anymore. His eyelids were low, his mouth barely open, and a deep brush of color had returned to his cheeks.

Jonas would have had to be made of stone to be unaffected, but it was the twist of anticipation at the base of his spine that told him this little exercise in indulgence had moved into dangerous territory.

"You saved my life." Sidney's voice was quiet, the tremor gone from it. Jonas's work beneath the blankets was likely done. If he was the sort who learned from his mistakes, he would have gotten out of bed.

"Well, better that than having Karolina dog me about it the rest of my life," Jonas said, more gruffly than he'd intended. Sidney drew his hand away.

"I appreciate the effort all the same."

"Just do me a favor and don't kiss any more strange creatures."

"She looked human," Sidney protested, smiling. Jonas couldn't look away from his lips.

"They often do."

When Sidney kissed him, Jonas had to choke down a moan. The sudden press of Sidney's cool mouth shocked Jonas's body as much as jumping in the Bittergate had an hour before. Jonas jolted, and Sidney jerked away.

"I am so sorry," Sidney whispered, his eyes wide, mouth open, lips flushed. Jonas could feel nothing except all the places where their bodies nearly touched. There was no graceful way to extricate himself, nothing that didn't reveal the absurd strength of his arousal.

So, he gave in.

Jonas threaded one hand through the back of Sidney's damp hair and pulled him close, pressing their lips together. Sidney opened his mouth for Jonas, and that was. That was something. Jonas leaned in, deepening the kiss into a slow, languid thing. He tasted salt on the seam of Sidney's lips and felt more than heard the whimper that came soft and sweet from Sidney's throat. He could have chased that sound all day, drawing it out of Sidney in a hundred different ways. But that wasn't going to happen. At all. Jonas pulled back; his breathing labored in a way that he could not account for.

"Stay there where it's warm," he said. And then he got up, holding the towel around his waist, as he pulled back the blankets and slid toward the end of the bed.

Why had he said that? Was he going to get back into bed? He'd told himself no more humans, and he'd meant it. At least, he thought he had. He could hear Sidney shift on the bed behind him, and steeled himself, refusing to look back. "I'll toss your clothes down."

8

idney put his clothes back on before they'd made it to the marina, and didn't say anything to Jonas as they got off the boat and into the truck.

Sidney was mortified. He'd let his fantasies get the better of him. Again. Jonas wasn't Mark. He hadn't crafted some perfect persona specifically meant to woo Sidney. He was Karolina's brother. A real person who didn't deserve to be mauled because Sidney couldn't control his urges. It was a relief, primarily to Sidney's ego, that his business with Jonas Rookwood was done.

Except. Except, if Sidney was going to research these other celestial skies, Jonas Rookwood's library seemed like the most logical place to begin. And if he was really going to try and build his dissertation around what he'd charted, he would need a better understanding of these different realms and what they meant. And, well, Jonas had kissed him back.

The thought of it, the way Jonas's hand had felt in the back of Sidney's hair, the heat and the hunger of it made Sidney's heart beat faster. He stared out the passenger side window as the sky turned a darker shade of grey over the bay. Sidney swallowed.

"You said there's a phone at the big house?" Sidney's voice was rougher than he'd anticipated.

"Yes." Jonas sounded perfectly even. Unbothered. Maybe this sort of thing happened to him all the time. The thought made Sidney blush all over again.

"Do you mind dropping me off?" Sidney asked as they rattled over the hill. "I need to make a call."

The foyer of Elmmond House was long and imposing. The floor was striped with light from open doors and hallways that sprouted off in all directions. A tall set of stairs was made of dark wood and lined with plush navy carpet that flooded down to the front door like a river. A grand tapestry in deep blues and greens hung above the mezzanine, where Sidney briefly thought he heard footsteps, though he saw no one.

"The nearest phone is in the first parlor on the right," Jonas had said, as Sidney hopped out of the passenger seat. "Verne's the head butler. Just tell him you're a guest of mine, if you see him."

There didn't seem to be anyone there, and Sidney was a little surprised that the front door had been unlocked. He found the parlor easily enough: a quaint room, all done up in various shades of sage. Along the same wall as the door stood a telephone table, matching stool tucked beneath it. The window directly across from Sidney had a lovely view of the garden cottage, and Sidney watched as Jonas parked the truck.

When Sidney lifted the receiver, the operator picked up almost immediately. There was a soft electrical hum while they connected Sidney to the Holyworth College Astronomy Department, the extension for which Sidney thankfully knew from memory.

He waited, wondering if he was about to make a colossal mistake. He was done in Hindry. He had his answer. He ought to go home.

Before he could hang up, the Astronomy Department secretary picked up the phone, cracking her gum in Sidney's ear twice, before agreeing to see if Karolina was available to take his call. The hold music was a particularly awful recording of the marching band playing "Hail the Holyworth Heroes," and Sidney lowered the receiver to his shoulder, stepping back as far as the cord allowed to grant him a better look at the adjacent bookcase.

"Hello?" Sidney lifted the phone to his ear, relieved to hear Karolina's voice.

"Karolina."

"Sidney. Is everything alright?" He laughed before he could stop himself.

"There are other realms, Karolina." A pause. Sidney's fingers closed around the phone cord. He watched Jonas walk around the side of the cottage toward the garden.

"He told you then?"

"You could have told me." Sidney tried not to think too much about the embarrassment that might have saved him. "You didn't tell me you had a brother."

"It didn't come up! And he's far more invested in the scholarship of it than I am. You know what my field of expertise is."

"Well, he's certainly not telling me everything."

"There's a bit to it, Sidney."

"I'm beginning to see that," Sidney huffed. He could almost hear her smile.

"So, what are you going to do?"

"I don't know," Sidney said honestly. She was flipping through papers.

"Why don't you stay until the Ascension, at least."

"The Ascension?" Sidney frowned. "What's that?" She hesitated. Sidney rolled his eyes. "Don't tell me to ask Jonas." Karolina sighed.

"When the planets in three celestial skies fall into alignment, the barriers between realms become thinner, and in certain places portals open up."

"What?" Sidney demanded. "Portals?"

"I'm not sure I can be much clearer than that. You ought to ask—"

"No. Wait." Sidney held up a hand as though Karolina was in front of him and took a breath. "What you're telling me is that the planets in other celestial skies can come into alignment with the planets in our sky and they have some concrete impact on life here on earth?"

"Uh, I suppose. But it's not that big of a deal. It happens every year."

"Jonas knows about it, then?" Sidney pressed.

"It would be hard for him not to. There's a big house party held at Elmmond every year to celebrate."

"I see."

"Did he not mention it to you?" Karolina didn't sound surprised. She did sound tired. Sidney let his silence speak for itself. "Look, try not to take it personally—"

"I wouldn't, if I hadn't asked him that exact question last night, and he shrugged and said 'I dunno.'"

"Jonas has his reasons," Karolina said simply. "Look, if it's going to help your dissertation to be there and use his library, do it. I can cover your classes until the Ascension. It's not far off. A week, I think."

"I don't think he wants me here. And I don't want to be an imposition." *And we just kissed!*

"Ignore him, Sidney. Do your research. See if you can find something salvageable in the project. You know you won't be able to let it go if you don't try." She was right, of course. Likely, she was the only person Sidney knew who thought of his stubbornness as a good thing. "Alright?"

"Everything I've read says interdimensional studies aren't taken seriously."

"Well, if anyone can change that, Sidney, it'll be you."

It was a nice sentiment, even if it didn't help much. Sidney said goodbye to Karolina and slid out of Elmmond House just as quietly as he'd slid into it. Until halfway down the steps when Delilah appeared in front of him out of thin air. He screamed and nearly fell down.

"Christ alive!"

"Sorry!" Her apology was at odds with the width of her smile. "What were you doing?"

"Making a call," Sidney said. He took a breath to steady himself and started for the cottage. Lord. Magical creatures. Sidney glanced at Delilah, who seemed content to float along at his side. If she was going to hover around, then perhaps she might be open to a conversation.

"Can I ask you something?"

"Sure," she said merrily.

"Are you magic? Or were you magic?"

"Ghosts are a bit of a grey area, no pun intended." Delilah cringed exaggeratedly. Sidney chuckled. "We do gain strength from interacting with humans, which is also how other magical creatures get their magic. Fae like to make deals and do tricks and the like. Demons have their crossroad dealings and soul sales. Ghosts remain earthside through the consistency of their interactions with other humans."

"So, if you stopped talking to people, you'd pass over?" Sidney asked. Delilah shrugged.

"Likely so. But I don't know. I'm still having a bit of fun here."

"You must've died quite young," Sidney observed. Then he winced. "Sorry, was that rude?"

"Maybe, but I don't mind. I was nineteen. In way over my head with the magical creatures. It's a sordid tale, really." They'd reached the front steps of the garden cottage, and Delilah looked up at the window on the second floor. Sidney followed her gaze. It was on the opposite side of the house from the guest room, but he couldn't see anything remarkable about it. Delilah smiled at Sidney.

"Has Jonas shown you the big telescope yet?" Sidney ignored the heat that immediately colored his cheeks at the thought of Jonas's big telescope and shook his head.

"What big telescope?"

"Like that bitty one you've been using, but much larger, and with far more of those colorful lenses that make the sky look different. It's on his balcony upstairs. I can show you if you like." The last thing Sidney needed was to sneak around in Jonas Rookwood's bedroom. At the same time, he was a little annoyed with the man for lying to him the night before.

"Shouldn't we ask Jonas first?"

"He's out in the garden still, and he won't care a bit. You really ought to see it before you go."

"I'm not sure I am going," Sidney replied. He stepped forward and opened the door of the cottage, letting Delilah glide through first. She giggled.

"Such a gentleman. Come on, then."

9

J onas had tried to make himself care about the garden. He'd looked at the overgrown weeds and the half-empty beds; the wind moved the leaves around plenty, but he still needed to rake. He'd gotten halfway to the shed before he admitted to himself that he wasn't going to be able to do any of those things in his current condition, which was almost painfully aroused.

Kissing Sidney had awoken something in Jonas that had been suppressed for so long that Jonas had genuinely thought he'd killed it, and he was rather unhappy about its unexpected rebirth. The feeling started in arousal, which was frustrating enough. But if that had been all it was, it would have been quelled in the shower, where he jacked off so fervently that it made his injured shoulder hurt.

He thought about their bodies, certainly, too close beneath the blankets in the bed on the boat. How Sidney's long, perfect fingers would feel around him. Stroking him. The problem was that Jonas came to the memory of that whimper of desire that he'd coaxed from Sidney when they kissed, the feeling of

Sidney's hair between his fingers. And those really weren't the sorts of things he generally masturbated about.

Jonas scrubbed his body in a perfunctory and intentionally abrasive manner, washing his hair with the same quickness, trying to cleanse himself of the urge to kiss Sidney again, which clung to him like a bad smell. Irritatingly, when he stepped out of the shower, he was half-hard again. Jonas resolved to ignore it. He towel-dried his hair and shaved his beard, first taking it short, then fully off. It felt better. More himself. Then he pulled on his glamour, draped his towel around his shoulders and walked into his bedroom at the same moment that Sidney and Delilah stepped in from the hall.

Delilah vanished in the blink of an eye, before Jonas could even speak to reprimand her. She might still be in the room, or she might have incorporealized through the floor. Jonas sighed. Living with a ghost was tiresome at times.

Sidney stood, staring, mouth agape. Jonas told himself that he felt nothing at all, and certainly not the urge to preen which would have been particularly stupid. Still, every moment that the fully clothed Sidney spent staring at fully nude Jonas made Jonas's arousal less avoidable or deniable. He tried desperately to remember that he was annoyed at the intrusion to his private room, and the rest of his life.

"Can I help you with something, Quince?" Jonas asked. Speaking seemed to remind Jonas that he could move, and he walked to his dresser to open the top drawer where his undershorts sat folded atop two marble phalluses, and why was he thinking about those now? Gods help him.

"Delilah had said you had a uh— a rather large, uh—" Sidney stammered, and Jonas glanced over his shoulder at him. "A telescope."

"Right," Jonas said, his hand resting on top of his underthings in the drawer. He should have taken them out and put them on. But the deep flush that colored Sidney all the way beneath his partially open collar was distracting for some reason. "And you wanted to see my rather large telescope?" he asked. Sidney coughed.

"Excuse me." Sidney put his weight on his back foot, edging toward the door.

"It's on the balcony there," Jonas gestured behind him as he turned his attention to his clothes. All business. Easy enough. "If you'd be so kind as to wait a moment..." he let the sentence hang, glancing up in the mirror to check that Sidney was appropriately abashed. He was still flushed, but his gaze seemed to have stalled on Jonas's backside. "I'll dress and then be happy to show it to you." Jonas cleared his throat, catching Sidney's eye in the mirror before Sidney turned to face the empty fireplace that stood opposite Jonas's bed.

"I'm sorry," Sidney said. "Delilah said you were in the garden."

"I'd caution you not to take her at her word. Ever. She may be having quite an extended afterlife," Jonas pulled on his undershorts. "But she's still nineteen at heart."

"That's good to know," Sidney said. Jonas strolled past him toward the armoire, and Sidney turned to face the balcony doors, obscured as they were behind a curtain. "I spoke to Karolina," he said. Neutral territory. And certainly de-escalating, as far as Jonas's arousal went. Jonas pulled a pair of trousers out the armoire.

"And?"

"You lied to me."

"About?" Jonas let his trousers hang open as he shouldered into his standard white button down.

"You said you didn't know if the celestial skies of other realms affected things here, but they do. Because that's how the Ascension works."

"Celestial alignments creating powerful flows of magic isn't precisely the same thing as gravity," Jonas replied, doing up his buttons. "Portals opening and closing is practically a mundane experience. It doesn't change the tides."

"So it was the semantics of my question you objected to?" Jonas glanced at Sidney, but Sidney's back was still to him. Jonas grabbed suspenders and clipped them onto the tops of his trousers.

"Get used to semantics if you're going to be investigating magical realms, Sidney. It wasn't a lie. You didn't ask the right question."

"Do you know if the celestial skies of other realms have any effects on earth aside from the Ascension?" Sidney demanded. Jonas laughed. He couldn't help himself.

"You have a lot of gall to come into my room uninvited, call me a liar and then demand answers from me! I'm not sure I owe you anything at all."

"You'll forgive me if I don't have a very clear sense of where our boundaries are," Sidney snapped. The sharpness in Sidney's voice shot a distinct prickle of arousal down Jonas's spine, which was concerning to say the very least.

"I believe," Jonas skirted around Sidney to pull back the curtain in front of the balcony doors, "you started it."

"Why did you kiss me?" Sidney demanded.

"Why did you kiss me?" Jonas let the door swing outward as he turned to face Sidney. Sidney's cheeks were red, his eyes bright. He swallowed, and Jonas watched the apple of Sidney's throat with interest that he hoped wasn't as plain on his face as he suspected it might be. The silence that fell between them was electric and strange and Jonas had to force himself to breathe through it. He shook his head, as if to dismiss his own question. As if he wasn't desperate to know the answer. "Come on, Quince. I thought you wanted a look at my telescope."

10

The balcony was a rectangle, perhaps eight feet by six feet. There was a small table and a chair directly in front of the door, and baskets held several hanging plants with barren vines that curled down over the balustrade. All of those things Sidney would notice later because his attention was immediately fixed on a massive telescope.

It was wedged into the far corner, overlooking the bay to the northeast. It had sleek black tubes and silver fixtures, nearly a foot in diameter and almost five feet tall. It made Sidney's mouth water almost as much as the sight of Jonas naked had.

"Good lord," Sidney said appreciatively.

"The most impressive of my telescopes," Jonas mused. Sidney's face reddened and he resolved not to respond. Instead, he walked over and lowered his face to the eyepiece. It was a little after midday by now and the sky had cleared. It would be a good night for stars.

"Did you make this one too?" Sidney asked. There was no response, and when he looked up he realized Jonas had gone back inside, and was coming out now with a large wooden case. "What's that?"

"I thought you were interested in the lenses." Jonas set the box on the wrought iron table and flipped open the latches with his thumbs. "The different celestial skies."

"Yes." Sidney managed to finally remember why he'd come into Jonas's bedroom in the first place. Jonas shrugged, taking out a wide red lens and gesturing to a silver band around the bottom of the tube above where the mirror would have been.

"Each color comes from a different realm or dimension." Jonas said, sliding the silver aside with a click and then slotting the red lens in on top of it. "They don't entirely act in place of witch sight, but they do enhance it quite a bit."

"Could you create something that gives witch sight? That isn't like taking a mark, I mean?" Sidney crouched down to examine the spot where the lens fit. The first silver band seemed to connect to the lens around the rim, holding the whole thing in place. He ran his fingers lightly around the metal. "This is an incredible design. You should patent this."

"I'm the only one who has a use for it," Jonas said. Sidney scoffed and rolled his eyes.

"I have a use for it."

"To study something that no one else can see?"

"You can see it," Sidney countered.

"Yes, but I don't care about your research. I'm not handing out grants."

"It's for my doctoral dissertation."

"I've got no power to give you a doctorate either. The only thing you'll get, Quince, is ridicule."

"Are you so afraid of being called a fraud that you'd hold back progress for the entire field?" Sidney pressed his hands to his knees to hoist himself to his feet, his injured calf throbbing. He shifted his weight, leaning back against the rail as Jonas watched him beneath a furrowed brow. "Even if people don't believe in what they're seeing, there would be other applications. Or can't see it, I mean. But there could be uses. Maybe not ones you or I could come up with, but—"

"Are you always so charitably minded?" Jonas folded his arms over his broad chest, biceps bulging. Sidney shifted his weight again. He really shouldn't have crouched. He could feel blood trickling down his calf.

"It's not the worst thing I've been called."

"You hurt your leg, didn't you?"

"It's fine," Sidney lied. Jonas rolled his eyes and started back inside.

"Liar."

"Karolina offered to cover my classes until the Ascension," Sidney said, hobbling inside after Jonas.

"So you can, what?" Jonas called from what Sidney thought was the bathroom. "Keep looking into the different celestial skies and doing research of no use to anyone without sight?"

"I was thinking I might try to examine the question I posed to you yesterday. If the energy flow created by a multidimensional planetary alignment can create portals. Which, I don't know what those are—" Jonas reemerged with gauze and a small jar filled with a green paste.

"Portals are how you move from one realm to another," he said. "Lean on the bed and take your trousers down."

"I'm fine!"

"I can see the blood on your pant leg." Sidney looked down at the blood on his pant leg. Shit and damn. He walked over to the edge of the high mattress of Jonas's bed and leaned his hips against it. Jonas grunted as he got to his knees in front of Sidney, and Sidney scrambled back into the conversation they'd been having as he undid his belt. His head wasn't clear when it came to Jonas in that position. Or any position of proximity. Focus, Quince.

"So, if the extra-dimensional bodies aligning can open

portals, perhaps the shifting gravitational fields of those bodies in other celestial skies impact other things on our planet." He shuffled his pants off and stared at the ceiling, as Jonas prodded at his leg, trying to keep his train of thought moving in a productive direction. "Tangible evidence, or at least chartable evidence, is likely the best route to being taken seriously by the establishment."

"Are you really so concerned with being taken seriously?" Jonas asked. Sidney laughed.

"I mean, it would be nice." Jonas scooted closer. Sidney could feel Jonas's breath on his thigh. He looked up at the ceiling again. "I'm trying to get tenure at Holyworth. I want a research position."

"So, you can do what?" Jonas asked, as he unwound the rest of the old bandage. "Make nickels instead of pennies?"

"Thanks to Karolina, the astronomy department has become one of the most prestigious on the east coast. It'll pay well, and I could even leverage it into a better job elsewhere, if it comes to that."

"You're content living like a spider— spinning your brains out for money?" Sidney cocked his head to the side. He knew the quote, but was surprised Jonas did. Never mind that it was a little ironic coming from someone who could afford to own a telescope larger than the University's.

"You read Louisa May Alcott?"

"She's quite popular," Jonas replied a little defensively. He opened the jar, dipped his fingers into the paste and then dabbed it on Sidney's wound. Sidney hissed.

"Christ on the cross! Fuck, Jonas! That stings!"

"Sorry. But it'll heal up overnight. Barely a scratch by morning." He smeared more green on and Sidney winced, clutching the bedspread as he groaned again. Jonas cleared his throat. "And you've read Alcott as well, otherwise you wouldn't have recognized it. You need to stop accusing people of things you're guilty of yourself."

"It wasn't an accusation, just an observation. She's a favorite of my mother." Sidney could feel his skin knitting itself back together, and decided not to look. Jonas began to wind a fresh bandage around his foot. "I heard Little Women annually, though I preferred 'The Mummy's Curse.' My brother read it to me when I was younger and it scared me to bits." Jonas winced as he moved to tie off the bandage behind Sidney's knee. "How's your shoulder?"

"Fine," Jonas said. Then he glanced up at Sidney with an arched brow. "Actually fine." Sidney hadn't been paying attention to Jonas's shoulder when Jonas was naked to know if this was true or not, but he wished he had been. Aside from pulling Jonas's shirt off, which he was not going to let himself do, he could think of only one way to find out.

"I don't believe you," Sidney said. Jonas blinked up at him, his amber eyes bright, not with amusement, but with something else. Darker maybe? Perhaps Sidney had made a major miscalculation.

"You don't believe me?"

"I doubt you've already healed." Sidney gestured to Jonas's shoulder. "Those weren't paper cuts."

Jonas huffed, but Sidney could clearly see the flush of pink that slid over his cheekbones. Jonas reached up and slid one black suspender off his shoulder, keeping his gaze intent on Sidney, and Sidney had the sneaking sensation that he might have miscalculated again. Standing over Jonas was doing strange things to him. It wasn't a position he found himself in that often. Not that he was in anything like a position now, but—

The gashes on Jonas's chest were still there, red, angry looking. The fact that Sidney had missed them before was embarrassing. He grabbed the jar of salve from where Jonas had left it on the bedspread and dipped his fingers into it, rubbing the green paste gently against Jonas's shoulder.

"I would have been fine," Jonas sulked.

"Of course," Sidney muttered. "Liar."

A silence fell between them as Sidney worked. It had been the same silence that had him nattering on about his research two minutes ago, but now he had nothing left to fill it. He was distracted by the heat of Jonas's skin and wondering what on earth Jonas could be thinking, as they both watched Sidney's fingers move over Jonas's chest.

"Stay and use the lenses and the library until the Ascension," Jonas said abruptly. Sidney looked at him, and Jonas met his gaze with a small smirk.

"Are you sure?"

"Certainly. If you think it'll help with your dissertation."

"Thank you." Sidney drew his hand back, at a loss for what else he ought to say. "You need gauze. That looks like it stains." Brilliant.

"Thank you," Jonas smiled, then leaned back on his heels and stood, half his chest exposed, lines of ink and all. Sidney's fingertips itched to skate over Jonas's skin. He wanted to kiss him again.

Oh, no.

Jonas started around the end of the bed toward the bathroom, juggling his medical supplies. "Just do me a favor, Sidney and knock before you come in next time."

11

Inviting Sidney to stay had felt, at first, like a dangerous breach of Jonas's 'no humans' rule.

But Sidney needed help. And it was help Jonas was able to give with only the most minor of inconveniences. Sidney didn't know that Jonas was a demon. Didn't know that he could have asked for so much more. And if Jonas had sent Sidney away without letting him use the library and telescope, Karolina would have given him an earful.

Jonas was going to have to offer to move the telescope down to the garden, though. And that would be an inconvenience, even if it was the only tenable option.

Yes, Sidney was as quiet as a mouse, stargazing on Jonas's balcony with nothing but an old oil lamp to make his notes by. But there was something about knowing he was out there, right outside the door, that made it impossible for Jonas to fall asleep.

When Sidney crept back inside an hour before dawn, his lamplight was so low it looked as though he was a single ember floating across the room. Only after Sidney gently closed the bedroom door was Jonas finally able to turn over and get some rest.

This was why he slept so late. He was, after all, a man of his habits, and he was very irritated to find he had woken up at half past noon. He staggered down the stairs, wrapping his dressing gown around his waist, brushing his hair back from his forehead. There were sounds and smells coming from the kitchen, warm and spicy things, music and singing, that had been foreign in the garden cottage for as long as Jonas had lived there.

In the kitchen, Sidney was staring down at a mixing bowl as he sipped from a tall glass of milky coffee over ice. A radio was on, a songstress trilling some slow jazz standard, and Sidney hummed along as he put his glass down. Jonas hadn't remembered he had a radio. Sidney bent over, digging in the cabinet below the counter, his white button-down loose without the sweater to tame it, draped over the knots of his vertebrae, and Jonas immediately forgot, again, about the radio.

It was very much as though he had woken up late and walked into a dream; a life that was not his own, but where he could have lived. There was a version of this early afternoon where he walked into the kitchen and wrapped his arms around Sidney's narrow waist, kissed the back of his neck. Whatever cinnamon and honey sweet batter was in Sidney's mixing bowl could be moved aside in favor of pressing Sidney's hips back against the counter and getting to his knees again.

Gods. He'd gone insane. Seeing Sidney's fingers clenched in his bedspread the day before had made him go insane.

Sidney pulled a loaf pan out of the cabinet, set it down on the counter and paused to look out the window, where Bittergate Bay sloshed merrily in the distance. The sky was grey and promised rain again.

"Is there any more coffee?" Jonas grumbled coming into the kitchen proper. Sidney didn't startle, but he did turn around quickly, as though he was surprised to see Jonas in his own house. There was a dish towel tucked in his belt and his shirt hung open, buttons undone to the center of his chest. Jonas was salivating and chalked it up to the smell of the cake. Or the coffee.

"Plenty of coffee," Sidney said. "I'm used to making a full pot for the whole house, so there's loads extra. Do you prefer hot or iced?"

"I've never had it iced," Jonas said. Sidney rolled his eyes and handed his own glass across the counter and Jonas sipped at it tentatively. It was more than just milky. There was vanilla in it and something sweeter. It was delicious. "How many people do you live with?" Jonas asked.

"Twenty-three residents. And they all drink coffee."

"Residents?" Jonas asked. Sidney nodded, grabbing up the spoon and stirring the batter again.

"Yes, I'm the faculty advisor for a student residency on campus. Primarily members of the football team, but there are a few who aren't sportsmen." Jonas had a vision of Sidney standing in a kitchen surrounded by twenty-three strapping college-aged sportsmen. He nearly choked and took a large gulp of sweet coffee as he composed himself.

"It's good, isn't it?" Sidney nodded toward the glass in Jonas's hand. "You finish that one. I'll make another in a minute. Just need to get this bread in the oven." He set down his spoon and grabbed a stick of butter, greasing the pan. Jonas looked at the ingredients spread out over the counter.

"Did we have all these things in the house?" Jonas asked.

"No," Sidney shook his head, smiling as he set the butter to the side and wrestled the oversized mixing bowl into a better position for pouring. "A delivery came up to Elmmond House this morning and I borrowed a few things as the grocers were unloading."

"You stole, you mean?" Sidney shrugged.

"Is it stealing? They didn't seem to object when I asked for a few things. Who orders the food for that place anyway? I didn't think anyone lived there."

"No one lives there," Jonas said. "But there's a big party for the Ascension, and it's been hosted at Elmmond House for years. It would be about now that they'd start to get deliveries for it."

"Who owns the house?" Sidney asked. Jonas hesitated. But then, what harm could it do?

"I do," he said. Sidney whipped around to look at him, eyes wide in surprise.

"What? Then why do you live here?"

"I told you the other night. That place is too big for me. And I've gotten the cottage just the way I like it."

"Well, then," Sidney stalled, and Jonas could practically see the wheels turning in his head. Jonas did regret his Alcott reference from the previous day. Comparing Sidney to a spider might not have been tactful, or accurate, especially coming from Jonas who could afford to staff houses he didn't even live in. Sidney opened his mouth to speak, but Jonas interrupted.

"People do use it. Not only for parties. It's become a sort of waypoint." All of that was true, but it didn't make Jonas sound any less like a wealthy benefactor. Sidney smirked, apparently untroubled.

"Who plans the Ascension party?"

"There's a planning committee, I suppose you could call it."

"And they don't communicate with you at all?"

"I'm perfectly happy that they don't. I'm not much of a host, as you well know."

"Untrue."

"No need to flatter me, Sidney. I've already said you can stay and use my things. What are you making?"

"Honey spice loaf. Calling it a bread would be generous. It's more like a cake."

"Where did you learn to bake?"

"My mother and her wife own a dry goods store in the town where they live, but they bake and stock their own loaves and cakes. Before I left for school, I spent most of my time in the kitchen. Or on the roof with a telescope, much to their chagrin."

"Not thrilled you decided to become an astronomer?" Jonas asked. Sidney laughed.

"I'm not sure they minded that much. Mostly they weren't pleased that I was climbing out of my third story window every evening." Sidney deposited the mixing bowl into the sink. "Of course, come the first of the month, we all wish I'd taken on a profession a little more financially hearty. Though my brother Leo's a lawyer, so he more than makes up the shortfall." Sidney hesitated for a moment and then scooped the spatula out of the bowl.

Here was the part where Sidney would ask Jonas for money. It was fine, really. He might actually give it to him. Jonas had lived long enough to know that everyone always wanted something. Humans especially.

Except Sidney seemed not to consider it at all. Instead, he licked off a stripe of the white batter, speckled with spices, and then glanced at Jonas.

"Let me guess, you've never eaten raw cake batter either?"

"I thought the point of batter was to bake it," Jonas said. Sidney rolled his eyes and held out the spatula to Jonas.

"I've worked out why you're so sullen," Sidney said, as Jonas found himself tentatively licking the ginger and honey flavored mixture off the spatula. Delicious, sweet and sharp and then sweet again.

"Am I sullen?" Jonas took another lick. Sidney grinned at him.

"You are a man of very few indulgences."

"I'm not sure you know enough about me to comment about

my indulgences." Jonas handed the spatula back, watching as Sidney stuck the tip of the spatula into his mouth and sucked the batter off with a sound that made Jonas's toes curl in his slippers. Indulgences indeed.

"I know you live in a very small cottage when you could live in a rather big house. And I know all you eat is fish stew—"

"Those were leftovers."

"And your only regular socialization is with a nineteen-year-old ghost. Did I miss any of your grand indulgences?" Sidney arched an eyebrow. Jonas scoffed.

"I'm indulging a pretty teacher from Holyworth by letting him live in my house and make sweets," Jonas countered. Sidney licked another stripe off the spatula before tipping it into the sink.

"That's indulging me. Not an indulgence for yourself." The entire interaction was proof to the contrary, but saying that aloud felt dangerously like exposing himself, so Jonas stayed silent. Sidney turned toward him and leaned his hip against the sink. A droplet of batter had landed on the center of his chest, and the most indulgent thing Jonas had ever wanted to do was pin Sidney to the counter and lick him clean.

"You've got batter on yourself," Jonas said. Sidney glanced down with a frown.

"Oh," he said, before swiping his finger up his sternum to collect the batter, and then popping his finger between his pursed lips with a satisfied hum that made Jonas unavoidably aware that he was naked beneath his dressing gown.

"Let me know when the spice loaf is done," Jonas grunted, taking his iced coffee and withdrawing back upstairs.

12

Sidney ate his spice cake in the library as he began the process of learning new celestial skies. It was fascinating to look at star charts for nights he'd never seen. Some of the names and notations looked familiar and others extremely foreign. But like learning anything, with repetition began the early stages of recognition, and something small and hungry inside Sidney delighted in the new knowledge of things strange and mysterious.

Jonas had pulled some of what he called 'foundational texts' and left them in a pile on the table by the window. Sidney switched to those after an hour or so of flipping through charts. Some of the texts were a little basic. His own understanding of astronomy helped him quickly through what looked like a child's encyclopedia of planets, albeit all planets he'd never seen before. Because he was nosy, he lingered on a compendium called 'Parables of the Stars' which was a book of stories about constellations. Not his constellations, of course, though it seemed like some of them had made it in other alternate names. But Sidney was really only interested in one:

Peregrine the Traveler was a demonic soldier, a mighty warrior of someplace called the Abyssal Planes. He was unmatched in battle and tales of his heroics traveled far and wide across the realms.

How many realms were there? Sidney added it to his list of questions and carried on.

Though he was the greatest of soldiers, Peregrine took no joy in his work. When the time of his service on the Planes ended, he took a vow of silence and left the demonic world to become a traveler and a seeker of knowledge. His journals were the beginning of the compilation of knowledge of the known worlds. They celebrate the beauty and life of the realms and remind us that all the worlds are more alike than they are distinct.

It was a lovely story and made Sidney wonder what sort of military service Jonas had seen and where. He couldn't have been older than thirty-five, Sidney had decided. So, where had he served?

It also made Sidney unaccountably pleased that what Jonas had told Sidney was verifiably true. He could have lied about his tattoos. He could have told Sidney anything or nothing. But this constellation was the same one inked on Jonas's ribs. That meant something to Sidney, even if he didn't care to think about what.

Sidney mulled this over as he went back to his own charts, relabeling them with the proper names of the celestial bodies, quizzing himself as he went along. As far as what effects these objects had on life on Earth, he had sort of reached an impasse.

There were the obvious things like tides and atmospheric shifts. Those would be easy to examine because there was data kept on them all over the world, and he could align them with his last six months of notes to see if there were any trends. It could be useful as a proof of concept, but wouldn't be world changing. Meteorology and oceanography were fairly outside his realm of study. His own re-education would be extensive. Not that he minded, just that it would take time. Sidney was beginning to understand why Jonas's resume was so extensive and varied.

Which brought Sidney's meandering mind back to Jonas. Sidney could see him out the library window, on his knees, a little way up the garden path. There was a basket beside him and a dirty trowel; his sleeves were rolled up to his elbows, tattooed arms flecked with soil. Jonas's hair caught the waning sunlight through the branches overhead, and it looked more red than it ever had, almost burgundy, against the darker stubble on his jaw.

Sidney shouldn't have started watching him because then he found he couldn't stop. All his questions turned toward Jonas Rookwood. How old was he? How long had he lived here? How had he gained witch sight? And was it in a sexy way or a boring one? Sidney shoved his head in his hands and stared down at the chart between his elbows. He didn't really care about the chart between his elbows at the moment. It had been hours, though. He could excuse himself one break.

Sidney got to his feet, grabbing and eating another slice of cake before walking out the kitchen door. The path to the garden led Sidney under an arboreal arch and onto paving stones lined with purple asters, aspiring toward the same brilliant hue that chased the setting sun across the sky. Stalks of goldenrod were overgrown in places, choking out the asters, and fighting the adjacent shrubbery for root space. Sidney took a deep breath as he walked, letting his fingers brush the tops of the leaves of the barren blueberry bushes.

"Seems like you've got a goldenrod problem," Sidney said. Jonas pressed his dirt covered palms against the knees of grey work pants and glanced over at Sidney. Sidney gestured to the yellow stalks, and Jonas nodded before turning back to his planting.

"What do you know about goldenrod, Quince?"

"More than I'd like. You need to dig it out at the roots, or it'll choke everything else. My mother planted them once and two years later we spent a whole weekend digging them out of the garden. The roots spread that quickly."

"I'll add horticulturalist to your resume too, then. Speaking of which, shouldn't you be working?" Jonas asked. His attention was on his planting, but he smiled all the same. It made Sidney smile too.

"I have a question for you."

"Of course you do."

"How did you get your witch sight?" There was a pause, and Sidney could practically hear Jonas considering an answer before giving it. Sidney minded that less than he had before.

"I was born with it," Jonas said. Not what Sidney had been expecting.

"That can happen?" Jonas nodded. It made sense, he supposed. It couldn't all be demonic dealings and illicit sexual congress. Sidney walked around to sit on the pavers beside Jonas. In the basket next to him were small bulbs that he was plucking up one at a time and pressing down into the dirt.

"Is there a way to... I don't know, temporarily grant sight, or something like that?"

"Still working on ways to make your research viable at Holyworth?" Jonas asked. Sidney shrugged.

"I'm weighing my options."

"There might be some kind of alchemical work you could do to create a non-permanent way to see the other realms. But you'd need a sorcerer for that, at least. And an alchemist."

"What's a sorcerer?"

"You've not heard of a sorcerer?" Jonas looked skeptically up at Sidney.

"I mean, I know about them from stories. Wizards and things."

"The stories are mostly right," Jonas said. "Magic wielders. People who study magic with the intent to grow and use their powers."

"Humans?" Sidney asked. Jonas went back to his work, broad shoulders hunching as he leaned further over the bed.

"They can be. Species doesn't matter as much as purpose."

"But humans can't do magic," Sidney said. Jonas snorted.

"Not with that attitude."

"What do you mean? How?" Sidney asked. Jonas sat back on his heels and studied Sidney with something that might have been satisfaction if it hadn't also seemed entirely bitter.

"You could make a deal for it."

"With a demon, you mean? Take a mark and get magic?" Sidney frowned. "That would make me a sorcerer?"

"No," Jonas grimaced, his gaze turning back to the bed of tilled earth in front of him. "It would make you a magic user. But that's how all sorcerers start."

"You don't like the idea." This much was obvious to Sidney. But why?

"Power always has a cost. That's all."

Power. It was perhaps a little silly that he hadn't thought of it in terms so frank. Magic was power, in this strange new world. The kind of thing humans would give up their soul for. What would someone like Sidney's father do, if he knew power like magic existed?

That was a stupid question. A better one would have been, what wouldn't his father give for it? How quickly would he ruin himself for a taste of something that he could lord over others?

It made Sidney nauseous to think about. And all of Jonas's warnings about marking made a little more sense now.

"Not worth it?" Sidney asked, already knowing his own answer. Jonas chuckled and shook his head.

"I don't really think I'm the best judge of that sort of thing."

"But you don't think it's worth it," Sidney pressed. Jonas pursed his lips. After a long moment, he met Sidney's gaze again.

"No. I don't think magic is worth the cost."

"Well," Sidney smiled and gave a shrug. "Consider it scratched off my list, then." Jonas blinked at him. Then he laughed, a wide, handsome smile splitting his face as he got to his feet.

"You're a strange man, Sidney Quince," he said, offering Sidney a hand up, which Sidney took.

"Likewise, Mr. Rookwood."

"Grab up that trowel and basket, would you?" Jonas asked as he lifted an obscenely large bag of soil up over his shoulder. The way his arms bulged under the weight made Sidney blush and nearly stumble in his hurry to gather up what Jonas had asked. By the time he'd straightened up, Jonas was halfway to the garden shed, and Sidney had to jog to catch up.

The shed was boxy and only lit from the light that snuck through the single window and the double doors, which Jonas had left wide open.

"Trowel on the wall," Jonas nodded Sidney toward a series of hooks which held all manner of gardening equipment. "Seeds on the shelves." Three shelves were mounted on the wall in one of the darker corners of the shed, and Sidney could see the spot on the top where the basket of bulbs was missing. He hung the trowel first, as Jonas hoisted the bag of dirt into its proper place.

Sidney wasn't used to having to get onto his tiptoes to put things away, but Jonas was much taller than Sidney, and he must have been the one to hang the shelves. Sidney stretched to slide the basket into its spot and froze as the basket knocked into something he couldn't see.

A lantern fell with a clatter and Sidney's brain told him to move, even as his arm reached up to try and catch it. He ended up doing neither. He missed the lantern and jerked back, flinching away from the anticipated shattering of glass. Instead, he collided with Jonas's chest.

Jonas caught the lantern by the handle, his front flush with Sidney's back. Sidney spun with an apology already on his lips to find himself between Jonas's outstretched arms. Against his chest. The words got lost and died somewhere in Sidney's throat.

The moment seemed to stretch out interminably. Jonas's arm that held the lantern brushed Sidney's hip. Jonas smelled like freshly tilled earth and the consistent warmth of a strong fire. If Sidney breathed too deeply, his chest would be against Jonas's. They were closer than they'd been in the boat, and that had already been very close indeed. Arguably too close. Not for Sidney; he suddenly had the inkling that he would actually never be close enough to Jonas Rookwood

His face began to heat and he realized he had no idea what to do with his hands. Last time he'd let himself touch Jonas, Sidney had ended up stroking his shoulder and he memory of that had Sidney glancing toward the bandage. Which probably looked more like he was staring at Jonas's chest, where lines of ink were just barely visible through Jonas's shirt, which was stretched tight over Jonas's muscles. Sidney wanted to peel Jonas's clothes off and lick the sweat from his skin. God, he was turning feral.

Jonas reached up above Sidney's head, putting the lantern back in its proper place. There was that darkness in his amber gaze again that Sidney still hadn't managed to parse, though now it looked a little like hunger.

"Sorry," Sidney's voice was low, the flush from his cheeks trailing down his jaw and along the lovely, slender neck that Jonas very much wanted to press his mouth against. Sink his teeth into. He wanted Sidney the way gasoline wanted fire. It was consuming him. Every heartbeat thundered in his ears, as he tried desperately not to let himself touch.

No humans.

He couldn't have Sidney the way he wanted him without changing everything between them. Even though there was nothing between them. Just because Jonas was a deviant, who couldn't stop thinking about the way Sidney's hands had looked clenched in Jonas's bedspread, and how good they would have felt tightening in Jonas's hair. The incident on the boat didn't bear thinking about. Entirely circumstantial. The result of fear and excitement, and Sidney hadn't known what he was doing. And Jonas still didn't know what he was doing.

"Supper?" Sidney asked, skirting abruptly around Jonas and moving to stand in the doorway. A safe distance, that Jonas should have appreciated more than he did. The empty space in front of him felt like a missed opportunity. Like he was watching himself actively fail at something.

"Let's go into town," Jonas reached up to adjust the lantern with one hand, as he reached down to discretely adjust himself with the other. "I just need a minute to change out of my work clothes," he said before he could stop himself. Hedonistic and ridiculous. Still, there were only so many showers a man could take in one day before it got suspicious.

"Great," Sidney said, footsteps already retreating. "I'll meet you at the truck."

13

Being invited out to dinner was more than Sidney had thought to hope for. He combed his hair in the hall bathroom and tried not to think too hard about why it had felt more likely that he and Jonas would have had a tryst in the garden shed than share a meal together. Sidney tried to slick back his hair with a handful of water and frowned as the strands immediately flopped back down over his forehead. He hadn't been at the cottage for many days at all, and he'd already misplaced his hat somewhere, and even though this wasn't a date—it just wasn't, it couldn't have been—Sidney had been trained by his brother that appearances were an important part of making a good impression.

Sidney didn't date much before college, but the few times he had, he'd always gone to Leo for help. Leo was four years older than Sidney, and he knew everything. He knew how to dress and flirt and talk to people in a way that made them feel like they were the most interesting person Leo had ever met.

"What do I say?" Sidney was suddenly vividly sixteen again, more stick than teenager, staring into their bathroom mirror, smearing a handful of pomade against his hair while Leo adjusted his bowtie.

"Why don't you talk about your new telescope?" Leo offered, half choking Sidney as he tried to adjust the knot at the base of Sidney's neck.

"The telescope?" Sidney pulled a face. Even the people who already loved him, Leo included, could only listen to him talk for so long about the telescope. "Leo... he's not going to care about the telescope."

"Where did you meet this boy again?" Years later, Sidney could barely remember the boy's name, but he'd never forget that tattoo of a naked girl on his arm. Or that they'd met behind the library, where the boy had been smoking by the trash cans.

"School," Sidney lied. Leo knew it was a lie, Sidney could tell by the scowl that briefly crossed his handsome face. That was the trouble about having a lawyer for a brother. Even before he'd been accepted into school for it, Leo had been very good at seeing through people.

"Well, the right person will want to hear about what interests you. They don't need to be fed lines." It was a difficult idea, even if it was easy enough for Leo to say. And Sidney wasn't sure he'd learned it then.

Or now.

Sidney's passions were strange, and people, he'd learned, often preferred the comfort of knowing rather than the danger of exploring. And he couldn't fault them for that. But Sidney just couldn't manage settling for comfortable, or comfortable lies. There was a vast universe, multiple universes as it so happened, of things out there, and Sidney wanted to know about them all, no matter what that really meant.

Was there anyone out there like Sidney? He'd thought Mark was, but Mark had only found him tedious in the end. To Mark, things were only worthwhile if they came with clout and admirers and fame. Sidney's father was the same. Pursuit of understanding, of learning for learning's sake, was a waste of time, no matter the subject. And Sidney had vowed to himself he could never be with someone like that. Not again.

So, he didn't know where things were with Jonas. Because, well, Sidney couldn't put a finger on it. It was easy to be with him, yes. They had similar interests, sure. And Sidney enjoyed the way they'd talked in the garden; the honesty of it, and the frankness. Jonas had told Sidney what he really felt about magic, and Sidney believed him and wanted to know more. And if Jonas was going to let Sidney keep asking him questions and giving him honest answers, well, that was something Sidney had never experienced before.

And Jonas didn't seem to find Sidney tedious at all.

The urge to be taken bodily by Jonas in a garden shed was also somewhat unique. For better or worse, Jonas was all the things Sidney liked to fantasize about in one massive package. The dirt-flecked work clothes and the heat that radiated off him had only unlocked new arousal in Sidney, which was sort of unfortunate, as Sidney had vowed that if anything else was going to occur between them, Jonas was going to have to start it.

Sidney thought about all this as they got into the truck and drove down into Hindry. It was a small town, wrapped in a crescent shape around the bay, where all roads lead to the harbor eventually. Clapboard houses hung ships' lanterns on their front stoops, golden lights swayed in the October wind, like stars that had dropped down out of the dark blue sky.

The main street had all the things that Sidney's hometown had: a bank, a hardware store, a corner market. But Jonas drove them toward the north side of town, closer to the docks. Residential began to mix in with the last remaining storefronts, and on a small hill was a silver-sided lunch car, with a red neon sign mounted on top. The words 'The Silver Platter' glowed down over them as they pulled into a half-full parking lot.

A bell jangled as they walked in, the smell of burnt coffee and bacon grease hitting Sidney in a delicious wall. The seats were worn and the sign beside the door which told them to seat themselves was precariously tilted. Exactly the way a good diner should be.

Jonas walked over to a vacant corner booth, only drawing brief glances from the other patrons, who seemed to recognize him. Instead of staring at the very tall, tattooed hulk of a man, people's gazes, if they lingered at all, sat on Sidney. Arched eyebrows. Quiet murmurs. Sidney did his best to ignore the sensation of being watched, even though it was making the hair on the back of his neck stand up. He settled himself on the cracked seat of the booth, and Jonas handed him one of two long laminated menus that were tucked between the condiments.

"Do you come here often?" Sidney asked. Jonas shrugged.

"What's often?"

"People seem to know you," Sidney hedged. Jonas rolled his eyes.

"I stick out. A bit. If that bothers you, we can leave." Jonas glanced around as though he was seeing the place for the first time, and when he looked at Sidney there was a flush on his cheekbones. "I suppose we could have gone somewhere else."

"This is fine with me."

"Nicer, I meant."

"I don't mind a change from fish stew," Sidney teased. Jonas chuckled, shaking his head, and Sidney dropped his gaze to the menu for something to look at besides the crooked smile that lingered on Jonas's mouth. The menu was the same as every other diner menu in the world. He put it back with the salt and pepper. Jonas followed suit.

"The food here is the best in town. Even if it's not what you're used to from the Holyworth dining hall—"

"Oh God, I never eat at the dining hall. Usually it's just a block of cheese and cheap scotch, hunched over my desk." Jonas snorted. Sidney grinned. "I doubt everyone you dine with has such a refined palate."

"Delilah doesn't eat," Jonas said. Sidney reminded himself how very casual this all was before he spoke again.

"So there's no one else?" All his thoughts of Mark and what's-his-name with the bad tattoo had made him wonder. Jonas blushed as he looked over the counter, suddenly very interested in the 'Specials' board.

"No."

"There are some decent restaurants near Holyworth," Sidney said, as though that was the normal next beat of the conversation. As though he wasn't extremely pleased by Jonas's response. "Karolina likes this seafood place—"

"Belle Vie?" Jonas grinned. "I can't believe she still goes there. It's horribly overpriced."

"And the drinks are weaker than a newborn calf. Barely better than sugar water." Jonas laughed, and Sidney was so enchanted by the sound of it and the look of Jonas smiling broadly, that he entirely missed the arrival of their waiter.

"I can do better than sugar water, if you like," the man said. He was handsome, with a massive pile of curls tied in a knot at the crown of his head. Gold spectacles stood out against his olive skin, and his apron was well-dusted with flour. "Good to see you, Jonas."

"You too, Dom," Jonas was still smiling. "This is Sidney. A friend of mine, visiting for a few days. I thought I'd show him the sights."

"These are the sights?" Dom asked.

"I don't get out much," Jonas conceded with a smile. "We'll be dining in."

"Well," Dom arched an eyebrow in Sidney's direction. "He really is giving you the five-star treatment. Usually he takes his order to-go and eats it all before he's pulled out of the parking lot." Jonas rolled his eyes, as Sidney chuckled behind his hands.

"Thanks, Dom."

"I try not to take it personally," Dom said to Sidney. Then he winked at Jonas. "Your usual?"

"Please."

"And for you, Sidney?"

"How are your flapjacks?"

"I keep my trophy cabinet in the kitchen," Dom gestured to the swinging door behind the counter.

"Alright, you've sold me," Sidney grinned. "I'll have a short stack with strawberries and whipped cream. And a coffee. Two sugars."

"Whiskey?" Dom offered with a smirk.

"Dry, thanks."

"Coming right up," Dom tapped the tabletop with his knuckles before vanishing as quickly as he'd appeared.

"He seems nice."

"I had no idea he was such a flirt." Jonas commented, aridly. Sidney tried not to smile.

"Well, how could he resist?" Sidney joked. Jonas sniffed but didn't comment.

"He's the owner. With his uncle over there," Jonas nodded to a man who was helping a customer at the counter. "Family business. Used to be his dad's."

"You really are a regular."

"I don't order to-go and then eat in my truck," Jonas grumbled.

"Maybe if you'd hang around a bit more, he'd flirt with you too."

"I think he's got better sense than that," Jonas said. Sidney pursed his lips.

"What's that supposed to mean?"

"This," Jonas gestured to himself, "isn't exactly a package you can bring home to your parents."

"I don't think my mom would mind," Sidney countered. "And I don't get along with my father, so no worries there."

"Ah, good. Family talk," Jonas grinned.

"Yes. Excellent date conversation," Sidney straightened up, wishing he hadn't just said the word 'date.' Jonas was still smiling broadly. "I walked out on dinner with my father earlier this very week, as a matter of fact."

"Rebel."

"Absolutely not. I'm just the disappointment. Not living up to my full potential, you see." Jonas snorted.

"I absolutely don't see. At all."

"My dad wanted me to talk to the dean. To see if Holyworth would award him an honorary degree." Jonas arched an eyebrow.

"A degree in what?" Sidney laughed.

"Oh, Jonas, that could not possibly matter less to him."

"Why does he want it?"

"He's running for senate, and he's weak on education. It'll look good in a newspaper. And it irritates me. Those are all his favorite reasons to do anything."

"He sounds like a treat."

"Then I've done a horrible job at describing him," Sidney could taste the bitterness in the back of his throat. His gaze dropped to the table as he realized with dread that he'd probably just fucked things up quite badly. When Leo had told him to talk about himself, he certainly hadn't meant like that.

Jonas nudged the side of Sidney's shoe with the toe of his boot, and Sidney looked up.

"He sounds like an asshole," Jonas said sincerely. "You're living up to the potential of at least five people. Possibly ten." Sidney shook his head.

"I'm sorry."

"Don't apologize. We all have families. Family bullshit. I grew up with Karolina. How do you think that was?" He smiled and when their eyes met, Sidney felt something unfamiliar slot in beside lust in his chest. He tapped the toe of his shoe against the side of Jonas's foot. A silent thanks, as their food arrived.

The food, however, brought the lust roaring back. Particularly the meticulous way that Jonas licked the whipped cream off the top of his chocolate milkshake. White cream speckled Jonas's stubble and Sidney bit down on his fork when he noticed it. And when it was nearly gone, Jonas sucked so hard on his straw that his cheeks hollowed, and Sidney had to pretend there was something extremely interesting going on in the parking lot before he came in his trousers.

"Sidney?"

"Hmm?" Sidney looked back, blushing when he realized Dom was at the end of the table. "Oh, sorry!"

"Dessert?" Jonas asked. Sidney frowned.

"You just had a milkshake."

"I think he means for you," Dom said, smiling. "You seem like an ice cream sort of guy."

"I can go for a cone now and then."

"Hard ice cream or soft serve?" Hard. Extremely.

"Oh, soft serve," Sidney said. "Vanilla."

"And the check," Jonas said. Dom nodded and walked off as Hector, the other owner, arrived with the bill, and to chat with Jonas. Sidney was still struggling with his wallet, when Dom returned with a towering cone of vanilla ice cream.

Jonas handed Hector a wad of cash, as Sidney scrambled to take a lick from the already tipping cone.

"Not fair," Sidney protested, as Dom and Hector walked away. "Also, he made it this big to embarrass me."

"I think he likes you," Jonas teased. Sidney glared at Jonas over the top of his ice cream before he attempted to take a bite off the top. He could feel the vanilla slip down against his chin. Jonas's eyes widened for the briefest of moments, before he suddenly became very preoccupied putting his wallet away.

Which was undeniably interesting. Maybe Jonas was just embarrassed to be seen with Sidney, as Sidney was making an absolute mess. Only one way to find out, he supposed.

When Jonas looked back up at him, Sidney took a long, slow lick of his ice cream from the top of the cone to the tip, his eyes fixed on Jonas. Jonas cleared his throat and arched an eyebrow.

"Are you ready to go?"

"Back home?"

"Not necessarily, but I don't want to keep you from the stars." It was so considerate that Sidney felt like a real ass for trying to be seductive with his ice cream. Which hadn't even been working anyway. To hide his blush, Sidney leaned over and looked up at the sky through the speckled tint of the window.

"I've got a little time yet. Did you have somewhere in mind?"

14

Jonas resolved to ignore the ice cream situation. It wasn't intentional. Dom had given Sidney far too much ice cream, and watching Sidney lick at it had been the worst seven to ten minutes of Jonas's preternaturally long life.

Sidney was still eating ice cream even after Jonas had gone to the bathroom and come back, and there was something a little like a knowing smile on Dom's face that made Jonas want to hide in his truck.

But he wasn't thinking about it anymore. They were driving down to a private little inlet of sea and sand that locals referred to as "the cove." It would be quiet there, and the angle on Sidney's star cluster would be similar to the one he'd get from the house But the cove was well away from the lights of Elmmond, which were always brighter around the Ascension.

As Jonas had anticipated, the gravel and sand parking lot that sat at the head of the tiny beach was empty. When Jonas turned off the headlights, Sidney leaned forward to look up at the stars and inhaled sharply.

"Christ, Jonas."

They were turned southeast, the town and the rest of the

country firmly behind them. Out in front, the bay met the ocean, and the ocean met the sky. The stars looked like diamonds spread out over a sheet of blue velvet. The rumble of waves on the shore, and the quiet hush of reeds in the wind were the only sounds aside from their own breathing. It was more romantic than Jonas had remembered. But then, he'd never have known. He'd only ever come here by himself.

"Oh, we should have brought the telescope," Sidney said. He was hunched forward onto his knees, still staring up into the skies. "Look, there's Leonidas. And Fiagnelle!" Jonas leaned forward to see if he could recognize anything in the clusters of stars.

"I did bring the telescope, actually," he said. Sidney tore his gaze from the stars to blink at Jonas.

"What?"

"The one you were using at Holyworth. I had this spot in mind when we left the house, so I put it in the truck bed. I know the angle won't be exactly the same, so we don't have to stay long —" Sidney still stared at him, and Jonas could feel his face heating. He hadn't meant anything by it, it had just occurred to him when he was getting changed, and it was easy enough to pack it up. "We can go back," Jonas said.

"No," Sidney said. "No, this is perfect." Then he leaned forward and kissed Jonas on the cheek.

For a moment, Sidney's hand was on Jonas's chest and his body was curled toward Jonas and Jonas thought about pulling Sidney across the bench seat and kissing him until neither of them could breathe properly. But that wasn't what this was. Jonas didn't know what it was. And before he could find out, Sidney was sliding away, climbing out of the truck.

Jonas gripped the steering wheel and took a deep breath. Humans wanted things from demons. He had no idea what humans wanted from other humans. A kiss on the cheek was innocuous. And Sidney hadn't made a move toward him in the shed, and Jonas was reading too much into all of it. Like he always did. He could hear Edmund saying so in his head, 'It's not that serious, Jonas. It doesn't mean anything.' And it hadn't in the end.

Sobered, Jonas got out of the truck in time to see Sidney picking his way carefully over the rocky shore toward the sand, telescope slung on his back. Jonas followed after him, the night air cool and refreshing. His stomach was pleasantly full and he realized as he walked that he'd had a nice time at dinner. The conversation hadn't lagged or strained. Talking to Sidney was easy. And who was the last person he'd met that he could say that about?

Sidney crouched in the sand, unfolding the tripod. He'd picked a place beside a large boulder, where his notebook was already resting out and open.

"I think this is going to be perfect, actually," he said the minute he noticed Jonas standing beside him. Sidney pulled the satchel off his shoulder and thrust it up at Jonas. "Can you get the scope out for me? It's hard to get these legs in the right position on the sand. How long do you think the tide will be out?"

"We've got plenty of time." Jonas said, glancing out at the water, where the shallow water rippled around a nearby sandbar. "It's moving out now."

"Excellent," Sidney said. He clicked the latch on the bottom of the tripod and got to his feet, dusting the sand off against his trouser legs.

As Jonas screwed the eyepiece into place, he could feel the soft heat off Sidney's skin in the cold night air. Jonas wanted to touch him. He wasn't going to.

"You're really quick with that," Sidney said, his tone appreciative as he leaned close, watching Jonas's movements. Jonas was glad it was dark enough to hide his blush.

"I invented it, remember? I do know how it fits together."

"Do you do much other mechanical work?" Sidney asked.

"Here and there," Jonas moved forward to slot the telescope into the top of the tripod. "I was toying with clockwork mechanics for a while. More out of curiosity than anything else." He leaned forward to glance through the scope, turning it left and right to make sure it was secure. When he straightened up, Sidney was beside him. They bumped arms, and Jonas stepped back to make room for him. Their hands brushed, and for a moment, Sidney glanced up at Jonas, the starlight reflected in his eyes.

Beauty was a strange thing to Jonas. He'd lived a long time, almost three hundred and fifty years, and certain types of beauty had become prosaic to him. Nature still caught him off guard sometimes: the color of the sky after a storm, or the first bloom of asters in the fall. With creatures it was different. Maybe it was oversaturation. Living with the fae, and Asterion in particular, beauty was as easy to artifice as air was to breathe, so maybe it had lost some of its charm.

But Sidney looked like the personification of the night sky that Jonas had loved for centuries. What little light there was on the beach illuminated Sidney's dark eyes. His hair fluttered down over his forehead, as soft as the wind. The small huff of his breath, the tension between them, like the moment before the crashing of a rolling wave. Watching it crest, the sound and sand shifting as the water collapsed in on itself, reforming into something the same and infinitely new.

Sidney's fingers slid between Jonas's, and Jonas looked down as Sidney drew their hands up.

"What are you doing?" Jonas murmured. He hadn't meant to say it aloud, but what little self-control he'd had was fast fleeting. Sidney smiled.

"You've got surprisingly nimble hands." Sidney dragged his

thumb over Jonas's fingertips and Jonas swallowed and tried not to shudder. He would have loved to show Sidney just how nimble his fingers could be.

Before he could punish himself for the thought, Sidney did something wholly unexpected. He raised Jonas's hand to his mouth and kissed Jonas's knuckles.

Jonas gasped. The softness of it caught him off guard. Sidney was watching him guilelessly, his eyes wide and mouth open ever so slightly, and while Jonas had been a variety of things over his lifetime, he was suddenly and uniquely vulnerable and full to the brim with longing.

He couldn't even blame himself for wrapping his free arm around Sidney's waist and pulling him close. They kissed, Jonas bowed forward over Sidney, as Sidney wrapped his arms around Jonas's neck and pulled him closer. Sidney's lips were pliant his mouth soft and warm and still tasting ever so slightly of vanilla, and when Sidney moaned Jonas ached to hear it again.

Sidney's mouth slid down to Jonas's jaw and then into the thin seam of Jonas's neck. It was heady to be manhandled. Jonas wasn't used to it, his skin tingling as Sidney slid his hands down beneath the collar of Jonas's shirt. It was intoxicating to be wanted. To be moved by someone else's pleasure. Sidney's fingers skimming across his skin had Jonas straining for more touch. He'd never considered how good it might feel. Wasn't sure how to ask for more of it now.

"Sidney—"

"Can you," Sidney's voice was muffled by Jonas's skin, his lips brushing the sensitive space beneath Jonas's jaw, "pick me up?"

Easily. Gladly. Jonas wrapped his arms around Sidney's waist and lifted. Sidney spread his thighs, his legs wrapping around Jonas, as Jonas got two good handfuls of Sidney's backside. Sidney shifted, and Jonas could feel Sidney's length, firm against his stomach. He tipped Jonas's chin back and kissed him, and

Jonas staggered forward in the dark slowly, knowing he wanted the rock to press Sidney against.

The moment he was perched on the boulder, Sidney began to move his fingers down the buttons of Jonas's shirt. Jonas shivered and tried to remind himself why he hadn't done this in half a century. There were reasons to avoid affection. There would be consequences.

"We'll freeze to death," Jonas muttered, not that he actually cared. Or would let them freeze. He was entranced by the way Sidney was undressing him. Jonas let his hands trail along the hem of Sidney's sweater. When Jonas grazed the skin of Sidney's stomach, Sidney's hips jumped. "Anyone could see us out here, you know."

"See what?" Sidney panted as Jonas dragged his fingers lower, across the soft hairs that led below Sidney's waistband.

"Just because the cove's deserted right now doesn't mean it always is." Sidney wrapped his legs around Jonas's hips. He leaned back on the rock, pulling Jonas down on top of him with a moan of pleasure.

When Sidney's thumb opened the top button of Jonas's trousers, Jonas forgot about the reasons and the consequences he'd been trying to enumerate earlier. Sidney's fingers were cool and soft, and his teeth were digging into Jonas's bottom lip with exactly the right amount of pressure. Jonas groaned.

"Do you care if someone sees us?" Sidney murmured, his breath warm against Jonas's jaw. No. God. He would have done this in the middle of town square if it was his only option.

"No," Jonas said. He could feel Sidney smile, his kiss turned soft as he pulled away slightly.

"I," Sidney began, his chest rising and falling before he started again. "I like you."

"Oh," Jonas said. Sidney smiled then, a small thing.

"I thought I was being obvious."

"I can be a little thick-headed at times," Jonas said. Sidney kissed him, and then got a good grip on Jonas's shoulder, holding, grinding up, and though he was looking down, Jonas saw stars. He reached for Sidney's hip, pushing him down against the stone and Sidney moaned, his eyes wide and dark, and Jonas wanted him. Wanted all of this. Wanted more.

It was dangerous. Stupid. Don't do it, said a small ignorable voice that was in no way attached to his cock. Barely attached to his brain.

Sidney slid his fingertips over Jonas's pectoral and rubbed his nipple. Jonas's body went tight and liquid at the same time; he grunted involuntarily when Sidney teased him again. Jonas could feel Sidney watching him. He could also feel Sidney's cock firming against Jonas's stomach with every twitch and moan that Jonas made.

"Is this—?"

"Good," Jonas agreed, nodding, as Sidney continued. "Yes. Gods, Sidney—" Sidney leaned forward, one hand sliding beneath Jonas's shirt to catch one nipple, flicking his tongue over the other. Jonas gasped and bucked his hips. He was so close.

"You're so sensitive."

"Observational science really is your forte," Jonas mumbled. Sidney smirked.

"I want to suck your cock."

Oh, no.

Oh, yes.

"I've got a better idea," Jonas said with his last modicum of common sense. He reached between them, pressing his palm against the thick bulge of Sidney's cock. Sidney hissed and rutted against his hand.

"Fuck, Jonas."

Jonas slid his fingers down into Sidney's trousers, beneath

the waistband of his shorts and stroked Sidney. Sidney bucked, his head thrown back and Jonas leaned forward, letting Sidney slide against his palm. Gods, that throat.

Jonas gave in, sinking his teeth into the skin of Sidney's neck. Not too hard, but hard enough that Sidney cried out, a sound a pleasure that Jonas wanted again and louder.

"I—Jonas—" Sidney pushed Jonas's stomach back, scrambling for Jonas's waistband, sliding Jonas's cock free. When Sidney stroked him, Jonas thrust forward into the friction, grazing the base of Sidney's cock. Then he did what only seemed sensible and took them both in hand.

Jonas watched Sidney thrust against him, hypnotized by the sounds, the small whimpers Sidney made.

"Jonas, I'm close." Jonas tightened his grip, leaning forward slightly, braced against the cold stone. Sidney's mouth was barely open, panting, and Jonas brushed the pad of his thumb against the bottom of Sidney's lip. There was no part of Sidney that Jonas didn't want to touch. When Sidney tilted his chin down and sucked Jonas's thumb into his mouth, Jonas nearly lost himself. Sidney's eyelashes fluttered closed and he came with a groan.

Before Jonas could give his own warning, Sidney looked up at him through those dark lashes. He took Jonas's thumb deeper, hollowing out his cheeks as he sucked obscenely, and Jonas came harder than he had in years.

Jonas's chest heaved, as he tried to catch his breath. He was dizzy. And when Sidney kissed him again it felt like an anchor. Like solid ground. Sidney leaned back, gasping for breath, and Jonas kissed Sidney's neck where he'd bitten it, reveling in the sensation of Sidney's pulse against his lips.

"Jonas," Sidney's voice was weak, his eyes wide as he looked up at Jonas. Jonas kissed Sidney again. He couldn't help himself. Jonas wanted to hold him. Wanted to kiss him and clean him up and take him to bed. It wasn't a good idea, but that didn't matter so much at the moment.

"It'll be about time for your stars," Jonas said. Sidney pressed his forehead onto the top of Jonas's shoulder, and Jonas could feel him laughing.

"I've never cared less about stars in my life."

"That's the endorphins talking."

"No, it isn't," Sidney said with such sincerity that Jonas had no idea what to say in response.

"Sorry if that was—" Sidney was packing up the telescope as the clouds rolled in. As far as stargazing had gone, it was a wasted night. As far as everything else was concerned, Sidney had no idea.

"Don't apologize." Jonas took the brown leather satchel from Sidney. Sidney grabbed his notebook. "I had fun."

Fun. Sidney snorted.

"I didn't think you hadn't."

"Then why were you apologizing? Was it no good for you?"

"Quite the opposite," Sidney ignored the heat rising to his cheeks. "You've got a gift for understatement."

"It was fun," Jonas smiled. "It was other things as well." Sidney nearly choked on his demand to know what exactly else those other things were. Though he supposed that it wouldn't do to ask when he didn't have an answer ready himself.

They got into the truck in comfortable silence. He was no closer to understanding what was happening between himself and Jonas Rookwood than he was before dinner. But somehow that didn't bother him as much as it had then.

Halfway into town, a question had begun to itch at the back of Sidney's brain.

"Why did you kiss me?" Sidney asked, a repeat of the conversation they'd had the day before. Jonas smiled to himself as he turned down a side street.

"If I'm keeping track, you're the one who keeps kissing me."

"I'm not sure you can say that this time."

"We met in the middle," Jonas said, looking smug. He paused and glanced at Sidney, his expression morphing into something softer, but largely enigmatic, before he looked back out at the road. "I like the way you want things. The way you crave things and then you just sort of... take them. I don't really know what that's like."

"I don't crave things," Sidney said. Even though he sort of did.

"I've known you for three days and you've done nothing but ask questions and pursue ends, despite being given only bizarre new information in return. You're not put off by ghosts or merfolk, or," Jonas paused, stopping at a light. "Or me."

"Was I supposed to be put off by you?" Sidney smirked. Jonas nodded.

"Most people are."

"I find that exceedingly hard to believe."

"I kissed you because I wanted to. Being the object of your craving, your wanting is," Jonas stumbled, biting his bottom lip, as he very clearly rifled through a mental catalog of words that weren't fitting right. Sidney knew what he meant though. The way it had felt when Jonas had pinned him down on that rock. The way Jonas wanted him had been intoxicating and largely indescribable.

"Magical?" Sidney offered, a gentle tease. Jonas groaned.

"Never mind. Forget everything I said." Sidney laughed out loud, resting his head against the window. Something brushed against his knuckles, and he looked down to see Jonas's fingers, slotting between his on the bench seat.

15

Jonas woke to knocking on the front door of the cottage. Groggy, he sat for a long moment, trying to get his bearings. The whole of the night before felt like a wonderful dream, and he wondered if maybe part of it had been. The cove hadn't really happened like that, had it? The knocking stopped and then started again, harder. Jonas pulled back the blankets at the same moment that Delilah appeared.

"Father Michaels is here with Mrs. Byrne. She's in a right state." That didn't answer as many questions as it raised, but it was enough to be getting on with.

"D'you mind telling them I'll be down in a moment?" Jonas asked. Delilah nodded and vanished. The fact that she didn't give him any grief for asking her to relay messages meant that Mrs. Byrne really was in a state. Jonas dressed more quickly than usual and only just remembered to pull up his glamour before he opened his bedroom door.

It was a good thing he had. Sidney opened the door to the guest room across the landing at the exact same moment. They both paused, Sidney squinting, half-asleep. Jonas tried not to stare at the purple smudge of a love bite visible just above the collar of Sidney's threadbare sweatshirt.

"I heard knocking?" Sidney scratched at the back of his neck. Jonas thought about biting it again. No. Focus, Jonas.

"It's Father Michaels and one of his congregants. Go back to bed."

"Were you expecting them?"

"No." Jonas was never expecting visitors, but it took him until Sidney asked to fully grasp how odd it was that they were here. Sidney seemed to sense this. He gave Jonas a small smile.

"I'll get dressed and start the coffee."

An unfamiliar warmth blossomed in Jonas's chest as he walked down the stairs. There was something comforting about not having to handle whatever this was by himself. Not that he thought it was anything that he would need assistance with; if it was truly dire straits no one would be coming to him for help. Not anymore. But it was still nice.

Mrs. Byrne was an older woman, short and in her late sixties if he had to guess. She had greying dark brown hair, a ruddy face and was turning a dog leash and collar over and over in trembling hands. Jonas remembered then that she was usually seen with some kind of little yellow wire-haired terrier, who did not appear to be present.

"Oh, Mr. Rookwood! I'm ever so sorry to trouble you." Her eyes were red, and Father Michaels had a comforting hand on her shoulder, his mouth folded into a frown.

"It's no trouble at all. What can I do for you?"

As it so happened, the little dog that Jonas remembered was named Ginger, and as Mrs. Byrne had been walking her along the cliffside by the church that morning, Ginger had pulled out of her collar to chase a chipmunk and had subsequently disappeared.

"I was near the chapel when it happened, so I went to Father

Michaels at once. I'm alright on flat terrain but my knees can't take the underbrush, and I know how the cliffside can be." Mrs. Byrne gave a watery smile to Sidney as he deposited a cup of coffee at her elbow.

"I went down the trail toward the slope," Father Michaels pulled his coffee closer, looking sternly at Jonas. "There were pawprints on the path to the caves."

"Well, there's not many places she could have got to from there," Jonas said. "It's a dead end. She must have come back up." Sidney delivered Jonas's coffee cup and set the rest of the spice loaf from the day before in the center of the table.

"That's the worry," Father Michaels said. "I went all the way down to the cave entrance and the bottom boards have fallen away. It's open enough. I'm afraid she might have gone in." Shit. Jonas sighed and sat back in his chair, as Mrs. Byrne began again.

"I told the Father that I could go in, and I'd happily—"

"No, Mrs. Byrne," Jonas interrupted with a shake of his head. "That's not a good idea."

"I didn't realize that was all your property," she continued on. Sidney slid a hand across Jonas's shoulder blades, and Jonas glanced up at him. His brow was furrowed, lips pursed slightly, an unasked question clear on his face. *Can we help?*

Jonas didn't like the idea of anyone else going into the caves. And he wasn't sure if he liked the idea of going by himself more or less.

"Sidney and I will go in and have a look around," he announced before he could second guess himself. "Give me a few minutes to collect some things."

"You should stay here and help yourself to more coffee and cake." Sidney leaned across the table and pushed the cake tin toward Mrs. Byrne, as Jonas stood. "We'll find Ginger in a heartbeat, I'm sure."

"I'm going out to the garden shed, Sidney," Jonas said, already making a mental list of the things they'd need. "If you have boots, wear them, and there should be a spare canvas coat in the foyer closet."

"Oh, thank you, Mr. Rookwood!" Mrs. Byrne was on her feet, eyes filling with tears again. Father Michaels ushered her back into her seat as she handed Sidney the collar and leash with praise so effusive that Jonas left the room with an uncomfortable flush on the back of his neck.

~

"What are the caves?"

Sidney found Jonas in the garden shed, a coil of rope threaded over one arm. Two lanterns sat on the workbench alongside a prybar, an impressively long hunting knife, and a shoulder satchel, empty and flat. Jonas was staring at the shelves, as though he was thinking he might take some gardening tools with him as well. Jonas turned, looking Sidney over with a critical eye.

"Are those the only boots you have?"

"I'll be alright," Sidney said. They were the only shoes he had and could only generously be called boots, but he wasn't about to be left behind. "What are the caves?"

Jonas turned to the workbench, his face the flat mask that he always seemed to slide on when he was choosing his words carefully. Ever since Sidney had worked out that was what it was, not necessarily a lie but rather caution, he'd found he didn't mind it so much. Sidney scooped up the satchel and one of the lanterns.

"I'll explain on the way," Jonas said finally. Sidney smiled and closed the distance between them, standing on tiptoe to press a kiss against Jonas's stubbled jaw. He liked kissing Jonas; after last night, it was hard for him to resist the opportunity.

Jonas's hand flitted against Sidney's wrist, thick calloused fingers against the sensitive skin, sending a shiver of delight up Sidney's spine. When Jonas moved to gather their supplies, he had a small smile on his face.

The grey October drizzle was the sort that made everything feel damp and cold. Little droplets perched on leaves, spangling the red, gold and brown with water that refused to move or merge until Sidney or Jonas brushed against it as they made their way down the path. Mist collected on Sidney's clothes and in his hair; it was doing as much as the coffee had to wake him up. Which was good, because Jonas chose then to begin talking.

"Some years ago, a friend and I were testing a theory that required the cultivation of several different strains of mushrooms."

"Alright," Sidney said. Simple enough to follow. If he could tamp down his questions about the 'friend' everything would be just fine. It wasn't any of his business. Jonas probably had lots of friends to test theories with.

"The mycete we were working with had very particular growing conditions, and the easiest way we could reproduce those conditions here was to use some of the limestone caves that exist along the cliffside."

"Did it work?" Sidney asked. Jonas glanced over his shoulder at Sidney, a smirk passing across his face.

"That's your question?"

"Well, it seemed like you were being intentionally vague about what your project was, so I thought it'd be best to skip to the end." Jonas snorted and turned his attention back to the path, which was beginning to slope downward.

"Do you think you're giving me too much leeway?" Jonas asked after a moment. Interesting. Sidney hadn't expected to be called out on *not* asking questions.

Knowledge was power, perhaps, but the intimacy that was

growing between him and Jonas wasn't a muscle to be flexed for more information. He was trying to be respectful. He would take what information Jonas wanted to give.

"What's the use in demanding answers? If you want to keep secrets, it's no business of mine to pry," Sidney said.

"You don't want to know, though?"

"I never said that," Sidney chuckled. "But I understand about not feeling like you can explain your work to people. I've never managed to have a casual conversation with anyone about astronomy."

"You don't say?" Jonas deadpanned. Sidney scoffed.

"What I *mean* is, it can be hard to backtrack. Explaining the nuances of a project, where it came from, what it means to you, those things are so much harder than just saying 'it worked,' or 'it didn't work.' Of course, I want to know, but I don't want to put you in the position of having to tell me what you were working on for the eight years before or whatever, unless you want to."

Sidney didn't really mean *project*. Or he did, but he also meant something else. He wanted to know about the people Jonas was with before, the life he'd had. But one tryst on the beach didn't make Sidney entitled to any information about Jonas, no matter how much he wanted it.

The trees were beginning to thin, and Sidney could hear the waves crashing against the cliffs below, filling the silence as Jonas came to a stop. Sidney slowed, coming up alongside Jonas at the exact moment Jonas looked over at him.

"I've never met anyone like you." The intensity in Jonas's amber gaze made Sidney warm all over. Maybe it was the sound of the water or the way Sidney's heart beat a little bit faster when Jonas looked at him, but all of a sudden, Sidney was faced with the realization that he'd never wanted to understand someone in the way he wanted to understand Jonas. He wanted everything and nothing all at once. And that was not a thought it was time to give voice to.

"You're pretty remarkable yourself. I hope that's alright for me to say." Jonas shifted toward Sidney and then away, his eyes finally flicking up and out over the water, like a gust of wind had changed his heading at the last moment. Sidney bit his lip, held his tongue, and turned his attention back to the path.

16

"This next part of the path is a bit treacherous. It hangs off the cliffside, so I'd prefer you go in front."

"So that you can push me off?" Sidney teased as he stepped forward. Logically, Jonas knew he didn't mean it, but it made his stomach twist all the same. The closer they got to the caves, the worse Jonas felt. And it wasn't helped by the fact that the path that sloped down the cliff face was narrower than he remembered. Sidney had a hand on the stone to steady himself, and Jonas glanced briefly toward the water below.

"Yes. I'm going to take all your charts and claim your research as my own," Jonas tried joke. It felt unnatural. Still, Sidney snorted.

"I've got bad news for you. It's mostly useless."

"Not so," Jonas protested, raising his voice to be heard over the sound of the waves. "Just because it's not what you thought it was doesn't make it useless."

"Was your mushroom research useless?" Sidney called. The research hadn't been useless, but everything that surrounded it had been. The project had turned so sour, Jonas hid it behind two by fours.

It wasn't that he didn't want to share with Sidney. The research, the testing, had been good. Interesting. Productive. But he'd been so focused on the work that he'd lost track of the larger picture. It was how Edmund had gotten away with so much before Jonas realized what was happening.

"My research partner and I were doing two different things. I was looking for a way to connect to the Mycelian neural network. To see if it could be accessed across realms."

"Sorry, the what what?"

"There's a fae race called the Mycelians. Mushroom people. They were in that bestiary you were looking at. Just like how mushrooms communicate with trees and other plants through their root networks, Mycelians do the same sorts of things. They don't live earthside, but I was trying to see if it would be possible to create a strong enough network that we could communicate with them in this natural thin space between realms."

"And can you?" Sidney asked, glancing over his shoulder as they came to the plateau of rock that jutted inward, forming the mouth of the cave. Jonas could see where the boards he'd nailed up years ago had been broken and washed away at the bottom. He reached into his satchel for the prybar.

"I don't know. The person I was working with, we had a falling out before I could test it. It's not safe to work down here by yourself. The tide gets high enough sometimes that it can flood the cave system. When he left, I boarded the whole thing up." He hazarded a glance at Sidney. It wasn't a lie, so he didn't really know why he was waiting for Sidney to call him a liar. But it wasn't the whole truth either. Sidney's face was neutral, his nose and cheeks pink with cold.

"I'm sorry about your friend," he said. Jonas swallowed. He wasn't really sure if he was sorry anymore. And he couldn't imagine trying to explain that.

~

SIDNEY DIDN'T KNOW THAT HE COULD BE WET, COLD AND AROUSED all at once, but watching Jonas pry old boards off the mouth of the cave did the trick. Questions about Jonas's mysterious research partner were all but forgotten; Jonas's coat strained over his back while he pried open the cave, and with a grunt, he loosed the last board. Sidney quickly busied himself lighting his lantern, which was what he should have been doing from the start.

Jonas stacked the plank to the side with the others, and Sidney swapped lanterns with him. Jonas held the light inside and looked around.

"It dips down before it goes up and in. I see paw prints." He pointed, and sure enough, muddy little paws had dirtied the smooth dark rocks well beyond where the light would reach. "Watch your footing here. It gets slick."

The darkness beyond the mouth of the cave was at a level Sidney had never really experienced before. One hand on the cave wall, the other tight around the handle of his lantern, Sidney followed haltingly after Jonas, who was careful never to get too far ahead. He pointed out to Sidney the hollow where the water from the bay would fill at high tide, and then Jonas paused, frowning down into the deep black.

"Any chance you have a watch with you?" Jonas asked. Sidney had slipped his pocket watch into his trousers more out of habit than anything else. "Does it have an alarm?" Jonas asked, holding the lantern up so they could look down at the shining watch face.

It did, and Sidney set it for an hour at Jonas's request.

"The cave won't be impassable, but we should be on our way out by then."

They walked for several more minutes, calling for Ginger at

random intervals, their echoes getting lost in the distant rumble of waves. Then, the floor began to slope upward, and the ceiling stayed put. Jonas's long gait meant it was easy for him to step up onto the next ridge of rocks. Sidney had to scramble, which reminded him distinctly of the discomforts of being a bookish child forced to play outdoors. He just didn't have the coordination that let other children climb trees and dash through forests and meadows.

A particularly high rise in the floor brought Sidney to a complete halt. Jonas was already two levels of stone above him, and Sidney, stuck, lifted his lantern to get a better look around. They might have been nearing the surface; something in the distance appeared to be giving off its own light. He turned back to look at where they'd come from, the darkness unfathomably deep.

"Here." Jonas's voice was so close that Sidney startled. He spun back around to see that Jonas had stepped down and was kneeling on the ridge above, reaching down for Sidney. "Lantern first," he instructed. Sidney gave Jonas his lantern. Then he gave Jonas his hand.

Jonas pulled him up with an ease that Sidney might have found unfair if he also hadn't found it extremely attractive. Jonas had also not pulled Sidney up onto the rock, but into Jonas's arms.

Sidney sat, stunned, on Jonas's knees. He forgot they were in a cave. He forgot how interesting and strange this all was. There was just the warm comfort of Jonas's body. The quiet that settled as they looked at each other. The way Jonas's hands smoothed carefully over Sidney's wrist and waist.

"Thank you for coming back here with me." Jonas's voice was low. "I'd always wondered what happened to this place."

"I think it's incredible," Sidney said. Jonas smiled, the first smile Sidney had seen on him since they'd started down the cliffside. Sidney tangled his fingers with Jonas's and squeezed. He would have kissed him, but he could feel the wariness in Jonas, and it seemed wrong somehow. They needed to keep going. Gracelessly, Sidney hoisted himself up onto the next rock, and when he got to his feet, he gasped.

THE MUSHROOMS WERE STILL GLOWING.

Long, orange and purple shelves of fungi pulsed all around the walls of the circular cavern. In the center, a pool of water was surrounded by moss, and a little dog lifted her head, then came bounding toward them when Sidney called her name.

"Christ," Sidney huffed, crouching to catch Ginger as she charged into him. "Are you part truffle pig?"

The soft glow from the bioluminescent mycete was impressively constant. Jonas and Edmund *had* intended to build a self-sustaining environment; he just hadn't known success would leave such a bitter taste in his throat.

Jonas kept his eyes down, hoping to find a couple of the medicinal mushroom varieties he'd planted before it'd all fallen apart. Instead, he found a few blue caps and fairy brollys and he scooped them up, reaching for the satchel before he remembered that he'd passed it to Sidney twenty minutes before.

Sidney's face was cast in the ethereal light of the mushrooms, his eyes wide, even as he held the little yellow terrier to his chest and stroked her head. The place was so spoiled by what had happened here, but Sidney still looked beautiful in it. Jonas wished, for a moment, that it had been theirs instead.

"Jonas, this place is amazing."

"Despite our best efforts."

"Could we salvage your project? Is there—I mean, we could test and see. This seems viable." Jonas turned away so that

Sidney couldn't see him grimace. Even though Edmund's experiments had long since ceased, Jonas couldn't imagine Sidney getting tangled up in all that ugliness. And Edmund's world was so deeply ugly.

Jonas walked back to Sidney, trying to shake the unease from his shoulders. When Sidney smiled up at him, he couldn't make himself smile back. He bent down and tucked the mushrooms into Sidney's bag. The little dog yipped and Jonas grit his teeth.

"We should go."

"Are you sure you don't want to look around?" Sidney asked, getting up with a groan. Jonas's stomach twisted at the thought and he shook his head.

"No. Mrs. Byrne is waiting for us."

Jonas's chest ached well past the point where the glow of the mushrooms had faded into darkness.

Sidney didn't have the coordination to carry Ginger and the lantern, and keep his footing, so Jonas took the dog. Aside from the occasional yip she was still, like she knew how much of an inconvenience she was being. Jonas still couldn't swallow around guilt that was lodged in his throat, but carrying the dog was a welcome distraction.

When they were a little more than halfway out of the caves, Jonas heard a sudden, loud rush of water. He held up his lantern and Sidney stopped at his side, squinting as though that would help him see better.

"What is that?"

"I don't know."

"My alarm hasn't gone off yet." Sidney tugged his pocket watch out of his pocket with grit-covered fingers and flipped it open. "Twenty minutes, still." Jonas grimaced. He hadn't been back here in too long. The place had changed, even though it still made him feel like he was in over his head.

Jonas slid from one ridge to the next. In the place where the ceiling finally opened up, he splashed down into three inches of fast-moving water.

"Fuck!" His curse echoed away on the water that was sloshing up from the gaps in the rock below. Sidney landed beside him, his mouth a thin line. He looked concerned. Not afraid. Probably because he didn't know he ought to be afraid. "We'll need to go fast. The tide's coming in more quickly than I expected."

"Alright," Sidney said. "Do you want me to go first with the lantern?"

"No." The thought of Sidney getting too far out ahead made Jonas's chest tight. He'd be left behind. Left to drown in the rising water. Trapped.

No. Sidney wouldn't do that to him. Jonas forced himself to take a breath.

"I'll go first and you follow me. Step where I step, alright?"

"Alright," Sidney nodded. Too trusting, Sidney. Did he know how stupid it was that he'd come down here? But it was too late for that now. Jonas took another breath and ducked, dropping into the lowest part of the cave, water rushing against his knees.

On Sidney, the water was thigh high. The roar of the waves made it impossible to hear. Jonas pushed ahead, his lantern smacking against the wall as he held Ginger tucked under his other arm. He had to trust that Sidney was behind him. This little outcropping of rocks was too narrow for him to turn back and look.

"Almost there!" he called out.

"Good!" Sidney shouted. "Because I hate this!" Jonas laughed, the ball of anxiety tightening in his chest.

Jonas felt the roll of water before he heard it. The ground under their feet shook with the reverberations of a wave. Jonas dropped his lantern, reaching for Sidney, turning his back to a massive wall of water. He leaned his head against the rock and tucked the dog into his chest, his grip furiously tight on Sidney's wrist. The wave smacked hard against them, pouring over his shoulders and then rushed backward, yanking Sidney out of his grasp.

"Sidney!" Jonas spun, feet slipping. Didn't see him. The water rushed out and the path was clear. Jonas ran for the entrance. Put the dog down. Find Sidney. Put the dog down. Find Sidney.

The water swelled as Jonas half tossed Ginger onto the higher rock shelf. Jonas moved to shuck his coat when he saw him.

Sidney's black hair shone against the far wall of the cave. He was pulling himself up when another wave crashed over his head. Fear made Jonas stupid. He should have been watching his feet, but he stepped too far and dropped off the shelf into the water.

Everything around him went dark. The water was so loud that it was like he'd stuffed his ears with cotton. For a moment he couldn't breathe, as water flooded his nose, mouth. His lungs. He'd fucked this so badly and now they were both going to die in this stupid cave.

Something thin and firm slammed into Jonas's chest with the force of a torpedo, and Jonas crashed back against the rock shelf. Jonas reached up and behind him, cold air chilling his skin, as he hauled himself up, head and shoulders, waist over the edge of the ridge. And Sidney was pulling himself up beside him, on top of him, hands slipping against the wet stone.

Jonas fumbled to help him, furious at the way fear wanted him to turn and vomit. Not now. Not yet. Sidney tumbled to the side, pushed himself up onto his knees, choking up mouthfuls of water. Ginger yapped at them from above, as Jonas tried to help Sidney upright.

"Fuck! Sidney—"

"You alright?" Sidney wheezed, his dark eyes bright and wide as he looked at Jonas. His hair hung over his face, and he raised a shaking hand to push it away.

"Am I alright!?" Jonas's raised voice echoed over the water. He was panting. Couldn't catch his breath. Still, Sidney was up and saying nonsense. That was a good thing.

"You dropped into the water!" Sidney accused. Jonas's brain scrambled through the last few moments. Water spilled over the rock shelf and pooled around their knees. "I was making my way back and I saw you step off the shelf! What were you thinking?"

"You saved me?" Jonas demanded. Sidney rolled his eyes.

"Well, if slamming you back against the rocks is the same as saving you, then I suppose—"

"Sidney. Gods," Jonas exhaled. And then he kissed Sidney.

Sidney's mouth, the warmth of him, his breath, cleared the fog of fear and regret from Jonas's mind. Everything that had happened with Edmund was so long ago. And Sidney was here now. And he was different. And Jonas wasn't sure that he deserved him.

17

It started to rain as they trekked back to the house, an almost laughable inconvenience, since they were already soaked to the skin. Sidney had Ginger on her leash, and Jonas's arm tight around his waist. Sidney was too exhausted to feel much beside the comfort of the warm weight of Jonas, and it was nice that Jonas didn't seem inclined to let go. When they reached the front door of the cottage, Jonas pushed it open and let Ginger run inside, leash trailing behind her. Mrs. Byrne shrieked with joy from the kitchen. Sidney moved to follow the dog, and Jonas put a hand on his arm.

"Just wait out here a minute," he said. Father Michaels came into the foyer, followed by Mrs. Byrne, her outfit newly muddy and damp. She thanked Sidney and Jonas a dozen times each, and at some point, Jonas slid the keys to the truck into Father Michaels' hand.

"We'll leave you boys to get cleaned up," Father Michaels said, taking Mrs. Byrne by the elbow and guiding her to the truck.

"That was kind of you," Sidney smiled. Jonas didn't smile back.

"I need to tell you something."

The walk home had been quiet, but Sidney had gotten so used to Jonas's silences that he'd been lulled into a false sense of security. Water trickled down his spine and Sidney tried not to shiver.

"Okay."

"My friend was trying to do some incredibly unethical experiments in the caves." Sidney sighed in relief, almost smiling, which were the wrong things to do. Jonas's eyes narrowed.

"No." Sidney tried to explain. "It's not— That's bad. Horrible. And I'm sure it put you in a terrible position. But I did figure that out already. Back in the spooky underground death trap."

"You knew?" Jonas demanded. Sidney frowned.

"Well, the location doesn't exactly scream 'this has been peer reviewed,' does it?"

"But the mushrooms—"

"You were working with the mushrooms to create a linked communication network between realms," Sidney said. He'd understood that much, after all. "What was *he* doing?"

"He was trying to create Mycelian clones. I've never been fully sure why."

"The people? The race?" Sidney asked. Jonas nodded. "Why?" Jonas shrugged, looking miserable. Sidney supposed it was hard to assume good intent, when the man had kept his work a secret from Jonas. "But you stopped him?"

"Or it didn't work and he gave up."

"Which was it?" Sidney asked. Did it matter? It seemed like it might. Jonas bit his lip.

"Both. I figured it out and told him it had to end, but he'd already given up. Then he left." Jonas's face was lined with worry, and Sidney wondered what had brought about this confession. And supposed he could guess at the nature of their relationship. The research partner slash 'friend' and Jonas. The omission was almost telling enough.

"I understand, Sidney. If you don't want to—" Jonas took a step back, his hand finally dropping away. Sidney caught him by the fingers.

"I want to go inside and take a hot shower. I want to eat lunch with you and talk about your mushrooms and my charts. Whoever that person was, you weren't him. And you stopped him when you knew."

"Is that enough?" Jonas asked, sounding hollow. Sidney's heart broke for him a bit, even as he nodded.

"It is for me."

Sidney meant it. Jonas stared at him for a long moment, waiting. Waiting for Sidney to call him a monster. To say that he was leaving. Sidney squeezed Jonas's hand.

"Come on. We need to get out of these clothes."

The house was uncomfortably cold. They stood in the foyer behind the closed front door and shucked coats and boots. Jonas sighed at the state of the floor where Ginger had left streaked, muddy paw prints. Sidney shivered, his shirt and sweater clinging to his skin. They didn't speak until Sidney was halfway up the stairs, Jonas several steps behind.

"Use my bathroom. I'll turn on the steam."

"You have a steam room?" Sidney asked, miffed that this was the first he was hearing of it.

"Sort of. I installed steam pipes and a valve. The whole bathroom is a steam room, if I want it to be. And judging by the way you're shaking, you need it." Sidney made a sound of dissension in the back of his throat, but his clothes were too waterlogged for him to try and argue the point properly.

The bathroom in Jonas's bedroom was larger than the one in the hall. Emerald tile lined the bottom two thirds of the wall; dark planks of wood along the top reminded Sidney of pictures he'd seen of rainforests. Copper fixtures and the oversized copper tub shone like beams of sunlight coming through a high canopy.

Jonas turned a couple of valves on the far wall. The shower head was wide, big enough for two to stand under, even if one of the two was the size of Jonas Rookwood. Sidney was cold enough that the thought of showering with Jonas was taking a back seat to the way he wanted to be able to feel his fingertips again. Feel them against Jonas's skin, maybe.

Jonas moved efficiently, perfunctorily, as though this was nothing to him. Which, it didn't have to be. Sidney knew, now, that there had been others. And that they'd just trekked through the places where Jonas and his 'friend' had worked most closely together. Maybe Jonas and his 'friend' had done this same thing once. Came back soaking wet from the caves and stood in these very spots. Maybe a dozen times.

Jonas kept his back to Sidney as he pulled his shirt off over his head. Dark lines of ink snaked over his shoulders, stars and plants and lines and curves, tempting Sidney to examine. To touch.

But, suddenly, nothing Sidney and Jonas had done together had context. How had it compared to this 'friend,' this 'partner?' Had it been more meaningful? Or less?

Sidney was momentarily overwhelmed by the sharp resurgence of embarrassment and doubt. Jonas glanced over his shoulder and arched an eyebrow at Sidney.

"Are you alright?" Jonas asked. Sidney ducked his head and tried to unbutton his shirt with slippery fingers.

"Fine. Sorry." He didn't look up again until he'd shrugged out of his shirt, his hands on his belt. Was he fine? Maybe. Jonas was still looking at him, but his mouth was a thin line, brow furrowed. Sidney frowned. "What?"

"How's your leg?" Jonas's voice was low and firm. Almost

impersonal. Sidney hesitated. "The injury from the merfolk, I mean."

"I know," Sidney said, because he had known. "It's fine. Healed." Jonas huffed, glancing toward the tub where the copper tubes were beginning to emit a slow line of steam. His huff hadn't been a happy sound. And Sidney wondered what response he would have preferred. Jonas's shoulder looked fine. He couldn't have expected Sidney's injury to linger much longer than his own.

Jonas turned on the shower, and Sidney unbuckled his belt and pushed his sodden trousers off his legs, holding the corner of the sink so he could step out of them. Jonas was twisting knobs and avoiding Sidney's gaze like it was his job. Which was frustrating. They couldn't both be embarrassed. The past was the past. At least, it was for Sidney. Compartmentalized, as best he could. And after the day he'd had, Sidney wasn't inclined toward any more discomfort. If he wanted to know where he stood with Jonas Rookwood, he was going to have to talk with the man.

Sidney took a breath and then a step forward.

"Jonas." Jonas looked over at him, expressionless. "What's wrong?" Jonas's shoulders hunched, as if Sidney was going to try and push him over.

"What are you still doing here, Sidney?" Jonas asked. Sidney frowned.

"Do you not want me to be here?"

"No." Jonas shook his head. "No, that's not what I—" He rolled his lips beneath his teeth, glancing toward the mirror and then quickly back to Sidney. "I mean, what do you want from me? From this place?"

"There isn't—" Sidney stalled, wishing for better phrasing and then plowed forward because there wasn't any. "There isn't anything I want from you. I'm just... well, I'm enjoying myself, I suppose."

"You nearly died today," Jonas said.

"But I didn't." Sidney shrugged. Jonas dragged a hand over his face and groaned. "You want me to leave?"

"I want you to stay. But I'm not good company."

"You're excellent company," Sidney corrected. "I enjoy talking with you. It's refreshing to share my work with someone who understands it. My passion for it. Whether or not it's 'worthwhile' or 'valuable.'" Jonas shook his head and took a half step forward, toward Sidney.

"Your work is valuable because it's yours. That's more than enough."

Sidney bit his lip. Respect was a surprisingly potent aphrodisiac. So was understanding. Sidney didn't let himself think too hard about either of those things.

"That might be the nicest thing anyone's ever to me."

"Nonsense," Jonas grumbled. His cheeks looked flushed.

"Yours too, then." Sidney said. "Your work is incredible. You've done so much, and I don't think you should downplay it the way you do."

"It hasn't all worked. And you nearly died."

"Failing isn't the point. Trying is the point. Learning is the point."

Jonas kissed him. Grabbed him by the wrists and pulled Sidney close. Sidney melted against the heat of him, the warmth of his skin. Jonas's hand barely brushed against Sidney's abdomen before he jerked it away.

"You're freezing! Gods. What are we doing? Get in the tub."

When Sidney took off his shorts, a shiver of anxiety traveled down his spine and he resolved not to look at Jonas. After what had happened at the cove, it was silly to be nervous about bathing together. It was perfunctory. Not sexual in the slightest.

Thankfully the shower was so gorgeously, perfectly hot, that it was easy to forget to be embarrassed. Sidney groaned as he leaned back under the water, letting the heat thaw him all the way to the bone. He could hear Jonas getting in on the other end of the tub and did badly want to look. Instead, he washed himself, scrubbing away the salt and silt residue from the bay water. When he opened his eyes, Jonas was leaning against the tile, watching.

Sidney had about three and a half seconds to appreciate the sight of Jonas fully nude. He could have been carved out of marble, each firm muscle well-defined, the black ink on his skin could have read like the labels of an anatomy poster. His thighs were thick and Sidney wanted nothing more than to be between them. Touching them. Biting them. He was hard. They were both hard. And Sidney was shaking again, but for an entirely new reason.

Jonas took two steps and slid his arms around Sidney's waist. Sidney leaned into him and all he could feel was the places where their bodies touched. The soft brush of Jonas's fingers across the small of Sidney's back. And the way their mouths fit together.

Jonas's skin was slick and firm beneath Sidney's fingers. The muscles in Jonas's thigh twitched at his touch, and Sidney shifted his weight onto his heel so that he could step back. Get onto his knees. Swallow around that perfect cock.

But Jonas pulled him close and they were kissing again and it was gentle. Tender and slow. Jonas skated his hand over Sidney's ribs almost reverently, and Sidney was caught off guard, made breathless by the touch.

There had always been a clean line in Sidney's mind between types of romantic encounters. There was being desperate to have someone physically. The skin crawling ache for sensation, mad with lust. Then the other sort, strictly the purview of fairy tales and romance novels: being held and kissed and caressed like something precious. To be cherished and maybe even loved.

The way Sidney wanted Jonas had become more complex. When they looked at each other, Sidney had the sense that he'd been granted witch sight all over again. His understanding of Jonas, and of himself, was new and shifting. And Sidney was eager to explore it.

18

Jonas stepped back, his large palms sliding over Sidney's hips and then off. He turned, reaching for a washcloth and soap. Sidney watched him, thunderstruck to realize that he needed Jonas like he needed air in his lungs and blood in his veins. It didn't make a lot of sense, but it was hard to think when Jonas was rubbing a bar of soap across the firm, muscular planes of his chest.

After they'd washed, Jonas turned off the shower, and Sidney felt that he should be commended for his great strength of character, as it was only then that he let himself slide up against Jonas and kiss him again. Their bodies were flush in a number of very perfect places and Sidney immediately lost the battle of keeping his hands to himself. Jonas smiled against Sidney's mouth, before he pulled away with a chuckle.

"You're a menace, Quince."

Jonas stepped out of the tub and handed Sidney a towel. Sidney dried off, but really he mostly just dragged the towel over his skin as he watched Jonas's muscles shift and flex. There was so much to Jonas Rookwood, both physically and metaphysically speaking, that Sidney's excitement was beginning to get the better of him.

Jonas glanced in his direction with a cheeky smirk, then walked over to the back of the bathroom door and took down a large dark green robe. He brought it over to the tub and draped it around Sidney's shoulders.

"Dry your hair. I'm going to light a fire." He already had, but Sidney wasn't going to be so obvious as to say so.

As Sidney dried off more intentionally, he could hear the rain still pounding down outside. A roll of thunder echoed in the distance. It was the perfect sort of day to spend at home in bed. Not that anyone had said anything about bed.

Sidney slid his arms into the sleeves of Jonas's robe and cinched it around his waist, then climbed out of the tub. The robe brushed against his ankles and gapped open over his chest. But the feeling of being exposed vanished as Sidney walked into the bedroom to the sight of Jonas in tight, black shorts, bent over in front of the fireplace. His ass looked incredible.

The top drawer of Jonas's dresser had been left open, and Sidney paused beside it to peek in. Not that Sidney was going to steal his shorts or anything, he was just being nosy. A brief glance, however, was far more revealing than Sidney had anticipated. A black marble phallus and a white marble phallus sat side by side against the corner of the wood, along with a small clear bottle of oil.

Sidney's mind spun, thrilling at the prospect of what Jonas might do with those particular instruments. About what they might do with them together. Jonas cleared his throat. He was sitting back on his heels, eyebrow arched, but Sidney could see the flush on his cheeks.

"See something you like?" Jonas asked. Did he ever. Sidney tried to be coy as he reached into the drawer. The black marble was cool and heavy in his hand, as he held it up for Jonas to see.

"I like the taper on this." Jonas's eyes widened as Sidney made a show of examining the stone. "A little heavy. But I think I could get used to it." That got Jonas to his feet. Sidney smirked, snatching up the bottle of lubricant before stepping back toward the edge of the bed. "Unless this one is someone else's?" Sidney asked, holding up the black marble again.

Jonas stopped beside the dresser and slid the drawer closed, as Sidney sat back on the mattress.

"They're both mine." Sidney had to bite back a groan. Keep it together, Quince. He fixed his face into his best approximation of an innocent expression.

"Do you use both at once?" Jonas's cheeks were crimson; his length twitched against the strained fabric of his little black shorts. "It's nothing to be embarrassed about. In fact, I'd be happy to hear details." Sidney slid his grip down the shaft of marble in his hand. Jonas bit his bottom lip and Sidney smiled. It was so satisfying to wind him up.

"You're a deviant." Jonas's voice was gruff. He was trying to pretend like he wasn't enjoying this, and Sidney loved it.

"There are far less pejorative terms, I'm sure." Sidney scooted back toward the pillows. The robe slid off his right shoulder and Sidney let it hang. "Are you going to join me, or do you prefer to watch?"

"Depends on what I'll get to see." Jonas crossed his arms over his chest. God, those arms. What Sidney wouldn't give to have them pinning him to the mattress.

"I could tell you about the last time I used something like this." He rested the tip of the stone cock against his chest. Jonas stepped closer.

"Were you by yourself?" he asked.

"Does it matter?" Jonas came up to the edge of the bed, his thighs bumping the mattress. Jonas's gaze raked the length of his body, and a shiver ran beneath Sidney's skin.

"I might get jealous."

"I was by myself," Sidney admitted, pleased at how Jonas's body canted toward him, like he was being drawn in by a magnet. "I actually invented a device, of sorts, during my years as an undergraduate."

"A device?" Jonas arched an eyebrow.

"Don't ask me to get into how because that *is* embarrassing. But many lonely evenings in a single dorm led to some exploration of how to affix one of these," he lifted the phallus again, "to the seat of a desk chair."

"How compelling." Jonas put one knee on the mattress. Sidney was thrilled; he knew Jonas couldn't hold out forever. His story was all true, of course. But it wasn't exactly something he was sharing at dinner parties.

"I still have it. And sometimes, when bad weather hits for a few days and I can't do any star gazing, I might tinker with it a bit. So to speak." Jonas's eyes followed the blunt tip of the phallus as Sidney ran it down his chest. He paused, taking a deep breath as it crested over his belly button. "So. I was riding my desk chair. Seeing how close I could get without going over. So to speak."

"So to speak," Jonas repeated. He crawled onto the bed, laying beside Sidney. His breathing was perhaps a little heavy as he watched Sidney untie the knot that held his robe closed. "And is this something you do often?"

"'Often' is a relative term. Imprecise."

"Fair enough," Jonas's amber eyes flicking back to Sidney's face. He ran his tongue across his bottom lip and Sidney had to take a moment to steady himself.

"So, as I was saying, I live in the attic all by myself. And it's raining. And I've got my nipples clamped—"

"Sidney." Jonas exhaled Sidney's name. Aroused? Surprised? Hopefully both.

"I suppose the rain is the important detail." Jonas's gaze dropped lower, his hand sliding beneath Sidney's robe, over Sidney's stomach. He moved carefully, slowly, almost, and again it knocked Sidney off balance, the gentleness of it.

Sidney took a sharp breath as Jonas's palm drifted down further, his fingers grazing the dark hair below Sidney's belly button. Jonas dropped his chin, pressing a chaste kiss to Sidney's collar bone.

"So," Jonas's breath was warm on his chest. "You're fucking yourself on your chair and?"

"The rain was heavy, and I was getting a little noisy. Tugging on the clamps and—" Sidney lost his train of thought, as Jonas wrapped his hand around the base of Sidney's cock and stroked him. He groaned, loudly.

"I see what you mean about the noise," Jonas murmured. Sidney pretended to ignore him, until Jonas licked his nipple and Sidney wasn't quick enough to bite back a whimper.

"So, I'm enjoying myself. Thoroughly. When there's a knock at my door."

"Oh no." Jonas smiled against Sidney's skin. "Who was it?"

"Captain of the football team. We'd had a meeting scheduled, and I forgot. Luckily, the door was locked."

"I bet you didn't think so at the time," Jonas teased.

"I might have brought myself off thinking about what would have happened if he'd opened the door," Sidney said. Jonas hummed in what sounded like approval, as he began to stroke Sidney again. Sidney couldn't help but moan, his hips jerking up to meet Jonas's fist. Sidney had lost the marble phallus somewhere near his hip, but he recovered the oil and slid the cap off with unsteady fingers.

"Would you have preferred the whole team?" Jonas twisted his wrist and Sidney nearly lost his grip on the oil.

"Fuck! Jonas." Jonas took the bottle out of Sidney's hands and leaned up to kiss him.

"Can I—?"

"Yes." Anything. Sidney was aching, desperate. He didn't have to know what he was being asked to know that he wanted it.

Jonas climbed between Sidney's thighs. Kneeling, Jonas towered over Sidney, and Sidney could have gotten off just by staring up at him. But then, oh. Jonas lowered himself slowly, one hand on either side of Sidney's arms, muscles bulging. He kissed his way down Sidney's chest, and Sidney could feel Jonas smile every time his touch made Sidney arch and moan. Jonas bit the sensitive skin just above Sidney's hip crease, and Sidney twisted against the blankets, hips held down by Jonas's broad shoulders. Jonas grinned up at him.

"Can I tell you what I would have done, if I'd found you like that?"

"Please." Oh, Sidney wished he'd had some kind of recording device. He knew he'd want to hear this over and over again for the rest of his life.

"First, I'd tease you." Jonas sank his teeth into Sidney's hip again, twisting Sidney's nipple at the same time. Sidney moaned and arched his back, aching for more.

"Jonas."

"I'd pick you up," Jonas kept talking as he slid his slick fingers against Sidney's entrance. "And then I'd take a seat on your special desk chair." Sidney groaned, thinking of Jonas working himself open with the same thick fingers that were now teasing into Sidney. Sidney's groan became a whimper, as Jonas pushed inside him slowly.

"Keep going," Sidney panted. Jonas made a soft, pleased sound and slid in deeper. Sidney arched his back, moaning Jonas's name, and Jonas kissed him gently on the thigh.

"Oh, God. Okay," Sidney was breathing hard, trying to keep focused. He was desperate to hear the end of Jonas's filthy story. "You were holding me up while you—while you fuck yourself on my chair?"

"One track mind, Sidney," Jonas teased, beginning to fuck Sidney with his finger.

"It's a compelling narrative." Sidney groaned as Jonas kissed his stomach. Mouthed against his cock.

"Once I've got a good rhythm going on your *device*, I would slide you onto my cock and fuck you. How does that sound?" Jonas slid a second finger into him and Sidney gasped and moaned. He was so aroused that every shift of their bodies was a new burst of sensation. He wanted it all. He was so close.

"So good. Jonas—"

"Oh, I'd be so good for you, Sidney." Jonas nipped at Sidney's hip crease. "Let the football team watch me take you." Sidney's whole body tightened, the fantasy tangling in the very tangible pleasure of Jonas's mouth, as he sucked Sidney off. Sidney barely managed to groan out a warning before he came hard, his hands twisting in the blankets, his body greedy for more.

Jonas eased back, swallowing, but Sidney needed him still. Sidney reached for Jonas, grabbing at his arms.

"No. No," he panted. "Keep going. Please."

"Keep going?"

"Where's the—?" Sidney felt around in the blankets. He barely had a coherent thought in his head. But he knew what he wanted. The black marble phallus was halfway beneath his thigh. Sidney grabbed it, grabbed at Jonas. "Slick this." Jonas looked at Sidney for a moment, his eyes dark, and it wasn't hunger Sidney had been seeing in them. It was desire, distilled and potent. How had he not recognized it? Maybe he'd never seen it before.

Jonas pulled out of Sidney carefully, before stroking the

stone cock. Sidney slid back, spreading his legs wide, propping himself up on one elbow as he took the phallus from Jonas. He placed it at his entrance and then pressed it in, letting his head fall back. It was thick, heavy. Exactly the way he imagined Jonas's cock would feel. Sidney moaned.

"Sidney." Jonas sounded desperate, letting out a soft groan as Sidney began to fuck himself slowly. Sweat prickled on Sidney's neck, and his spent cock twitched as he could feel Jonas shifting over him on the bed.

Sidney opened his eyes and watched Jonas watching him, palming himself through his shorts. And that wouldn't do at all. With fumbling fingers, Sidney pulled down Jonas's waistband, freeing his massive, leaking cock and began to stroke him.

It was incredible to watch Jonas lose himself in pleasure. Jonas arched his back and thrust into Sidney's fist with a moan. His hand was clenched into the tender skin of Sidney's thigh, and Sidney was still shallowly fucking himself. Their knuckles brushed, and before Sidney quite knew what was happening, Jonas reached down. He took the phallus out of Sidney's hand and began to fuck Sidney in the same rhythm as his thrusts. Sidney moaned, stroking Jonas faster. He'd never wanted to see a man come so badly in his life.

"Jonas, come on me. Please. Jonas!" Jonas lost control of the phallus almost immediately, hand stuttering forward to grab Sidney's hip as he came, streaking Sidney's chest with his spend.

Jonas leaned forward, one hand braced against the mattress, the other still on Sidney's hip, breathing hard. He looked at Sidney, just as Sidney dragged his hand through the cum on his chest, lifting his fingers to his lips.

Jonas stretched up and grabbed Sidney's wrist, casually pinning him to the pillows. Jonas smirked at Sidney's small gasp. But before Sidney could say anything, make an excuse for himself, Jonas was kissing him breathless.

19

Jonas panted, staring down in awe at the man beneath him. Stretched over Sidney, Jonas could feel the slick heat of their bodies with every rise and fall of Sidney's still heaving breaths. Jonas was no better, but he couldn't stop watching Sidney, his body arched up against Jonas, eyes closed, clearly waiting for another kiss. Jonas couldn't stop himself from dropping down to Sidney's lips, relishing the plush, delicious taste of Sidney's mouth.

Jonas hadn't known. Jonas hadn't known how he needed Sidney until he was having him. And he couldn't stop himself now, even though things had almost gone wrong in the worst possible way.

If Jonas marked Sidney, if they committed an 'exchange of component fluid,' maybe Sidney wouldn't notice. Jonas hadn't exactly been making lots of deals and what little magic he had was nowhere near as strong as it used to be. Even his glamour had felt thin as of late. Maybe he couldn't leave marks anymore. He hadn't been having sex, and there wasn't any other way to test it out.

But none of that was the point. It wouldn't be honest. That was the point.

And if Sidney got marked and did notice, he'd have questions. And Jonas's only available answer was that he was a demon, and that would change things. It always did. After what happened with Edmund, Jonas wore mistrust more easily than any glamour. He wasn't ready for questions. Not yet.

Sidney wriggled an arm free and slid it up over Jonas's broad shoulders. The touch was gentle, Sidney's brown eyes were droopy and soft, and the feeling of their bodies together, the satisfied look on Sidney's face, made Jonas all but forget the bolt of fear that had pierced his chest when he saw Sidney drag his cum-covered fingers to his lips. All Jonas wanted was to admire Sidney in the afterglow. Which was a bad sign, and likely meant Jonas was fucked as far as not having feelings for Sidney was concerned. No humans. He did know better. He really did.

"Are you alright?" Jonas asked. His voice was rougher than he'd expected. And more sincere. Damn. Sidney smiled so handsomely, and Jonas ducked his head, kissing Sidney's neck to hide his blush.

"I'm amazing. Although—" Sidney adjusted his hips, and Jonas eased back slightly, giving him space to make himself comfortable. After a moment, Sidney sank back into the pillows with a contented sigh. His hair spread out on the pillow, his body relaxed. Was this the first time Jonas had seen him relaxed? He was beautiful. And Jonas couldn't stop himself from thinking it. "Are *you* alright?"

"You look so good in my bed," Jonas said because apparently he couldn't be trusted to filter his thoughts before they emerged from his mouth. He had fully lost control. Sidney was grinning, though, so Jonas tried not to care about the flush staining his cheeks and laid down next to Sidney on the bed.

In the silence, Jonas's mind began to race. Now was the time to speak up. Tell Sidney the truth about who and what he was. Or perhaps this would be the worst time. 'Maybe I should have mentioned this before I came on you, but I'm a demon. Hope that's alright.' It didn't sound good. And it wouldn't do anything to mitigate the larger problem.

The larger problem was still that humans always wanted things from demons. They wanted boons: magic and talent and power. And for years Jonas had not looked like himself when there were humans around because he wasn't interested in making any deals anymore, or in anything else to do with humans either.

But things with Sidney had escalated so quickly, so dramatically, Jonas hadn't thought about what he was going to do with Sidney until it was already happening. Part of that was because Sidney was not inclined to act in the ways the Jonas had determined humans normally acted. Sidney wasn't supposed to be hanging around. He was supposed leave on the Ascension. So none of Jonas's secrets really mattered.

Maybe this was going to be a one-time encounter. They'd both wanted it. There had been something simmering between them, but this would quench it. Sidney would be gone in a few days and it would all be over. Jonas's chest tightened uncomfortably at the idea.

In an attempt to ignore that discomfort and what it might mean, Jonas moved closer to Sidney on the blankets. Sidney hummed contentedly, eyes still closed, and Jonas tried to hate himself for giving in to the urge to be near Sidney. But it felt right to lay with Sidney. To press his mouth against Sidney's shoulder. Sidney curled onto his side and tipped Jonas's chin up so they could kiss. The soft brush of lips shouldn't have left Jonas aching so badly for more tenderness.

"I'm starving," Sidney murmured.

"You know where the kitchen is," Jonas replied. Of course,

Sidney could have asked for any food in the world and Jonas would have found a way to get it. But Sidney didn't have to know that. Sidney snorted.

"You're a terrible host."

"I think we've moved well beyond the 'host and guest' portion of our acquaintance," Jonas said. Then he kissed the flushed skin above Sidney's collar bone, when he should have stopped kissing him altogether.

"I want to sleep and I want to eat." Sidney carded his hand through the back of Jonas's hair and Jonas leaned into the scratch of Sidney's blunt fingernails. His lack of self-control was appalling. "I don't know which I want to do first."

Sleep would be good. Exhaustion was beginning to tug at Jonas's limbs. And maybe when he woke up his head would be clearer. The post-sex haze would be gone, and he'd know what to do about Sidney, and about his own secrets.

"Stay here," Jonas said. Sidney glanced at him and Jonas allowed himself one more kiss, before rolling out of bed. He went to the bathroom and cleaned himself up before bringing out a washcloth for Sidney, and in those few brief minutes, Sidney had fallen asleep.

Jonas didn't stand at his bedside and look down at Sidney breathing peacefully. Jonas's grip on the washcloth didn't tighten; Jonas's chest didn't ache with the desire to have Sidney beneath him again. Jonas didn't clean Sidney gently, and then crawl back into bed beside him so carefully that Sidney never stirred. No. None of that happened.

At least, not that anyone other than Jonas ever knew.

20

Jonas woke later to a window-rattling roll of thunder. Rain slammed against the balcony doors and the bedside lamp flickered, as Jonas pushed himself up onto an elbow, trying to get his bearings. Sidney sat beside Jonas on the mattress. His back propped against a pile of pillows, a burgundy cardigan open over his bare chest. Sidney had a tome spread across his lap, pencil loose in his fingers as he glanced over at Jonas.

"There you are," Sidney smirked. "I was getting worried when the last couple of rumbles didn't wake you."

"What are you reading?" Jonas mumbled, half asleep and trying not to be too pleased by Sidney's continued presence in his bed.

"A book I found in your library yesterday about shifting climate patterns," Sidney said. "It's likely too broad a study to be useful to me, but it's still interesting. Cookie?" He gestured toward a plate on the nightstand. Jonas should have been irritated by Sidney eating in his bed, but he was also hungry, and he didn't actually care, he just felt like he ought to. He nodded. Sidney handed him a cookie.

Cinnamon sugar melted against his tongue as Jonas laid

back against the pillows and listened to the rain. Weirdly, his first thought was that he'd missed waking up with someone beside him. Was it possible to miss something you'd never really had? Empirical evidence said yes. He rolled onto his hip and looked down at the book.

"Tidal data would be easier to find."

"But are tidal shifts already accounted for by lunar orbits?"

"Deviations from the norm in tidal charts could possibly sync up with the shifts in other celestial bodies," Jonas offered. Sidney hummed and leaned back against the pillows. He rolled his bottom lip between his teeth, and Jonas thought about kissing him.

"So, you're suggesting we observe the effects of the moon on the tides to get a baseline, and then examine the tides for any anomalies and see if the anomalies can be explained by the movements I've charted."

"Yes." Jonas admired the way Sidney's brow furrowed when he was thinking hard. "Can I have another cookie?" Sidney handed him a cookie with one hand and began scribbling in his notebook with the other. "The harbormaster should have some record of the tide charts for the bay, if you want to start around the Bittergate. A limited area might be a good first step."

"You said it's thinner here. Between the realms, I mean." Jonas made an affirmative sound, his mouth full of cookie. "If that's true, then it's possible we'd see more evidence of unusual shifts here than in other places. Good proof of concept. If the data backs it up, of course."

"Of course," Jonas agreed, noticing a mug behind the cookies on the bedside table. "What's that?"

"Coffee." Sidney handed Jonas the coffee, without looking up, hair falling down over his face as he made copious notes.

Jonas sipped the lukewarm coffee and tried not to think about tucking that errant hair behind Sidney's ear. Or closing the book on Sidney's lap so that Jonas could lay on top of him and kiss him.

As it turned out, the clarity a nap had afforded him was not the clarity he'd been expecting. He'd thought he was going to wake up to an empty bed and know that what happened between he and Sidney earlier was an outlier. Instead, he'd woken up in a fantasy, where he could have someone who would stay. Who would have interesting conversations with him and bring him cookies in bed. It didn't seem possible. But then, it was actively happening; the evidence was all right in front of him.

Jonas took another drink of coffee. Lightning flashed outside the drawn curtains, thunder roared. Sidney jumped as the lights went out. The bedroom turned dim, everything suddenly in shades of grey.

"I guess that settles that." Sidney closed the book and his notebook, pencil still inside.

"We're not going down to the harbor in this weather," Jonas said. Sidney took the coffee mug from Jonas and set back on the nightstand.

"I really wasn't going to suggest it." Sidney stretched back across his pile of pillows. "Truly, I've had enough of being soaked to the skin to last me for several months."

"Your aquatic adventures have been rather dangerous as of late."

"It's not a problem I had until I met you," Sidney smiled.

"I hardly think you can blame me," Jonas defended, fighting the temptation to slide his hands over Sidney's bare ribs.

"Should we find candles or a flashlight, or something?"

"Are you afraid of the dark, Quince?" Jonas teased. Sidney rolled his eyes, and Jonas couldn't hold out any longer. It was a bad idea. It was self-indulgent and mildly dishonest. But the storm wouldn't last forever.

Jonas pushed himself up, tucking his nose next to Sidney's chin. Sidney hummed, as though Jonas had made a salient point worth considering. When Sidney tilted Jonas's jaw up Jonas sighed in pleasure. He was too weak for Sidney, but he was going to let himself be. Just this one last time.

Jonas crowded Sidney against the pillows. Their kisses lingered. They touched each other gently, unhurried, and Jonas couldn't remember the last time he'd done this slow. It felt indulgent. Luxurious, even.

Jonas's hand grazed the smooth skin of Sidney's chest, and Sidney arched closer, pulling Jonas down on top of him, shifting beneath him. Jonas wanted Sidney. He wanted Sidney in ways he wasn't going to let himself think about.

When Sydney nudged Jonas onto his back, Jonas went willingly, ignoring the fact that he shouldn't. He moaned when Sidney slid his hands over Jonas's ribs. Sidney's soft teasing kisses turned into hot sucking bites over sensitive places on his skin. The pounding pulse of the rain began to sync up with Jonas's heartbeat as he lost himself to Sidney's touch.

Sidney mouthed against Jonas's hip crease. His eyes fixed on Jonas. Their gazes met as Jonas reached down for him, sweeping that beautiful dark hair out of Sidney's face.

Sidney tilted his head down, watching Jonas through thick, dark lashes as he licked the length of Jonas's shaft with the flat of his tongue. When Sidney took the tip of Jonas's cock into his mouth and sucked, Jonas's whole body shuddered, alarm bells in his brain desperate to be heard over the thick arousal that fogged his senses. Sidney moaned around Jonas's cock, and Jonas closed his eyes, carding his hand through Sidney's hair at his temple, before pushing him gently off.

"No," Jonas breathed. He couldn't. They couldn't. The mark.

Stillness fell and Jonas closed his eyes, not wanting to watch the tenuous thing they were building between them fall apart.

"No?" Sidney's voice was quiet, but because Jonas couldn't sense any emotion behind it, Jonas looked. Sidney had a hand on Jonas's thigh, one lip tucked under his teeth, biting pensively as he studied Jonas's face. It was Jonas's turn to respond. He had to say something. 'I want you to suck my cock, but you can't because I'll mark you because I'm a demon.' It would be a thorough destruction, at least.

But Jonas couldn't. He wanted Sidney too much. Wanted to press the wrinkle from between Sidney's brows, kiss his throat, push him against the mattress and make him know how perfect he was. How much Jonas wanted to hear him talk. Wanted to wake up with Sidney in his bed.

"Let me." Jonas pushed himself up onto one elbow.

"If you want to stop, I'm perfectly—"

"I won't last," Jonas said. That was true at least. "I just want... I'm enjoying this." Sidney's expression softened slightly. He ran his fingertips over Jonas's thigh and Jonas tried not to arch into his touch.

"We don't have to," Sidney said again, firmly. Jonas's chest ached from the kindness of it.

"I know that," Jonas said. "I do. But I want you."

Now that he'd said it, it felt ridiculous that he hadn't before. Sidney's eyes widened, his head cocked to the side like he was trying to understand words in a language he'd never heard before. Perhaps he hadn't, and that... that wouldn't do at all.

Jonas reached out and tugged Sidney closer. He smoothed his hands over Sidney's skin as they kissed, and tried to say with his body the things he was afraid he wouldn't be able to say ever.

When he pulled back, they were both breathless. Sidney's eyes were still wide, his mouth flushed and wet.

"I want you, Sidney." Jonas said again. Sidney climbed on top of Jonas, so close that Jonas had to tilt his head back into the pillows, as Sidney slid his tongue slowly, deeply into Jonas's mouth.

Jonas pushed Sidney's cardigan off Sidney's shoulders. He wanted to feel Sidney's skin under his tongue. He wanted to memorize the angles of him. He wanted Sidney desperately. It wouldn't be right. He should have explained, but he wasn't sure he could.

And then Sidney's hands were on him, lower and perfect. Jonas moaned, his fingers digging into Sidney's hips, desperation shifting as Sidney drew their bodies together. Jonas gave into the sensation of it, lost in Sidney's movements. He wrapped an arm around the small of Sidney's back, pulling him close enough that Jonas could taste the sweat on Sidney's skin. Sidney swore beautifully, his gaze fixed on the places where Jonas was teasing, biting, his hand working furiously between them. When Jonas sucked a love bite onto the pale skin of Sidney's ribs, Sidney moaned, and Jonas tipped over the edge. He could feel Sidney follow, his hips shuddering as he came against Jonas's stomach.

Sidney stared at the small space between them, mouth open, panting; the small reddish bruises on his chest were a shade darker than the flush on his skin.

"You're the most beautiful man I've ever seen," Jonas said, because it was true, and he was desperate to tell Sidney the truth.

"You want me." It was a statement, but it sounded painfully like a question. Sidney looked up at Jonas, his brown eyes searching, again. Always asking questions, but never the right ones.

"I want you," Jonas confirmed. It was a bad idea to want Sidney. Dangerous and foolish. He'd said 'no humans' for a reason, but then he hadn't known there would ever be a human like Sidney Quince. "It's my indulgence," Jonas admitted, and Sidney laughed, as Jonas pulled him down into another kiss.

SIDNEY SLID OFF JONAS, THIGHS PROTESTING. IT WAS A GOOD ACHE, made all the better by the euphoria of knowing Jonas wanted him. For all Sidney knew, he might have floated to and from the bathroom.

Sex wasn't usually like that for Sidney. There was a line between wanting sex and wanting a person, and Sidney had told himself, especially as things had begun to fall apart with Mark, that one was as good as the other. But to hear it during sex was not the same as hearing it after.

Sidney returned to the bedside, still trying to parse out what he was supposed to do with this new feeling, when Jonas tried to take the damp washcloth out of his hands. Sidney batted his fingers away.

"No. My turn."

"I'm perfectly capable—"

"I know you cleaned me up earlier." Sidney was a little embarrassed that he'd fully expected to wake up sticky, and instead found that Jonas had been so sweet to him. And that Sidney, like an idiot, slept through it. "Let me take care of you, please." Jonas frowned and Sidney gave him a coy smile. "Consider it another indulgence for your ever growing list."

"I can take care of myself."

"Can you?" Sidney asked as he swiped his spend off Jonas's stomach, and then climbed back onto the mattress. He crawled onto Jonas's lap again, and leaned down to kiss Jonas's chest, as he pretended there was more cum to clean up. Sidney liked Jonas's chest. He liked everything about Jonas, and he wasn't inclined to deny himself any indulgences the way that Jonas was.

"I've been taking care of myself quite efficiently for a very long time."

"Have you?" Sidney snorted, looking up and brushing a stray hair off Jonas's forehead. "You'd never had spice loaf before I got here."

"I'm sure I must have."

"Says a man truly enjoying the opulence of life!" Sidney exclaimed. Jonas rolled his eyes.

"What about you?" Jonas attempted a counter. "Scotch and a block of cheese, wasn't it?"

" I cannot live on fish stew alone," Sidney grinned. Jonas pushed Sidney off him, and Sidney landed with an exaggerated grunt, more than a little pleased that Jonas was over him in moments. Jonas nipped at Sidney's neck, and Sidney squirmed away from him. "No. Don't start that again. We need food." Sidney's breath caught in his chest as Jonas hummed against his throat.

"The power's still out," Jonas said. Sidney laughed and pushed him off.

"Cold sandwiches it is."

THE POWER CAME BACK HALFWAY THROUGH THEIR SANDWICHES, the hum of electricity filling in the cracks of comfortable silence that had fallen as they ate.

"No stars tonight," Sidney sighed, glancing out into the rain.

"Likely not. Storms always linger over the bay for longer than they do anywhere else. That might be—" Delilah materialized in the seat beside Sidney, startling him so severely that he nearly fell out of his chair.

"Hello you two," she cooed, grin very wide and of the shit-eating variety. Jonas grimaced. "Welcome to 'out of bed.'"

"We were out of bed," Sidney replied more sharply than he would have if he hadn't just nearly been scared to death. "Then we went back to bed."

"Oh, believe me, I'm very aware." Delilah winked at him. "I've been listening."

"You could have left," Jonas said. Delilah crossed her arms over her chest and huffed.

"It's raining!"

"You're incorporeal," Jonas retorted. Delilah rolled her eyes.

"You owe me a favor."

"Do we?" Jonas sniffed.

"What is it?" Sidney asked, intrigued in spite of himself. What sort of favor could a ghost need? Jonas rolled his eyes.

"You're too nice, Sidney."

"You're exactly the right amount of nice, Sidney," Delilah returned. "Plus it sounds like you have a very nice—"

"What do you want, Delilah?" Jonas interrupted. Sidney didn't know whether he was blushing at the implication or at Jonas's defense of him. Maybe both.

"I can't find my copies of Vogue. The old ones. I think they're in the attic and the boxes are too heavy for me to move. Be a pair of sweet lambs and fetch them for me?" Jonas glanced at Sidney, who shrugged. He hadn't realized the house had an attic, and he was immediately intrigued. It must have shown on his face, because Jonas sighed and shook his head.

"Fine," Jonas grumbled. "Give us a few minutes."

21

The attic was a wide-open space, cool and damp. Rain streamed down the matching round windows on opposite sides of the room, the peak of the roof high above, slanting sharply down on either side. Piles of old furniture, couches and cushions, and several bookshelves loaded with stacks of boxes that spilled out onto nearby trunks were providing most of the insulation for the lower floors.

"What is all of this?" Sidney asked. Jonas snorted in lieu of a response and shook his head, nudging a milk crate to the side with his calf.

"If you think this is bad, you should see the cellar."

"You could furnish three houses."

"Unfortunately, I've only got two." Jonas wandered off toward one side of the attic, and Sidney watched him go, still a little lust drunk. Jonas bent low and dragged a dark crate out from under the slope of the roof. His shoulders bulged with the effort, and Sidney turned away in an attempt to focus.

"Are all these Delilah's things?"

"Likely half." Sidney tried to determine by sight alone which box or boxes looked most likely to contain fashion magazines.

He ended up picking one at random and lifted the lid. Inside was a stack of alarmingly lacy table linens.

"Whose are these?" Sidney asked, holding up something that looked like it belonged in his great grandmother's house. Jonas glanced over his shoulder and smirked at the smug look on Sidney's face.

"You never know when company's going to come by." Jonas shoved aside the crate he'd unearthed and pulled over another.

"Strange that you didn't rush upstairs and break them out when I got here."

"Curious," Jonas deadpanned. Sidney chuckled.

Normally bad weather had Sidney stir crazy and sour for not being able to look at the stars. But this was fascinating. It granted Sidney insight into what Jonas found valuable or worth keeping.

Sidney discovered a box of wrapped glassware and another which appeared to be full of half-empty decanters in varying levels of dustiness. Sidney slid his way between several crates toward the wall, where a low bookshelf overflowed with loosely wrapped papers.

"Delilah really wants to reminisce over old fashion plates?"

"She probably wants to change her appearance for the Ascension," Jonas said. "She does from time to time."

"I suppose I thought ghosts just look the same as they did when they died."

"I can't imagine I'd want to be trussed up in the clothes I died in for the length of my afterlife. What if you die in your sleep? Pajamas for eternity?"

"I rather like my pajamas," Sidney considered.

"If I die in my sleep during the summer, am I supposed to be nude forever?" Jonas asked. Sidney's cheeks warmed at the thought. He kept his head down, unwrapping a bundle of papers, which looked primarily like old school notebooks.

"Does it take a lot of concentration, I suppose? Magic?"

"Ghosts do have some magic that binds them to their realm."

"Delilah mentioned that," Sidney said, thinking back to the conversation hey'd had earlier in the week. "She said they gain magic by interacting with humans. Talking about their deaths. Scaring them. That sort of thing."

"Making them engage with the afterlife, or at least, the concept of it," Jonas amended. "Which, I suppose for some means scaring, yes."

Sidney considered this as he set his first packet of papers aside. There was another stack below where he'd pulled the first one from, and behind that was a wine crate full of photographs. It wasn't Vogue, but Sidney pulled it forward anyway. He sat on the floor, thumbing through the yellowing prints.

The first few were of Elmmond House, bedecked with sparkling lights as though it were Christmas. Then there were people. Or perhaps not people.

Some had wings, others crowns and horns. Some shots were posed and others candid. A room of beings sitting, staring rapt at a woman wearing little more than strategically placed leaves, mid-recitation. A table bowing under the weight of food. Blurred figures dancing in a bedecked ballroom. The evidence of an Ascension party from long ago.

Or maybe not so long ago. The next snapshot had clearly been matted and framed at one point. The center was sun damaged, the edges in a crooked square were far paler than the print.

On the right side of the photo was a fireplace, where a man in a finely-tailored suit stood with his shoulders pressed against the mantle behind him. He was exceptionally hand-some and was mid laugh. A pointed chin and long nose barred perfectly symmetrical lips, his long hair looked light grey in the silver nitrate. There was a circlet atop his brow and the stone in the center of it was nearly the size of Sidney's pocket watch.

The man's arm was wrapped around the shoulder of a thinner man. Pale with more angular features, his gaze came out from beneath thick dark lashes as he looked askance at the man who was laughing. His shirt hung open at his chest, collarbone leaving a stark shadow against his skin.

Beside them was Jonas, smiling broadly. His eyes were bright and crinkled at the corners, his body turned partially away from the camera, placing him in profile against the other two. That strange angle must have been the reason his skin looked so much darker, though the tattoos on his visible forearms marked him clearly out. A large metal pendant hung off his neck, a strange ornament, reflecting the light in an odd way. It must have been part of his fancy dress, along with the rams horn that curled back behind his ear, black tip pointing to the corner of his jaw.

"Any luck?" Jonas asked. Sidney startled as he looked up to find Jonas standing over him, only a wine crate between them. Jonas stared at the photograph in Sidney's hands, his brow furrowed, mouth open as though he was about to speak.

"An Ascension party?" Sidney offered. Jonas nodded, crouching down to take the photograph gently from Sidney.

"Masquerade was the theme that year, I believe," he said slowly.

"I might have guessed by the costumes. That's quite the getup."

"I'm partial to the horns," Jonas said dryly.

"They suit you," Sidney smiled. "What's that giant thing hanging off your neck?"

"It's a livery collar. A replica." Jonas handed Sidney back the picture and turned away, looking around the attic again, though, his shoulders seemed oddly straight and tight. Sidney pursed his lips, and glanced back at the photo. He should let it go. He knew he should. It wasn't his place. Not any of his business. But the picture had been framed.

"Who's this with you?" Sidney asked, trying to keep his tone light. But the silence that fell was hard. Sidney should have dropped it; he knew it. But he was so curious. Had one of these men been the partner who'd worked with Jonas in the caves? Betrayed him? Jonas walked away as he began to speak.

"The one on the left is Asterion. He's a prince of the fae realm Andurnei. And the other is Edmund Morrow. A sorcerer." Jonas crouched down out of Sidney's eyesight to shift more boxes, and Sidney knew he should apologize, even if he wasn't sure for what. He tucked the photograph away and pushed the box back to where he'd found it while he tried to think of something to say. On the other side of the attic, Jonas grunted.

"And here they are." Jonas shifted backward and tugged a stack of yellowing magazines from beneath a dusty desk. "Here, Sidney." Jonas hoisted the pile up as Sidney made his way through the maze of crates toward him. "Do you mind taking that down to the library while I put things right up here? It'll just be a minute."

Sidney understood he was being dismissed and felt guilty enough for asking about the photo that he wasn't going to argue. And he definitely wasn't going to think about how, when Jonas put the magazine's in Sidney's arms, he hadn't looked Sidney in the eye.

22

That night had been the last night they'd all been friends.

"I don't think it's a good idea," Asterion had said. He'd been hanging off Jonas's shoulder by then, drunk enough that his words were beginning to slide together.

"The evidence supports—" Jonas replied, eating a cracker as he glanced at Asterion over his shoulder.

"I'm not worried about the evidence, Jonas," Asterion interrupted, his fingernails digging into Jonas's arm. "And I like a human as much as anyone."

"Believe me," Jonas rolled his eyes. "I know."

"But he's cleverer than you," Asterion said. Jonas could still hear it in his head. He'd liked that Edmund was clever. And that Edmund was always pushing the limits of Jonas's knowledge. If Jonas said magic could grow a flower, Edmund wanted to know if it could grow a tree. Jonas had been too young, too foolish to see how that desire for more could be a bad thing.

"He's not cleverer than me," Jonas sputtered, almost laughing at the absurdity of it, his ego too long untested. "You're more drunk than I thought."

"You give him your magic, and then what?"

"Just enough so he can build his own portals if he needs them."

"Enough to come visit you in Z'ahrend, you mean?"

"I'm going to stay here," Jonas said. He was drunk too, or he would have hesitated before he said it.

"Here?" Asterion released Jonas's shoulder and stumbled backward, sloshing some golden bubbling drink down his arm. "You're not serious."

"Edmund needs my help. I'm still teaching him."

"Did you talk to your mother about this?" Asterion asked. Jonas turned to pick up his flagon from the table.

"I've made my choice. She's aware of it." Were the same conversation to happen today, he would have known better than to look back at Asterion. To see the distress writ large over his best friend's handsome face.

"Jonas..."

"I'm not welcome back in Z'ahrend."

"What did Karolina—?"

"She doesn't know."

"She's your sister!" Asterion blurted.

"You never tell Kephisto anything."

"Because he's a massive prig, isn't he?" Asterion ran his hands through his hair, midnight blue tinged with teal, shining against his fair skin. His golden eyes were wide in distress. "This is a huge mistake," he said finally.

"I know what I'm doing, Asterion."

But he hadn't. He hadn't known how quickly giving some of his magic to Edmund Morrow would backfire. How Edmund would use it against him. How quickly Edmund would leave, and how much damage he would do before and after he went.

Jonas knew now that not all humans were this way. He lived among them easily, if not comfortably. He'd worked with them and collaborated and gotten drunk. Karolina had married one.

But Jonas had been careful not to get too close. Not again. They always wanted something, even if they didn't understand what it was going to really cost to get it. And sometimes even if they did.

Jonas put the photographs back in the wine crate and stuck it in the gap beneath the desk left by Delilah's magazines. He tidied up the eternally messy attic, a pang of distress vibrating in the center of his chest.

Thankfully Sidney hadn't seen what was right in front of him; honestly, the true circumstances of Jonas's life were so absurd they would have been impossible to conjecture from a single image alone. But Sidney had said he liked Jonas's horns. That was nice, at least, he supposed. Perhaps the sight of Jonas without his glamour might not send Sidney screaming from the house right away. Jonas considered his reflection briefly in a dusty silver platter that sat atop an ancient sideboard. A creature with two worlds, two houses and no home. Ridiculous.

Jonas climbed down out of the attic, but hesitated on the landing. Sidney and Delilah were both downstairs, not waiting on him for anything. He didn't want to seem upset by staying away for too long. He was upset, but it wasn't Sidney's fault. It wasn't anyone's fault but his own.

Remnants of Jonas's old life were everywhere. He didn't focus on them, generally, and so over the years they had faded into the woodwork. The side table Asterion had bought when he lived here was now covered with books and bric-a-brac and dust. The vase on the windowsill had been a gift from his mother, back when she tolerated him enough to give him gifts. Jonas had never really bothered to go through his things and so many of them had lost their emotional attachments. It made him uncomfortable to think of how divorced he'd become from all of it. And yet his past still had the power to reappear and turn his mood sour all of a sudden. Perhaps that was the way with unfinished business. Business that would always remain unfinished.

Jonas shook his head, a weak attempt to derail his extremely depressing train of thought. He walked into his bedroom and then the bathroom, fully intending to splash water on his face and snap himself out of this, whatever it was. Miasma of emotions. Silly, self-indulgent. He tripped on the leg of Sidney's still soaked trousers, and bent over to scoop them up, hang them over the side of the tub. As he did, Sidney's pocket watch tumbled to the floor with a clatter.

It was sort of a miracle that it hadn't gotten swept away into the bay, but as Jonas grabbed it up, his heart sank as water trickled out over the hinge.

It was a pretty little watch, and the hinge and the latch looked clean which meant it was likely fairly new. Jonas grimaced down at it. Based on the state of Sidney's wardrobe, the fact that he was still living in undergraduate housing as a professor, and that Karolina had explicitly said that he was poor, Jonas inferred Sidney didn't have very many nice things, and it was such a shame that this one was now likely broken. One more good thing that Jonas had destroyed.

Jonas opened the watch, thinking he could at least assess the extent of the damage. There was no water under the crystal, which was a good sign. But an engraving on the inside of the cover, a series of stars Jonas didn't recognize, and the words '*May you always find your north star. Love Mom and Annie*' made Jonas feel worse. A gift from Sidney's mother; Jonas was going to have to try to fix it.

23

"So, you found the picture and then what?" Delilah asked. Sidney couldn't tell if she was actually paying attention. Her elbows were splayed on the table, one hand propped up her chin as the other flipped idly through a yellowed issue of Vogue.

"I mean, I didn't ask a lot of questions."

"But you did ask some?"

"Well," Sidney hesitated, "it would have been strange not to ask any."

"You mean 'polite,'" Delilah said without looking up. "It would have been *polite* not to ask any."

"Do you know which of the two men in that photograph he used to—" Delilah interrupted him with a snort.

"I may enjoy giving Jonas a hard time—not as much as you do, of course," she added with a wink. Sidney rolled his eyes. "But that's his story to tell, not mine."

"But Delilah—"

"He's secretive, Sidney. He's always been that way. And you bedding him isn't going to change it. As a matter of fact, it might make it worse."

"Why? What do you mean?" Sidney asked, trying to ignore

the way anxiety churned his stomach. He really needed to eat. Delilah finally deigned to look at him, her lips pursed as she considered. When she spoke, she started with a sigh.

"Jonas believes, not always incorrectly, that people only bother getting close to him when they want something from him. You know, like you have with the telescope."

"Uhh, no," Sidney protested indignantly, even as the truth of what she said began to sink in. "That's different! I'm— Karolina sent me here!"

"And now you're using his library. And his knowledge. And his body, and his bed, and his—"

"I'm not using him!" Sidney insisted. Delilah only hummed and tilted her chin down, her gaze back on the magazine. "Delilah, I *like* him."

"Of course you do. He's very likable. Even when he's pretending not to be."

"No, but—" She cut him off with a shrug.

"Genuinely, Sidney, it's not what I think that matters." Before he could ask her what Jonas might be thinking, there was a knock at the door. "Be a doll and get that, won't you? If Jonas is sulking upstairs, he won't hear it." The knock came again and Sidney sighed and got to his feet.

He paused for a long moment in the foyer, watching the stairs to see if Jonas really wouldn't come down. The bedroom door at the top of the landing was shut. With a deep breath, guilt swimming in his stomach, Sidney went to answer the door.

The woman on the stoop took a step back, and so did Sidney. She was strange and beautiful. Her hair was the color of moss, and the tips of her tawny ears were pointed and pierced with shining gold links. She was short and full-figured, her waist pulled in by a wide black belt. Everything she wore was black. A turtleneck sweater did nothing to diminish the impressive size of her bustline, and sharply skirt and patent pointed heels put him in mind of the secretary of the dean of the astronomy department. Her mossy hair was pinned back, dark eyeliner in two sharp slashes at the corner of her eyes all came together to make Sidney feel quite like he was about to be reprimanded for turning in his supply request for the semester two days after the deadline.

"Hello," Sidney said.

"Where's Jonas?" the woman asked, her voice a stern flute, snappish and arch.

"He's indisposed," Sidney hedged. The woman's brow furrowed.

"I see. Who are you then?"

"I'm Sidney Quince," Sidney returned. "Who are you?"

"Ellery Van Ahlberg, personal assistant to his royal highness Prince Asterion of Andurnei." Maybe Sidney was supposed to be intimidated by the full title, but it only annoyed him more.

"Is there something I can do for you or his majesty?" Sidney glanced over her head, to see if perhaps 'His Majesty' was in attendance. Asterion was one of the men from the picture in the attic and Sidney's curiosity was piqued, in spite of himself. Ellery Van Ahlberg narrowed her eyes.

"Do you live here, Mr. Quince?"

"Temporarily," Sidney said, which was probably mostly untrue. Before he could decide whether or not he wanted to clarify, Ellery leaned into the house and inhaled deeply, her nose not more than six inches from Sidney's chest. Then she leaned back and looked at him again, her lips pursed. "Can I..." Sidney trailed off, as Ellery's head slowly tilted to one side, her gaze boring into him.

"Ah," she said. "I see." She sighed and bit her lip, glancing around the front of the house before looking at Sidney again. "Well, shit."

"Sorry? Is there something I can help you with?"

"Do you know when Jonas will be *less* indisposed?"

"No," Sidney said, which at least had the benefit of being true.

"Of course not," Ellery grumbled under her breath. "Is Delilah home?"

"Elle?" Delilah chirped from the foyer behind Sidney. He heard no footsteps, of course, but the dramatic shift in Ellery's demeanor indicated that Delilah had arrived. Or at least made herself visible.

"Lilah! How are you, darling?" Ellery's voice took on a decidedly kinder tone. Sidney grimaced as Delilah floated up beside him, bestowing air-kisses on Ellery's cheeks.

"Oh, you know," Delilah drifted casually into the doorway beside Sidney. If she was corporeal, it would have been a tight squeeze. As it was, Sidney felt like a palace sentry wedged into an archway beside his partner. "A bit bored if I'm honest. But Sidney's been a welcome addition to the house."

"Has he been here long?" Ellery asked, addressing Delilah as though Sidney was a new pet, unable to answer for himself. Unsurprisingly, Delilah responded in kind.

"Not terribly long, but he's settled in nicely. Doing some astronomy and that sort of thing."

"I'm right here," Sidney interjected. They ignored him.

"I don't suppose Jonas is going to break his streak and actually come to the party this year?" Ellery asked.

"Likely not," Delilah shook her head. "Sidney would love to come, though."

"Would I?" Sidney asked.

"Without Jonas?" Ellery scoffed, glancing at Sidney like he was a noisy toddler covered in mud. "They'll eat him alive."

"I'm not sure I want to—" Sidney began. Delilah interrupted.

"No. It'll be fine. I can look after him. And you can help."

"I don't work for Jonas," Ellery said, her tone suddenly barbed. "Or you."

"Oh, Elle," Delilah batted her lashes. "Come on. You should see Jonas with him. He's practically a kitten."

"What?" Sidney demanded, cheeks heating. Ellery snorted.

"As pleased as that makes me," Ellery said, though she neither looked nor sounded pleased. "It makes my job a hell of a lot harder."

"Can he have an invitation? Please, Elle?" Delilah pouted.

"As if that's my decision." Ellery produced two envelopes from behind her back. "I'll speak to Asterion about it," she said, handing Sidney the heavy cream-colored stationery. "If you really want to go, that is."

"I don't—"

"Of course he does," Delilah said. Ellery glanced up toward the sky, her hand curling around the handle of her umbrella.

"Coffee in the garden tomorrow, Lilah?" Ellery asked.

"Sounds lovely, Elle. I'll be there."

"Goodbye, Mr. Quince." Ellery gave him the falsest of smiles. "Lovely to make your acquaintance."

"Was it?" Sidney asked. She laughed, short and sharp, and then turned, lifting her umbrella as she started back toward Elmmond House.

"She's wonderful, isn't she?" Delilah sighed, drifting back into the foyer.

"She's horrible." Sidney closed the door more firmly than necessary.

"Well, you're no prince yourself," Delilah snipped, floating down the hall. Sidney followed her, a prickle of apprehension standing up the hairs on the back of his neck.

"Asterion's coming to the party?"

"He hosts it. Did Jonas not tell you?" she asked, glancing

back at Sidney's face. He shook his head, and she grimaced. "Don't think too much about it. Jonas never goes."

"But I thought…" Sidney didn't know what he thought, really. His mind was all jumbled. Maybe Asterion wasn't Jonas's research partner. Or maybe he was? "Asterion still comes around then?"

"Sometimes," Delilah shrugged. Her edges seemed to waver and she turned toward the kitchen, like she was looking for an escape. "Ask Jonas about it," she said. "Likely not right now. Though he is having an awful long pout. You ought to go check on him. Take him those envelopes. That'll cheer him up."

"Will it?" Sidney asked, as Delilah floated away with a chuckle.

"Well done, Sidney. You're cleverer than you look." And then she was gone. Sidney looked at the envelopes in his hands. He tapped them together, as he tried to think. They were an impressive, expensive looking weight; commissioned by a prince of Andurnei.

Sidney turned his gaze to the steps. Knocking on the bedroom door felt intrusive. Things were uncomfortable and it was Sidney's fault, but he didn't want them to stay uncomfortable. And avoiding Jonas wasn't going to help. They were going to have to talk about it.

Sidney set the envelopes on the table near the door, and took a deep breath, steeling himself before he started up the stairs.

24

It had been a long time since Sidney had rehearsed an apology, but that was exactly what he did as he walked upstairs. *'I'm sorry for prying.' 'I'm sorry for dredging up unhappy memories.' 'I'm sorry, but I'll likely do it again.'* That was the most honest of them, and it might not have actually counted as an apology at all. Sidney sighed.

Leo was the only person Sidney had ever really made a habit of apologizing to. His mother never required one, and he'd given up on his father very young, and frankly, Sidney didn't really have many friends to wrong, so apologies weren't something he was well-practiced in. And he knew his own faults. He would do everything he could not to delve into Jonas's private business again, even if he did want to know it very badly.

The door to the bedroom wasn't shut like Sidney had thought from downstairs; it was cracked. When Sidney stuck his head inside, he didn't see anyone. He stepped in and glanced around. Everything was still a mess, the bedclothes and their clothes scattered around the mattress and the floor. Sidney could feel the heat on the back of his neck, not embarrassment. Not in the least. His desire was almost foreign to him; he didn't recognize the strength of it. The way he wanted Jonas again, already.

It wasn't just that though. When Delilah had accused him of using Jonas, something deep inside Sidney had balked, and he'd been too upset to realize it then, but now, in the empty room, when he could see the minor destruction they'd wrought together, Sidney knew the part that he had enjoyed the most was when Jonas woke up beside him. When they'd talked and shared a mug of coffee. It had been the easiest conversation that Sidney'd had in a long time. Maybe his entire life. And he wasn't so foolish that he didn't recognize that that meant something. Something he wanted to explore more than the stars. Which was a very strange realization indeed.

He jumped when a light in the corner flickered brightly. Sidney whipped around to see that there was a door ajar in the corner. A door he'd thought was a closet. But through the crack he could see a window, and the flickering light along with it.

Sidney had never met a minor mystery that he wasn't inclined to solve, and he was still looking for Jonas, so he went over and nudged the door open. The cool air from the new room he'd revealed mixed with the warmer, dampish air from the bedroom and drew goosepimples on his ankles. Paper and notebooks cluttered every available surface. Every shelf was packed to its edges with further ephemera balanced precariously atop yellowing pages and cracking spines. And in the center of it all, sat Jonas.

The space on the large desk in front of him was clear of documents. Instead it was cluttered with hand tools, and Jonas was peering through a large, lit magnifying glass at a stand which held a deconstructed pocket watch. A bruise in the shape of Sidney's mouth was visible below the open collar of Jonas's shirt. Sidney's heart fluttered strangely in his chest, and the next thing he knew he was smiling. Why was he smiling? Penitent people, people who needed to apologize, ought not be skulking and smiling. Luckily Jonas hadn't looked up yet, so Sidney had time to get his rogue facial features in order.

"Jonas," Sidney said. Jonas glanced up, his tools stilling. For one moment his amber iris was magnified by the lamp in front of him before he lifted his head. His mouth hung open, a bit like he was trying to come up with something to say, and Sidney smiled again, even though he'd told himself not to, goddammit. "Sorry for— Sorry for interrupting, I just—"

"No, it's my fault." Jonas set the tools down with a nervous clatter. "I didn't hear you come in."

"What are you working on?"

"It's uh... It's your pocket watch." Sidney stiffened in surprise, and Jonas began to apologize. "Sorry. I should have asked. I only thought—It was so waterlogged, but I thought if I could take it apart and dry the components—"

"Can you put it back together?" Sidney asked, stepping up to the other side of the desk. There was a chair there, stacked with papers, a large book open on top. Sidney carefully picked up the pile and moved it to the corner of the desk, as Jonas looked down at the watch parts.

"I can definitely put it back together."

"Then it's no problem." Sidney sat, curling his legs up beneath him, and leaned on the edge of the desk, looking at all the parts of his pocket watch. He could feel Jonas staring at him. Finally, he looked up at Jonas's furrowed brow. "It's fine. I didn't even think of it, honestly. And it's not like you can break it any worse than me dunking it in the water."

"I think it'll still work." Jonas's attention dropped back to the gears on the towel in front of him. He picked up a set of tweezers. "It's well-made."

"It was a gift," Sidney said, as though he needed an excuse to have something nice. Jonas nodded, his expression hidden by his bowed head as he went back to work.

"I saw the inscription. Who's Annie?"

"My mom's wife."

"Ah." Jonas said, as though this was a statement that required no further questions. A lesson in good manners and not prying. Sidney sat back in his chair and looked around. On top of the pile that he'd moved to the desk was a liturgical looking book, a leather bookmark resting in the open valley of its cracked spine. The text was all in ecclesiastical Latin, which Sidney was not fluent in, though he could identify astronomical terms on sight. Here, there were none.

Sidney turned his attention to the bookshelves, where a cursory skimming of titles was enough to inform Sidney that whatever cataloging system Jonas had devised was one that Sidney would need instruction to understand. Perhaps bizarrely, he was thrilled and charmed by this. An unparsable cataloging system was an appealing addition to all the other things he already found appealing about Jonas. Unfortunately, there wasn't a way to say that aloud that didn't make him sound deranged. And anyway, he was supposed to be apologizing.

"I, uh," Sidney cleared his throat. "I'm sorry about earlier."

"No, it's fine," Jonas said too quickly, gesturing dismissively with a thin pair of tweezers.

"I shouldn't have pried. I—I always ask too many questions."

"I'm quite used to your questions by now, Quince." Sidney could hear the smile in Jonas's voice when he said it, and Sidney tried not to be pleased about that.

"Still, I apologize."

"There's really no need."

"It's none of my business," Sidney said. Jonas glanced up at him then, one eyebrow arched. Sidney abruptly remembered what Delilah had said to him downstairs. About people using

Jonas. Only wanting Jonas for what he could do. That wasn't Sidney's intention. He cleared his throat again. "I only want to know what you're comfortable telling me. Or what you want to tell me. And if that's nothing, that's fine."

"Is it?" Jonas bent back down over the watch, but Sidney could see the flush high on his cheekbones. Was that good or bad? Fuck.

"I just mean, I want to know everything about you. But I'll take what I can get." No. That didn't sound right either. Shit, he was bad at this. Jonas stopped what he was doing and looked up at Sidney.

"Unfortunately, I'm a bit out of practice when it comes to talking about myself."

"That's alright. Apparently, I'm out of practice at talking in general." Jonas snorted.

"I think it's nice."

"You're being incredibly generous with me."

"It's been quite some time since anyone's shown an interest in my life. Any aspect of it. I don't mind it." Jonas looked incredibly sincere, a small smile on his closed lips. Sidney wanted to crawl over the desk and kiss him. Instead, he put his foot in his mouth.

"I don't have any ulterior motives," he said, like an idiot. Jonas's eyebrows lifted sharply. Fuck, shit and damn. "I mean— Delilah said—"

"Oh, Gods." Jonas shook his head, chuckling. "What did I tell you about listening to her?"

"The thing is, I sort of believe her," Sidney said. Jonas didn't laugh at that, and Sidney could feel his face getting red. "I like you, Jonas. I feel myself around you and here, and I just... I really like it. And I like you." Jonas blinked at him. Sidney got to his feet. "I'm sorry. I'm so bad at this. Forget I said anything. I—" he broke off and forced himself to turn. Leave, Sidney. For the love of God, get out of this room. He was almost to the doorway before he remembered that Ellery had come by. Fuck. Sidney groaned and turned back.

"Ellery Van Ahlberg came by with your invitation to the Ascension party. I left it downstairs on the entry table for you."

"I don't want it." Jonas was standing behind his desk. Odd. Why had he gotten up?

"She said you'd say as much. Delilah asked her for one for me, which. I mean, if you're not going—Not that I—" Sidney clamped his jaw closed. No more talking. At least not in front of Jonas Rookwood. He shook his head to indicate this. A crooked smile flitted across Jonas's beautiful mouth. He picked up Sidney's watch off the desk, and closed it with two firm clicks, then he held it out toward Sidney.

"It needs to be wound. But it should work."

Sidney walked slowly back across the floor of the study, trying to ignore that his heart was beating rather quickly in his chest. When he took his watch out of Jonas's palm, he couldn't help but feel the warmth of Jonas's hand against his fingertips. And he couldn't help but notice the way Jonas's palm twitched, like he wanted to close it around Sidney's.

"Thank you," Sidney said. Jonas nodded.

"Of course. My fault it got damaged in the first place."

"I don't mind," Sidney said. Jonas grinned and shook his head.

"That's an insane thing to say."

"Yes," Sidney agreed. "It is true though." Weird, Sidney. Could he not be normal for sixty seconds in front of this man? Sidney swallowed and slid his watch into his pocket before turning to go. He had one foot over the threshold when Jonas spoke.

"Sidney?" Sidney bit his lip and turned.

"Yes?"

"I like you too."

"Oh," Sidney said. It was probably more like a gasp, which was embarrassing. But Jonas was smiling, and then Sidney was smiling too.

"The rain's letting up. Do you want to go to the diner for supper?"

"Sure," Sidney said, even as he heard the rain pounding down against the eaves. "I'd love to."

25

The cold, wet morning clung to Jonas's work coat as he walked the perimeter of the Elmmond House property. He was groundskeeping, dragging a wagon around behind him, picking up the sticks and branches that had blown into the yard from the storm the day before.

It didn't need to be done so early in the morning, but Jonas was restless. After they'd gotten home from the diner the night before, Sidney had gone to work on his charts in the library. Jonas had fallen asleep in his study by accident; the sound of the rain rhythmic and tranquilizing.

When he first woken up, it'd been so early that it was still dark, and maybe, ridiculously, he'd checked out on the balcony for Sidney before crawling into bed. No stars could be seen through the thick layer of clouds. Sidney had probably gone to his own room hours ago. And that shouldn't have bothered Jonas at all, but he was still thinking about Sidney as he tugged his wagon full of halved branches around the western edge of the woods.

He liked Sidney. He'd said it out loud the day before and had been turning it over in his head ever since. It was true, of course, but he still wasn't sure why he'd said it. Why he'd exposed himself like that. It was dangerous, wasn't it? But 'No humans,' as a rule, suddenly felt silly and reductive. And Sidney had been so pleased, that it charmed the fear right out of Jonas's head. Jonas wanted to please Sidney. He wanted more things than he'd realized.

The windows of Elmmond House were dark, condensation catching on the glass revealing that the rooms inside were being heated and, therefore, occupied. Jonas cared for the house, even though he didn't live in it. He'd pushed himself out of it at some point; told himself that he didn't want the big old thing because it came with too many responsibilities and bad memories. Instead, Jonas built a garden cottage in the corner of his heart for the things he wanted and couldn't let go of. Jonas condensed everything about himself, covered it with a blanket and pretended like that meant it wasn't there anymore.

It was stupid to be surprised that everything under the blanket still existed. All the things he wanted. The life he'd thought once of building for himself. He'd forgotten that Elmmond House could look welcoming. Could be warm and lived in. Experienced from the inside, instead of picking up branches on the periphery. It made him wonder what Sidney would think of it. If Jonas could make room for him, would Sidney be willing to take up the space?

He was blushing, ridiculous on a man of his age, but he couldn't stop himself. He'd forgotten the way affection warmed him, the way it made him hungry. Foolish.

Still, when he saw Sidney coming across the lawn toward him, all bundled up in his grey peacoat and borrowed garden boots, since his were still soaked from the caves, Jonas turned toward the trees so that he could fix his hair and straighten his coat.

"It's fucking cold out here," Sidney grumbled, hoisting a heavy thermos toward Jonas, who took it.

"What's this?"

"Coffee, obviously." Sidney glanced down at the wagon full of wood behind Jonas. "What are we doing?"

"I'm cleaning up from the storm yesterday. You don't have to join me. I've got to go all the way up to the chapel."

"So, that's why Delilah told me to go back to bed."

"The one time she was being helpful, and you didn't listen."

"To my credit, it's impossible to tell the difference."

"No," Jonas took a sip from the thermos, before smirking at Sidney. "If you hang around long enough, you'll figure her out." Was that an invitation? It sounded like one, though Jonas hadn't realized he meant it until it was out of his mouth. Sidney's eyes widened, and his cheeks pink. From the cold. Jonas handed him back the thermos. "Really, you don't have to come with me."

"I don't mind," Sidney said. "I went to bed early. No stars, you know. Plus, I made breakfast sandwiches." He tugged his satchel around to the front of his body and produced a steaming bundle of wax paper. The smell of bacon hit Jonas with almost tangible force. His mouth watered.

"For me?"

"No, just for me." Sidney rolled his eyes as he shoved the sandwich into Jonas's hands and then pulled another out of his bag. "I know you didn't have breakfast because the kitchen's still clean."

"I'm not sure what you're insinuating," Jonas lied. It was his kitchen and he could leave it as messy as he liked. And he hadn't had breakfast.

The sandwich he unwrapped dripped grease onto his palm, and when he bit into it he moaned at the bright, salty flavor that melted against his tongue. Sidney laughed. He held his sandwich in one hand and grabbed the wagon handle with the other, heaving it into motion. Jonas followed along, trying not to bask too much in the warmth of Sidney's presence, and how nice it was to not be tending to the house alone.

TREES LINED THE DIRT ROAD BETWEEN THE COTTAGE AND THE chapel. The bay crashed against the cliffs below, but the sound of it was almost drowned out by a wind that was furiously shuttling clouds across the sky.

"How long have you lived here?"

"A while," Jonas evaded gracelessly. Sidney let him have it.

"Is it a family property? Like—"

"Delilah's family," Jonas said. "Her mother was an Elmmond before she married Heatherington. I bought it several years after she passed. Delilah, not her mother."

"You bought it?" Sidney knew it was unreasonable to be startled by this, but he was anyway.

"I told you I own the property."

"It must have cost a fortune."

"But if I'd inherited it, that would have been fine?" Jonas arched an eyebrow, and Sidney considered the paradox. How *had* he expected Jonas to own the place? Sidney was woefully inexperienced when it came to real estate; he'd been living in college housing for far longer than any grown adult ought. "If it helps, I'm not nearly as rich now as I was before."

"I thought it went, '*When I had the youth I had no money; now I have the money I have no time,*' or something like that."

"More Alcott?" Jonas grinned. Sidney shrugged.

"I'm appallingly well-versed."

"Indeed. Unfortunately, I've ended up in quite the opposite state of dear Louisa."

"Nonsense," Sidney teased. "I bet you have *investment portfo-*

lios," he imbued the words with an absurd amount of disdain and Jonas snorted.

"Out of all of the things people have decided to dislike about me, I'm not sure it's ever been that my finances are in decent order."

"That's because you're friends with princes and sorcerers and ghosts."

"I don't think Delilah worries too much about her stocks and bonds these days."

"I genuinely have no idea what those things are." Sidney shrugged. "I'm not a prince, remember."

"I'm fairly certain Prince Asterion doesn't know what those things are either," Jonas chuckled. Sidney shook his head in mock disappointment.

"You need to meet better princes." That made Jonas laugh out loud. It was a gorgeous sound that made Sidney's joints go all wobbly.

"I certainly don't need any more princes," Jonas arched an eyebrow at Sidney. "I can barely handle one rogue Astronomer as it is."

"On the contrary, I think you've handled me quite admirably." Jonas snorted, and Sidney was inordinately pleased by the flush that spread across Jonas's cheekbones.

"Admirably?"

"I'm practically tame now," Sidney said. Jonas leaned close, and for a moment, Sidney thought Jonas was going to kiss him.

"I certainly hope not," Jonas murmured. Every part of Sidney tensed, his pulse turned rapid, and his mind blanked.

But only their fingers brushed, as Jonas took the wagon handle out of Sidney's grasp and kept going up the path. Sidney couldn't see Jonas's face, but he knew Jonas was smirking. Fine. The wagon was getting heavy anyway. Jonas could take it, if he wanted.

Sidney knew he was being toyed with, and he liked it so much. It was a game he'd never gotten right before. The trust, the balance of feeling, in previous relationships was wrong for it. But Jonas wasn't like that. Of course, Sidney wasn't a fool. He knew Jonas had secrets. But everyone did. Sidney couldn't fault him for it.

Sidney took a deep breath, resolved to ignore that he was half hard, and caught up with Jonas in several quick strides, as though nothing had happened at all.

"How did you get rich in the first place? Maybe that will make it better."

"I doubt it, but like I said, I'm poorer now. Hopefully that'll make all the difference. My family is titled."

"Oh, Christ," Sidney gave an overexaggerated groan. Jonas grinned at him. "I should have guessed. What are you? An Earl?"

"I was a Duke. A long time ago. I've been disinherited though. No money. No title," he shrugged, his gaze flicking back to Sidney. Sidney smiled.

"A plebian like the rest of us, Duke Rookwood?" Sidney teased. "I like the sound of it." Jonas pulled a face.

"Ugh. No."

"Of course. Anything for his lordship." Sidney affected a little bow, and Jonas swatted at him with his free hand. Sidney ducked away, so distracted by the easy, lovely smile on Jonas's face that he immediately tripped over a worn groove in the dirt road.

Jonas dropped the wagon handle and caught Sidney by the extra fabric of his coat at his waist. With a sharp jerk, Sidney was against Jonas's chest, Jonas's arm wrapped around him to steady him. Sidney bit back a gasp, his body immediately relaxing into Jonas's embrace. Jonas frowned down at him in concern.

"Alright?"

"I'm fine," Sidney said.

"Your ankle's okay?" Did Sidney have ankles? He had no idea.

"Perfectly fine, Your Grace." Jonas scowled and kissed him hard.

Jonas was more than Sidney had ever wanted. Strong and smart. Handsome and clever, with a sense of humor. There was nothing for it. Sidney was ruined. He knew it as he clung to the damp lapels of Jonas's worn canvas coat. He'd never wanted to kiss someone so much in his entire life.

Sidney tried to give as good as he got, but Jonas was pressed against him, hands grasping at Sidney's waist like Jonas was afraid he was going to blow away. Sidney leaned into Jonas and slid his arms around Jonas's neck, running his fingers through the back of Jonas's thick, dark hair. Before Sidney could make a move, Jonas straightened up, holding Sidney firmly by the waist as he lifted him off the ground.

Sidney's gasp of surprise ended in a moan, as he wrapped his legs around Jonas's waist, reveling in the moment of perfect friction between them. Jonas growled in response, nuzzling Sidney under the chin with his mouth, nipping at his throat. Jonas had a penchant for biting that Sidney was growing quite fond of.

"Not very duke-like behavior," Sidney chastised breathlessly. Jonas chuckled against his skin.

"Clearly you haven't met very many dukes."

"Anyone could see us!"

"As though that's not what you'd prefer," Jonas said, his voice low again. Sidney felt his cheeks heat, not at the accusation itself, but that Jonas knew him well enough to make it. "Besides, this is my property. If I want to have you in the middle of the road, I don't see that there's much anyone else can do about it."

"Spoken like a true aristocrat," Sidney barely managed. His brain wasn't working as quickly as it had been before, as all his blood had vacated for points south. "So demanding."

"I could be," Jonas offered. And that was certainly tempting. Sidney leaned down and kissed him lightly, gently, and the hum of approval that emerged from Jonas's chest was delicious. Jonas tightened his grip on Sidney's hips. Like he wanted Sidney desperately; barely clinging to composure. No one ever wanted Sidney like that. Sidney would have let Jonas take him in the road. He would have let Jonas have him anywhere.

"Trees," Sidney murmured. Jonas arched an eyebrow at him. "Into the trees. Carry me." Jonas smirked as he did, abandoning the wagon in the road.

"I said I don't mind if people see."

"We have your reputation to think of," Sidney murmured. "Pillar of the community to vicars and ladies who walk dogs." Sidney trailed off, as Jonas pressed Sidney's spine against the rough bark of a tree and smiled up at him, wolfish, hungry almost. Some feral part of Sidney thrilled at the thought of being Jonas's prey. The game, again. Teasing, chasing. He squirmed, just enough to slip out of Jonas's grip, relieved when his ankles didn't give out as he balanced himself on the roots beneath their feet. He put his hands on Jonas's lapels, braced against his chest, and looked up into Jonas's gorgeous amber eyes.

"Go on, then." The challenge. Sidney said it mostly to see what Jonas would do. Gratifyingly, Jonas pounced on Sidney in moments, his hands beneath Sidney's coat, mouth against Sidney's neck. Sidney leaned into it, relishing his attention.

Jonas dropped to his knees, fingers pulling roughly at the button of Sidney's trousers, like he couldn't get them undone fast enough. Sidney whimpered watching him. It felt incredible to be wanted in a fervor. To see the way he desired Jonas mirrored in the desperate way Jonas was undressing him.

Jonas freed Sidney from the confines of his trousers, shorts, and licked his lips before taking Sidney at once into his mouth.

Sidney groaned, his head falling back against the tree. He threaded his fingers through Jonas's hair, moaning as Jonas hummed his approval. Sidney's heaving breaths echoed in his ears, as the fingers of his free hand clutched the bark of the tree.

"Jonas! God—" Jonas slid a hand up, his fingers curling around Sidney's hip bone. Sidney's mind had turned to mush. The cold wind on his cheeks, the warmth of Jonas's hand on his skin, and the frantic heat building in the base of his spine. Sidney was gasping, so close to release, and desperate for more. For desire that was tinged with affection like this. It was intoxicating, and destroying him, he knew. He could never settle for anything less. For anyone else. He wanted Jonas Rookwood in every imaginable way.

"Jonas," Sidney moaned. Gasped, as Jonas looked up at him. His eyes were bright in the strange light of the woods, pools of molten copper that Sidney wanted to sink into. Still hungry for Sidney, even as he feasted. Sidney's head dropped back. "I'm going to—" Jonas tightened his hand on Sidney's hip and took him to the base in one fluid motion, swallowing around Sidney as Sidney came with Jonas's name on his lips.

Before Sidney managed a coherent thought, Jonas was up, pushing Sidney back against the tree. Their mouths were pressed together. He could taste himself on Jonas's tongue and the thought of them being mingled together, pleasure and desire, overwhelmed him.

Sidney was only vaguely aware that Jonas's hands were tucking Sidney away, doing up his trousers. Jonas licked into Sidney's mouth again, and Sidney grabbed weakly at the back of Jonas's coat and that was when Sidney heard the sound of footsteps crunching through the leaves.

He stiffened immediately, but Jonas kept kissing him. Slower, though. He'd heard it too. Jonas smoothed his hands down the front of Sidney's coat between their bodies. When had Jonas first heard it? Who had caught them? A throat cleared. Jonas stilled, his lips soft against Sidney's. Sidney could feel Jonas's mouth curl into a smirk before he turned his head.

"Father Michaels," Jonas said by way of greeting. Was there a worse position to be caught in by a priest? Sidney's mind very unhelpfully provided several immediate examples, so by the time he met Father Michaels' gaze, his cheeks were bright red.

"Good morning, gentlemen," the vicar said, without even a hint of irony. He was wearing a pair of binoculars around his neck and had a notebook in his hand.

"How goes the birding?" Jonas asked.

"Oh, very well. How goes the...?" he trailed off, looking between Sidney and Jonas with a look of absolute innocence. Like he'd encountered them at the corner store.

"We were gathering up the sticks and branches that had fallen on the road. Tidying the place up a bit before the festivities."

"Good of you. Actually, quite a large one came down outside the rectory. I've got an axe, if you don't mind taking a whack at it for me. I'm afraid with my back, I'd only hurt myself."

"Of course," Jonas said. Sidney was amazed at him. Amazed at both of them, really. But then all of a sudden, Jonas's hand was threading through Sidney's, leading him back toward the road. Father Michaels followed alongside.

"You ought to see this tree on the far side of the graveyard Jonas. It's really quite extraordinary. There are about three starling nests in it. Only the birds living there have different wing markings than your normal starlings."

"I'm afraid I don't know a starling from a blackbird, Father," Jonas said as he grabbed up the wagon handle and glanced at Sidney. "Sidney?"

"Ornithology hasn't really ever been an interest of mine, I'm afraid. A mockingbird nested outside my bedroom window when I was young, and it was so loud, it put me off the class of creature entirely."

"Here it is. See? And with some green still on the leaves as well!" They followed the curve of the road toward the chapel, and it was very quickly clear which tree Father Michaels was talking about. Jonas stopped to look up at it, a frown creasing his brow.

It was a strange enough sight that Sidney's worry about being caught faded more quickly than he would have thought possible. While most other trees were brilliant shades of orange, red, and yellow, this one tree, with low branches stretching wide, was still full of green leaves. A strange shade of green too, a deep emerald. Not all of the branches. But some. Enough that it stood out.

"I have to confess, I've not noticed it before," Father Michaels said. "Not the tree, I mean. It's been here longer than I have, I'm sure. But the foliage, and the birds."

"Strange," Jonas agreed. He let go of Sidney's hand to walk up the slope toward the tree, and it was only then that Sidney realized they'd been holding hands the whole time. He lurched to go after Jonas, and Jonas held up his palm toward him without looking back. "Wait a moment, Sidney. You too, Father." And with that, Sidney was left standing beside the vicar next to the wagon full of branches, and embarrassment returned.

"It's alright, Mr. Quince," Father Michaels said, apropos of nothing. "I'm well beyond being shocked by any bog-standard debauchery. Ascension parties cured me of my prudishness years ago."

"Pardon?" Sidney arched an eyebrow. Debauchery at the Ascension parties? This was a new bit of information.

"It's alright, my boy. I didn't see anything. Even if I had, this is Rookwood's land, and he's—"

"No, sorry," Sidney shook his head. "I meant about the Ascension parties."

"Aren't you...?" Father Michaels asked, frowning at Sidney's confusion. "I assumed you knew."

"Knew what?"

"About the Ascension party. About the—" he stopped and glanced up the hill at Jonas, his brow furrowing. Sidney pursed his lips.

"Father?"

"Never mind." Father Michaels shook his head as Jonas started back down the hill toward them.

This Ascension party, that according to Ellery Van Ahlberg, Jonas never went to, was becoming more curious by the minute. The pictures he'd seen hadn't looked all that different from any other party Sidney had been to in his life. But then it was a gathering to celebrate the opening of portals into other realms, and what did that mean, exactly?

"It's strange," Jonas said, clearly referring to the tree, as he got closer. "Do you mind if I keep an eye on it for a bit?"

"Not at all," Father Michaels shook his head.

"Could you write me up a bit about the starlings. Or the not-starlings, I suppose. Just what makes them different from the normal ones."

"Of course," Father Michaels agreed. "I'll have it done by the time you boys have chopped up that branch for me."

Sidney tried to listen to their conversation as they walked up the hill toward the church, but he couldn't stop looking at Jonas. For every bit of knowledge Sidney gained about Jonas and the world of magic he inhabited, it seemed like Sidney also gained about six more questions. Everyone assumed he already knew what was happening, or they were actively keeping things from him, and he couldn't always pick out which was which. Unfortunately, there wasn't time to dwell on any of that, as the branch that had come down in front of the rectory was quite large, and was going to take some serious effort to hack apart.

26

The head butler at Elmmond House, Verne, had been employed there for longer than Jonas had owned the property. He was supposedly a human, though Jonas was almost certain that someone somewhere along the line had either gifted him a preternaturally long life or he had dealt for it. Verne was a small man with salt and pepper hair and a straight line for a mouth that never betrayed a single errant thought. He was a consummate professional, and Jonas was very intimidated by him.

Jonas stood at the servant's entrance to the kitchen, down a narrow ramp on the northeast side of the house where they took deliveries. Sidney had gone back to the cottage at Jonas's insistence, so Jonas stood there alone, facing Verne's judgment.

"Thank you, sir," Verne said, as he looked down at the wood-filled wagon beside Jonas. His expression was entirely impassive, and his voice didn't betray a single emotion. Jonas felt judged anyway.

Jonas wasn't the sort of employer Verne was used to. A disgraced duke who lived in an outbuilding on the property and didn't even come to his own parties? Who insisted on doing his own groundskeeping? Who gave blow jobs in the woods behind the house? He was a disaster. Normally, that didn't matter to Jonas. But sometimes he felt like maybe he should be doing something else. Playing his part better. Trying to impress.

Of course, Sidney hadn't been impressed by who Jonas had been. He didn't know Duke Rookwood to be impressed by him, and Sidney liked Jonas as he was. Which, excepting that he wasn't human, was a truer version of himself than he'd ever been before.

To people who had known Jonas as Duke Rookwood, he was diminished. To people who hadn't, he'd tried to become as standoffish and strange as possible. Keeping everyone away had been his primary goal, but it hadn't worked on Sidney. And now that Jonas had decided he did want Sidney around, he was at a loss for how to keep him interested.

Jonas didn't know much about romance. By all accounts, every attempt he'd ever made at it had ended poorly. But he thought he understood what Sidney wanted. And there was only one avenue for navigating that at the moment.

"Is Asterion in?" Jonas asked. Verne stepped aside immediately at the barest indication that Jonas would be coming into the house. Jonas did come into the house, inhaling the warm air of the kitchen, trying to pick out what was for dinner amongst all the delicious scents.

"His majesty's entourage and personal effects have arrived," Verne said, holding his hand out for Jonas's coat. It took Jonas a moment to realize that's what he was doing, but the two-hundred years of aristocratic training won out in the end. Jonas handed his coat to Verne. "I believe his majesty is due later this evening. But we've put him in the gold suite, per your standing request." It had been a grand joke for nearly a quarter of a century. Asterion swore gold clashed with his hair.

"Thank you," Jonas said. "I just need to leave him a message."

"I'd be happy to take something up for you, sir."

"No, that's quite alright." Jonas moved to step off the mat, and then remembered to wipe his boots off first. "I'll see to it myself."

"As you wish." Verne nodded, with no indication that this was highly irregular. Jonas was going to have to give him a raise.

Jonas had arrived before most of the guests, and as such, he encountered no one in the halls and stairways leading up to Asterion's suite. He could hear people. There were murmurs, quiet movement behind closed doors. But he saw no one, thank the Gods.

The halls were as pristine as ever before the grand event. Everything had been polished and even the dark wood of the walls shone. The plush carpet muffled the heavy step of his boots as he made his way to the east wing of rooms.

The gold suite was so called because of the extreme, almost tasteless, amount of gilding on every fixture and piece of furniture in the room. Jonas had never had an eye for aesthetics, and when he'd bought the house it had almost seemed like sacrilege to make any changes. He winced at the high shine on everything from the drapes to the carpets. If he was ever going to move back in, he would have to redecorate.

"Ellery?" he called. No response. He'd never known what she got up to when Asterion wasn't around to need her minding. She was organized and clever enough to overthrow realm governments, and Jonas thought they were all very lucky that she chose court machinations and colluding with Asterion instead.

"Ellery?" Jonas called again, making his way to Asterion's bedroom. The door was ajar, but he tapped on it anyway. With Asterion, one could never be too sure.

The room was empty and had slightly more muted gold tones mixed in with amber and dark wood. Overall, it gave the impression of falling asleep inside a caramel chocolate bar. Two large navy trunks sat in the corner. The first was locked, which was deeply unfortunate. Jonas bit his lip as he frowned down at the latch.

Asterion wasn't here and Jonas needed to get into his trunk. He didn't want to have to share with anyone why he needed to get into Asterion's trunk, but he needed to get into it all the same. He pursed his lips and tried to decide what would be more humiliating: pulling rank to get someone to unlock the trunk for him or having to ask Asterion or Ellery for help. Not getting in at all wasn't an option, with Sidney on the line.

On a whim, Jonas tried the lid of the second trunk and found it unlocked. It had mostly been unpacked, which gave Jonas another avenue for searching the room. The black leather pouch he'd been wanting was safely tucked away where he should have begun his search: in the drawer of the bedside table.

Jonas was alone, but he still found himself blushing as he shuffled through Asterion's bag of sex tricks. They'd lived together for a few years, and had been in bed together a few times on either side of that, but there were plenty of things in the bag that Jonas didn't recognize and didn't want to know the use for. He was going to have to wash his hands and, if possible, some parts of his brain, but none of that mattered if it meant being able to please Sidney.

Sidney wanted Jonas. Jonas wanted Sidney, and Jonas didn't want to explain why it would be dangerous for Sidney to hop into bed with him because, well, because there was only so much one person could take, wasn't there? Surely Sidney was nearly at his upper limit by now. And Sidney liked Jonas as he was. Why ruin that?

Alchemically-laced prophylactics were hard to come by.

Demand was traditionally quite low and they were complicated to make. Most creatures with magic wanted to mark their partners. That was half the point of sexual congress with humans anyway, and anything else, like pregnancy and most diseases, could be prevented using normal human contraception. Magic, though it was tied to bodily fluids on some level, followed intent. Wanting someone the way Jonas wanted Sidney was risky, even though he wasn't anywhere as powerful as he used to be.

Still, Jonas knew two things about Asterion, and one was that he really enjoyed sex, and the other was that he didn't always enjoy being marked by partners. If anyone was going to have what Jonas was looking for, it was him, and there, near the bottom of the bag, was a small black tin with copper lettering. Exactly what he'd been looking for.

Jonas tugged it out, and flipped it open. There were five. He could likely take two, deposit them in a tin of his own, and then bring this one back. It wasn't as though Jonas wasn't going to tell Asterion he'd taken them, he just also didn't want to have to ask. Not because they'd been lovers, but because they were friends, and Asterion had spent years telling Jonas to get back out into the world, and he was going to be insufferable when he found out Jonas had done exactly that.

A knock on the doorframe froze Jonas in his tracks. He looked up, trying to pretend like he absolutely belonged where he was. His house. His ex-boyfriend's room. Desdemona Briarthorne blinked at him, her mauve eyes wide in surprise. A single white fang pressed into the plush coral skin of her bottom lip. Shit.

She was a confectionary creature. Her skin was bright pink and dusted in white freckles, like only her nose had been out in a snow flurry. Her hair was a shade of pink so light that it could have been mistaken for spun sugar, if not for the iridescent ivory of the horns that curled away from the crown of her head. A robin's egg bodice set of several inches of lightly glittered cleavage, as she leaned heavily on the doorway, peering in at him like he was a strange animal in a cage.

"You're the absolute, very last person I thought I'd see here," she mused. Her eyes dropped to the bag in his hand and her smile widened, teeth bared like a shark smelling blood in the water. "Well, maybe not the *very* last person. What the fuck are you wearing?"

It took Jonas a moment to realize she was talking about his glamour. To remember he was wearing one. He tried to ignore the heat crawling up the back of his neck.

"It's good to see you too, cousin." Jonas kept his voice carefully measured. Desdemona scoffed.

"Drop the glamour, Jonas. I can't take you seriously while you're playing dress-up." Jonas swallowed. Desdemona required delicacy in all situations because she was a horrible combination of spoiled and capricious. One wrong move, and she'd have a field day. And even if he said everything right, there wasn't a single doubt that she'd be telling everyone she saw in the next twenty-four hours that she'd seen Jonas in Asterion's bedroom, rifling through his 'intimate' items. Fuck.

Jonas dropped his glamour and straightened his shoulders.

"What are you doing here?" he asked her before she could ask him. She arched an eyebrow and provided the obvious answer.

"Looking for Asterion, of course."

"Why?" He knew it made him sound like a jealous lover and he didn't care. It wasn't jealousy. He'd long ago stopped caring who Asterion bedded, except when it was unsafe for Asterion to do so. And Desdemona was certainly not to be trifled with when it came to matters of the heart.

"Goodness." Desdemona batted her lashes and covered her

mouth with her fingertips in a mock gasp. "I didn't realize you two were still involved."

"We're not. I'm just borrowing something."

"Well, I can see that." Desdemona stepped forward into the door frame, leaning her hip against the gilded wood. She stared at him like she was trying to see inside of him. Perhaps she was. Jonas stiffened.

"Asterion's not here yet. If you're looking for him, you'll have to come back later."

"Which just leads me to wonder why you're in here, borrowing something from that bag in particular, if he's not even here yet." Desdemona wrinkled her nose, as though Jonas was doing something distasteful. He pursed his lip and slid the condom tin from his palm into his pocket as discreetly as he could.

"Are you traveling this Ascension?" he asked. Desdemona snorted.

"Good lord, Jonas. You're truly terrible at this! Sneaking around and being subtle are not your strong suits. No wonder you stay holed up in that little cottage all the time." She was right. Jonas grit his teeth, and Desdemona laughed. "Not that you actually care, but yes. I'm going back to Halmorn."

"Halmorn?" The capital of the fae realm. Not what he'd expected from the demon baroness. Unless she'd been compelled to give up her title too.

"I've got a new apartment in the city. Come through and visit sometime. You've got enough magic left for that, surely?" He didn't. And even if he had, he wouldn't have wasted it on a trip to see Desdemona. Still, his silence seemed to speak for him. For the first time, the smile dropped off Desdemona's face and she shook her head. "Ruthless," she muttered.

"What?"

"Nothing, dearheart." Her smile was back, horribly apologetic. It made his stomach sink.

Jonas's loss of magic had been a scandal in demonic circles. It was a circumstance entirely of his own making, of course, so there was little sympathy to spare for him. But it was strange how, even now, his shame lingered. The way it felt to have everyone know what a fool he'd been. And that they still knew it. He'd become a cautionary tale to people he'd once thought of as friends, and it stung.

Jonas closed Asterion's bag and put it away. When he turned back toward the door, Desdemona had straightened up, and in doing so, lost some of her softness. For a moment, she looked stiff.

"Give my congratulations to Karolina, won't you? I was so sorry I couldn't make it to the wedding."

"Of course," Jonas nodded. The formality which he'd hated for so long was now a relief to him. Polite conversation was fully navigable. She stepped out of the doorway, and somehow it was enough of an opening that Jonas knew he was being freed. She'd taken pity on him. He didn't like it, and he wasn't sure why it was happening, but he wasn't about to look a gift horse in the mouth. He'd made it halfway across the suite before Desdemona spoke again.

"It was good to see you, Jonas." Jonas made a noise that sounded affirmative, and left quickly down the servant's stairs, before he could encounter anyone else.

He shouldered into his coat as he walked back toward the cottage. The ruffle of his hair catching the wind and settling on either side of his horns was the thing that made him realize he still had his glamour off. His cheeks heated immediately, as his glance darted to the cottage up ahead, as though Sidney was going to be standing with his nose pressed to the window, eyes wide and jaw hanging in shock.

Jonas ducked his head and yanked the magic back up over his shoulders like a cloak. The thought of Sidney made him feel nauseous. So did the thought of Desdemona, Elmmond House. All of it. What was he even trying to do anymore? Wanting Sidney was stupid. He could tamp down his own longing; he'd been doing that for years. And if Sidney just wanted him for sex, then what was the problem, really? Jonas could do that without having gone shuffling through Asterion's things. Exposing himself to ridicule and age-old hurts. That had been supremely foolish.

Except, it wasn't just that he wanted Sidney in his bed. They got along so well. It was another stupid thing to think. Self-indulgent. He likely could have gotten along with plenty of people if he didn't stay locked up in his house all the time. But Sidney liked him even though he did stay locked in his house all the time. And he was so clever and handsome and nice to talk to. And Jonas had nothing to offer him for all of that. Not even sex, which was why he had gone into Elmmond House. Because even if he couldn't give Sidney anything his real self, at least they could do that.

Jonas skirted the edge of the cottage and stomped down into the garden. The breeze off the bay was growing stronger, and the goldenrod was practically bowing in the wind. Goldenrod he'd planted for Edmund Morrow. Edmund had wanted marigolds, but they didn't do well so far north. Jonas had tried anyway. But it hadn't been enough.

His eyes were stinging, suddenly, hot tears collecting just beneath his eyelids. He blinked them away and walked up to the garden shed to get his trowel.

27

Chopping wood was an exhausting task, and Sidney had gone back to the house and immediately drawn himself a hot bath. Perhaps it had been a bit presumptuous to use Jonas's bathroom but the tub was bigger, and if Sidney was going to be able to use his arms at all he needed to soak his throbbing shoulders as quickly as possible.

And maybe it was also presumptuous to leave both the bathroom and the bedroom doors ajar. But it didn't matter. Sidney stayed in the tub until his fingers were wrinkled, and Jonas never came in. Sidney got out, dried off, went back to his room and dressed, discovering that he was on his last clean outfit. He hadn't planned on staying so long.

But now, he wasn't sure he could bring himself to go. It was silly. He hadn't been invited to stay. And there was work to consider. But the world Jonas had shown him was so compelling, so endlessly, infinitely study-able, that he couldn't imagine pretending it didn't exist. All his months of charts had brought him here, and it seemed only natural to keep going. The thought of it energized him like no other proposed dissertation topic had, and he didn't really know what that meant, except that he wasn't willing to give it up just yet.

And of course, that didn't even begin to broach the question of Jonas himself. Sidney wasn't much for big words like 'love.' It just never seemed important to him before. Or maybe he'd just told himself it wasn't important because it always felt so far out of reach. Nothing to do with him in any conceivable sense. But now he couldn't help but think that he didn't want to leave Jonas. The way he wanted to talk about everything with Jonas meant something. And Sidney knew he should pay attention to it.

He tried not to, of course. He wasn't crazy. Could you fall in love with someone in a week? He genuinely had no idea, and thinking about it made his stomach hurt. Sidney gathered up his notebook off the desk in the guest room and went back into Jonas's room. A half a step out onto the balcony told him it was too cold to go without his jacket, but he did anyway.

Sidney set his notebook down and put a small, potted plant on top to keep it from blowing away. The gust died down and in the quiet that followed, Sidney heard a grunt and the distinct sound of a shovel biting into cold, wet ground.

Below the balcony, in the garden, Jonas was hunched over a half-empty flower bed. Beside him was a stack of goldenrod, roots and all, as high as Sidney's knees.

Sidney watched in silence for a minute or two, as Jonas dug out the roots like a man possessed. Sidney tried to decide if he should be able to parse out whatever was happening down there on his own. It simply didn't seem possible.

"What are you doing?" he called down. Jonas twisted his torso, his dirt covered hand and the handle of the trowel braced against his knees as he looked up.

"Digging them out from the roots," Jonas said. He paused

and then looked at the goldenrod and then back up at Sidney. "Like you told me to."

"Shit weather for it," Sidney said lightly. Jonas snorted. His head dropped down and his shoulders began to shake, as laughter caught on the wind and lifted to Sidney.

"Gods, Sidney," Jonas ran a hand beneath his eyes as he looked back up at him.

"I mean, you could have waited for a warmer day, at least."

"I've let them go for far too long."

"Do you want help?" Sidney asked. Jonas looked around him and at the bed out in front of him and shook his head.

"I'll be alright. I probably won't finish it all today." He looked back up at Sidney. "What are you doing?"

"Getting the telescope into proper alignment. Should be a decent night for stars, if the weather holds."

"You ought to put on a coat."

"Yes, thank you." Sidney rolled his eyes and Jonas scoffed.

"If you're sick you can't stargaze."

"You actually aren't my mother, you know," Sidney said. He ought to start doing things with the telescope, but Jonas was still looking up at him and Sidney couldn't bring himself to pull away.

"I don't think your mother has the monopoly on caring about your health, Quince."

"I'm not sure anyone else has ever bothered."

"Well, then let me take some of the burden off your poor mother by telling you to go put on a fucking coat!" Sidney snorted derisively, but he was beaming as he straightened up and went back inside. At the front door, he pulled his peacoat off the hook, and then hesitated at the foot of the stairs. The telescope was fine. No one had touched it since he last used it. There were hours before the stars yet. He pulled his arms into his coat and went out through the front door, around the side of the house and into the garden. Jonas glanced over at the sound of his footsteps and then turned back to the stalks, shaking his head.

"Oh no, Quince. You've forgotten how stairs work?"

"Shut up." Sidney got down onto his knees beside Jonas.

"I don't need help, Sidney."

"You were really enjoying our little Romeo and Juliet routine?" Sidney said before he could think better of it. Jonas glanced at Sidney out of the corner of his eye.

"I'm not quite sure we're what Shakespeare had in mind."

"Star-crossed lovers," Sidney joked, waggling his eyebrows. Jonas huffed and went back to digging. Sidney leaned forward, pushing his hands into the dirt. He tugged at the nearest stalk of goldenrod and let himself talk, because he knew Jonas wouldn't mind it. "Do you think Shakespeare ever visited the other realms? He wrote quite a bit about magic."

"It's possible. Edmund Spenser certainly did."

"Is there really a faerie queen?"

"There are several," Jonas said in a tone that indicated this was obvious. Sidney chuckled.

"How does anyone get a decent grasp on this stuff? I feel like every time I ask a question, I get a fully new piece of information, entirely unrelated to anything else you've told me."

"Well, to be fair, you ask a lot of questions."

"What did you make of that tree, earlier?" Sidney asked. He'd been thinking about it in the tub.

"The one we cut up?"

"The one in the graveyard."

"Strange," Jonas said. Obviously. Sidney rolled his eyes.

"Not any stranger than the mushroom cave. Or everything else about this place."

"I suppose not," Jonas chuckled. Sidney pressed on.

"If the birds aren't from here. If they're not some new species of starling with different markings or something, I mean... you said this place is a thin space between the realms. Portals open up, right? Maybe the birds came through with the tree?"

"The tree came through a portal?" Jonas asked. Sidney shrugged.

"I don't know. I don't know how portals work."

"They require sacrifice and magic, both. Unless you've got a strong enough caster, I suppose. But that's rare."

"What do you mean by sacrifice?" Sidney asked. Jonas heaved a fistful of goldenrod out of the earth and tossed it on the pile before he turned to Sidney.

"Blood is easiest. But it can be anything. Usually, for humans, the creature providing the magic also sets the terms of the sacrifice. So, if you were making a deal with a demon to open a portal, they'd probably want some part of your soul."

"Right, I remember you said. What use do demons have for human souls?"

"Interacting with humans nets more magic for creatures. Taking a soul is nice because souls are self-regenerative. Not forever, of course, but a little. And a human willing to give up part of their soul once is often an easy target for more deals later."

"Hence the marking."

"Exactly," Jonas nodded. Sidney wrinkled his nose. The thought of this power exchange made him uneasy. Reminded him too much of his father, again.

"Sounds sinister."

"It is a bit," Jonas agreed. "But, if you do your research beforehand, you can get a sense of what to expect. Still doesn't tell us why anyone would make a sacrifice to put a tree through a portal with a bunch of birds in it."

"The portals opening at the Ascension, do those require sacrifice?" The pieces of the puzzle that was the Ascension were beginning to float nearer to each other in his mind. Not that he had a whole picture, but there was a picture there, if he could get the right angle on it.

"Ascension portals open because of the magic generated by the alignment of the celestial bodies. Humans still have to be marked to use them. But no one has to give anything to make them appear."

"And why don't you go to the Ascension party?" Sidney asked. It wasn't tactful, but it felt like a natural progression of the conversation. Jonas bit his lip. His gaze dropped to his knees. Sidney backpedaled. "Sorry. We don't—"

"I'm not really a part of that world anymore," Jonas said. He ran a dirt covered hand over the roots of the goldenrod. "I don't have much to offer them."

"That can't be true," Sidney said, sure of this even if he was sure of nothing else. "You're brilliant."

"Not always."

"Well, you could have fooled me," Sidney said. "I think you have plenty to offer." Jonas looked at him then. The ghost of a smile crossed his face. Then he cleared his throat.

"What should we have for dinner?" Jonas asked. Sidney pursed his lips, trying to decide if he was going to let that incredibly ungraceful maneuver stand. He should have. Jonas had been more than forthcoming, but then Jonas laughed and shook his head. "Go ahead. Ask."

"I don't think I have to ask. I think I can guess," Sidney tried to sound casual, but he could tell by Jonas's smirk that he sounded as smug as he felt.

"Can you now?"

"You told me you got disinherited. You're not titled anymore. And you used to be friends with a prince and a sorcerer, I've seen the pictures. And I don't know about sorcerers, but I don't know how often princes and commoners get together for tea." Jonas laughed, his eyes crinkling at the corners.

"Alright, Detective Quince."

"Maybe you feel like you don't have anything to offer them without your title and your money, but I think you do. You're incredibly intelligent—"

"Alright."

"Funny."

"A court jester, then?" Jonas smirked.

"And handsome."

"Sidney, you're going to make me blush," Jonas deadpanned, but he was blushing. Sidney smiled.

"How'd I do?"

"Aside from your questionable list of my positive qualities? About halfway right. Fifty-fifty."

"I can take that."

Jonas opened his mouth to respond, but before he could, the roar of a car engine broke the silence. Sidney jerked around as a cavalcade of long, sleek luxury cars, followed by horse drawn carriages began to file in around the loop of Elmmond House's driveway.

There was a cacophony of sounds as revelers began to spill from the vehicles. Each carriage was spangled with crystal lanterns that swung with the stamping of the white and black horses that pulled them, forced to halt by footmen in metallic livery. The passengers disembarking were similarly marvelous, luminous skin and shining hair in a rainbow of colors that seemed both natural and unnatural to Sidney. Bodies were swathed in fabrics that could have been made from starlight or stiff silk depending on the angle and tailoring. Some had wings that emitted showers of sparkles as they unfolded, others were bedecked with crowns that wrapped around horns, or jewels that were so large that they were visible even from Sidney's distance. With each new arrival, there were cheers and laughter, the sound of a stringed instrument and the soft smell of magnolias drifting through the gardens on a gentle and strangely warm western breeze that hadn't been there even three minutes before.

"Good Lord." Sidney was in awe.

"Yes, they do put on quite a show, don't they?" Jonas's voice was arid.

"They're beautiful." A woman with blue black skin as radiant as the midnight sky was being twirled by a man who was almost silver in his iridescence. Among them, humans, looking more as Sidney expected them to look, stood out as plain, homogenous. "Who are they? What are they?" Sidney was so enraptured, it took him a long moment to realize that Jonas hadn't responded. "Jonas?"

"They're creatures. Fae, mostly. But there'll be demigods, demons, lycanthropes. The Ascension brings all kinds."

"Are they all so...?" Sidney trailed off. Beautiful didn't really seem to be a strong enough word. Ethereal?

"Strange?" Jonas incorrectly substituted. Before Sidney could disagree, Jonas shrugged. "The other realms are very different from this one. Appearance is a sort of game to them. Most of them can change it at will."

Jonas's attention was back on the goldenrod, as he yanked stalks out of the ground with vigor. Sidney winced. Another painful memory, clearly. There was no reason to press Jonas's bruises any further. Sidney put his hand on Jonas's shoulder.

"We should go in and start dinner." Jonas glanced at him out of the corner of his eye, and Sidney smiled. "Seriously. I can't possibly be expected to peel carrots with my shoulders as sore as they are. That's your job."

"Would you like me to introduce you to them?" Jonas asked. Sidney rolled his eyes.

"Yes, cavorting with werewolves is very high on my list of things to do this evening." Jonas gave him a small smile, and Sidney shook his head. "No. I don't really enjoy parties at the best of times. And I'm starving and my back hurts." Jonas's expression softened.

"Thank you, Sidney." Sidney leaned forward and kissed him on the cheek. For a moment, Jonas stiffened. Maybe it was the wrong thing to do. But he didn't pull away.

Sidney let his hand slide over the back of Jonas's neck, stroking the top of his spine, and slowly, Jonas relaxed into the touch. The breeze picked up again, and for a moment, the world faded away in the rush of wind and waves. Their bodies, warm and pressed together, felt more real than anything Sidney had ever experienced before.

28

By the time Jonas had put away his trowel and washed up, Sidney had the radio on in the kitchen and the wine poured. He was humming along to the music, a dish towel over his shoulder, as he pointed Jonas toward a bag of carrots and grater that were sitting on the counter.

"What are we making?" Jonas asked, unbagging the produce.

"Chicken cacciatore," Sidney said without looking up from the pan on the stove. "And carrot cake."

"Why carrot cake?"

"Because I'm indulging your sweet tooth." Sidney swept past Jonas toward the fridge, but not before dragging his hand over the small of Jonas's back in a perfectly casual display of affection that Jonas had never encountered before. Jonas wanted more.

Sidney made affection seem easy. Maybe it was easy. It was certainly fun. The music, the lightness of Sidney's hands on Jonas's waist and on his arms. Every time Sidney touched him, Jonas's heart skipped a beat.

The conversation in the garden reminded Jonas that Sidney really seemed like he could take anything in stride. He'd pulled Jonas out of his sullenness and into the bright warmth of the kitchen with little more than an unflappable attitude. A small voice in the back of his head said, 'he's good for you,' and Jonas tried to ignore it. What did that even mean? But as Sidney made the most delicious smelling supper the garden cottage had ever seen, Jonas had to admit, at least to himself, that Sidney was good. Good for him, very probably. Even though Jonas had little to offer in return.

Dinner went off without a hitch, and their conversation stayed firmly in the celestial realm for the length of it. Sidney was going to stargaze that night, which, of course he was. It was why he was there in the first place. But it did bring a thought to Jonas's mind.

"I wonder..." Jonas began. His cheeks were flushed, his gaze dropped to the last of his third, possibly fourth, glass of wine. "Would you have an interest in using my telescope for an extended study of the star clusters that pass over the bay? You could use it as the basis for your dissertation, if you decide to keep investigating the influence of the celestial realms here on earth." He glanced up, a little surprised to see Sidney's smile widen over the rim of his wine glass.

"You're offering me your telescope?"

"Well," Jonas stammered, afraid the critical suggestion had been overlooked. "Not just the telescope."

"Of course."

"To study the stars here, where the thin place between the worlds is—"

"You're asking me to stay here?" Sidney's cheeks pinked. Maybe he was drunk. Jonas wasn't drunk. Was he drunk?

"To stay, I mean... It doesn't have to be here. Elmmond House is perfectly—"

"For how long?" Sidney asked. He was still beaming, and Jonas couldn't help but shrug and smile in return.

"As long as you like."

Sidney leaned back in his chair and picked up his wine glass. He looked so content, so pleased, and Jonas was thrilled he'd had some small part in making Sidney feel that way.

"We should probably talk about this again when you're sober."

"I'm not drunk."

"I think you might be."

"Well, then you ought to take advantage," Jonas teased. There was a line of tension in it that he hadn't meant to put there. But it was at his own expense. And it was alright. It really was. Sidney wasn't going to hurt him. Somewhere along the last day or so, Jonas had finally managed to square that in his mind. Still smiling, Sidney shook his head and got to his feet.

"We'll talk about it again later."

"Alright," Jonas said. And then Sidney was beside him, grabbing up his plate, kissing him on the cheek.

"I need to go check the telescope and get my supplies together. I'll be back down in a few minutes to ice the cake. Do not eat it until I've iced it." Jonas nodded obediently and Sidney left, his footsteps echoing down from the floor above. Jonas put away the leftovers, and then went into the library to avoid the temptation of the carrot cake, where he promptly fell asleep in the armchair by the window.

Several hours later, he woke up. It was properly night, and through the library window he could see the stars glittering in the deep black sky. There was only the slightest pulse of a headache behind his eyes. He needed a glass of water, an aspirin and a slice of the cake he could still smell sitting in the kitchen.

The cool water from the fridge went miles toward clearing his head. Jonas ate his cake in silence, trying to puzzle through what on earth he was doing with Sidney Quince. It was stupid to deny the way he felt. He'd invited Sidney to stay with him for God's sake. And if Sidney said yes, maybe Jonas could figure out how to explain. How to apologize for not telling Sidney that he was a demon sooner. Time would be a good thing. It would help.

Jonas made his way upstairs, where he could better hear the wind whipping violently over the roof. But, of course, the very first thing Jonas saw as he stepped into his room was the rapidly flickering light from Sidney's oil lamp, Sidney's silhouette hunched over the wrought iron table. Sidney was wild, and Jonas's heart beat a little faster at the sight of him.

When Jonas pulled open the balcony door, the cold took the air from his lungs in a gasp.

"Good Lord, Sidney. Come inside!"

"I'm nearly done." Sidney's teeth were chattering.

"You're nearly a popsicle, Quince!"

"I'm f-f-fine."

"If you're not inside in three minutes, I'll bring you inside myself," Jonas said and closed the door.

He spent the next three minutes lighting a fire. Warmth was the objective, not romantic ambience. He couldn't help it if his room looked more inviting in the firelight. Jonas was just the last bastion of good sense between Sidney and his goal of getting hypothermia.

When the room had reached a comfortable temperature, Jonas steeled himself and went back outside. The minute the door opened, Sidney began to protest.

"It's not been three minutes."

"Likely closer to five." Jonas stepped behind Sidney, reaching around him to close the notebook. Sidney smacked his hand and Jonas smacked Sidney's ass.

It wasn't intentional. Reactive would have been a more accurate word. In the same moment that Jonas tried to apologize, Sidney looked over his shoulder with a suggestively arched eyebrow and a heavily lidded gaze. Jonas swallowed, apology dying on his tongue.

"A compelling argument."

"You're being irritating," Jonas managed an arch tone. Sidney turned, grabbing his things up from the table, purposefully rubbing his ass against Jonas's crotch. Two could play at that game.

Jonas let his palm settle on Sidney's right hip. Sidney shifted into the touch, pushing back ever so slightly. Invitation. Encouragement. Jonas couldn't suppress the shiver that ran down his spine.

"It's far too cold out here for that, Quince."

"Is that your only objection?" Sidney murmured. If he listened for it, Jonas could hear sounds of music, laughter, on the wind, down from Elmmond House. The thought of having Sidney up here on the balcony, in view of anyone with a light and a mind to look their way, was intoxicating.

Jonas leaned forward, letting his weight pin Sidney briefly to the edge of the table. When Sidney leaned back against his chest, Jonas couldn't stifle a satisfied hum of approval.

"I don't mind if you don't." Jonas said truthfully. Sidney tilted his head back, and Jonas bent forward to kiss him. Sidney's lips were frozen. "Too bad you won't make it until the warmer months when we actually could. At this rate, you'll freeze to death on my balcony before April."

"I thought you offered to take me inside and warm me up."

"I did no such thing," Jonas chuckled. Sidney's mouth curled into a smile.

"But you will, won't you?"

"If you like." Jonas couldn't stop himself. Should have. But Sidney kissed him then, ground against him, and Jonas pulled Sidney back against his chest and steered him inside.

29

For all of fifteen seconds, Sidney thought how gorgeous Jonas's bedroom looked in the firelight. His fingers prickled as they thawed in the warmth. And then Jonas pushed him toward the bed.

Sidney let himself stumble forward, elbows beneath his chest as he bent over the edge of the mattress. Jonas made a half-feral noise of approval, almost a growl, and Sidney licked his lips.

Jonas seemed to be trying to keep his arousal on a tight leash. Excepting their encounter in the woods that morning, Sidney had been the one to initiate every time. There might have been reasons for that, but Sidney couldn't help but enjoy being the one to snap Jonas's tether. Jonas was starving for so many things, and Sidney was absolutely prepared to feed him.

Sidney rolled onto his back, hoisted himself onto the end of the mattress. Jonas's hands were tugging at the buttons on Sidney's coat before Sidney had fully balanced himself. He watched Jonas's brow furrow in concentration. Sidney toed off his boots, before threading his fingers beneath the collar of Jonas's shirt. Jonas hissed, pulling his shoulders up to his ears.

"Your hands are freezing!" Sidney grinned, trying to slide the offending digits into the crack between Jonas's chin and his neck. Jonas snorted, reaching up, yanking Sidney's left hand away with warm, firm fingers. For a moment, Sidney could see Jonas's mind spinning, and Sidney thought he was going to be pinned down. But then, perhaps surprising them both, Jonas drew Sidney's hand up to his mouth and pressed a kiss to his knuckles.

It was so romantic that Sidney couldn't stifle a small sigh. The energy shifted immediately, feral heat replaced with desperate longing. Sidney wanted Jonas. Wanted him so much. Sidney leaned forward, tugging his hand down, replacing it with his mouth, and Jonas moved into the kiss, pulling them together.

Sidney slid off his coat as Jonas crowded him, crawling over him onto the mattress. In one fluid movement, Jonas was over him, their kiss finally breaking, leaving Sidney breathless. Jonas's eyes skated over Sidney, as he sat back astride Sidney's thighs, palms flat against his own knees, like he'd been given a plate at a buffet and wasn't sure where to begin. Encouragement was something Sidney was more than happy to provide.

Sidney began unbuttoning his own shirt. He wriggled his hips just enough so Jonas could feel his erection. Feel the way Sidney wanted him. Jonas bit his lip and spread his legs just enough so that Sidney could have something to grind against. Perfection. Sidney let his cold fingers trail against his bare chest as he thrust up against Jonas's ass. Jonas's chest was rising and falling heavily as he dropped his fingers to the sensitive skin just above Sidney's belly button.

"You're impossible," Jonas said. Sidney cocked his head to the side. He caught Jonas's fingers in his own and dragged them up his chest.

"Thank you?"

"I just mean—" Jonas paused, eyes widening as Sidney lifted

Jonas's hand, kissing Jonas's fingertips. Then Sidney opened his mouth and dipped Jonas's first and middle finger down against his tongue. He sucked lightly and Jonas grunted, hips twitching. "Sidney." Jonas sounded desperate for air. Sidney released his grip on Jonas's hand, let Jonas's fingers slide out of his mouth and trail against his bottom lip.

"I want you," Sidney said, and Jonas descended on him.

The kissing was breathless again, frantic. Jonas's deft hands made quick work of Sidney's clothes, and Sidney was pleased to find it was fairly easy to keep up. The dark lines of ink over Jonas's chest looked etched in the dim light, and Sidney dragged his fingers over them, leaning up to kiss them, lick them as Jonas stretched for his nightstand. Jonas looked down at Sidney between his arms, and Sidney smiled up at him. Shrugged.

"I like your tattoos."

"I can see that." Sidney licked his lips and sucked a sharp kiss over one of Jonas's nipples. Jonas groaned, arms going weak for just a moment before he shifted himself back onto his knees. There was oil in his hand and he tossed a small black tin onto the blanket. Condoms. Good. Fantastic actually. Not that Sidney needed Jonas to wear one, unless, well... unless there was a reason he ought.

Sidney thought back to when Jonas had pushed Sidney off him the day before. He glanced up at Jonas, a question (several questions) on the tip of his tongue. Jonas blushed.

"Not—We don't have to."

"It's perfectly fine with me," Sidney said gently. "We don't have to do anything if there's..." He'd been very close to Jonas's cock and hadn't seen anything alarming. How to insinuate your partner might have some kind of sexual disease without killing the mood? "We don't have to if there's a reason not to." Sidney attempted. It wasn't good. Jonas looked flummoxed, the furrow returning to his brow.

"What do you mean?" Jonas asked. Sidney blinked.

"I know you were a soldier," he tried to say without insinuation. As though he was teaching a class. "Venereal disease is—"

"Oh! No. No," Jonas shook his head with such a fervor that Sidney almost laughed. "God. No. I'm just— I prefer to be careful."

"Okay," Sidney said, bemused and appreciative. He sat up enough that he could wrap his arms around Jonas's neck and kiss him. "That's actually very sweet."

"Are you not careful?" Jonas asked, eyebrow arched. Sidney snorted.

"I get off on *pretending* to be easy." Sidney pressed a kiss to the corner of Jonas's mouth as Jonas rolled his eyes. "It's been a little while for me."

"Me as well," Jonas admitted, gaze softening. He wrapped his arms around Sidney's waist.

Jonas kissed him, laid on top of him. Their bodies were flush and Sidney moaned at the feeling of Jonas pressed against him. The heat of his erection, the firm planes of his muscles.

"I want you so badly." Sidney rolled his hips and Jonas pressed his forehead to Sidney's shoulder, grunting, and shifting for more pressure. Sidney gasped at the sensation, wanted more of it. And then Jonas slid his hand into the back of Sidney's hair and kissed him so deeply that when Jonas pulled away, Sidney was panting.

"I want you inside of me, Jonas. Please."

Jonas didn't answer. Instead, he began kissing his way down Sidney's torso. Soft, reverent kisses that made Sidney squirm with their gentleness. Sidney didn't think he had a body to be admired, all thin and long and boney. But Jonas hummed against his skin, nipping, groaning like Sidney was a decadent dessert to be devoured slowly. Sidney didn't know what he liked more, the fevered, frenetic encounters, or this. The slow, languid pace of Jonas's hands dragging over Sidney's hips, spreading his thighs, made Sidney squirm and buck. Jonas sucked a love bite into the tender skin of Sidney's hip crease, and Sidney moaned, as Jonas moved lower, mouth and tongue and hands, deliberate and unhurried.

And then, Jonas answered Sidney's request. He began to open him up, achingly slow. Soft caresses, firm but gentle. Sidney moaned at the first finger. Began to beg at the second.

"Jonas! Oh, Jonas, please."

"Don't rush me, Sidney." He was smiling, the bastard, his chest flush and gorgeous, looking very pleased with himself.

"Or you'll—" Sidney couldn't bite back the groan as Jonas began to fuck him slowly with his fingers. "Jonas!"

"Yes, Sidney?" Jonas purred. Bastard. Sidney arched his back.

"Fuck me! Please, Jonas."

"I am," Jonas said. Sidney moaned, grinding down again. He reached up to push his hair out of his face, stretching into the pleasure of it. Jonas grunted his approval and his hand began to move ever so slightly faster. Yes. God. Perfect.

Sidney kept his back arched and dropped his free hand down, sliding his palm over Jonas's cock. Thick, heavy and leaking. Sidney stroked him, and Jonas's eyes closed as he rocked forward into Sidney's fist.

"Like that," Sidney said. "Please. Yes." Jonas shifted his hips back, out of Sidney's grasp, sliding his fingers away at the same moment. "Jonas!" Jonas reached up and grabbed the condom tin off the bed, as he got to his knees again.

"On your back?" Jonas asked, his attention on the rubber. It had a strange, almost iridescent shine to it that caught Sidney's eye. And then Jonas had it on, and Sidney rolled over, pressing up onto his knees.

Jonas leaned down, kissing the knots of Sidney's spine, kneading Sidney's ass. Sidney pushed back against him, wanting to be touched in every place all at once, and he could feel Jonas smile against his skin.

"Greedy, Sidney."

"Fuck me, Jonas." Jonas slid his hand down Sidney's hip, then to Sidney's cock, stroking him slowly. Sidney moaned. "Jonas!" And then Jonas was at his entrance, pushing into him. Stroking him. Sidney's arms nearly gave way all at once. He tried to bite back a groan and it still came out a whimper.

"Sidney." Jonas's voice was ragged, his body still. His fingers curled into Sidney's hip hard enough to bruise, and all Sidney could think was that he wanted more.

JONAS BIT HIS BOTTOM LIP AND TRIED NOT TO COME ALL AT ONCE. Sidney was perfect. Tight, and gorgeous and trembling just a little. Every time he made a sound, Jonas's hips wanted to thrust. He was trying to be still, let Sidney adjust. And then Sidney grunted and began to slide forward and back, fucking himself on Jonas's cock, and Jonas lost all coherent thought.

"Sidney. Oh, God, Sidney."

"Harder, Jonas. Fuck! Please." Jonas reached around to stroke Sidney, as he slid deeper. Faster. Sidney was begging for him, moaning. Sidney braced himself against the bed and slid too far forward, turning the angle bad. Jonas caught himself on Sidney's hip, as their bodies slid apart. Sidney looked over his shoulder at Jonas, eyes dark, pupils wide in lust.

"Over there," Sidney nodded toward the headboard, breathing hard. Jonas went, not a single thought about anything other than Sidney's pleasure. He would have gone anywhere. Done anything.

Jonas fell back against the pillows, reclining against the headboard. Sidney crawled over to him, kissed him, slow and gentle. Then harder, sliding his hand up Jonas's slick cock. Jonas twitched and moaned. Sidney stroked him and then pulled away.

Before Jonas quite knew what was happening, Sidney had turned, and leaned back against Jonas's chest. He kissed Jonas that way, his neck at an angle, the soft, smooth heat of his body pressing against Jonas's chest. Sidney hitched one thigh over Jonas, and then reached for him, slowly sliding down onto Jonas's cock.

The space between their bodies shrank as Sidney took him, and Jonas watched, entranced. His body was moving on its own; he slid his hand beneath Sidney's thigh to help support him, and when he squeezed, Sidney moaned. Sidney rolled his hips slowly, head thrown back onto Jonas's shoulder as Sidney took him to the hilt.

"Sidney. Fuck." Jonas gasped. Sidney whimpered, and Jonas kissed him. Kissed his jaw, sucked a love bite into his neck. Sidney moaned and began to move, and then Jonas was clutching Sidney's thigh, as Sidney rode him.

The pace Sidney set was perfect. Gorgeous. Jonas sank his teeth into Sidney's shoulder and Sidney cried out, his back arching. Sidney braced himself with clenching fingers against the slick, hot skin of Jonas's ribs, as he pulled Jonas flush against him. However they'd fumbled before, they were perfectly in sync now. Jonas thrust and Sidney moaned his name. When Jonas shifted his hand down, stroking Sidney's cock, Sidney whined, nodding, frantic.

"Oh, fuck. Yes! Jonas, please! I'm close. I—" Sidney came, head falling back against Jonas's shoulder again, moaning into Jonas's ear, and Jonas spilled inside him.

Sidney's chest was heaving, flushed and gorgeous, and he leaned up, licking his way into Jonas's mouth. Somehow, Jonas was desperate for Sidney than he had been when they'd started.

It wasn't the sex he wanted more of. Or, it was, but it was something else too. Jonas kissed Sidney, could feel Sidney's eyelashes flutter against his cheek. Jonas wanted to curl around Sidney's body and cling to him forever. He'd kept Sidney from getting marked but felt like the magic had reversed on him somehow. He was enchanted by Sidney. He might be in love with him, and he was elated and terrified both, by the realization.

Sidney turned his head, shifting forward, off Jonas. Jonas helped as best he could, his energy spent, body aching to be close. Not to let him get too far away.

"Oh," Sidney said quietly. "Oh, uh."

"What's wrong?" Jonas frowned, pushing up off the pillows, the headboard. "Are you okay?" He slid his hand over Sidney's hip, trying to pull him back, look him over, as Sidney slid to the side.

For a moment, all Jonas could see was Sidney's back, shoulders. Sidney half collapsed onto his hip, as he picked something up off the bedspread. The condom. Empty.

Dread hit Jonas like a bucket of cold water.

"It's alright," Sidney was saying. "I don't mind, honestly."

"Are you okay?" Jonas asked. It was the wrong question.

"I'm fine," Sidney said quickly. He frowned at whatever Jonas's face was doing. Shit, what was his face doing? "Are *you* okay?"

"I'm alright. Fine." Jonas couldn't stop watching Sidney, desperate to remember if there were any physical signs of a mark he might see. He'd fucked this so badly. He'd tried so hard to be careful. "As long as it doesn't bother you, there's nothing to worry about." Liar. Gods, it made the bile rise in his throat.

"It doesn't bother me." Sidney blinked, his cheeks pinking further. "I like it, actually."

Jonas didn't deserve the way Sidney's expression softened.

But telling Sidney now would be pointless. The mark would make Sidney stay, even if he wanted to leave. But without an oath or a binding, it wouldn't last long. A few days at most.

Sidney was saying something. Was grabbing Jonas's arm and tugging him down on the bed.

"...But I appreciate it all the same. I'm sorry I wasn't more careful. When we changed positions, I wasn't paying attention."

"Neither was I," Jonas said. Stupid. Selfish. Sidney kissed him, and Jonas's rib cage tightened with guilt.

"That was incredible," Sidney murmured against Jonas's chest as he curled against Jonas. Jonas wrapped an arm around Sidney's waist and tried to breathe.

"You're too good for me," Jonas said. Sidney snorted, as though that was an absurd thing to say. As though it wasn't absolutely true.

30

Sidney woke from a deep sleep, curled under Jonas's arm. Morning light eked in through the seam in the curtains. Or maybe it was afternoon. Sidney shifted beneath the blankets and smiled when Jonas's grip on him tightened. He slid closer to Jonas's chest, tucking himself beneath Jonas's bulk. Sidney inhaled the warm scent of Jonas's body, his gaze on the narrow space between them. He'd never been so comfortable before.

The lines of ink on Jonas's chest rose and fell slowly with his breath, and Sidney watched them, wondering if it was possible to feel this way every morning. To want nothing except the man already laying next to him. If Jonas had meant what he'd said the night before at dinner, if he really wanted Sidney to stay, Sidney would be a fool not to accept. And Sidney could tell himself he was doing it for access to the library, to the telescope, for his dissertation. But truthfully he was doing it for opportunity to have more mornings like this one.

Sidney ran his thumb along a tattoo that followed the shadow of Jonas's pectoral muscle. He kept his touch light, but Jonas still blinked open his eyes. For a moment, his gaze was so soft, so open, that Sidney nearly couldn't breathe.

"You're a menace," Jonas mumbled as he lay his head back down, his eyes closing again.

"I wasn't doing anything," Sidney protested, letting his fingertips trail up over Jonas's nipple. Jonas's eyes opened slowly above a smirk, searching Sidney's face, like he was expecting to see something unusual.

"How are you feeling?" Jonas asked. Sidney yawned.

"Nicely achey." He nudged his knee between Jonas's thighs, tugging himself closer to Jonas's body until they were flush hip to chest. He could feel Jonas's length hardening, and he couldn't help but be a little pleased about that. "How are *you* feeling?"

"Like this conversation is entirely pretense," Jonas murmured as he leaned into the soft caress of Sidney's fingertips. "I have some errands to run today."

"I need to go into town and meet with the harbormaster." Sidney ran his palm over Jonas's hip, skating lower, but not too low.

"You can take the truck. I'll borrow one of the cars from Elmmond House."

"Where are you going?" Sidney asked. Jonas was watching him again in a peculiar way, like he was waiting for a certain reaction.

"Visiting a friend," Jonas said. Vague. Sidney arched an eyebrow and then let it go.

"Will you be home for supper? I could pick something up when I'm in town."

"Not sure," Jonas said. "But don't worry about me. I'll be fine either way."

"Alright," Sidney shrugged. It was, somehow, the oddest conversation they'd ever had. But also, Sidney couldn't bring himself to care about that at the moment. His hand snaked low enough that he could run his fingers along Jonas's shaft, and Jonas moaned as Sidney did so. Christ, Sidney could have lived with that sound in his ears all day. He leaned up, kissed Jonas, teased him again, shivering at the whimper of desire hidden just behind the pant of Jonas's breath.

Sidney rolled onto his back, desperate, aching. Jonas followed him, crowded him back against the pillows and the sheets, pressing bruising kisses against Sidney's mouth, and the column of Sidney's throat as Sidney arched into his touch.

When Jonas pressed inside Sidney this time, they were face to face. Sidney couldn't help but meet Jonas's gaze, enraptured by the intensity of it, the way Jonas watched him. Jonas was beyond careful, pacing himself, reacting to each and every one of Sidney's sounds and movements. Meanwhile, Sidney was making noises he'd never heard himself make; barely sensible, the longer Jonas was inside him.

Jonas fucked him slowly, but not too slowly, and Sidney came apart beneath him. It could have been ten minutes; it could have been an hour. All Sidney knew was Jonas's mouth on his neck, one of Jonas's massive hands against his hips, his body taut under Jonas, straining in pleasure. Jonas slid into him at precisely the right angle, and Sidney nearly came untouched.

"Jonas! God!" Sidney grabbed for his shoulders, and Jonas ducked his head and thrust again. Sidney groaned, and then gasped as Jonas took him in hand.

"I've never wanted someone like this." Jonas's lips brushed against Sidney's neck, the praise nearly tipping Sidney over the edge. "I need you, Sidney. Please."

Sidney came. He dug his fingers into Jonas's shoulders and moaned, rolling his hips down until Jonas pulled out and spilled over Sidney's hip crease. Sidney tugged him down into a kiss, the heat of Jonas intoxicating, his limbs all but turned to rubber.

"I don't know what you've done to me," Jonas murmured. His eyes were bright, wide like he was in shock. No one had ever said anything like that to Sidney before, and his orgasm addled brain couldn't begin to imagine what it meant. So Sidney said the only thing he knew.

"I love you, I think."

Jonas smiled for a moment. A small thing that faded as he leaned forward and kissed Sidney like he was drowning, and Sidney held the last supply of air in his lungs. It was a good reaction, Sidney thought. Not what he'd expected. Though he hadn't really expected anything because he hadn't planned on saying it. When Jonas pulled away, his head was bowed, looking down between their bodies. Jonas was touching him like Sidney was something precious again, deliberate and delicate, but it took him a moment before he met Sidney's eye.

"I want you to stay here. Use the telescope." It wasn't, 'I love you too.' But it also was, in a way. Sidney smiled.

"Have you been drinking again?" Jonas rolled his eyes.

"You'll stay? You'll think about it, at least?"

"I'll talk to Karolina. It may have to wait until the semester's over."

"I'll cover your expenses," Jonas said. Sidney laughed, shoved Jonas gently with the flat of his palm.

"I'm not for sale, Duke Rookwood. I'll find a job."

"Whatever makes you happy." Sidney stretched up and kissed him.

"Remember that you said that."

"Oh no."

"Too late. You can't take it back," Sidney said, pushing Jonas off him, and rolling out of bed. "I'm going to go take a shower."

By the time he was dried and dressed, Jonas was downstairs in the library with a cup of coffee. Sidney poured himself one as well, and cut an overly generous slice of carrot cake, which he'd eaten half of before Jonas emerged with a stack of paper.

"I found some charts I made, oh probably ten years ago now." Jonas laid the pages down on the table. "Only about a month's worth. But they're from here. They might be helpful if you're looking for a baseline to place against the tide charts."

The charts were expertly composed, all thin lines and cleanly labeled. Sidney admired them as he took a swallow of his coffee to clear his throat.

"These are perfect."

"Far from it," Jonas said, though he was smiling. "I just thought you might want the dates so you can get those tables from the harbormaster too. Though, ten years back, they might be at the library or the historical society. I don't know who keeps those records. Or if anyone does."

"I can still borrow the truck?" Sidney asked. Jonas nodded.

"Of course. Keys are on the hook in the closet."

"I can take one of the Elmmond House cars, if that's easier."

"Easier?" Jonas frowned.

"So, you don't have to. For your errands." Jonas's mouth crumpled in a frown of confusion. "Visiting your friend?"

"Ah. Right." Jonas nodded, his expression neutralizing almost too quickly. Suspicious. "No, I'll be fine."

"Do they live far?" Sidney asked. A reasonable question. Jonas shook his head, turning to look out the window.

"Not terribly. But if it looks like rain, I may stay put." The sky was blue and cloudless. Sidney cut a bite of cake with his fork.

"Is your friend a real person? Or did you make them up?" He put the cake in his mouth as Jonas whipped back around to look at him, his cheeks pink.

"I—" Sidney cocked his head to the side, and Jonas sighed. "I didn't know if you'd want space. After last night. And I just thought—"

"You'd make up some errands to sound like you had other things going on that I couldn't do with you."

"I do have friends that I could visit," Jonas offered. Sidney tried not to grin. "I know that just saying that makes it sound like I have no friends who could possibly want a visit from me, but—"

"I believe that you have friends, Jonas," Sidney chuckled. Jonas huffed and shook his head, turning around and going back toward the library.

"You're insufferable."

"Should I bring back dinner?" Sidney called after him.

"Yes," Jonas replied. "From the Silver Platter."

"Your usual?" Sidney asked. Jonas huffed.

"Surprise me."

31

Jonas waited until Sidney was out of sight, down the hill in the truck, to walk to Elmmond House. He left a note for Asterion with Verne, who said he'd deliver it right away. If Asterion was awake before three in the afternoon, Jonas would eat a hat.

Sidney didn't seem to have been marked. Or, if he had been, it was so inconsequential that it didn't change his behavior toward Jonas in any noticeable way. Except, of course, one rather large way, which was that Sidney had said he loved Jonas.

Jonas wanted to dismiss it. He wanted to say it was a part of the mark and move on, and not let himself feel the elation that he did very much feel. He'd barely managed to admit to himself that his feelings for Sidney were running in that direction too, and he knew all of this should have been thrilling.

It was. But more than that, it was overwhelming. Until he came clean with Sidney, he couldn't let it go any further. Jonas had fallen in love once with a man he didn't know, who'd built their entire relationship on a lie. He couldn't do that to Sidney. He wouldn't.

After dropping off his message for Asterion, Jonas went back to the house. Because he truly didn't have any other errands to run, he went into the garden. After an hour spent removing goldenrod, clouds began to crowd into the blue sky from the west, and Jonas caught himself wondering if they'd be gone by the time Sidney was back to stargaze.

Jonas turned on the radio in the kitchen while a new pot of coffee percolated, and glanced around for Delilah in several rooms before he realized she was likely up at the big house. Once guests started arriving, he usually didn't see much of her, which was fine. He was glad she could visit with her old friends and have fun. But with Delilah gone and Sidney gone, Jonas found he was at a loss of what to do with himself.

Which was absurd because he had moved into the garden cottage precisely so that he could be alone with his work and his thoughts. Instead of either of those things, Jonas sat at the table with a plate and fork and a cup of coffee, indulging his sweet tooth and wondered what he was going to do with the rest of his day, and all the days after that.

Not that there was plenty of work to do. And he ought to call Karolina because she would know the best way to approach Sidney about the demon issue. Asterion had been the first person Jonas had thought of, and, upon reflection, likely wasn't the best. Once Sidney got back, they would have to look at the tide charts and compare them to Sidney's notes and Jonas's notes. He ought to go get his notes, actually.

The echo of his own footsteps in the empty foyer made him shudder, and thankfully the sound of them was interrupted by a commotion at the big house. Car horns honking, voices shouting. Jonas stepped up to the narrow window beside the front door and peered out to see what looked like a traffic jam. Several florists carrying massive flower sprays, as well as two grocery delivery vans, had come up against a long black car full of revelers who were trying to execute an unnecessary three-point-turn in a circular drive. Jonas sighed and turned back toward the stairs.

Everything about the Ascension was tiresome. It would mean people for days after the party had been over, new creatures knocking on his door when they realized they'd been left behind and they'd have to survive with humans for a full year before they could get back. And this year he'd have less sympathy than usual. They'd be taking away his time with Sidney.

~

"Yeah, I'm not sure I can just give those out." The harbormaster wasn't in, and his clerk looked to be about twelve years old, in spite of (or perhaps because of) his pencil moustache and the wet nub of a cigarette clenched between his teeth.

"I'm a researcher from Holyworth College," Sidney said. Then added a lie, to see where that would get him. "I spoke to someone about this on the phone."

"Like I said," the clerk shrugged. "The harbormaster's not in, and the whole town is closing down for the Ascension. People are already turning up missing, the damn thing hasn't even happened yet." He flicked his cigarette into the trashcan and looked at Sidney with narrowed eyes. "That why you're here?"

"I'm here to see the tide charts for the last six months." The clerk folded his arms across his narrow chest.

"Come back on Monday." Four days from now. Shit. Sidney sighed.

"Is there a requisition form I can fill out or something?" The clerk snorted.

"Sure. And you can file it for me too." The man-child kicked the trashcan at the side of the desk with his toe, nudging it pointedly in Sidney's direction. Sidney thought of a half dozen rude things to say, and swallowed all of them. Instead, he gave a thin smile and left.

The clerk didn't seem to be lying about the town being shut down. Half the shops had 'closed' signs in the windows, and there were small clusters of people milling around on front porches and stoops, like they were waiting for a parade. Sidney wasn't sure The Silver Platter would even be open, but when he pulled up, he could see people sitting inside at the front windows, and smoke rising from one of the vents near the back into the crisp fall air.

The bell above the door rang merrily. The bitter smell of coffee mixed with the saccharine tinge of syrup or cherries jubilee. All the stools along the counter were empty, and before Sidney could decide where he ought to sit for a to-go order, Dom came out of the swinging door of the kitchen. A chambray shirt strained across his biceps as he tossed a dish towel over his shoulder. He smiled at Sidney as he pushed gold rimmed glasses up his nose.

"Sit anywhere," he said.

"It's just a to-go order," Sidney said. Dom nodded.

"I guessed as much. Still staying up at the cottage then?" Sidney nodded and took the nearest counter stool, and Dom returned with a menu. "I guess Jonas wants his usual. What can I get for you?"

"It smells like cherries in here," Sidney said. Dom smirked.

"I've got cherry tarts in the oven, but they'll be a few minutes."

"I've got time," Sidney said, settling in.

"Coffee while you wait?" Dom asked. Sidney nodded, and Dom moved to the massive metal coffee maker on the back counter. Jonas had said Dom owned the place. Maybe he'd know more about why everything closed for the Ascension. Or why the harbormaster's clerk had been so unhelpful.

"I'm a little surprised you're still open. Everything else seems like it's shuttered for the weekend." Dom nodded, as he slid Sidney a full mug of coffee.

"That's the Ascension for you." He brought a sugar shaker within Sidney's reach, but Sidney could see that Dom was stiff, the soft curve of his mouth crumpled into a grimace.

"Why? It's not a holiday, is it?"

"No," Dom said, glancing at Sidney for a long moment. "Not for us, anyway." Sidney met his gaze with one that he hoped read total innocence. "It shuts business down in town because people tend to leave."

"Leave town? Why?"

"Some of them leave town." Dom drummed his fingers on the counter and then glanced up at Sidney. "Some of them disappear."

"Disappear?" In everything he'd learned about the Ascension, this was perhaps the strangest bit of information he'd gleaned so far. Dom didn't seem pleased that Sidney didn't know what he was talking about. He leaned forward and lowered his voice.

"Jonas hasn't spoken to you about it at all? He didn't warn you?"

"Warn me? No. He doesn't… well, he said he doesn't go to the Ascension party." Dom scoffed.

"Of course he doesn't. He'd have vanished by now. Look, I don't know much about it. It's a big, well," he hesitated, glancing around once again before continuing. "It's a sort of big orgy. At least, that's what I've heard. And all these strange people come into town for it. And I don't mean— I don't mind strange. But these folks are different. Faeries, I mean. Creatures. Things that shouldn't exist." Dom's eyes were so wide and earnest that Sidney could see flecks of silver in the circles of his dark brown irises. Probably this was the part where people called Dom crazy, and he seemed to be holding his breath, waiting for it. Sidney knew better, of course. When Sidney nodded that he understood, Dom looked relieved. "You're better off avoiding the whole thing. People who go don't often come back."

The pieces of this Ascension were finally connecting in Sidney's mind. Marking made it so humans could travel through portals. People who wanted to travel into the other celestial realms would need to be marked, so the debauchery that Father Michaels had alluded to, and that Dom was calling an orgy, as well as the disappearances, made sense. People left through the portals. Creatures too. Comings and goings.

"People from the town attend, though?" Sidney asked.

"They get enchanted, some people say. Or trapped. And I've heard you can make bargains for things. Magically, you know? So maybe some people do know what they're getting into, but..." Dom faltered, trailing off.

"I believe you," Sidney said. Dom's eyes narrowed, scrutinizing Sidney, as though Sidney might have been lying.

"You haven't heard anything else about it?" he asked. Sidney shook his head.

"Only little things, here and there."

"I'm surprised Jonas hasn't said anything." There was judgment in his tone that made Sidney bristle.

"Like I said, he doesn't go." And that was more defensive than he needed to be, but Sidney couldn't help it. Maybe it was a little odd that Jonas hadn't mentioned anything. Especially if the Ascension really was dangerous, but Jonas had told Sidney that he didn't go to the party anymore, and Sidney had no reason to believe that wasn't true. Ellery Van Ahlberg and Delilah had both confirmed it.

Maybe Jonas didn't know how sinister the whole thing had become, or maybe there was something else. Sidney pursed his lips. He could guess all day, but the easiest thing to do would be to go ask Jonas.

"Did you want anything else?" Dom asked.

"No," Sidney shook his head, mind reeling slightly. "Just the tart."

"Alright. It'll be up in a minute," he said brusquely, before going back into the kitchen, leaving Sidney to try not to theorize without all the data.

32

Jonas was shuffling through more charts in his study when he heard a knock at the front door. With a grunt, he got to his feet and made his way back through the house. He'd been looking for anything that would be helpful for Sidney's research and had come up woefully empty handed. The desire to find something was at least half (but likely more) an unspoken apology from his guilty conscience. Still, it would be useful to have more data, no matter what the impetus for gathering it was.

He'd just reached the bottom of the stairs when another knock rang out, impatient and demanding. The sound of it practically identified the visitor; Asterion might as well have called out his own name.

Though Jonas had just pulled open the door, Asterion somehow managed to already be leaning against the doorframe. The Prince's long cobalt hair curled around the angles of his chin and cheeks, framing his flawless, glowing skin. His eyes were gold, crinkling at their narrow corners as his mouth curled into a smirk.

"Jonas," he said, his voice low and ridiculously breathy. Jonas arched an eyebrow.

"Good morning, your highness." Asterion huffed at the use of his title and peeled himself off the doorframe, shouldering his way past Jonas into the foyer. Asterion was broad across the chest, but his waist was as narrow as if he was corseted. He'd always been that way, and due to the nature of Fae magic he likely always would be. Asterion looked around the foyer with an appraising eye and made a small hum that was neither approval nor disapproval, but likely dismissal. When he looked back at Jonas, he put one hand on his hip.

"Don't be a prick. You asked me to come. Why are you wearing that?"

"What?" Jonas looked down at himself. The glamour. He'd forgotten again. "Oh. I've been entertaining a human."

"Entertaining? Is that what we're calling it now?" Asterion leaned around Jonas to look into the parlor. "Ellery did mention something to me about him. I think she called him a 'finicky weed,' or something like that. She said he wanted an invitation to the party." Asterion produced one of the heavy, embossed envelopes from inside a billowing sleeve and smacked it against Jonas's chest, before striding into the parlor. "There you go. No need to thank me." Jonas swallowed. He'd forgotten that Sidney had asked for an invitation to the party. Or Delilah had asked for one for him. It was hard to imagine Sidney in his threadbare sweaters and corduroy trousers carousing with Asterion, who was busy sweeping his short, velvet cape to the side as he swanned into the parlor.

Jonas set the invitation on the entry table and closed the door. When he turned back, Asterion had already collapsed artfully on the far end of one of Jonas's least comfortable couches: a baroque thing, upholstered in blue damask that Jonas had inherited with the house. Jonas stepped into the room as Asterion dragged his fingertips over the fabric of the arm of the chair.

"Well, where's your schoolboy? I want to steal him away from you."

"He's out at the moment," Jonas said.

"You always did love having a student." He smirked, but before Jonas could tell him to fuck off, Asterion fixed Jonas with a golden stare, his eyes narrowed, as a long, perfectly manicured finger tapped against his chin. "Can you take your glamour off, since the human's not here? I need to get a good look at you."

"Why?"

"Humor me." Jonas sighed at the silliness of the whole thing, as though it wasn't a relief to have one of his oldest friends here to help him. Jonas shrugged the glamour off his shoulders, and Asterion pursed his lips, his gaze intense and oddly humorless. For a moment, Jonas could have sworn that Asterion even looked sad. Before he could ask why, Asterion was smiling again.

"It's actually disgusting how satisfied you look. I mean, really. Have a sense of decorum, Jonas. Some of us are languishing, you know. It's cruel of you to be so thoroughly well-fucked."

"I've never known you not to be well-fucked, Asterion."

"Touché, darling. Still, just by looking at you I'm not sure what's wrong. Your note said you had some problem that you wanted to talk through. And I warn you, if it's science related, I've already had two glasses of champagne, so I'm not going to be of much use to you. You know I don't have the mind for it."

"I know you pretend to be stupid because you think it's interesting," Jonas reprimanded. It was absolutely his least favorite thing about his friend.

"You wound me, darling. No one wants a clever libertine. It doesn't play well in the bedroom."

"I like you as you are."

"Aren't you a treasure?" Asterion purred derisively, batting his ridiculously long eyelashes at Jonas. "Either way, I'm at least two drinks in—"

"It's two in the afternoon." Jonas glanced at the clock. And then at Asterion, and then at the clock again. "Wait. It's two in the afternoon. You might as well be paying me a visit at six in the morning. What are you doing up so early?" Asterion sniffed, waving a hand dismissively.

"Trouble sleeping. Too much excitement with the Ascension. Don't worry your pretty little horns about it. What's the problem?"

It was now or never. Jonas sat on the opposite end of the horrible couch from Asterion and turned to face him.

"He hasn't seen me without the glamour."

"What?" Asterion wrinkled his nose. Jonas sighed impatiently, as Asterion's expression shifted, eyes widening into understanding. "Oh. Wait. No—You've been fucking him in the glamour?"

"The sex isn't the issue."

"I beg to differ."

"You fuck everyone in a glamour," Jonas accused.

"I live in a glamour! This is me," Asterion pressed his fingertips to his chest. "Perhaps the prettiest version of me, but I don't go around dressing up like a demon or a—"

"He doesn't know," Jonas said, needing desperately to curtail Asterion's rant and keep them on track. "Sidney's never seen me like this. He doesn't know I'm a demon."

"Did you mark him?" Asterion asked, his eyebrows annoyingly high. Jonas huffed.

"Maybe? I've got so little magic left it's hard to—I mean, if I did, it's not—"

"He's not in here salivating over your every word, so I suppose that's a good sign." Asterion collapsed back into the corner of the sofa and stared at Jonas, one hand sliding up to cover his mouth. "Is he leaving soon?"

"I asked him to stay," Jonas said. Asterion was silent, his eyes as wide as dinner plates, the hand over his mouth now clutching his jaw. Jonas grit his teeth. "Don't."

"I assure you, I'm quite speechless." Jonas growled, crossing his arms over his chest. The silence stretched out between them, as Jonas kept his gaze firmly fixed out the front window, where long grey clouds were rolling in over the tops of the trees to the west. The carving on the back of the sofa was digging into his shoulder. He hated this room. When everyone left, the first thing he was going to do was redecorate it.

Asterion slid over on the couch, so his knee was pressed against the side of Jonas's thigh. Jonas looked down at him, and Asterion leaned forward and took Jonas by the chin, staring into his eyes.

"I love you, my darling. But you're not going to like what I have to say."

"That's nearly always true."

"You have to tell him."

"I know I have to tell him," Jonas grumbled, jerking his chin out of Asterion's grasp. "*How* do I tell him?"

"Gods, Jonas. Aren't you supposed to be the smart one? You just fucking tell him."

"Historically, that hasn't gone well for me," Jonas snapped. Asterion pursed his lips, drawing back in surprise.

"This is about Edmund?"

"It's not about Edmund," Jonas lied. "Humans always want something. When they find out you can do magic. Grant wishes. Whatever—"

"Well, first of all, you're not a fucking genie."

"I mean—"

"So, if you like him, bestow some favors on him. Give him

some gold. Shoot some sparks out of your cock. Whatever he likes. What's the problem?"

"I can't do magic without a reagent! The glamour is practically all I have left. Anything more complicated than that is gone. If Sidney wants to see me shoot sparks out of anywhere, he's going to have to forfeit something for it."

"So what?"

"So, I don't want to be a magical well for any human who decides to toss a fucking penny in, Asterion!"

"I thought you said this wasn't about Edmund," Asterion said, then pursed his lips pointedly. Jonas groaned and ran his hands over the sides of his head, tucking his fingers around his skull behind the curve of his horns. As though he could squeeze the effects of Edmund's betrayal out of his brain. He didn't want this to be about Edmund. He didn't want to be afraid forever. Alone forever.

"Look," Asterion leaned into him again. He hooked his fingers into the crooks of Jonas's elbows and tugged his arms down, catching Jonas's hands in his own. Asterion's smile was thin and almost pitying. Jonas groaned.

"Are you going to be nice to me?"

"I've never once been nice to you." Asterion's smile strengthened briefly. "We've been friends a long time, haven't we?"

"We have," Jonas admitted, begrudgingly. He had too few to deny the existence of any.

"Were we ever in love, do you think?" Asterion asked. Jonas stilled; his head cocked to the side. It was rare that either of them talked about the time after Edmund. The years Asterion had stayed with Jonas. In the cottage. In Jonas's bed. Asterion had been trying to help, in his own way. Jonas had wanted it to be romantic, for a little while. Maybe it had been.

"I don't know," Jonas said after a moment. Asterion's mouth crumpled in the middle, his eyes strangely damp. In a hundred years of knowing Asterion, Jonas realized he'd only seen him cry once or twice. Usually from mirth. Never like this.

When Asterion kissed him, Jonas both was and wasn't surprised. He wasn't surprised that it was happening. He was surprised he felt nothing in it, except desperation in the way Asterion's hand had tightened on his wrist. Jonas stilled, his own body foreign in that moment. Something was wrong with Asterion, and suddenly Jonas was worried about him. He cupped Asterion's cheek with his hand, meaning to gently push him off—

A crash, a splatter of something wet, had Asterion and Jonas jerking away from each other. Sidney stood just inside the front door, eyes wide. How had Jonas not heard it open? Oh, Gods. Oh, shit.

"Sidney—" Jonas lurched to his feet, nearly knocking Asterion off the couch. His lips prickled where blood rushed back into them.

"I..." Sidney's voice was a breath. Milkshake, Jonas's hamburger, a cherry tart, was all over the floor and Sidney's boots and pant legs. "I left something in the truck," Sidney managed, before turning around and walking back out of the house.

33

Sidney couldn't hear. It was strange. The blood rushing in his ears reminded him of being swept under a wave. The crushing tightness in his chest. The way he couldn't take a full breath. His fingers fumbled with the keys in his hand. He nearly dropped them as a distant rumble of thunder echoed across the sky.

Maybe the man on the couch hadn't been Jonas. Sidney knew it was, but he gave himself half a moment to pretend it wasn't. Jonas's skin wasn't the bright red-orange of a flame and he didn't have two onyx rams horns. Just like the ones Sidney had seen in the photograph in the attic. The photograph that Jonas had said was him in a costume. Not a costume. A lie. So, what was he?

The dark lines of ink on Jonas's skin, the burgundy and black hair. The size of him. The heat. A demon? Sidney's hands were shaking so badly he couldn't unlock the door to the truck. He tried to breathe and instead his throat made a strangled little gasp. Pathetic. Panicking. Running away.

When he'd walked out on his father at the restaurant, Congressman Quince had called him selfish. Ungrateful. *'After everything I've done for you.'* The panic thrashing in Sidney's chest was the same now.

"Sidney. Sidney!" Sidney couldn't face Jonas. Didn't want to face him. Jonas had been lying to him. Why? Sidney didn't know. Did it even matter? "Sidney, please!"

Jonas's footsteps crunched in the dying grass. If Sidney didn't turn now, Jonas would get too close. Close enough to touch. Sidney would be trapped. His face was hot, but at least he hadn't started crying yet. Sidney clenched his hand around the keys and turned.

Jonas looked distraught, eyes wide and imploring, a frown drawing down the corners of his handsome mouth. There was something more real about him now. He was more beautiful than he'd been before, like his features made better sense this way, in these hues. He was taller, broader, and Sidney was barely surprised to find that he still wanted Jonas. He wanted to swipe the frown from Jonas's face. Smooth the wrinkles that crowded his forehead. Even though Jonas didn't want him. Even though it had all been a lie.

"I have to go," Sidney said. Swallowed. Fuck. Don't cry.

"Please, Sidney. Let me explain."

"Which part?" Sidney asked. Should have demanded. There was suddenly so much that warranted an explanation. Jonas gestured back toward the house.

"He's not—"

"You lied to me," Sidney interrupted. "About everything!" He'd meant it to be an accusation, but desperation made it sound like a question. Fuck. He could feel the heat behind his own eyes. If he started crying he was going to stab himself in the thigh with Jonas's truck key.

"No," Jonas shook his head. "No. Not everything." But some things. Obviously.

"What are you?" If he was going to leave now, he had to at least know that much.

"A demon. From the ninth realm of the—"

"A Duke?"

"That was all true. My past. What I told you—" Jonas kept speaking. Explaining. But it was all beginning to make sense to Sidney.

If Jonas had been a duke, even if he'd been disinherited, why would he be here? Why would he be fucking around with silly, useless Sidney Quince? Sidney had been so caught up in the bliss of it, of being appreciated and wanted, that he hadn't stopped to think about how none of it made sense. Sidney's own father didn't invite Sidney out for dinner unless he needed something. Mark only wanted to be admired and lauded and put on a pedestal. Why would someone like Jonas want Sidney without a reason?

"Why me?" Sidney interrupted. Jonas looked lost.

"What?"

"Why. Me. What do you want from me?"

"I don't know what you're—"

"Why did you let me in? Why did you ask me to stay?" Jonas had asked him to stay. Had he not meant it? Sidney's voice was rising and he could barely contain himself. "What do you want from me?"

"Sidney, *you* came to *me*. For help." The mark. Right. Christ, that felt like an age ago. Jonas had removed Sidney's mark, so that was—

And then Sidney understood.

"You marked me."

Jonas's mouth snapped shut. His eyes were wide, desperate. Sidney was going to throw up.

"I didn't want to."

"For your magic. To make you stronger. Is that what this is? Is that what I am to you?"

"No. Sidney, no. I never wanted to—" Sidney closed his eyes and tried to swallow around the bile that was rising in his throat. At least he had all the pieces now. At least everything made sense. He'd wanted to know, and now he did. Right question, wrong time. Sidney opened his eyes.

"Is that why it feels like this?" Jonas shook his head.

"What do you mean?"

"The mark. Is that why...?" Sidney pressed his hand to his chest where it still felt like he could barely breathe. Jonas hesitated.

"I don't—"

"Never mind." It didn't matter. There was nothing he could do to fix it either way.

For a moment, they stared at each other. Sidney wanted to collapse. Beg Jonas to tell him that it wasn't true. Not that Sidney could believe him; it would be a waste of breath for both of them, and Sidney didn't have much left to spare. He needed to leave before he suffocated.

Sidney turned. He managed to jam the key into the lock and open the door of the truck. The roaring was back in Sidney's ears as he climbed inside and turned on the engine, backed out of the grass and drove away.

WHEN EDMUND MORROW HAD LEFT JONAS IN THE CAVE, THERE had been a moment where Jonas sense of the world and his place in it flooded away from him. Blood seeped out of his arms onto the stone, he had been so weak he couldn't even call after Morrow, beg him to help. The weight of Jonas's own body worked against him then, too depleted to even crawl across the unforgiving stone to higher ground. He had made his deal with Morrow willingly. There was no one to blame for his agony but himself.

It was strange to feel that way again. He stood rooted in the grass, watching Sidney drive away in his truck, and Jonas knew that it was his own fault. Something that had seemed so good and bright and precious was gone in the crunch of gravel, the roar of thunder overhead.

"Oh, Gods." Asterion came up beside Jonas as the rain began to fall. Jonas barely heard him speak. Asterion steered him back toward the cottage, nattering the whole way, as Jonas tried to will himself into believing he could come back from this. But despair was a more familiar companion than hope. And a stronger one.

"Jonas!" Asterion pushed Jonas, both hands against his chest, and Jonas felt himself recoil. They were in the foyer. Asterion was glaring at him. "There you are! Gods, I half thought—"

"This is your fault," Jonas bit, a sudden burst of rage clenching his fists.

"Fuck you, it's my fault," Asterion retorted. "You were in this mess well before I got here."

"Why did you kiss me?" Jonas demanded. "Why?"

"If my kiss is the wedge that drove you apart, I apologize for it. Truly." Asterion's voice was low and bitter, his eyes nearly incandescent with anger. "Shall we chase him down and explain that it was my keeping you from telling him the truth the entire time?"

"Leave me be." Jonas turned on his heel, striding away. It wasn't Asterion's fault. Jonas had fucked it all again. There was no going back now, and he wanted to destroy himself in peace. Thankfully his liquor cabinet was well-stocked.

"You're being stupid." Asterion was hot on his heels. "Jonas, listen to me."

"Leave me alone, Asterion." Jonas stopped in front of the pantry and Asterion ran into him.

"You asked me to come here!"

"Now I'm asking you to leave."

"You're not even going to try to talk to him?" Asterion raised his voice. "You're just going to what? Build an even smaller cottage inside this one? Live in the cellar?" That didn't sound like such a terrible idea, actually. At least it would be quiet there.

"Go away, Asterion," Jonas grumbled, squinting into the darkness of his liquor shelf. What was that at the back? Some unmarked bottle from a hundred years ago. That would burn going down for sure. He leaned in to reach for it, and Asterion slid himself under Jonas's arm, blocking his path. Fucking rat bastard. Jonas grit his teeth.

"You like him, Jonas. And he's not gone yet."

"I lied to him."

"You can apologize to him. You can explain about Edmund and the magic and the whole thing."

"It's not an excuse." Not a good enough one.

"It's not an excuse, but it is a reason. Jonas. You looked happy. For the first time in years. Glamour or not, you looked more like yourself than I've seen in a long time. Do not ruin this."

Jonas's heart was still pounding in his chest. Adrenaline coursed through him, begging him to move. But Sidney was gone. And Jonas deserved what he'd wrought.

"It's over, Asterion."

"It doesn't have to be!" It was almost funny how earnest Asterion was, his gesticulations wide and wild. "We can go now!"

"Why do you care?" Jonas asked. He reached around Asterion's waist and grabbed the first bottle he could get his hand around.

"Because I care about you, you insufferable ass!"

"That's not what I meant." Jonas turned, carrying his prize to the counter. It wasn't the bottle he'd had his eye on, but any would do, really. "It's not like you to care about something as trivial as heartbreak."

It wasn't until he glanced over his shoulder into the silence of Asterion's response that Jonas realized he'd said something wrong. Jonas opened his mouth to apologize. He hadn't meant to be mean. But before he could say anything, Asterion turned and left, slamming the front door behind him.

That seemed about right.

Jonas cracked the seal on the bottle. The liquor inside smelled acidic and saccharine in equal measure. He doubted he'd be receiving house guests any time soon, so there was no need to leave any undrunk.

34

Halfway back to Hindry, it started to rain properly. Sidney pulled into the small parking lot at the train station and strode up to the ticket window barely feeling the downpour on his skin.

"No trains to Bainbridge until tomorrow morning," said the ticket agent. They looked up at Sidney for the briefest of moments, their face contorting at whatever dour expression Sidney was wearing. He knew he looked disheveled, flushed and frustrated; he never had found his cap. "There's a freight arriving at seven tomorrow morning that sometimes has a commuter car, and a passenger train at two in the afternoon."

Sidney could sit in the truck in the parking lot until seven in the morning. That seemed reasonable and fine. He thanked the ticket agent and stumbled back to the truck.

The hammering of the rain on the roof did its best to drown out Sidney's thoughts. His coat was heavy with damp and the stupid cab of the truck smelled like hamburger and Jonas beneath that. Sidney pressed his forehead against the steering wheel and tried not to breathe. Great. Now he just had to do that for the next eighteen hours and hope that Jonas wouldn't report his truck stolen in the meantime. Very manageable.

Unfortunately, it was then that Sidney reached the end of his emotional tether. Objectively, lasting nearly half an hour past the worst thing that had ever happened to him was pretty impressive. He still fucking hated that he was crying.

The first tears that slid down his cheeks were hot, burning with embarrassment. Sidney had thought Jonas wanted him. Sidney told Jonas that he loved him! What a fucking fool.

Jonas was perfect, and that should have been Sidney's first clue that something wasn't right. He tolerated all of Sidney's too personal questions, the way he'd put himself in Jonas's space like he belonged there. And for all of that, Sidney had been too stupid to see what now seemed so obvious. Jonas was pretending. Jonas had even tried to warn him, in his own way. But Sidney had been stubborn. An idiot. And he deserved this.

Sidney's sobs turned ugly, shoulder shaking. It didn't matter. There was no one there to see him. No one could hear him over the sound of the rain. A train pulled into the platform, and people began to disembark, little more than shadows through the rain. Sidney took a shuddering breath as he watched them for a moment. Black suits and dark umbrellas. Suitcases.

If he'd had money, he would have gotten out and purchased a ticket. It didn't really matter where the train was going. He didn't have to be back at Holyworth until Monday. His research was fucked without Jonas's telescope and library. No university would take it anyway. And now he didn't even have his charts.

Sidney rested his chin on the top of the steering wheel and closed his eyes. Crying was useless, and he hated useless things. He'd wasted time. A lot of it. But now, he just needed to get back to Holyworth and figure out something else. No use dwelling on what had happened. It was over.

Perhaps unsurprisingly, that didn't exactly make it any

easier. Months of work had gone to waste, all because Sidney hadn't been able to put two and two together to make four. And somehow that wasn't even the most upsetting thing about it, when it really should have been.

A knock on his window made Sidney jump. He lurched sideways, away from the rain-streaked glass and the sight of a very unexpected face.

"Sidney?"

Sidney's brother Leo stood under an umbrella, his cloud of dark brown curls untouched by rain. His eyes were narrowed, his head cocked to the side as if to counteract the odd angle of a twice broken nose.

"Sidney?" Leo's voice was an echo of Sidney's own, always surprising people with its lightness, when his broad shoulders and chiseled features usually had admirers expecting something deeper. Now, it was laced with concern and loud to be heard over the rain. "What are you doing here? Are you alright?"

And then Leo opened the door and climbed inside.

Sidney slid out of the way out of habit, letting Leo have the driver's seat. Leo folded his umbrella, then stood and waved to two people, a man and a woman standing on the train platform watching him.

"You two go ahead and take a cab! I'll catch up!" He said, then sat on the bench seat, putting his bag between himself and Sidney on the upholstery. Leo pulled the door closed and dropped his umbrella near his feet. Newly wet curls sagged against his forehead as he looked at Sidney.

"What are you doing here?" Sidney asked before Leo could.

"Work," Leo said, waving a dismissive hand at the people who were already gone from the platform. "A sort of party thing, with a client." He wrinkled his nose and shook his head, as if it was nothing. Maybe it was. As far as Sidney could tell, most of Leo's life was parties for his law firm and fundraisers for their father. Once, Sidney had teased him about never actually doing any lawyering, and Leo had looked so defeated by the jibe that Sidney immediately apologized.

"Are you okay?" Leo asked again. "What are *you* doing here?"

"I'm great," Sidney wiped at the tear tracks he could still feel on his cheeks. "Really good, actually. Just leaving town. Well," he swallowed. He never liked lying to Leo. "Tomorrow."

"Tomorrow?" Leo frowned. "But—What's all over your trousers?" Sidney looked down at his trousers, the bottom hem of his coat, both flecked with chocolate stains.

"Milkshake."

"Milkshake?"

"Yeah," Sidney nodded. The whole thing was too embarrassing to put into words.

There was a time when Sidney had been closer with Leo than anyone else in the world. They were born almost six years apart, and Sidney had admired Leo since the moment he was able to form coherent thoughts. After their parent's divorce, when their father began to try and play them against each other, they'd drifted apart. Not because their father's games had worked. Sidney knew Leo was trying to protect him from their father's cruelty, his absurd expectations and terrible temper. But Leo'd gotten swept up in their father's business as a result.

"If you're not leaving until tomorrow, come to this party with me," Leo said at once. "You can stay in my room. We'll see if we can get you some clean clothes. You're about Paul's size. My coworker." Leo gestured again to the train platform where Paul no longer was and gave Sidney a smile. "I'm sure he has a spare pair of trousers you can borrow."

"I'm not good company," Sidney said. Heard Jonas's voice say the same thing in his memory, and he winced as the rest of that conversation came rushing back. *What are you still doing here, Sidney?*

"Well, that's okay. You never have been good company." Leo teased gently, nudging Sidney with his elbow. Sidney tried to smile.

"Your hosts won't appreciate it."

"Nonsense," Leo shook his head. "They won't even notice you're there. It's supposed to be a big to-do. One more face in the crowd." Sidney wasn't great at crowds in the best of times, but Leo countered Sidney's protest before he could vocalize it. "Or stay in the room. You look like you might need to lie down." It was a gentle pry, artful even. Leo really was better than Sidney at everything. Sidney sniffed and nodded.

"Alright."

"I can drive if you want. Where'd you get the truck?"

"Borrowed it," Sidney said, sitting back and reaching for his seatbelt. "Do you know where you're going?"

"I've got instructions in here somewhere." Leo felt around the inside pockets of his coat. "Gordy said it was a straight shot from the train station though. Then again, if you've been here long, you might know better." He pulled a folded half sheet of paper out of his pocket. "How long *have* you been here?" Leo handed Sidney the folded sheet.

"About a week," Sidney said, opening the directions written in Leo's tidy looping script. His eyes darted to the address at the bottom, and he blinked at it, waiting for the words to sort themselves out into other words that made more sense. When that didn't happen, he looked over at Leo.

"Elmmond House?"

"That's the place. You know it?"

"Who invited you to this party?"

"One of the firm's big clients attends every year, and he always passes a few invitations to us. Just another high-society weekend house party. Tiresome, really, though the food is supposed to be pretty good. And—"

"And they come back every year? The lawyers who go?" Sidney demanded. Leo frowned at him.

"Yes? What a bizarre question."

"I don't think you should go," Sidney said. Fuck, was he going to have to explain faeries and demons and magic to Leo? Leo pursed his lips.

"Well, unfortunately, I have to go. The firm is paying me to be there. And Paul and his wife already took a cab up. I wouldn't leave without them." Of course, Leo was going to be wholly decent and practical about it. Shit.

Sidney looked out into the rain and tried to puzzle out what he was going to do as quickly as possible. Shockingly, somehow, he hadn't asked Jonas enough questions about the Ascension party. Were all the attendants in glamours? Did the humans who go get a primer, a pamphlet, on the basic principles of magic? Getting marked? Sidney winced.

The simplest thing to do would be to go up with Leo. Keep an eye on him. Pretend like he was as ignorant as everyone else of the whole thing. And technically, Sidney did have an invitation.

"Sidney?" Leo prompted. Sidney took a breath.

"Sorry. No, it's been a long day. I'm being stupid. It'll be fine."

"Are you sure?" Leo's voice was firm. It was comforting almost, to be trusted implicitly. Sidney nodded, wiping away at the phantom sensation of tears on his cheeks.

"It'll be fine. Let's go," Sidney folded up the directions and put them on the seat beneath Leo's bag. "I know the way."

35

As long as Sidney didn't look in the direction of the garden cottage, he might be able to survive this. Leo followed the driveway around to the garage near the back of the house, and when they'd gotten out, a butler took the keys with narrowed eyes, his gaze darting between Leo and Sidney. And then to Jonas's cottage.

"You can take it back," Sidney said, gesturing vaguely eastward. The man nodded, climbing into the driver's seat in Leo's place, while another staff member came up to take Leo's umbrella and bag. The rain was tapering off, but it didn't matter. Before they could get too wet they were shuttled into a rear foyer, where a maid held a wide leather ledger.

"Leo Quince," Leo said, and the woman began turning pages in the book. "And my brother Sidney Quince. He'll be rooming with me, and he might not be on your list, but—"

"No, sir. You're both here. Mr. Quince wasn't down for a room," she added, glancing at Sidney. "But plenty of guests elect to share. If you'll follow me, sirs, I'll see you up." Ellery had come through for Delilah, it seemed. Leo gave Sidney a quizzical look, but Sidney only shrugged and started after the maid.

The house was all dark wood and thick carpets, warm orange light from wall-sconces cut the dark from the pressing clouds outside. It would have suited Jonas; the colors, the lighting. Knowing it had been his house, that it was still his house, made him feel present. Sidney tried to shake it off, glancing out a window as raindrops began to patter against it. Another terrible night for stars. It was good Sidney wasn't going to be staying in Hindry much longer. It would have been impossible to keep up with his charting.

Not that Sidney had any use for his star cluster now, of course. He was going to have to put the whole business of it behind him and come up with a better dissertation topic. And, if he changed topics, he wouldn't have to go back to the cottage for his charts.

Their room was comfortable, both in size and furnishings. Sidney collapsed into an armchair by the north facing window, ignoring the view of the backyard, the trees and the path that led to the chapel. Leo had followed the maid to Paul's room and returned in short order with not just a pair of trousers, but a long, charcoal grey suit that was at least the right height for Sidney, if not the right width.

"There's a cocktail hour in a little bit," Leo said as he hung the suit in the armoire. "I wanted you to have something to wear, if you felt up to joining us. Paul's always got a spare. He's the best dressed man I know." Which Sidney supposed was saying something, coming from the best dressed man he knew. Sidney thanked his brother, then watched Leo unpack in silence.

Once Leo's bag was stowed under the brass frame of the double bed in the corner, Leo sat back onto the mattress and began to toe off his shoes. He glanced at Sidney briefly, and Sidney knew Leo had finally calculated a question that was precise enough that Sidney wouldn't be able to worm out of it.

"I broke up with someone," Sidney said, before Leo could ask. "This morning."

"I didn't know you were seeing anyone." Leo braced his palms on the mattress, his shoulders broader and squarer than Sidney remembered.

"Are you still boxing?"

"Why?" Leo arched an eyebrow. "Do you need me to kick someone's ass?" Sidney smirked at the thought.

"He's bigger than you."

"I'm quick," Leo smirked. "And mean."

"You're a kitten."

"Not when it comes to you," Leo said. Sidney tried to smile, but he couldn't manage it. Instead, he shook his head, hoping Leo would know it meant he didn't want to be babied. Now that he stopped crying, it was fine. It wasn't fine, but it was over. And that meant it was fine. No more wasting time.

"It's alright, Leo. It wasn't even really... It wasn't real."

"Whatever you say, Sidney," Leo said, raising his hands and leaning back on the bed. "He's not going to be here tonight, is he?"

"No." At least that Sidney could be sure of.

"Good. Then I think we should get dressed and go get very blitzed on company time."

By the time Leo and Sidney made it down to the foyer an hour later, there were already fifty people milling about. Gone were the wings Sidney had seen as the fae paraded into the house the night before. Some still had the colorful hair, though. Or a sort of ethereal glow that might have been able to be chalked up to wealth and good hydration if he didn't know better.

The drinks were good. Strong and pretty, too. A waiter handed Sidney a coupe filled with liquid that shimmered like gold and tasted like oranges and honey. Leo hung close, mentioning the names of people he knew and keeping a running commentary on people he thought they needed to meet. Sidney hadn't been to many of his father's campaign events, but he recognized the behavior immediately.

"Leo. I'm not running for office," Sidney told him firmly after Leo speculated that the tall blonde man in the corner was either called Ellis or Elias or Silas or Sullivan. "I don't need to know what his name is before I talk to him. And also, I'm not going to talk to him."

"Well, you could," Leo waggled his eyebrows. "You look sharp in that suit. And you're newly single."

"Oh, Christ," Sidney chuckled. "Please don't wing-man for me. I'm your embarrassing little brother."

"We share the same good genes."

"I make an eighth of what the least paid person in this room makes."

"You're a passionate young academic with a world full of possibilities ahead of him." Leo made a grand gesture, sloshing his gold drink over the edge of his cup. A tall man with dark brown skin and close-cropped hair, strode over to them from the stairs, smiling widely.

"Is he drunk already?"

"Shut up, Paul." Leo gave the man a crooked smile before he turned to Sidney. "Sidney, this is Paul. Paul, my brother Sidney."

"Pleasure to meet you." Paul's handshake was firm and warm, and he had a very handsome smile.

"Thanks for the suit."

"No trouble," Paul said. "I hate when the trains lose luggage, it's—"

"Where's Evie?" Leo interrupted, looking around Paul toward the stairs.

"Still unpacking. Some of the pieces of her headdress got crushed in the suitcase."

"Headdress?" Sidney asked. He didn't know much about women's fashion, but it sounded a bit extreme for a lawyer's wife.

"For the costume party," Paul said. At Sidney's look of confusion, he continued. "Tomorrow night. It's the big event of the weekend, so I'm told." Ah. That made more sense. Sidney's stomach tightened. Maybe he was going to have to explain about magic to Leo after all. "Leo, it's Maude Hoffman and her husband. We'd better go shake hands."

"You'll be alright, Sidney?" Leo asked, squeezing his arm. It was kind of Leo to be checking on him. But it was hard for Sidney to pretend that nothing was wrong with Leo constantly reminding him that nothing was wrong. It would be nice to have a few minutes to himself.

"I'm fine," Sidney nodded. "Go ahead. I'm going to explore a bit." Leo nodded, shooting Sidney one last, overly sympathetic smile before he and Paul were off into the crowd.

Sidney wandered on his own, thinking about what Leo had said. *'A promising young academic with a world full of possibilities ahead of him.'* But it could have been *realms* full of possibilities. Universes. A hundred new celestial skies. But Sidney's doorway into all that had closed. He supposed maybe there could have been other ways to keep studying it. To make his charts useful still. He was in a room full of glamoured magical creatures, after all. But the thought of venturing forth without Jonas made his stomach clench uncomfortably. Better to just leave it all behind. Wasn't it?

As he walked, the crowd began to thicken somehow. People were coming in, more and more of them, but from where Sidney was standing, the front door had only opened a couple of times. There must have been a portal somewhere.

He thought about looking for it, as he backed out of the crowd and went down the first hallway. There were still people milling around, but with more breathing room between them. On Sidney's left was an open parlor door, where several small groups were listening to someone play a jaunty tune on a piano. A buffet table was set out in the hall, and Sidney picked off a few petit fours as he walked past. And then walked past again for a few more because they were delicious and he hadn't eaten anything all day.

Sidney stood in the hallway eating petit fours until three women sauntered up to the table talking loudly. Sidney drained his drink, and started off to find a waiter with more drinks, but before he could take two steps, there was a collective gasp from the women. A man being swarmed by an extensive coterie stepped into the hallway, and Sidney bit his tongue.

Asterion, Jonas's prince, wore a sapphire suit with ornate silver embroidery on the lapels and waistcoat. His cobalt hair was brushed back away from his face, and long emerald earrings trailed his collar. Sidney's first, bitter thought, was that Asterion hadn't looked so put together when he was on top of Jonas in the parlor.

Unfortunately, Sidney had stopped directly in the path of the prince and his coterie. Stepping to the side would have been the polite thing to do. Sidney didn't want to engage with him, no matter how much the citrus honey drink seeping into his bloodstream said otherwise. Before Sidney could move or speak, Asterion was in front of him.

The expression on Asterion's face wasn't a smile. It looked like one on the surface, but there was a sharpness to it, like Sidney expected to see fangs among his teeth.

"Mr. Quince." Asterion's voice was cold. "What a surprise."

"I was on the guest list."

"You're welcome for that."

"I suspect you didn't do it for me," Sidney said. Asterion arched an eyebrow and looked Sidney over, head to toe.

"Would you join me in the study for a moment?" Asterion asked. A murmur went through the crowd behind him. "In private." Like a spell had been cast, the crowd dispersed. Or rather, had taken a collective step back. Sidney could feel them watching him and he knew he didn't have a choice.

"Of course," he nodded. "I'd be happy to."

36

The study Asterion led Sidney to was dark. A fire was lit in the hearth, but the walls looked like they were painted black, and the lamps were low. Somehow, still, Asterion shone. The embroidery on his jacket caught the light and played it across his face, as he walked in front of the fire toward the drinks cart.

Sidney stepped into the room and startled when someone pulled the door closed behind him. Across the sitting area, Asterion was pouring drinks, unbothered.

"I'm afraid we didn't have a chance to be properly introduced earlier," Asterion said. Ice clinked in the glass in front of him.

"I don't think it's necessary," Sidney said. Asterion straightened up, two glasses with ice and amber liquid in his hands. Sidney dearly hoped it was scotch.

Asterion stepped into the middle of the rug and held a drink out to Sidney, coaxing him into the golden circle of light cast by the fireplace. Sidney half suspected a trapdoor would open up and swallow him whole if he stepped into it, but he hated Asterion enough that he couldn't not rise to the bait.

When Sidney took the glass from Asterion's hand, Asterion

stepped back. He sat in a black, leather armchair, his gaze never wavering from Sidney's face. Sidney took a large gulp of scotch, and sat on the edge of the armchair's twin, turned toward the fire.

"You're wrong about him, you know," Asterion said.

"So I've learned." Sidney replied dryly. Asterion smirked.

"I kissed him. He didn't kiss me."

"I think that's probably the least of our problems." Sidney sipped his scotch, watching Asterion's gold eyes settle on Sidney's face.

"Jonas cares for you."

"He has a funny way of showing it." Sidney didn't even try to keep the bitterness from his voice. "He lied to me. He used me."

"Used you for what?"

"Magic," Sidney said. Asterion arched an eyebrow, and Sidney was suddenly reminded of Karolina. The way her expression would immediately telegraph when a student said something that was not only wrong but also stupid. Sidney tried to ignore the heat crawling up his neck. "He marked me."

"He doesn't have enough magic to mark you," Asterion said. Sidney frowned.

"What do you mean?"

"Magic comes from interacting with humans. Making deals. Oaths. Bartering for power," Asterion explained. Sidney knew all of that. Jonas had told him.

"So what?"

"Jonas is a recluse. He doesn't talk to anyone. He doesn't fuck anyone. He doesn't even come to this party." Asterion set his glass down on the arm of the chair. "A major hub for power exchange. People come from worlds away for it."

"Why not?" Sidney asked. Asterion cocked his head to the side, and Sidney huffed. "Why doesn't he come? Why doesn't he have magic anymore?" Asterion's mouth tightened at the corners, and Sidney could see that he was biting the inside of his lip. Whatever it was, Asterion didn't want to say. Sidney took a stab. "Does it have to do with his old research partner?"

"Research partner." Asterion cocked his head to the side. "Yes. He told you about him?"

"As much as he told me anything," Sidney said. Asterion took a deep breath and picked up his glass, staring down into the ice.

"It's not my story to tell. But I will say this: what that man did to Jonas was beyond any cruelty I've seen or heard of. Before or since. Jonas barely made it out of that relationship alive, and it changed him." Sidney tamped down all the questions that this raised with a deep, steady breath. And then he rolled his eyes for good measure.

"So, he's allowed to lie to me?" Sidney snipped. It wasn't really about him, this conversation. He knew that. But he wasn't about to be drawn into feeling bad for Jonas by the man Jonas had been kissing earlier that afternoon. What little pride he had wouldn't allow it.

Asterion sniffed, clearly irritated by this response and drained his scotch before getting to his feet.

"He didn't actually do anything to you, aside from not tell you who he was. And he has his reasons for wanting to keep that to himself when he's dealing with humans."

"His research partner was a human?" Sidney hadn't given it much thought before, but now it seemed incongruous. If Jonas was a demon, what was he doing living here? Working with a human? It would stand to reason that a magical being would know so much more. Wouldn't it? Asterion shook his head, eyes casting toward the ceiling, as though he was looking for the strength to go on.

"I get the feeling, Mr. Quince, that you have the unfortunate ability to always be asking exactly the wrong question."

"What should I be asking, then?"

"Instead of asking anything, why don't you try paying attention? Maybe then you'll be able to piece some of the answers together for yourself." Asterion looked down his nose at Sidney. "I have a hard time believing Jonas would sleep with anyone who was truly an idiot. But perhaps you've proven me wrong."

"Fuck you," Sidney snapped. He'd had enough. Asterion chuckled and shook his head, starting toward the door.

"Pleasure to meet you, Mr. Quince." Sidney got up. For no reason. An apology hung heavy on the tip of his tongue. Who knew what sort of power Asterion had? This was his party after all; Leo would be so upset if Sidney had gotten them kicked out.

Asterion turned back to Sidney, his hand on the doorknob, and Sidney drew a small breath, holding it in his chest.

"Just for future reference, and as a matter of personal safety, I would caution you against drinking or eating anything handed to you by a faerie. Or any magic user for that matter. You never know what kind of enchantments might be in the recipe." He lifted his empty glass to Sidney and then swept out the door, pulling it closed again behind him.

Sidney looked down at his half-drunk scotch. Shit. Too late to worry about it now. He took another sip, and then sat back down in the chair, trying to make sense of what had just happened.

37

Another glass and a half of scotch later, a gaggle of people crowded into the study, giggling and talking excitedly, and Sidney took that as his cue to leave. He put his empty cup on the sideboard and went back out into the hall.

The crush of people was so dense, that he almost immediately retreated into the study again. This was not the kind of party he did well in. What kind of party did he do well in? He tried to imagine one as he twisted toward the less sparsely populated side of the hall and started down it, looking for another set of stairs to the upper floor, back toward Leo's room and solitude.

He wished he was back in the garden cottage. And then he tried to make himself not wish it. He didn't actually have to be at the party, he just had to survive until the morning when he could call a cab to take him back to the train station. To Bainbridge and his old life. A life that would pale in comparison, now that he knew how much else might be out there.

That didn't matter. A world with assholes like Asterion and liars like Jonas was not something he wanted to be a part of.

Sidney passed a waiter with another tray of the citrus and

honey drinks, and took one just before turning a corner where he almost immediately ran directly into a beautiful man.

He was as tall as Sidney, willowy, with pale skin and a sweep of thick golden hair across his forehead. He wore a well-tailored black suit which was now covered in sparkling cocktail. The man's cheeks were flushed in surprise.

"Oh my God!" Sidney exclaimed, his free hand flying to cover his mouth. "I am so sorry!"

Before the man could speak, they were flanked by waiters with napkins who began taking turns dabbing at the man's waistcoat and glaring at Sidney.

"No, no. Really. It's alright." The man's voice was low and soft. Kind. When he shot an apologetic glance at Sidney over the heads of the waiters, Sidney felt himself blush. He was more tipsy than he'd realized. "Really, gentlemen, really. It's quite alright. I promise. I won't melt." The man gave them a final shoo with his hands, and begrudgingly the waiters left.

"I really apologize."

"It's a house party," the man said with a shrug. "I have three more just like it upstairs. Besides, whatever you were drinking smells delicious."

"I think it must be a house cocktail or something. All the waiters have them."

"Well, then, I know how you can repay me for the inconvenience." The man smiled. Sidney's stomach turned over and he did his best to ignore it. Leo had been the one to suggest rebound. Sidney hadn't thought that he would want to. No prospects. No interest.

But spite was a funny thing, and Sidney's mind was buzzing. Maybe a distraction from the dull ache in his chest was precisely what he needed. It didn't have to mean anything. Apparently when Sidney thought things meant something he was wrong, so adjusting his aim a bit would be a recipe for success. That made sense.

And if Jonas could fool around with someone else, Sidney could do the same thing. Maybe Sidney could find a way to keep studying the other celestial skies after all.

"One moment."

Sidney had to go two steps around the corner to find another waiter carrying drinks. As Sidney lifted two drinks off the tray, a bitter voice in his head said that by the time he got back around the corner, the handsome man would be gone. It had just been a ruse to get him to leave. No one wanted Sidney. But, he told himself firmly, if that was the case, then at least Sidney would get two drinks out of it. And that was good too.

The blonde man was still there and his smile widened as Sidney handed him the drink.

"Cheers," he said. The edges of their coupes clinked and the man took a sip. His eyes were the darkest brown Sidney had ever seen, almost black, and fixed on Sidney.

"I'm Sidney," Sidney said. He sounded like he was about twelve years old, introducing himself to the cutest boy at the school dance, but the man gave a gentle chuckle.

"I'm Zac. Zachariah Mears. Call me Zac, please."

"It's a pleasure to meet you," Sidney said, offering his spare hand. Zac's handshake was firm, calloused on the side of his palm.

"Where were you off to in such a hurry?" Zac's fingers trailed against Sidney's as their hands dropped apart. Thinner than Jonas's. He'd had too much to drink. He took another sip of his cocktail.

"I was going back to my room," he said, gesturing vaguely upward. And that sounded like an invitation, didn't it? He blushed and pressed on. "Parties like this aren't really my strong suit."

"Mine either." Zac's smile was handsome, but not as wide as Jonas's. "If you're looking for someplace to hide out there's a conservatory at the end of this hall," he gestured behind him. "It's quite beautiful, even at night. They have it all strung up with lights."

"Sounds lovely," Sidney said.

"I'd be happy to show you. I know a bit about flowers."

"A gardener?" Sidney asked. He couldn't imagine this man digging in a flower bed, dirt under his pristine fingernails, uprooting goldenrod by the fistful like Jonas. Zac turned and started back down the hall, and somehow, Sidney fell into step beside him.

"I'm a botanist," Zac said. Sidney brightened immeasurably. He knew how to talk to other scientists.

"That's fascinating!" Zac smiled at him.

"It's not often that gets such an enthusiastic reaction."

"I've always loved the natural sciences. I'm an astronomer. I teach at Holyworth College," Sidney said.

"Oh, really? Where's that?"

"Just down in Bainbridge." Zac shook his head, no recognition on his face.

"Sorry, I'm not from here," Zac said, as he pushed open the door to the conservatory.

The room was verdant and several degrees warmer than the hall. Tall leafy plants stretched up around them, and the high panes of glass that made up the pointed panel of the roof were all draped in twinkling lights that framed the starry night sky.

On the far side was a sitting area, where a glass top table held more sweet and savory appetizers. The same petit fours Sidney had wolfed down in the hall filled an overflowing plate.

"I guess not many people have made it back this far yet," Sidney said.

"More treats for us," Zac chuckled, starting toward the spread.

"You said you're not from here?" Sidney asked, as Zac began to fill a plate.

"No." Zac didn't meet his eye, busy getting food.

"Where *are* you from?" Sidney pressed. Zac looked over at him then, hand frozen in the air halfway to some mini tarts. He cocked an eyebrow in Sidney's direction. And two half-ideas congealed into something whole. This man wasn't human. Sidney stiffened. "I know about magic. Faeries and things."

"Ah," Zac straightened up. Then with a shake of his shoulders, the man in front of Sidney was transformed. His skin was a deep crimson, the color of welling blood, and his golden hair turned ash grey, laced with strands of shining silver. Horns spiraled out six inches on either side of his head, white at the base and grey at the tips. His black suit looked even more striking now. And Sidney could see one white fang pressed against the corner of his lip. Did Jonas have fangs? Sidney hadn't seen. He wished he had. No. It didn't matter. He wasn't thinking about Jonas now.

"I appreciate you telling me," Zac said, returning to the tarts. "Those glamours are damned uncomfortable."

"Are they?" Sidney asked. Jonas had kept his up all the time. That was how much he didn't want Sidney to know the truth about him. Sidney sniffed, irritated. Zac didn't seem to notice. He turned his back, trying to balance his plate, setting the coupe down on the table. "Oh, can I take anything from you?"

"No, I've got it." Zac gave a small grunt, and then turned back around. He stepped close to Sidney, offering him the plate of treats. "I've heard the petit fours are particularly good."

❧

Drinking alone wasn't something Jonas liked to make a habit of, so his tolerance had decreased considerably over the recent decades. As a result he was currently extremely, almost uncomfortably, drunk.

Jonas slouched against the high table in the library, staring down at charts he'd offered Sidney that morning. Sidney's own charts were there too, rolled up beside him. There were fingerprints near one bent corner of the roll, the whorls of Sidney's thumb and fingers, hands that had traced the skin of Jonas's body, a horrible, tempting reminder of his existence.

After another hour or more, Jonas might have passed out or dropped off, he pushed himself up out of his seat. He wasn't so young that he could sleep in chairs and not feel the effects of it the next day. In his time in the military, magic had kept him rejuvenated. Forever youthful. Healers cleaned him up after fights, and he knew enough to wipe a hangover from his brain. But this, what he'd done to himself, it would hurt tomorrow. Jonas relished the thought, as he dragged his feet through the kitchen and into the foyer. Hurting physically would distract him from the pain of losing Sidney.

There was still spilled food all across the foyer floor. Jonas staggered to a halt and stared down at it. Chocolate milkshake puddle had sunk beneath the treads of his boots. His hamburger had slid into its component parts across the rug. Jonas's stomach growled. Truly, there was no point in trying to feel less awful, so he ignored his hunger. He ignored everything because he had to give all his attention to making it up the stairs to the landing. Then into his bedroom. Into a bed that would still smell like Sidney.

The thought made him growl in frustration. The guest room was out as well. Sidney's bag was probably still in there. His clothes. Somehow, after little more than a week, Sidney permeated everything in Jonas's house. He was a part of the place. A part of the routine of Jonas's life, a routine that Jonas never thought he'd be able to fit another person into again. Sidney managed it though. And it had been easy. And Jonas ruined it.

A step forward and the banister was there to hold him up. Jonas turned slowly, and something red caught the corner of his eye out of the front window. When he moved his head to look back, he moved too fast. For a moment, his vision spun, and when it congealed into reality again, Jonas still didn't believe it.

His truck was parked outside. The truck Sidney had left in. Which meant Sidney had come back. The truck was back, so Sidney had to be back. There wasn't anything else that made sense.

Jonas stumbled trying to step off the bottom stair and dropped to a knee, scrambling to get himself upright again. His legs were impossibly heavy, but he still heaved himself to the front door and yanked it open. The cold was bracing, and as effective at sobering him up as dunking his head in a bucket of ice water. Jonas held himself up against the doorframe and let the cold October wind rush over his skin and into his house. He took two deep breaths, and then started forward again.

What was he going to say to Sidney? How to apologize. Where to begin? *Let me explain. I'm so sorry.* Jonas fumbled, tripping over nothing and caught himself on the window of the driver's side door. He winced, another apology ready on his tongue. A rude awakening for poor Sidney who was sleeping inside the cab of the truck.

Sidney wasn't there.

Jonas pressed his face against the glass. The truck was empty. The key was on the seat, as well as Sidney's satchel, his notebook poking out of the top of it. Sidney wouldn't have left Hindry without his notebook.

Jonas pulled open the door to the truck and leaned inside.

The lights from Elmmond House in the distance caught on the key as he fumbled in the dark. And then he stopped.

The cold was doing wonders for his sobriety. If Sidney hadn't come back to the cottage, then there was only one place he could have gone. Jonas grabbed Sidney's bag. Having it would be a weak reason for coming to find Sidney, but that didn't matter in the slightest. Jonas would have taken any excuse. He had to find him. To apologize properly. To do anything to salvage what had blossomed between them.

Jonas closed the door of the truck and started toward Elmmond House.

38

It had been a long time since Jonas had come into Elmmond House through the main door. He should have always been using the main door; Verne would have preferred it. But this time it proved to be a colossal mistake.

Jonas stepped into a packed foyer, his head spinning immediately as his drunken brain was assaulted with noise and music and the smell of food and drink and bodies. Well-dressed. Everyone was so well-dressed, and Jonas was in his garden clothes. He nearly backed right out the front door, but he caught himself, the strap of Sidney's bag still clutched in his hand as he braced himself against the wall.

A footman he didn't recognize approached him with an efficient and practical expression that morphed quickly into shock. Clearly he'd not been expecting the owner of the house. The young man's step faltered, and he looked around as though he was hoping someone else with more experience would swing in and rescue him. Jonas could help with that.

"Where's Verne?" he slurred.

"Ah. In the kitchens, sir."

"Take me to him." Jonas pushed himself off the wall, took two steps and was immediately intercepted by a short thin man with tan skin and a dark moustache. Jonas didn't recognize him.

"Duke Rookwood? My lord." He bowed reverently and Jonas winced. No. He could not navigate this.

"On second thought," Jonas said to the footman, who had thankfully come closer, but was unhelpfully trying to take Sidney's bag from Jonas's fist. "I'll wait for Verne in the—" he glanced toward the front parlor. Full of people. The library would also be full of people. As would the drawing room and likely also the study. There was an office upstairs that would be vacant, but then he would have to navigate stairs. "Where is there quiet?" The footman stammered, looking between Jonas and the man who was still bowing in front of him, clearly not wanting to interrupt.

"Uh, well, the west wing is—" West wing. Tea room. Conservatory. Armory.

"Have Verne meet me in the conservatory. I need a sobriety potion. A strong one. Double strength."

"Yes, sir," the footman said, and scurried off.

It was nice to have someone do his bidding. Jonas had forgotten about that. He ignored the bowing man. A social faux pas, but he didn't care, as none of the people in that building, aside from Asterion, had bothered reaching out to him after he disappeared from their society all those years ago. Their good opinion didn't matter. He needed to talk to Sidney. He needed to do it sober. More sober than he was at any rate. And Verne would know where Sidney was. Verne always knew where everything and everyone was in Elmmond House. Jonas really needed to give him a raise.

The crowd was dense, but Jonas's size was useful in cutting a swath through it even as he kept one hand on the wall to steady himself. He knew the house (not as well as Verne, no one did) even though it had been a long time since he'd really been through it. In the crush of people, he could feel heads and eyes turned toward him, as he went down the hall. The odd man out by a nautical mile. Everyone was dressed to the nines. Everyone looked human. Except him. Oops.

Magical creatures didn't reveal themselves until the night of the Ascension itself. Tomorrow. The costume party. The portals opened for a few days on either side of the alignment, but the humans weren't really brought up to speed until the day of. Plenty of them already knew, of course. Jonas didn't really care. Let the fae and the demons and whoever else was there in glamours make excuses for him. He had no intention of disguising himself again.

Jonas fumbled around a corner. Sidney's bag caught on the edge of a table of appetizers. Jonas tugged, and a clatter of glass and food followed, as he staggered. People were scowling at him. Waiters and guests. Jonas winced, panic edging in at the corner of his consciousness. A day full of mistakes.

"Jonas." A hand caught the center of Jonas's chest as he lurched forward. Gently, Jonas was nudged against the wall, braced by a shoulder. Asterion's voice was smooth and calm, laced around the edges with concern. "What are you doing, darling? Come on." Asterion threaded his arm through Jonas's elbow and pulled him into the nearest doorway. The back entrance to the billiards room. A half dozen people were milling about the pool table. Another seven were playing cards.

"May we have the room for a moment?" Asterion's voice was loud, but he hadn't shouted. The command dressed as a question shattered the camaraderie in the air as easily as Jonas had shattered the cake stand in the hall. Heads turned toward them and then, like a wave receding, everyone moved toward the doors.

Asterion dismissed his coterie with the shake of his head,

and Jonas watched Ellery leave out the main door, where he knew she would stand watch outside.

Jonas braced his hands against the green felt, billiard balls duplicating in his vision and then reforming into one. Asterion was looking at him.

"I'm sorry about what I said earlier." Jonas hadn't meant to mumble, but his tongue kept getting caught behind his teeth. He exhaled and forced himself to look up. Asterion was a shining, handsome blur. Then he was Asterion, his mouth curled into a frown. "I am so sorry. I didn't mean to be—"

"I know you didn't." Asterion's voice was soft. "You never do." The silence was heavy. Jonas wanted to shake it off but moving felt dangerous. Like he was liable to break something again. "You've done a number on yourself."

"He came back," Jonas said.

"I know." Asterion rounded the table, slid his cool hand onto the back of Jonas's neck. "I saw him."

"He's here?"

Asterion didn't respond. His magic sunk into Jonas's skin and burned the alcohol out of his bloodstream. It was like dipping a fingertip in melted wax, hot and then too hot. Fae magic wasn't ever comfortable in demon veins, a thick thread forcing its way through a narrow needle. Jonas's fingertips curled into the felt, as he gritted his teeth against a noise of pain. His head was clearing. Any errant sounds would be fuel for a gossipy fire that was sure to already be burning quite brightly.

"Sidney's here," Asterion confirmed, pulling his hand away. Jonas straightened up and winced against the searing headache at the front of his skull. Asterion was still frowning. "Better?" Jonas nodded.

"Thank you. Where is he?"

"Jonas—"

"I'm going to apologize."

"Get your bearings first," Asterion warned. That was ominous.

"Did you speak to him?" Jonas asked. Asterion pursed his lips. Oh no. "Asterion."

"I was nice." A sure sign that Asterion had not been nice. It was exasperating. The situation with Sidney didn't need any more animosity. Still, a little voice in the back of his head, reminded Jonas that Asterion was truly his friend. Anything he'd threatened Sidney with had been well-intentioned. Jonas would have done the same thing had their roles been reversed. And Sidney was still here somewhere, which was all he really cared about.

Verne appeared, Ellery ushering him in with an arched eyebrow at Asterion. Asterion nodded his approval, which was ridiculous, as it was Jonas's house.

"Here you are, sir." Verne approached, two rounded glass bottles held in one hand.

"Thank you." Jonas took one, though he likely didn't need it after Asterion's handiwork. Asterion was quite the master of sobriety spells. Still, he had asked for them, and it might help with the headache. He popped the cork with his thumb. "Where's Sidney Quince?"

"Mr. Quince is in the conservatory," Verne said. Jonas nodded and downed the potion in two gulps before handing the empty bottle back to Verne.

"Thank you," Jonas said.

"Can I glamour you up a better outfit?" Asterion asked. Jonas shook his head.

"No more glamours."

"You've caused quite a stir, you know," Asterion said. "Coming in here all big and orangey."

"Tell them I got drunk and was trying on my costume for tomorrow."

"I already have," Asterion smirked.

"I'm sorry for the trouble."

"I know." Asterion reached up and patted him on the cheek. "Good luck."

39

Zac led Sidney around the conservatory twice, while Sidney ate petit fours and asked asinine questions about plants. He was starting to feel the effects of the scotch and the cocktails, the gentle haze of alcohol fuzzing the edge of his memory, so that on their second lap, he had to ask the names of some plants a second time.

"That's a jack-in-the-bush."

"I thought you said it was a pitcher plant?" Sidney didn't actually care. He'd only remembered 'pitcher plant' because it sounded good to say. Pitcher plant. Jonas ought to plant one in his garden. He'd have room with all the goldenrod gone.

"Ah, yes. Well, a jack-in-the-bush is a type of pitcher plant." Zac might have been full of shit about plants, but Sidney didn't really care. His skin was warm, like Jonas's. And Sidney had begun to lean heavily on him as they neared the seating area again. Zac had long fingernails, almost claw-like, and Sidney was really only thinking about what they might feel like digging into his skin. The way Jonas had clutched at him had awakened something in Sidney, that was all. The way he had said Sidney's name with so much wanting.

"Have you ever worked much with goldenrod?" Sidney asked.

"Ah," Zac smirked as though Sidney had made a joke. "No, I can't say as I have."

"The root system is dense." Sidney gestured with his hands. "Expansive. Once it takes root it can really dominate the space."

"Fascinating," Zac's voice was patronizing in a way that Sidney didn't like. "Do you have an interest in particularly *dominating* plants?"

That was... stupid. So stupid actually that it had the opposite effect of the intended innuendo. Eugh. Sidney imagined Jonas snorting in derision. *'Come on, Quince. You can do better than that.'*

He could have, normally, but he was drunk. And he wasn't supposed to be thinking about Jonas. And he didn't need to impress Zac. He just needed to forget.

When Zac bowed his head toward Sidney, Sidney kissed him. He tried to relish the aftertaste of the citrus and honey on Zac's tongue. But Jonas tasted better. Zac's arm snaked around Sidney's waist, and Sidney let himself be moved.

It was probably some kind of sign that every coherent thought Sidney had was about Jonas still. It was infuriating. Jonas was firmer than Zac. Broader, heavier. Kinder, more handsome.

Moving was easier than thinking. Sidney knew the steps of the dance. He didn't have to feel anything about them. He didn't have to miss the way Jonas touched him and teased him and wanted him. He didn't have to think about anything aside from pleasure. His own. Not Zac's. He didn't know Zac. He didn't care about Zac. And no one cared about Sidney. Sidney knew that. Had been painfully reminded earlier that very day.

Sidney was on top of Zac on the chaise. They'd gotten there wordlessly. Zac dug his fangs against the skin of Sidney's throat and that was good. Like Jonas. Sidney groaned, grinding down.

"Good boy. Just like that." Zac didn't quite sound like Zac. His voice was rougher. Deeper. Something in Sidney balked against the praise. He wanted it to be Jonas's voice. Jonas's hands untucking the back of his shirt. Zac's long pointed nails dragged up Sidney's spine and Sidney shivered. "That's it. Feels good, doesn't it?" It did. Didn't it?

Not really.

Before Sidney could say no, Zac's tongue was in his mouth, hot and long. Sidney trembled, some last sliver of coherence in him desperate to regain control. This wasn't right. He didn't want it. They weren't even undressed, and his skin was so sensitive, hot, tingling that touching almost didn't feel good. Like he'd overindulged and nausea was about to set in.

Sidney pulled back. He rested his forehead against Jonas—no, Zac's, trying to catch his breath. A moment was all he needed. Just to come up for air. Zac chuckled.

"Alright?"

"No." Sidney's heart was still racing. Were all demons so hot? Jonas had been warm, always. Sidney liked the heat of him. Sleeping beside Jonas had thawed Sidney out. Softened the walls Sidney had built around his heart after all the times he'd tried and failed to fall in love. Walls that he desperately missed now that they were gone.

But he could rebuild them.

Zac stroked Sidney through Sidney's trousers. Sidney told himself he liked it, even though he didn't feel like he liked it. When Sidney leaned forward and bit down on the curve of Zac's neck, Zac growled in pleasure. It was a good sound, similar enough Jonas's growl that Sidney could pretend it was him. He was going to pretend it was him.

Sidney bit him again. Jonas growled again, and Sidney moaned, grinding down against him as the door to the conservatory opened. He didn't bother looking up. He didn't know any of the people at this stupid party. He'd never see them again, and they could watch if they wanted.

Sidney could feel Jonas turn his head, the rumble of a strange voice against Sidney's lips, Sidney's mouth still on his throat.

"Can we help you?"

"Sidney?" Jonas's voice cracked.

The real Jonas.

Sidney's Jonas.

The one beneath him wasn't real. Too sharp and too small. The heat of him stung, and Jonas had never hurt Sidney. Not like this. Jonas was here, and Sidney was desperate to put his thoughts in order. The more he strained to find clarity, the more things clouded, his head throbbing. Why had he done this? To get back at Jonas? To stop himself from feeling things? But now everything was magnified and muddled.

He didn't care if Jonas's feelings got hurt, did he? Jonas had broken Sidney's heart, goddammit.

But Sidney had gone too far. He had to say something. There were tears behind his eyes and his head was spinning. He felt sick. He wanted to go back to the cottage. To sleep. And then maybe later they could talk, and—

Zac's grip tightened on the back of Sidney's thigh, sending a searing, burning sensation up Sidney's leg. A hornet sting that Sidney tried to jerk away from. But Sidney's body wouldn't move.

"We're a bit busy at the moment." Zac sounded prim again. Sidney stayed still, frozen in place. His arms were shaking with the strain. He couldn't move off Zac's chest. "Is he yours or something?" Sidney tried to speak, even though the question wasn't directed at him. His tongue stuck behind his teeth. Sidney's stomach soured. He jerked his shoulders. No movement. "Is he yours?" Zac repeated.

Say 'yes.' Please say 'yes.'

Jonas didn't answer. Maybe he was gone. Zac's fang nicked the shell of Sidney's ear, as he sniffed Sidney's neck.

"I don't smell a mark."

Jonas hadn't marked Sidney? But Sidney had thought—

A sudden sharp pain made it impossible to put two thoughts together. Sidney's body numbed, a limb left in one position for too long, held in a roaring fire. Zac's mouth curled into a smile; his tongue flicked against the edge of Sidney's jaw.

"He doesn't want to see you." No! No, that wasn't true. "And you don't have a claim on him. So why don't you fuck off?"

SIDNEY'S MOAN ECHOED IN JONAS'S EARS SO LOUDLY, THAT JONAS couldn't think.

He didn't know the demon beneath Sidney. He was long-limbed and his horns and his nails had been filed to sharp points. When he turned his head to Jonas and smiled, he could see the demon's fangs. The creature winked as he ran his tongue across the fang tips.

"Sidney." It was all Jonas could say. What else was there? But Sidney wouldn't even look at him.

Jonas had gotten the whole thing wrong. Sidney hadn't come back for him. He'd just come back because he had nowhere else to go. And Jonas hadn't said the right things. He hadn't looked right or been right. He'd lied. And now—

The other demon spoke, and Jonas couldn't hear him. Sidney wouldn't even look at him. The demon squeezed Sidney's thigh and before Jonas could behead him, Sidney whimpered.

Jonas's whole body went rigid with hate. Was Sidney enjoying this? Was he pretending like Jonas wasn't even there? Mocking him?

You deserve it. You deserve this.

"Is he yours or something?" *Yes. No.* "I don't smell a mark."

Jonas hadn't marked him. Of course he hadn't. He didn't have any fucking magic left, and he'd lied and ruined everything over nothing. Jonas had been a fool. And Sidney couldn't even look at him. Wouldn't speak to him. They were finished.

"Why don't you fuck off?"

So Jonas did.

He was out the door and down the hall, and then, thank the Gods for Asterion's sobriety spell, Jonas dipped into the narrow servants' hall. He pushed past people carrying trays and he just still couldn't hear anything besides Sidney's whimper.

You pushed him though, didn't you? Straight into the arms of another man. Another demon, no less. He knows about the mark and doesn't care. You lied. You deserve this.

Did he though? Did anyone?

The cold night air rushed into his lungs as Jonas stormed outside and across the lawn toward the cottage. He was so furious he couldn't think straight. He needed to destroy something. Shatter some plates, punch a wall. Something. Anything. Jonas's fist tightened around the strap of Sidney's satchel and, for the first time since he'd stepped into the conservatory, he remembered he was carrying it.

Jonas stopped and stared down at the bag. The top of Sidney's notebook was still peeking out, and Jonas yanked it free.

He stared down at the notebook in his hands. All of Sidney's work. Months of studies and notes. Fuck him. Fuck that stupid man and his dissertation and all his questions. *You always did love having a student.* Gods. Jonas was so predictable. He should have known it would all end like this. It always did.

Jonas strode toward the edge of the cliff, his blunted claws leaving divots in the cover of the notebook. He hated humans.

He hated how callous they were. Self-serving, power-hungry, rushing in like a hurricane and destroying Jonas's life before rushing back out to sea again. It happened every time, didn't it? Past indicators of future results. Sidney didn't deserve to know about magic. He didn't deserve any of the things Jonas had told him. Fickle, stupid Sidney. Couldn't he see that Jonas loved him? Didn't he know?

As he reached the cliffs, Jonas could hear the steady rush of waves below, promising that they would take away the notebook. He'd never have to see it again. He'd never see Sidney again.

He hated Sidney for breaking his heart. And he hated himself for breaking Sidney's heart first.

Jonas's hands were shaking. The notebook was open, Sidney's hurried, slanted script, barely visible in the moonlight. Jonas had already destroyed so many good things today. What was one more. Beneath his fingertips, he could feel the indentations Sidney's pen had made on the page. He squinted down at it in the dark.

Peregrine the Traveler is made up of seven stars, two almost parallel lines, representing the demon and his staff.

Sidney had sketched the constellation on the page, Jonas's stars, in neat lines. When Jonas had left home, when Jonas had left the military, when Edmund had nearly killed him in the caves they'd built together, it was always Peregrine that Jonas had come back to. Maybe it was just a story, but Peregrine had been the sort of creature that Jonas had always wanted to be. A knowledge seeker. A good person. Not a creature of destruction.

And Jonas could no more destroy Sidney's notebook than he could hate Sidney. He loved Sidney, and he should have told him. And now it was too late.

Jonas retraced his steps in the dark. He found Sidney's bag, and shoved the notebook back inside it.

Then he walked back to his truck and got inside. He couldn't be in the cottage knowing Sidney was curled around another man fifty yards away. Especially not when it was Jonas who had pushed him there. So, Jonas drove to the end of the driveway of Elmmond House and hung Sidney's bag on the post box. Verne would find it and deliver it to him. And that was as close to good as Jonas could be.

~

SIDNEY HEARD THE DOOR TO THE CONSERVATORY OPEN AND CLOSE.

No. No. Fuck. No.

Sidney was crying, and he should have been moving. Shoulders shaking. Sobbing. Anything. But he wasn't even blinking. Zac's chin brushed against Sidney's nose, as he looked down at him.

"Oh," Zac cooed, the tip of his tongue darting out to lick a tear off Sidney's cheek. "Too bad. He seemed nice."

40

Jonas's chest felt empty. Heartbreak shouldn't have been so foreign to him. It was simple: Sidney loved him, and Jonas had betrayed him by lying about who he was. And Sidney had lied about loving Jonas; if he'd really been that quick to climb onto some other man's lap, he must have been lying.

Or he was lashing out. Hurt changed people, Jonas knew. After Edmund, Jonas had withered. He had become someone wholly different from who he was before, doing things he hated just to feel disgust. Locking himself away to revel in the loneliness. The thought of Sidney scrambling to feel something other than Jonas's betrayal shouldn't have been so repugnant to him. Shouldn't have made him so feral and furious. But that wasn't real disgust. It was jealousy. And grief.

Jonas had loved Sidney. And he'd been stupid not to act like it.

He gripped the steering wheel tight and tried to focus on the road and not the throbbing ache in his chest.

The sign for The Silver Platter was a slash of red in the sky. A motorcycle was stopped in the turn-in for the diner, its front tire half in the roadway. The back tire was flat. A driver stood beside the bike, waving for help.

Jonas pulled onto the side of the road, and took a deep breath, grateful, almost for another person's problem to occupy his time. He put on his flashers. He might still have that tire repair kit in the glove box.

No. He'd used it, or removed it, but he'd already stopped, and the motorcycle driver had taken off his helmet. Dom was recognizable by the long hair that spilled down from a loose topknot on his head.

"Are you alright?" Jonas asked, climbing out of his truck. Dom stared at him, brow furrowed, head cocked ever so slightly to the side, eyes widening slowly. It was sort of a strange expression, like Dom didn't recognize him. And then Dom took a step back.

The glow of the restaurant's sign reflected on Jonas's orange skin, as he raised a hand in greeting, and he stopped mid-step. He hadn't put on a glamour.

Jonas's mouth dropped open, but no explanation came out. *I've been lying to you for years. I'm not at all who I say I am.* That would be fine. The perfect end to his day.

"Jonas?" Dom asked.

"Yes," Jonas said, lowering his hand. He wavered by the hood of his truck. Don't scare him. "Are you alright?"

Silence settled in the air between them, tense for a long moment. Dom exhaled slowly, gathering up his hair in his hands. He looked at the bike, re-tying the bun at the crown of his head. When his hands dropped, he looked back at Jonas.

"I'm alright." Dom sighed. "You couldn't give me a lift, could you?"

"Of course," Jonas stammered. He hadn't thought... But then, needs must, he supposed. Something about the devil you knew, perhaps? Jonas rolled his eyes at himself. Dom took a step back and looked at his rear tire, with an exasperated grimace.

"Are you sure you don't mind? I don't live far. But it'll take a minute if I have to lug this thing." He pointed up at the sky, where clouds were beginning to roll in from the south. "Looks like rain."

"I'm happy to." Mostly it was a relief that Dom wasn't running away screaming; Jonas didn't think his ego could take it. He took a step forward, fully anticipating that in better light, closer, Dom would flinch. Or he'd do the other thing humans did: start probing. General questions about magic would morph into 'what can you do?' and that was a short jump away from 'what can you do for me?'

But Dom didn't say much, aside from what basic communication was needed for the two of them to maneuver the unwieldy motorcycle into the bed of Jonas's truck. Jonas was back behind the wheel and Dom was tugging on his seatbelt when he asked his first question.

"So you're a demon?" Succinct and to the point. Jonas nodded. Then realized Dom was still buckling his seatbelt and hadn't looked up.

"I am."

"I guess I should have figured, since you live right next to Elmmond House." Jonas adjusted his grip on the steering wheel.

"Where do you live?"

"Through two lights. The next street after, take a right." Jonas nodded and pulled off the shoulder.

They made it to the first cross street, pulling up slow. The signal flicked from yellow to red.

"Sidney said you don't go anymore. To the party at Elmmond House."

Sidney had been talking about him to Dom. Affection fluttered in Jonas's chest. He ignored it.

"I don't," Jonas said. "Do you?" Lots of the locals attended, but Dom shook his head.

"No. We were always— Hector always told me and Ares to steer clear." Jonas nodded. Hector had always seemed like a practical man. "What goes on there? I mean. Not like—" Dom glanced over at Jonas, and the light turned green. Jonas looked back at the road. "The people who go missing. What happens to them?"

"That depends." Jonas knew what Dom was talking about. He'd seen the missing signs that popped up in the post office every November. "When planets align the right way, portals open up at Elmmond House. Portals to other worlds, other dimensions. People go through. Some don't come back."

"They're trapped?"

"No." Jonas shook his head. "Not trapped. They could come back, they just don't. I don't know anything about growing up mundane, since I didn't, I mean," he gestured to his horns. "But I imagine a world full of magic and sorcerers and faeries has quite the appeal when you're not born into it."

Dom frowned as they pulled up to the second light. Jonas turned on the windshield wipers, as droplets splattered on the glass.

"Why do you live here?" Dom asked. Jonas chuckled. It was stupid how easy this conversation was. How it was the exact conversation he should have had with Sidney. It made the words bitter on his tongue.

"I don't have much magical ability anymore. Just enough for a glamour."

"I guess that makes sense." Did it? It used to, in Jonas's mind. But now he wasn't so sure. "They won't let you come back? Since you don't have magic?"

"No, I could." Maybe he should. Would that be any better? Or differently worse? "I like it here," he admitted. "It's quieter."

The light changed and he pulled forward. When they came to the next intersection, Jonas took the right.

Guillemot Street was mostly dark. A row of two-level clapboard houses sat back from the sidewalk behind a variety of different styles of fence. Jonas slowed the truck. Dom was still frowning, his gaze distant.

"Here?" Jonas asked. Dom startled.

"Sorry. Three down. 701. You can pull into the alley and I'll get the bike out."

701 was a little narrower than the other houses on the block, and seemed to have two front doors.

"Is it an apartment?" Jonas asked as he turned onto the gravel backstreet.

"A duplex. I rent out the top floor sometimes. Not at the moment."

Jonas glanced over at Dom, watching his mouth open and then close. He'd swallow his question and then try again. Jonas was so used to Sidney's rolling stream of questions, he'd forgotten that it wasn't so easy for everyone. By the time they parked at the shed around the back of the house, Dom had started and stopped himself at least three times.

Jonas genuinely felt bad for him. He'd recently experienced the frustrating inadequacy of words. Maybe Sidney prompting Jonas to tell the truth would have helped.

"What do you want to know?"

"My brother lived on the top floor." Dom gestured to the house. The dark windows. "He went to that party ten years ago and... We looked everywhere. Questioned everyone, and I can't believe he wouldn't come back if he could." And that was not at all what Jonas had been expecting. A totally different sort of heartbreak.

"Maybe he can't come back," Jonas offered. "Depending on what he sacrificed to get into the other realms, it's possible."

"How do I figure it out?" Dom's eyes were fiery, his tone fierce.

"I mean, ten years," Jonas managed as delicately as he could. "Most binding contracts don't last that long. It takes a lot of magic to hold things together. And, well—"

"What?" Dom demanded. Jonas hated being the bearer of bad news.

"Even if something kept him in another realm, he would have been able to contact you." Dom' s mouth drew into a thin line as he turned to look out the window.

"Right."

"I don't mean—" Jonas tried, but Dom cut him off.

"He wouldn't just leave." Dom's conviction was so firm, Jonas could have built a house on top of it. From the sound of things, Dom already had. "He wouldn't do that to me."

But people, Jonas had learned, were capable of all kinds of things Jonas never would have believed. Jonas thought that Sidney never would have ignored him when he walked into the conservatory. Sidney would have stormed out, maybe. Or told Jonas to get fucked, very possibly. But Sidney wasn't vindictive. Or Jonas hadn't thought that he was.

"People can surprise you." Jonas offered. Dom glared at him.

"I know my brother," he snapped. Did Jonas know Sidney?

He thought he had. And now that he was letting himself dwell on it, Sidney's behavior seemed even more strange. Something wasn't right.

Jonas stared at the back of Dom's house, as he let his thoughts congeal.

"Creatures can take advantage of humans. That happens, sometimes." Dom narrowed his eyes, as Jonas began to piece things together aloud. "There are contracts and then there are enchantments. People can get tricked into things. Eating, drinking..." Prolonged physical contact. That demon had been all over Sidney.

"How would we know? Is there any way we could find out?"

"I can ask," Jonas said, thinking only that he needed to get back to Elmmond House. To Sidney. He needed to talk to him. To make sure he was alright.

"Would you?"

"Of course," Jonas agreed, without thinking about it. "I'll go now."

41

Sidney's head ached. What little light was in the room seared his brain as he opened his eyes. Pain sent him wincing, and nothing congealed beyond a flickering glow, diffused by dust in the air.

He was lying on something cold, hard and a little gritty. When he tried to get a hand beneath him, his limbs barely moved. But they did move which was better than before.

Before. What had happened? It was all so fuzzy in his head. His mouth felt chalky. A whistle split the silence and made Sidney wince again. He tried to lean back but his shoulders pressed against something heavy and cold. A circle of pillar candles surrounded him, came into his field of vision as shadows shifted. Where the fuck was he? And what had he gotten himself into?

"Hello?" Speaking made his throat ache. His voice rasped, coated with the sugary residue from the petit fours. The ones in the conservatory. The ones Zac had offered from his plate. There'd been something wrong with them. Asterion had warned him.

And then there was Zac himself. He'd done something to

Sidney. The pain that had shot up Sidney's thigh and frozen him in place. Stopped him from speaking to Jonas. How could Sidney have been so stupid?

Panic tightened his chest. What was he going to do?

"Jonas?" But he wasn't there. Of course, he wasn't there. Why would he be, after what he'd seen Sidney doing?

Footsteps to his right brought Sidney's mental spiral up short. A door opened and a ball of brightness made him shrink back, as multiple lanterns came into the room.

"Hello? Who's there?"

"He's awake?" The voice was masculine and unfamiliar to Sidney. Not Jonas. His vision was still spotty, and everything except Sidney was cast into shadow. Concentrating made his temples throb.

The orbs moved around the outside of the room, and there was the scraping of wood on stone. Sidney could hear voices, but he couldn't focus on them. Couldn't hear them. He wanted to start screaming, but he wouldn't be loud enough to get the attention of anyone outside of whoever was already in the room, and they didn't seem particularly worried about him. Slowly, Sidney dragged his arm up to his forehead, to try and press away the ache. His fingers came away tacky with blood...

From when Zac knocked him unconscious. He remembered. Zac had pushed Sidney's frozen body onto the floor and cracked him on the head with a ceramic pot. Son of a bitch. He'd drugged Sidney? Magicked him? Was it the same thing?

A vague memory of Leo sitting him down years ago, when Sidney was barely more than a teenager, trying to lecture him about not leaving drinks unattended at bars, made Sidney shudder with an inappropriate wheeze of laughter. If Leo could see him now. If Leo would ever see him again.

And Jonas. Jonas. He'd wanted to call out to him. Jonas had come to find Sidney. Why? And Sidney had been on Zac's lap.

Sidney hadn't wanted to be. He had wanted to be. But he hadn't meant it.

"Mr. Sidney Quince." A man walked into the circle of candles, holding a lantern and a scroll in one hand. As he came closer, Sidney could make out that he was not particularly tall or wide. Average, mostly. His hair was dark and slicked back, and so was his outfit— black with shining lapels and sturdy looking boots. The only color at all was a startling shade of turquoise that lined his cape, and a bright yellow marigold tucked into his lapel.

Sidney looked up at him as the man crouched down in front of Sidney and set the lantern on the floor between them, shadows strange over the long angles of his face.

"A last-minute addition to the guest list by none other than the prince of Andurnei himself. Lucky lucky."

"Who are you?"

"That's not relevant at the moment," the man said. "The most pressing matter is you. And how cooperative you're interested in being."

"Fuck off," Sidney hissed. The man smiled, a line of teeth beneath a stupidly thin moustache, above a patchy goatee. His eyes were dark and narrow. Sidney hated him. But he did also look familiar. Had he seen him at the party? He would have remembered the outfit, surely.

"There's another Quince on our guest list." Leo. Shit.

"It's a common name," Sidney said. The man snorted.

"Not even sort of."

"Our father is a congressman."

"So Leo Quince is your brother?" Shit. Shit. Fuck. Sidney was not coherent enough for this.

"My father is a very important man. He—"

"I don't give a shit about your father," the man snapped. In any other circumstance, that would have been hilarious. "How do you know Asterion?" Sidney didn't respond. The man already had Leo as leverage. Why did he care how Sidney knew Asterion? Know was a strong word, anyway. Asterion—

Asterion was where Sidney had seen this man before. Beside Asterion in the photograph in Jonas's attic. The narrow nose, the pointed chin and high cheekbones. The dour expression.

"You're Edward Morrow," Sidney said. The man scowled.

"*Edmund* Morrow," Morrow said, one eyebrow arching. The sorcerer then. Sidney could tell he'd struck a nerve, getting the name wrong. Thanks to Mark, Sidney was now very adept at recognizing a pretentious ass when he encountered one.

"A sorcerer." Sidney tried the word in his still slow mouth. Morrow's scowl deepened. There was a chuckle from outside the circle of light, soft and feminine.

"How do you know Asterion?"

"I don't. He's a friend of a friend."

"Asterion doesn't have any friends," Morrow snarled.

"*You've* known him a long time," Sidney said, thinking of the photograph. Morrow sniffed.

"To know him is to loathe him." Then he paused. "Wait, how do you know that?" Sidney shrugged. Tried to shrug. His body was stiff, sensation still eking back into it. "Who told you that?" Sidney stayed quiet, and Morrow glared at him. Then he leaned back. "Zachariah!"

The Zac that stepped forward, to the edge of the circle, looked nothing short of bored. His spectacles were tucked in his pocket. He was checking his nails.

"Yes?"

"Tell me again about the demon who stumbled in on you and Mr. Quince in the conservatory." Oh shit.

"Big fellow." Zac's voice was deep and rough. Not the polished accent he'd had with Sidney in the hallway. Fucking bastard. "Grey horns. Flame-y sort of skin. Dark hair. Looked a right mess."

Morrow glared at Sidney.

"You know Rookwood?"

Sidney kept his mouth shut. With a growl of frustration, Morrow dropped onto his knees, moved the lantern to the side, and slid closer to Sidney across the stone. Sidney tried to move backward, but the large stone, whatever it was, was still behind him.

Morrow reached out and clamped his hand around Sidney's throat. He pushed Sidney's still throbbing head against the rock and glared down at him. Then he leaned forward, his nose almost touching the base of Sidney's throat, and inhaled. All at once, Morrow drew back, dropping Sidney to the floor.

"Well, fuck me!" Morrow laughed, a hard, joyless sound, as Sidney wheezed, trying to catch his breath. "What else did Jonas tell you about me?"

"Nothing," Sidney gasped. He tried again to get a hand under himself and finally succeeded. He straightened up, arms trembling, and his pocket watch dropped out of his pocket and clattered against the floor.

"He told you nothing?" Morrow demanded. "I don't believe it." Sidney swallowed down a groan of pain.

"He barely mentioned you at all."

Fury was an ugly look on Morrow. His brows crumpled as his mouth curled into a sneer. He snatched up Sidney's pocket watch and clambered ungracefully to his feet.

"That's mine!"

"Shut up!" Morrow barked. "Desdemona, bring the knife! We're doing this now."

42

Zachariah grabbed Sidney by the shoulders and dragged him up on top of the large stone. An altar. Dark stained glass windows stared down at him, colors desaturated, hued orange in the candle light. If he was in Bittergate Chapel then it *might* be possible to make it out of this alive.

The long-bladed knife in Morrow's hand begged to differ. Sidney tried to shift to the side, marble slick beneath his sweaty palms. His body still refused to move properly, and Sidney collapsed onto the stone.

"Stay away from me."

"We're going to make a deal," Morrow said.

"I'm not making any fucking deals with you."

"Need I remind you, your brother is still in Elmmond House."

"Leo's a hell of a lot smarter than I am."

"I doubt that's among his greater achievements." Morrow smirked. "In exchange, for your soul, I will assure your brother's continued safety. Throughout the weekend, my associates will guide your brother away from any threats toward his personhood, and protect him from himself, if need be."

"Why?" Sidney stalled. He needed to get more sensation back in his limbs before he could escape. Father Michaels's house wasn't far. Morrow arched an eyebrow at him.

"Why?"

"Yes, why. Why do you want my soul? You're not a demon or a fae. You're a human. What use do you have for it?"

"Gods, you're nosey. I bet Jonas loved that."

"Fuck you," Sidney snapped, enraged suddenly. Jonas had tried to warn him about sorcerers. About the whole thing. The cruelties people would commit for power.

And that slotted two disparate thoughts together in Sidney's head. Asterion told Sidney that Jonas's former research partner had been horrible to him. Jonas's behavior after their caving expedition. And his warning about sorcerers. Sidney's mouth dropped open.

"You're Jonas's research partner."

"Partner?" Morrow snorted. "That's one word for it."

"What did you do to him?" Sidney wanted to be screaming. Morrow laughed.

"Oh, he certainly has you wrapped around his claw, doesn't he?" Morrow winked. "I'd guess he enchanted you, but then, that never was his style. Loyal to a fault, our Jonas. Not to mention I took all his magic—"

"*You* took his magic?" Sidney felt like he'd been hit with another ceramic pot. "You— How?"

"Well," Morrow leered, so obviously pleased with himself. "To say I took it would be untrue. He gave it to me. All I had to do was ask. And he's so stupid, so guileless, that he actually did it." Sidney as hollow with rage. Morrow chuckled. "Don't look all put out. Jonas wanted me to be a part of his world even more than I did. He didn't even make me work for it. Unless you count all the stupid cuddling and caressing work." Morrow's tone turned simpering, as he batted his eyelashes. "*Oh Edmund, do you love me? I'll do anything for you, darling.*" Morrow snorted. "What an idiot!"

Sidney's fists clenched. For the first time in his life, Sidney didn't want to run. He didn't want to hide. Sidney wanted to fight. He understood what Asterion had meant now. He felt like he understood everything. And he hated this man more than he'd ever hated anyone else in his life.

But Sidney couldn't move to fight him And he wanted, desperately to hit him squarely in his stupid, smug smirk. So, he did the next best thing.

Sidney's spit hit Morrow square in the cheek, and slid down his face. Morrow's eyes widened and he flinched, shocked, fingers wiping at his face and coming away damp.

"You little shit!"

"Fuck you," Sidney hissed. "You're a monster."

"Oh, Quince," Morrow snarled. "You have no idea how monstrous I can be."

JONAS PULLED UP TO THE COTTAGE ALMOST EXACTLY TWO HOURS after he'd driven away, even more certain that something hadn't been right when he'd left. Maybe it was wishful thinking. He didn't think so, but Jonas wasn't going to storm back into Elmmond House and charge through the halls just yet. If Jonas's intuition was wrong, then he'd just embarrass them both.

Except, he didn't think he was wrong. He hadn't known Sidney long. But he did know him well. '*Seven years would be insufficient to make some people acquainted with each other, and seven days are more than enough for others.*' Sense and Sensibility had not been his favorite of Austen's works; Marianne Dashwood particularly at odds with his own sensibilities. But Dom's conviction about his brother had made Jonas really think about how well he knew Sidney.

Barely more than seven days, perhaps, and maybe Jonas hadn't been honest with Sidney about what he was. But they had connected over things deeper than that, in ways that mattered. And the Sidney in the conservatory wasn't the Sidney he knew.

When Jonas climbed out of his truck, he only had the beginnings of a plan. He wavered on the gravel drive: to go back to the cottage and strategize or go up to the house and enlist Verne or Delilah to help him check on Sidney. Verne wouldn't like being relegated to spymaster, but he would do it. Delilah would be willing, if she wasn't busy, because she loved to snoop.

He glanced at Elmmond House, all imposing shadow speckled with glittering lights, like pinpricks through a piece of black paper. And that was when he noticed two figures walking across the lawn toward him.

It was early for him to be getting stray visitors from the house. People didn't usually wander over, lost and confused, until a few days after the Ascension. The light from beside his own front door caught the cerulean shine of Asterion's hair. What was Asterion doing coming back over here? Had one of the servants told him how Jonas had rushed from the house?

Asterion's boots crunched on the gravel, and the man beside him came into the light. He was short, with square, muscular shoulders. It was the build of a boxer, someone meant to be quick and strong. When he looked up at Jonas, Jonas startled.

The man's eyes were the same as Sidney's, downturned at the corners and narrowed in scrutiny. The same mouth, full bottom lip, over a different, squarer jaw. Where Sidney had black straight hair, this man's hair was a nest of dark brown curls. For each thing about him that looked soft, there was a different feature that read hardness; the obviously broken bridge of his nose, the final piece of this handsome, if incongruent, puzzle.

"Is Sidney here?" Even his voice had a melodic note to it. Just like Sidney's.

"This is Sidney's brother Leo," Asterion sighed, giving Jonas a look that very clearly said: *You owe me for dealing with all of this.* "I told him Sidney was most likely to be found here, since you'd come up to the house to—"

"I just got back," Jonas said turned toward the cottage with all its darkened windows, before looking back at Leo and Asterion. "When I last saw him, he was in the conservatory with a…" He trailed off, glancing at Leo. Leo shook his head, abrupt and exasperated.

"With a what? A faerie? A vampire?"

"He's been well-briefed by his law firm," Asterion inserted. "Or *reasonably* well-briefed. Baron Sarceda is one of their clients." Sarceda was a member of the fae aristocracy with some of the most extensive landholdings Earthside and in Andurnei. It made sense that he'd have a human law firm on retainer.

"Sidney was with a demon in the conservatory," Jonas said. "I didn't recognize him. The demon," Jonas added for Asterion's benefit.

"Sidney's not in our room," Leo said. "Or in any of the common areas."

"Desdemona's the only demon with a room at the house this year," Asterion said. "So, if they were going to…" he trailed off, glancing at Jonas apologetically. "Not that they couldn't slip into any unlocked bedroom, I suppose."

"That's not like Sidney," Leo frowned. Jonas took a breath, fortified by the fact Sidney's brother saw it too. Leo's worry made Jonas's own feel justified.

"We can check the cottage." Jonas turned to the door. "And if he's not here, we'll go to Verne."

"I don't know why I didn't just go to Verne," Asterion muttered from behind Jonas, as Jonas turned on the light in the foyer, stepping around the spilled food that was still on the floor.

43

Morrow's contract was written in impossibly small script. Not that Sidney could read it, laid out on the altar like some kind of occult sacrifice. Morrow had explained the parts he'd thought relevant through gritted teeth, bound by some magical rite to explain certain elements of their agreement.

Sidney tuned him out, trying to come to terms with the easiest hard decision he'd ever made in his life. Could Leo keep himself safe if Sidney refused to sign away his soul? And was dying with his soul intact really that important to Sidney in the first place?

Because Morrow would kill Sidney, one way or the other. Zac had stepped into the circle with a long knife in his hand too. And this one wasn't fine bladed and sharply tipped. It looked more like a machete.

His body still wasn't responding much. Fighting wasn't going to get him anywhere. He was going to have to keep stalling, and he was running out of time.

"What about Jonas?" Sidney interrupted Morrow's reading. Morrow snorted.

"What about him?"

"What if I want to add him to the contract? Return his magic and I'll sign willingly." Morrow laughed. Threw his head back. It was a high pitched, irritating sound.

"Impossible. The clause itself is too complicated. And he'd need to be present. He's not likely to accept an invitation from me any time soon."

"He would from me," Sidney said. Morrow rolled his eyes.

"You think he still cares for you? After what he saw?" Morrow lifted his eyebrows, his gaze darting across Sidney to Zac. "Do you think he wants anything to do with you?"

Sidney's stomach clenched painfully. It was true. Sidney had misunderstood what had happened between Jonas and Asterion, and he hadn't listened to Jonas's attempts to explain. But he thought Jonas might listen to his? Jonas wouldn't forgive him after what he'd seen in the conservatory. Why should he, when Sidney hadn't been willing to grant him the same?

"If he ever loved you, he doesn't now. Take it from me, Jonas doesn't stomach betrayal well." Morrow chuckled, and rage bubbled up again in Sidney's chest.

His pain wasn't limited to his throbbing head or the tingling of his half-numb limbs anymore. He'd never felt so guilty. Been so ashamed. If he'd really wanted Jonas so badly, he should have been willing to fight for him before. Not now, when it was useless. When it was too late. Morrow had almost killed Jonas in his pursuit of power. And now if Sidney didn't sign away his soul, they would kill him and go after Leo too.

Zac leaned his elbows on the top of the altar, his breath hot and sickly, honey sweet in Sidney's nostrils. He smirked as he slid a claw down Sidney's temple, dragging blood into Sidney's hair.

"I can buy you another fifteen minutes or so, if you like. Finish what we started." Sidney nearly retched.

"Get away from me."

"Let's not test the proprietary mesmer, Mears," Morrow grumbled, shooing Zac away from Sidney with the flat of his blade. Zac rolled his eyes, but he stepped back. Morrow turned the knife, the point of the blade pressing into the base of Sidney's throat. "Quince, do you agree to the terms?"

Sidney's heart pounded in his chest. He tried to shift his shoulders, his arms. He could move, but he wouldn't go anywhere fast. And agreeing was the only way to keep Leo safe. Sidney was going to die, no matter what he said. He didn't have a choice.

"Yes."

"Good boy," Morrow smiled. Before Sidney could retort, Morrow brought his knife down. He flipped Sidney's hand over on the stone and punctured Sidney's thumb. Sidney winced but could barely feel the prick as blood welled up over the pad of his finger. Maybe it should have hurt more, but Sidney was numb with the agony of everything he'd lost. Jonas, first. Now his own soul.

Would he still be alive without it? Would he wither and die? Did it matter? Everything he'd wanted, thought he had, was gone. He'd saved Leo. That was going to have to be enough.

Morrow pressed Sidney's thumb to the signature line of the contract, and Sidney watched as the paper shimmered suddenly, a sheen of gold overlayed the text for the briefest of seconds, before disappearing from existence.

"Someone's coming," the woman said. She was still in the shadows, the outline of her horns visible in the moonlight through the stained glass.

"Who?" Zac demanded.

"Probably just some guests from the party looking for a good place to—"

"Quickly then," Morrow huffed. He pulled Sidney's pocket

watch out of his trouser pocket and pressed it to Sidney's hand. "Hold that."

"Why?" Sidney asked, mostly out of habit. And he'd thought signing away his soul would have hurt more.

"It's a binding agent," Morrow snorted. "Shall I explain the technical aspects of the spell as we go along? It only seems right, seeing as you're Jonas's little protege."

Morrow began to talk as he slid the knife down Sidney's arm, and there was the pain. Blood seeped into the fabric of Sidney's borrowed dress shirt. His grip tightened around the watch, as he swallowed down a groan of agony, and he tried to think about Jonas. Jonas had fixed this watch for him, an unnecessary kindness. He'd cared for Sidney; he'd shown it in his own way.

A twist of the blade at his wrist made Sidney whimper, his stomach souring. Jonas had pulled out his own magic for this horrible man. He'd given something and never tried to get it back. Morrow had taken advantage of the way Jonas was generous with his whole heart.

Maybe Sidney shouldn't have still loved Jonas. But he did, and there was no use denying it now.

When Morrow pressed the knife into Sidney's palm, Sidney screamed.

"Shut him up!" Zac shouted.

Which meant there was someone to hear him.

Sidney screamed again. Louder, and kept screaming, until Zac pressed the blade of his knife against Sidney's throat.

"Mr. Quince left with a Mr. Zachariah Mears, a little over an hour ago," Verne said, without looking up from the dish he was plating.

"Never heard of him," Jonas said.

"Neither have I," Asterion agreed, which was concerning, as Asterion knew everyone there was to know.

"Mr. Mears was an invitee of Ms. Desdemona Briarthorne," Verne added. Jonas and Asterion exchanged a glance. That didn't bode well.

"Where did they go?" Leo demanded. Verne shot him a look that would have curdled milk, and Jonas was impressed that Leo didn't flinch.

"My business," Verne said, primly, "is the inner workings of this property. What people do outside of the property is not my concern."

"They left the property?" Jonas asked.

"Yes, sir," Verne replied. "By way of the northern road."

Armed with flashlights, Jonas, Asterion and Leo set off. As they crossed the lawn, Jonas hazarded a glance at Asterion again.

"You really don't have to—"

"You've said that to me twice already," Asterion said, dryly. "If you tell me again, I'm going to hit you."

Had he already given Asterion the offer to stay behind? Jonas couldn't remember. He'd started to get nervous when they'd gone through the cottage and found it empty. Verne's revelation that Sidney had gone off the property chilled him to the bone.

The chapel was on the northern road, true. So were the caves. So was a vast expanse of forest. Technically, the caves were still on the property, just beneath it. But Jonas had no idea how far Verne's powers of observation reached. Or how deep magically imbued property boundaries sank.

The night was cold, and the half-moon spent a good portion of their trek behind fast-moving storm clouds. When they reached the graveyard, Jonas paused as the strange starlings began to chirrup, like they didn't know it was night.

"What is this place?" Leo asked, apparently unfazed. Perhaps a lack of self-preservation instinct ran in the Quince family.

"This is the edge of the property," Jonas said. "Right up to the graveyard. Everything here and up the hill belongs to the chapel."

"What denomination?" Leo asked, as he started up between the headstones.

It was a good question. One that, somehow, Jonas had never considered. All churches were sort of the same to him. He knew about them in vague swaths. Knew the stories. Appreciated how easily their blasphemes rolled off the tongue. He shrugged and glanced at Asterion.

"Don't look at me," Asterion chuckled. "How on earth would I know?"

"Is that a light?" Leo pointed toward the chapel. From their position down the hill, they hadn't been able to see inside. But now—

A scream of pain split the air and silenced the starlings. Leo took off running toward the church, and Jonas caught up with him in three strides.

He needed it to be Sidney. He desperately needed it *not* to be Sidney.

Jonas slammed his shoulder into the chapel door, expecting it to be locked. Instead, it burst open and he fell inside, just catching himself on a nearby pew.

The soft wash of gold from the candles in the center of the room illuminated a grisly scene. Sidney's long limbs were dangling across the altar. The demon from the conservatory, Zachariah Mears, held a blade to Sidney's throat. Morrow was standing beside Sidney, behind the altar like some unholy priest, his hands red with blood, casting. A silver-green light shimmered over Sidney.

Sidney's eyes were wide, his face pale, as he turned his head toward the door. Blood stained his shirt. Jonas could smell it in the air, the scent of it somehow unmistakable. Sidney's jaw dropped at the sight of Jonas, and the only thing Jonas could hear over the roaring of rage in his head, was Sidney's sharp inhale of breath.

Jonas had frozen, but Sidney's gasp sent him lurching forward. Leo was faster, bursting across the room with a shout.

Jonas's fingertips brushed the back of Leo's collar, reaching to stop him too late, as Leo careened across the room, scattering candles. He threw himself at Mears, knocking the demon and his knife to the stone floor.

Morrow jerked back in surprise, the thread of the spell lost and the green glow vanishing with it as he watched Leo lay fists into Mears. Jonas moved, seizing his opportunity to rescue Sidney a moment too late. Morrow had seen him out of the corner of his eye and laid his own bloody blade against Sidney's throat.

"No!" Jonas barely recognized his own voice. As though he'd cast a spell, everything stopped. Even the candlelight seemed to hold steady. Slowly, Morrow's mouth pulled into a smile.

"What a surprise. Jonas Rookwood. After all these years."

Leo scrambled back from an unconscious Mears, a slash across his forehead.

"Let him go," Jonas said.

"He has something of mine." Morrow held up the paper. Gestured down to Sidney. A contract. "I intend to take it." Jonas grit his teeth. Tension raced through his shoulders.

"Void it."

"This isn't your property, Jonas. You don't have any power over me here. Neither of you do," he sneered, his eyes darting to Asterion, who stood at Jonas's side. "Though, to my credit," Morrow's voice simpered. The meekness, the falseness of it, made Jonas's stomach clench in disgust. "I didn't know he was yours when they brought him to me. I would have killed him outright. So much kinder than a soul-drain. Or so they tell me."

Sidney's soul.

"I'll kill you," Jonas said. It was as much a threat as a practical solution. Morrow's death would void the contract. Return Sidney's soul back to his body.

In fact, when Jonas considered it like that, it made perfect sense. He took a step forward, remembering vaguely his military training, thinking of death in a practical sense. A tool he would gladly wield. Maybe his thoughts showed on his face. Asterion put a hand on Jonas's shoulder, as Morrow pressed the tip of the knife more firmly against Sidney's skin, his eyes narrowing in concern. Morrow was afraid. Good. He ought to be.

"You don't want to do that," Asterion murmured, his mouth as close to Jonas's ear as he could get. "He's Assembly Viceroy now. There'll be an inquest and a—"

"Anything Sidney agreed to was done under duress." Leo was on his feet, swiping the blood out of his eyes. Morrow smirked at Leo. "All contracts are—"

"Unfortunately, the contract is already signed. In blood," Morrow waved the contract in Leo's direction. Leo staggered forward, and both Jonas and Asterion winced.

"Leo—" Jonas warned. Leo held up his hand toward Jonas and moved around the altar. "Leo." No response. No survival instinct in either of the Quince brothers.

Leo reached toward Morrow for the contract. When Morrow held it out to him, Leo punched Morrow in the center of his face and broke his nose.

44

Sidney needed a moment to process the scene, and he barely had it.

The sound of bone breaking plunged the room into chaos. Leo reached forward and hauled Sidney off the altar, hoisting him up. Sidney groaned, pain making his head spin. He landed hard on Leo's shoulder, unable to see where they were going. His palm burned, flesh searing, clenched tight around his watch. Morrow howled, cradling his nose as blood gushed from between his hands. Leo jerked to a halt, and Sidney turned as best he could, looking over his shoulder. Zac was on his feet.

Jonas plowed into Zac like a freight train. Zac was knocked backward, and Jonas roared, huge and fearsome and gorgeous, his dark orange skin flushed crimson in anger. Relief and pain were a heady mixture. Sidney's vision was starting to double. Leo gave a low whistle, and then Asterion was there, his metallic embroidery gleaming as he ushered them out a side door and into the graveyard.

"Take him—" Leo started.

"Here! Come here! What's going on?" Father Michaels was

pulling on a coat, rifle in his hand. Asterion stepped forward and took the gun from him.

"Your cottage is still warded, no?" Asterion demanded. Father Michaels nodded. "Shelter them. I'll be back." Father Michaels apparently needed no further instruction, but Sidney couldn't leave Jonas behind.

"Leo, no! We can't—"

"Rookwood can take care of himself." Leo tightened his grip on Sidney's hips as Sidney began to squirm.

"No, Leo! Stop! I need to—" He reached back, accidentally clipping Leo's injured forehead. Leo grunted in pain, and Sidney jerked himself to the side, tumbling to the ground.

He smacked his shoulder against a gravestone and scrambled to his feet. Too fast. Oh, Christ. He was going to be sick. He had to get to Jonas. Sidney tried to get his bearings, and he slipped, crashing back to the ground, his vision blurring, fingers clenching around the watch, as he slid into unconsciousness again.

"Enough," Morrow said.

Jonas grabbed Mears' knife off the floor and turned toward him. Blood ran in thick rivulets down from Morrow's nostrils. Jonas couldn't stop himself from smirking.

"Void the contract."

"Fuck you," Morrow sneered. "I'm the Viceroy of the Assembly, and I'll do as I damn well please."

"The Assembly is going to have a hell of a time taking orders from a Viceroy with no head," Jonas retorted, spinning the knife in his hand. Morrow fell silent, glaring, teeth bared and bloody.

"Jonas," Asterion's voice was even. Jonas glanced over his

shoulder to see Asterion in the doorway with a shotgun. "It's treason."

The Sorcerer's Assembly was a major governing body across the magical realms. How Morrow had become one of their viceroys, Jonas didn't really want to know. Jonas took a deep breath. At best, murdering Morrow would put him in prison for the rest of his life. But it would keep him from Sidney.

"You have something I want. I have something you want," Morrow said slowly. Winced. "Let's trade."

"What do I have that you want?" And did it even matter? Was there anything he wouldn't give for Sidney's soul?

"I want Elmmond House. The property. All of it." Jonas frowned, confused, and Morrow rolled his eyes. "When you banished me, I lost access to the social event of the Ascension season," Morrow's tone was light, but Jonas could hear the rage in his voice and almost wanted to laugh.

"Power brokering. Really, Edmund?" Jonas chuckled at the look of twisted rage on Morrow's face. "You never fail to disappoint me."

"I don't have to offer you anything at all. I have what I need." Morrow waved the contract, and Jonas only sighed.

Elmmond House, the cottage, was the only place Jonas had left. But even that wouldn't feel like home without Sidney.

"Fine," Jonas said. He stepped forward and Morrow took a step back.

"And an apology." Before Jonas could open his mouth, a shotgun cocked behind him, and Jonas glanced back at Asterion.

The prince had the shotgun raised to his shoulder. A sporting stance, but it would still be effective.

"The contract, Morrow," Asterion prompted.

"You wouldn't," Morrow said, though he didn't sound sure.

He glanced at Jonas, and Jonas shrugged, a little unsure himself. Asterion had been acting strangely.

"Fine," Morrow sighed, as though they were all being unreasonable. Then he stepped forward and held the casting knife out to Jonas, still slick with Sidney's blood.

Jonas drew the point of the blade across his palm and then handed the knife back to Morrow, without giving in to the urge to stab him to death.

"I can't undo the binding until the full moon," Jonas said. It was a practical matter only. Morrow scowled as he sliced his own hand.

"That's what? Fifteen days?" He asked, not looking at Jonas. "That's fine. It'll give you time to move your things. Do me a favor and ask Verne if he'll stay on. He always had a good handle on the place." Jonas's rolled his eyes, as Morrow set the knife down. He held out his hand, and Morrow shook it.

Sidney's contract fizzled out of existence in a burst of blue and gold sparks, a lingering haze of grey smoke the only evidence it had ever existed at all. Morrow watched Jonas with a look of smug satisfaction, and Jonas was surprised to find he didn't care in the slightest. He turned on his heel and walked out of the church, Asterion following closely behind.

"You deserve an award for your restraint," Asterion said. Jonas snorted.

"So do you."

"Where are you going to go?"

"It doesn't matter." Jonas paused. Leo and Sidney were nowhere to be seen. His chest was throbbing, his palm stinging, and it was hard to breathe in the cold night air. Panic was pressing back in. "Where are they?"

"Michaels' house," Asterion said, and Jonas started up the hill.

45

When Jonas walked into Father Michaels' narrow living room, the only thing he could see was Sidney.

Sidney was breathing, but otherwise unconscious on the couch. Jonas stumbled for the first time since leaving the church. He staggered forward, and Leo slid to the side to make room for him. Leo was kneeling beside the couch, Jonas had nearly tripped over him, and now, Leo was granting Jonas a space Jonas didn't deserve, not after everything he'd done. But Jonas knelt beside him anyway.

There was so much blood on Sidney's shirt, across his arms and chest. Jonas should have looked at Leo, waited for permission, but Sidney's brother looked hollow. Haunted. So, Jonas shook the tremble out of his own hands and began to peel aside the damp fabric.

"It's just the arm." Father Michaels walked into the room. He was holding a rag stained red, wiping his hands with it. "And—"

"He wont let go of the watch," Leo interrupted, glaring at the time piece. Jonas looked to Asterion, the only one of them with any power, who hesitated behind Father Michaels in the doorway.

Before Jonas could ask Asterion for help, Sidney whimpered, his fist tightening around the silver casing. Jonas's heart lurched as he reached for Sidney's right hand, which was, indeed, clenched around his pocket watch. He slid his fingertips against Sidney's skin gingerly, feeling the places where the silver was melded to his flesh.

"How?" Leo asked. "How did it melt?"

"The heat from the spell getting cut off, I would guess."

"I can heal him," Asterion offered. "But I've never toyed with soul stuff. That's your area of expertise." Jonas felt sick. The last time he'd tugged at a soul was his own, unbinding his magic from it to give the magic to Edmund.

"Was Sidney's soul in the watch?" Leo asked. "Is it still in the watch?" An excellent question. "What do we do?" Another excellent question. If Jonas had more power he would have been able to press in and see. Again, he glanced at Asterion, the only source of magic in the room. Asterion bit his lip. He looked so much younger when he was unsure of things.

"The soul should have retracted when the spell was unfinished, and the line should have been sealed with the breaking of the contract." Jonas was confident of this much. He was the one who had built the spell with Morrow in the first place. He knew how it worked. "Asterion, can you check the watch?"

Asterion nodded and came around to Jonas's side. As he leaned over Sidney, his hip pressed against Jonas's shoulder, and Jonas tried to appreciate the contact. That Asterion was here with him again. He always seemed to turn up just when Jonas was about to fall apart, and Jonas loved him for it. Asterion pressed his fingertips against the front of the watch and closed his eyes.

"It feels hollow," he said after a moment. "Mechanical only. But you should check. You'll be able to get a better sense than I can. Here."

Before Jonas could protest, Asterion lifted Jonas's fingertips to the back of the watch and pushed. Fae magic blistered against his bones. Jonas breathed through the tingling pain and concentrated.

Sidney felt a certain way to Jonas. Brilliance and kindness and curiosity were all wrapped up in the essence of him. The sharpness of fresh dirt in springtime, and the caress of fingers down the center of Jonas's chest. There was a glimmer of it in the watch, and Jonas could feel his energy trip over Sidney's. Jonas swallowed and closed his eyes.

"Can I borrow—?"

"Yes," Asterion said. Exhaled. And in that soft rush of breath, just above Jonas's head, Jonas felt himself catch the tether of Asterion's power.

It was a rush and relief both at once. In some other world, in some previous life, it would have just been a thrill to feel the sparks in his veins again. A limb that he'd learned to live without, miraculously reattached.

He wielded Asterion's magic as carefully as he could, letting the heat of it wrap around the parts of the watch that felt like Sidney. Coaxing the soft curls of Sidney's essence off the cogs and springs of clockwork, and up into Sidney's hand. Jonas pushed whatever threads of his own magic that were left in his chest out of him, sealing Sidney's soul back into Sidney, leaving Jonas empty. It was the least he could do. He would have given more if he'd had anything left to give.

The loss of Sidney's energy, even though it had gone exactly, precisely where Jonas had pushed it, left Jonas's own soul aching. Below his chest, below his heart, something essential in Jonas was desperate to be with Sidney again. To wrap itself up in the warmth of Sidney's love and be whole.

But that wasn't Jonas's privilege anymore. He'd ruined it. The emptiness, like the void left by his absent magic, was just something he was going to have to get used to.

The cut on Sidney's arm closed and the connection with his soul severed at the same moment. Jonas fell back with the force of the sealing, his hand stinging, and even Asterion stumbled away, shaking out his arms and cursing.

The pocket watch tumbled to the couch cushion, revealing small lines of silver embedded in the creases of Sidney's palm.

MICHAELS APPEARED WITH CUPS OF TEA THAT WERE SUPPOSED TO be fortifying. Jonas's dissolved in his mouth like ash. After a quarter of an hour spent mostly in silence, Jonas, Asterion and Leo walked back to the cottage. Jonas carried Sidney, still unconscious, through the night.

A fine mist began to fall from the sky all around them, a great atmospheric curtain of cold fog that was perfectly suited to Jonas's mood. Sidney looked relaxed now, limp in Jonas's arms, as though he was in a deep sleep. Jonas watched Sidney's face more than where he walked, desperate to make sure there were no signs of pain. The weight of Sidney was almost comforting. And it was nice, Jonas told himself, to be able to hold Sidney one last time.

He began making a mental catalog of things he needed to do. Planning the way the rest of this hour, this day, the rest of his life was going to go, and what he would need to take with him from the cottage. And what he might be able to leave for Sidney.

Elmmond House was still lit up, more foreign to Jonas than it had ever been. People spilled out onto the back patio, flitted around behind curtains. Laughter and music echoed through the cold. The only music Jonas wanted to hear was whatever Sidney put on the radio when they were cooking together. No laughter sounded as sweet as Sidney's.

But these truly were the last moments they would ever have together. Sidney would wake up still angry with Jonas. More furious than before, it stood to reason, since it was Jonas who'd dragged Sidney into this mess. Almost lost him his soul. There wasn't a way to apologize for all of Jonas's compounded wrongs. He would do his best, of course. But then he would move on alone.

"Asterion." Asterion had been walking ahead of Jonas with Leo, but fell back at once, looking over at Jonas with a frown. "Can you call Karolina? Have her come up with Claire in the next couple of days and pack up the library?" Asterion's gold eyes were sharp in the dim light.

"I think she'd rather hear from you."

"I don't have time for one of her lectures. I need to go."

"Go where?" Leo demanded. He'd slowed his gait to be on Jonas's other side. Jonas doubted Leo would understand, but he wasn't about to lie to one of the Quince brothers. Not again.

"I need certain alchemical components to be able to unbind the property. It'll take me a few days to gather them up."

"What do you mean, unbind the property?" Leo asked. "Are you leaving?" Jonas tried to ignore the way the reality of the answer to that question slammed into him. Yes, he was leaving. Only he couldn't get his mouth to say it.

"It was the only way to get your brother's soul back from Morrow," Asterion explained. "Morrow wanted the property, and Jonas gave it to him, so that Sidney could keep his soul."

"I see," Leo frowned. The pause lingered, and Jonas tried to breathe in the silence, waiting for Leo's anger or derision. Instead, Leo asked, "where will you go?"

Gods. Did that really matter?

"I'll find my way, Mr. Quince."

"But Sidney—"

"He'll be fine," Jonas said. It was the only thing Jonas was sure of. Sidney would heal and go back to Holyworth. He would be brave and curious and successful and Jonas longed to be with him. To see Sidney happy.

But Sidney wouldn't want that. Jonas knew it. And he had to trust himself, otherwise he would stay. It was a selfish, horrible, self-indulgent urge to sit at Sidney's bedside and wait for him to wake up. To beg for Sidney to take him back.

He would spare them both the indignity of that. It was the least he could do.

46

Sidney woke to near silence. His head felt fuzzy and he lay still with his eyes closed, trying to guess by touch and sound and smell where he had ended up.

Not in the graveyard. The smell of loamy earth and cold stone was gone. Instead, he was surrounded by the warmth of spice and the soft tang of body that was familiar and comforting.

Jonas's bed was soft, and Sidney was relieved to find himself there. It meant that Jonas couldn't be far, which was good for a number of reasons. Primarily, it meant that Jonas had survived dealing with Edmund Morrow. That no-good, scheming, two-bit asshole. On Sidney's list of absolute fucking bastards, Edmund Morrow slotted in right above Sidney's own father, which was quite an accomplishment.

That Sidney was waking up in Jonas's bed also hopefully meant that things were mended between them. After learning about what Morrow had done, Jonas's lie about his identity seemed like little more than self-preservation. It would have been foolish for him to do anything less, and if Sidney knew anything about Jonas Rookwood, it was that Jonas was not a fool.

Sidney opened his eyes, half expecting to see Jonas sitting at his bedside. It was a cliché and dramatic, even Sidney could admit that to himself, but he was a little disappointed to wake up and discover he was alone.

He was in Jonas's bed though, still a good sign. Sidney pushed himself up with stiff arms, and glanced down at his bare skin. Someone had undressed him. And there were no injuries that he could see. Had the last twenty-four hours been a bizarre fever dream?

The light in the room was dim. Early morning or dusk? Or just another rainy Hindry day? Sidney glanced down at his palm, where lines of thin silver had been painted on his skin. Rubbing at them with his thumb did nothing. It was like they had been poured there, molten, and filled the natural creases. The last thing he could remember holding was his pocket watch, his hand clenched around it painfully tight.

It didn't hurt now, at least. The silver bent as he flexed his hand, moving as though it had always been a part of him. He would ask Jonas about it. Where was he?

"Finally! You're up!" Delilah materialized two feet away from him, cross-legged on the end of the bed. Sidney nearly had a heart attack.

"Christ, Delilah!"

"Karolina and Claire will be here soon, and someone has to open the door for them. Your brother's still asleep," she added.

"Where's Jonas?" Delilah's expression faltered, her mouth folding in a brief frown before she shook her head.

"He's gone."

"Gone?" Sidney shook his head. That didn't make sense. Obviously, he wasn't gone. He'd probably gone into town.

"He said not to expect him back for a week. Five days at least."

Five days? Sidney's head ached as he furrowed his brow, and

he pressed his silver-lined palm to his forehead and tried to take a breath. There could still be a perfectly reasonable explanation.

"Where?" Sidney demanded. It was the wrong tone to take. Delilah crossed her arms, levitating two inches off the mattress in irritation.

"Not that it's any of your business, but he's gone to Clement's Island to get some supplies."

"He didn't want to make sure I—" Sidney stopped himself, trying to swallow down the way Jonas's disregard stung. Delilah's eyes were wide, an extremely skeptical *Are you stupid?* written into the over-exaggerated arches of her brows. "I just meant—"

"Did you read the note?"

"What note?" Sidney asked. Delilah pointed to the nightstand.

On the corner, beside the lamp was the satchel that held Jonas's telescope. The telescope that had brought Sidney to Jonas in the first place. On top of it was a folded piece of paper, Sidney's name in Jonas's slanted handwriting.

Sidney's stomach turned over as he reached for the paper. He flipped it open with his thumb.

> *Sidney,*
>
> *Karolina and Claire will be here this morning to pack up some things for me, and to take you back to Bainbridge. I hope you are well and remain so. Please accept this telescope as a token of my deep regret. The telescope on the balcony is also yours to take with you back to Holyworth. I hope it will be useful to you. The lenses are in the study, along with my designs and measurements, should you desire to make more. I wish you the very best in all your future endeavours.*
>
> *— J. Rookwood*

"I wish you the very best in all your future endeavours?" Sidney stammered through the sentence aloud. Delilah snorted.

"Sounds like you got let go. Ever been fired before, Sidney?"

"No," Sidney shook his head. It was hard to breathe all of a sudden. It didn't make sense. He'd woken up into a nightmare. "Delilah, he rescued me."

"And it cost him everything," she snipped. Sidney dropped the note onto the bedspread and glared at her.

"What are you talking about?"

"He told me not to tell you."

"Oh, so now you're going to listen to him?" Delilah pursed her lips, straightening her arms as she considered him. "Delilah. Please."

"If I tell you, you have to do something for me. And you have to promise not to tell Jonas that I told you."

"I'm a bit leery of making deals at the moment."

"Oh, so you have learned something after all?"

"Delilah, please."

"I just want you to introduce me to your brother," she flattened her skirt over her knees as she said it, her eyes drifting downward as though she was embarrassed, and Jonas was right, Delilah was still very much nineteen. Sidney barely managed not to groan.

"Yes. Fine."

"He's very handsome."

"Delilah, you said Jonas rescuing me cost him everything. What does that mean? Why isn't he here?"

"He had to give Elmmond House and the cottage and the whole property to Edmund Morrow in exchange for your soul."

Sidney felt as though he'd jumped into the icy waters of Bittergate Bay all over again. His chest was tight, brain scrambling to process this new information.

"What?"

"He's going to Clement's Island for some of the supplies he needs to unbind the property. And unbind me from the property, because I'll be fucked if I'm living anywhere near Edmund Morrow. The day Jonas banished him was—"

"Why didn't he tell me?"

"You left, remember? You accused him of using you for magic, which is a little ironic come to think of it, and then you left."

Oh.

Oh, no.

Sidney couldn't let Jonas go off thinking that Sidney hated him. Sidney didn't hate him. Sidney understood Jonas better than he'd ever understood anyone in his life. More than that, Sidney loved him. And Jonas had given up the last things he had to keep Sidney safe.

"Where's Clement's Island?" Sidney asked as he got out of bed. His knees wobbled, his joints still stiff and achy.

"North of here," Delilah shrugged. "I don't know. You can't see it from the cliffs. There might be a map." She gestured toward the study, and Sidney took a step on his stupid, wobbly fawn legs. When he didn't collapse, he kept going.

The bedroom door opened, and Delilah disappeared with a small screech before Sidney could turn around. For the briefest of moments, he thought it would be Jonas, and he scowled when instead, in the doorway, stood Leo.

"Why are you out of bed? And who on earth are you talking to?" Sidney had already turned back and was halfway through the study door.

"Nevermind about that, I'll explain later. Can you give me a ride?"

47

Leo's pigheaded insistence on breakfast meant that they might have missed Jonas entirely. Sidney chugged his coffee, had taken half a bite of a day-old scone and then was out the door, pulling on his boots, as he hopped toward Elmmond, leaving Leo in his wake.

When they finally drove through town, Sidney bounced his knee impatiently, scanning every parking lot they passed for Jonas's truck.

He directed Leo to the marina in very few words, anxious, trying to sort out what to say. How to apologize. Lines he was rehearsing in his head flooded out his ear as they pulled into the marina. Jonas's truck was parked in the corner of the lot.

Sidney was out the door of the car before Leo had put it in park.

"Sidney, Christ! Slow down!" No time. He had to find Jonas. He couldn't let him leave without explaining what had happened. Without telling Jonas he was sorry.

Sidney jogged through the misty gravel lot and ducked under the slanted tin roof of the covered slip where Jonas's boat was. Had been.

The trawler wasn't there.

Jonas would be gone for five days. St. Clement's Island. Sidney had found a map in Jonas's study, not that he really knew how to read nautical maps or sail a boat. But he was willing to try.

He stalked up and down the wooden planks, eyes narrowed, half looking for Jonas, half assessing the other boats for one he might be able to steer. The only sound aside from his footsteps was the clanking of riggings against masts and the gentle slosh of water against hulls. He didn't know how to steal a boat. He didn't know what he was doing. And Jonas was nowhere to be found.

Sidney tried to take a deep breath, looking at his options for commandeering, as Leo appeared on the docks behind him.

"What are you doing?" Leo demanded.

"He's not here," Sidney said. Then he turned. "Do you know how to sail?"

"Yes, I've been taking boating lessons for the last fifteen years."

"Really?"

"No. How hard did that demon hit you?" Sidney groaned, throwing his head back.

"Leo, Jonas is gone."

"He'll come back."

"I need to—" Sidney insisted, trying to pull away as Leo grabbed him gently by the shoulders.

"Sidney. Breathe."

"Leo!"

"Sidney."

"He shouldn't be out there alone!" Untrue. Jonas was more than able to take care of himself. But Sidney needed to be with him.

"We're not stealing a boat so you can chase after your ex-boyfriend."

"He's not my ex-boyfriend."

"Well, he's not your boyfriend either," Leo said. A slap in the face would have been kinder. Sidney jerked out of Leo's grasp, furious. Primarily at himself. "Where are you going?" Leo called after him as Sidney stormed back into the parking lot.

"I'm going to charter a boat."

"With what money?" Sidney came up short. Fuck. He did have no money. Leo's footsteps crunched on the gravel behind him, and Sidney spun to face him again.

"Leo..." Sidney immediately resigned himself to begging. "Please, Leo—"

"Stop." Leo held a hand up toward Sidney in a wonderful imitation of their mother when she wanted them to quiet down. "Where were you going to go to charter a boat?"

"The harbormaster's office is just down the street." Leo took a deep breath and stared at him, unblinking. "Leo, I know I—"

"Stop," Leo said, far more gently this time. "You don't have to do all that. We'll see how much they cost."

The harbormaster's clerk looked up from a newspaper. The cigarette hanging from the corner of his mouth emitted a thin line of smoke. He'd shaved his moustache at least. Sidney might've believed he was twenty.

"You again?" The clerk chuckled. "Let me guess? More charts? And who's this? Your, ah..." The clerk trailed off, his mouth drooping open slightly at the sight of Leo's smirk. "Your lawyer?" The clerk straightened up, stubbed out the cigarette in an ashtray, and didn't bother looking back in Sidney's direction as Leo ruffled his damp curls with his fingertips. "Welcome to the harbormaster's office, sir."

"Thanks." Leo could make a single word into a flirtation and in other circumstances, Sidney would have gagged. As it was, he grinned, mentally jumping for joy. Thank God for handsome older brothers. "We're looking to charter a boat."

"Sure, I've got the names of some local charter companies," the clerk reached below the desk and produced a ledger, still not taking his eyes off Leo. "Most of 'em will be closed for the holiday, but—" Sidney grimaced, ready to argue. But Leo was leaning against the counter with one elbow, wearing a charming smile.

"We're only in town for the weekend, and we were hoping to take a little tour of the coast." The clerk glanced over at Sidney, disdain flooding back into his expression for the briefest of moments.

"Both of you? Cause I've got a boat, but it's small. More than two would be a tight fit."

"Hmm," Leo pondered. "That's a shame."

Oh, God. Sidney walked over to look at a map on the wall, and acknowledged to himself that he was not going to be able to stomach much more of this. And it was wasting time. Maybe Dom had a boat.

When he looked back over his shoulder, the clerk was leaning heavily toward Leo, and his voice had dropped, and Sidney was mere moments away from pretending he needed a cigarette so that he could go outside and wait for Leo to possibly seduce them into a boat ride with the world's most annoying clerk, when the door to the harbormaster's office swung open. Sidney thought he'd be grateful for any distraction, but when he turned, his stomach leapt into his throat, and he had to clutch the wall to keep himself upright.

Jonas looked tired. His shoulders sagged beneath the straining seams of his work shirt. There were rust-colored circles beneath his eyes and a thick layer of stubble on his jaw. He took two steps into the building before glancing around, his eyes widening as they landed on Sidney. Jonas flushed a deep cherry red across the top of his cheekbones, and he took a step back.

"Mr. Rookwood," the clerk prompted, entirely oblivious to the way Sidney's heart was thundering in his chest. "How can I help you?"

"Uh, yes." Jonas's eyes dropped from Sidney to a piece of paper clutched between his hands. His grip was so tight, he was going to tear it. Jonas stepped up to the desk, his gaze fixed downward. "This is a temporary cancellation form," he laid the paper on the counter and smoothed one hand across it. "I needed a permanent cancellation."

"Ah. Sorry about that." The clerk reached below the counter, and then bent down, ducking fully out of sight. Leo was staring at Sidney with wide eyes, and Jonas was determinedly looking at neither of them, shuffling with something in his pocket.

"Jonas?" Sidney managed. Jonas didn't turn. His shoulders stiffened and the clerk reemerged. Jonas put his hands on the counter.

"Here you go." He slid a single sheet of paper to Jonas, and Jonas took it with a nod.

"Thanks, Freddie."

"Mr. Groen isn't back until next week," Freddie the clerk said to Jonas's already retreating back.

"I'll come by and speak to him," Jonas replied. And then he was gone.

Jonas had barely looked at Sidney. He hadn't acknowledged him or spoken to him or... or anything. Was Jonas furious with him? He had every right to be, Sidney suddenly realized. It was Sidney who had cost him everything. It was Sidney who had been so unreasonable. It was Sidney who had left.

The reality of it hit Sidney all at once. Karolina and Claire were coming to pack up the library. Jonas had given up his home. Shame pressed in around Sidney's lungs and suddenly it was hard to breathe. He wanted Jonas back, but Jonas didn't want him.

"Oh no. He forgot his watch."

Sidney jerked around. His silver pocket watch was dangling from the chain in Freddie's tobacco stained fingers. Sidney lurched forward, hitting his ribs hard against the edge of the counter and snatched the watch out of the clerk's hands.

"Hey!"

"I'll take it to him," Sidney said in a breath, and then ran out the door.

48

Thankfully, Jonas was large enough that it was hard for him to disappear into the misty fog. Sidney made up the distance easily, watch clenched in his fist.

"Jonas!"

Jonas jerked to a halt the moment Sidney called out to him. He glanced over his shoulder and then turned slowly, frowning. Sidney stopped in front of him, limbs rubbery, ribs aching.

"I thought you'd gone," Sidney panted. Jonas's gaze dropped, like he couldn't bear to look at Sidney.

"I was. I am. Leaving."

"We went to the marina and your boat wasn't in the slip. I thought I'd missed you."

"The refueling dock is on the other side of the inlet," Jonas said, glancing off in the direction of the shipyard and gesturing northward. "It's not a far walk."

"Are you—Delilah said you're—" Damn. He wasn't supposed to say that Delilah had told him. Jonas grimaced, but he didn't speak. "I'm so sorry about the house."

Jonas barely nodded, and still didn't respond. Perhaps it hurt too much to talk about.

"Where are you going to go?" Sidney asked. Rubbing it in. Stupid. Jonas rolled his bottom lip between his teeth. Two fangs, small points, dug into his skin. He took a deep breath.

"I left your watch in the office," Jonas said. Sidney blinked.

"What?"

"And you can take whatever you like from the house. Wherever I end up, I imagine I'll be downsizing. I can—" he stopped himself, glancing out at the water. "Karolina can help you find whatever might be useful for your dissertation in the library. Take whatever you need." As though Sidney cared about his dissertation now. It had never meant less to him.

"I thought you said I could stay," Sidney tried, desperate. Jonas huffed, a small, unhappy sound.

"Well, Dom, the diner owner, has a room for rent. I don't know how the lights will be so close to town. Might be bright for stargazing, but uh…" Jonas pushed his dark hair back between his horns and looked up at the cloudy sky. "I don't really know anyone else in town. There might be a notice board in town hall —" What on earth was he talking about?

"I don't want to rent a room," Sidney began. Jonas sighed.

"I'm not a real estate agent, Sidney. I'm not—I—I have to go." Jonas turned away, and Sidney caught him by the elbow.

"Jonas, please!" For a moment, Sidney thought Jonas might throw him off. Jonas expression crumpled. Jonas pressed his palms to his eyes, almost covering his face, and Sidney's hand fell away. He had done this to Jonas. This was all Sidney's fault. Jonas took a deep breath and lowered his hands.

"I'm sorry, Sidney," Jonas said. "I want to do more. I do. But I think it'll kill me to be with you, to spend time with you and know…" he trailed off, eyes fixed on Sidney.

"To know what?" Sidney pressed.

"To know that it's my fault we're not together. I know you can't forgive me for what I did. I don't expect you to—"

"I do," Sidney said. His face felt flush all of a sudden, as he reached for Jonas, desperate to be understood. "Jonas, I forgive you. I'm sorry I didn't listen to you." Jonas kept his gaze on Sidney, giving him the courage to press on. "I should have waited to hear you out. I shouldn't have run off, and I'm so sorry you gave up your house for me. I never would have—"

"You forgive me?" Jonas stammered. Sidney smiled. Stupid. Not good at apologizing.

"Of course I do," Sidney said. It nearly came out as a shout. "I forgive you. I understand. I know why you didn't tell me about your glamour. Or the mark."

"That doesn't make it right," Jonas insisted. Maybe it didn't, but somehow Sidney couldn't see all the ways that it wasn't right and could only see the man in front of him. Not the demon, or the human he thought he was, but Jonas. The way he'd always been to Sidney.

"It doesn't matter. I understand it. I know not wanting to be used. I know how hard it is to try again after someone lets you down. I—"

Jonas kissed him. Jonas leveraged Sidney's grip on his arm to tug him close, and then they were really kissing. Jonas was solid and warm and gentle all at once, and Sidney felt more himself pressed against Jonas's chest. Real and whole.

They separated, for a moment, just enough to breathe, Sidney had thought. But when he leaned up again, Jonas pulled back.

"I *am* sorry."

"I know," Sidney nodded. "I'm sorry too." Good. Perfect. Sidney leaned in for another kiss, and Jonas took a step back.

"Maybe when I get settled somewhere we can work together again. I doubt you'll need much help, though. The library is full of really decent astronomical texts about the celestial skies and the—"

"Wait, what?" Sidney held up his hands. "What are you talking about? You're still leaving?"

"I don't have a house anymore," Jonas said, a sad smile tugging up the corner of his house. "Or I wont two weeks from now. And I don't have anything else you need. No magic. I can't — Or, I mean, I suppose I could try and deal for something with you, if you wanted. Is there something you," Jonas swallowed, his shoulders stiff. Sidney's heart nearly broke for him. "Is there something you want?"

"No," Sidney shook his head. "Jonas, no. I just want to be with you."

"But I don't have any—"

"I don't care," Sidney said. "I don't need anything from you. I don't ever need to see the stars again if it means we can be together."

It was true. It was all true. Jonas cleared his throat.

"I have something else I ought to tell you," Jonas said. Sidney nodded. It wouldn't matter. Nothing Jonas could tell him would change how Sidney felt. He knew that now. Jonas slid his fingers against Sidney's. "I love you."

Except for that.

It changed everything and nothing all at once. Sidney was elated. He was smiling and he wanted to cry and all the while, Jonas was carrying on, trying to explain himself:

"Ever since the caves, I just— and not because you saved my life. There's just something about you that I can't— I love you, Sidney. And I should have said it before."

Sidney threw himself into Jonas's arms and kissed him. And then Jonas lifted him off the ground. Sidney wrapped his legs around Jonas's hips. He could feel Jonas smile against his lips, and Sidney never wanted him to let go.

∽

IF HE'D HAD A HUNDRED YEARS TO GUESS WHAT THE REST OF HIS life was going to include, Jonas would have never dared to dream that he'd have Sidney in his arms again. Perfect, glorious Sidney.

Sidney, who was carding fingers through Jonas's hair as he kissed him. They stood in the middle of the sidewalk, Jonas unglamoured, Sidney trailing his fingers around the base of one of Jonas's horns, Sidney's mouth against his. He might have been dreaming. Maybe exhaustion was making him delirious.

Sidney paused to take a breath, and Jonas lifted him slightly higher.

"Sidney," Jonas murmured, "are you—"

"Don't bother asking me if I'm sure. The answer will always be yes." Jonas grinned, even as he snorted.

"I was going to ask how you're feeling? Are you alright?"

"Perfect." Jonas rolled his eyes and tugged Sidney's hand down out of his hair. His palm still had a line of silver in it, but otherwise looked fully healed. Jonas ran his thumb over it gently.

"It doesn't hurt?"

"No," Sidney said. When Sidney looked back up at Jonas, he smiled. "Thank you. For last night."

"I love you," Jonas said. It was like a gulp of fresh air after having held his breath for too long.

"I love you too." Sidney straightened up, sitting taller in Jonas's arms. Jonas tilted his head back to look up at him. And then to kiss him. Sidney curled into Jonas's body, and all of Jonas's fear and exhaustion ebbed away at his touch. They could do this. He could do this.

"I take it we don't need a boat?" Leo's accusatory tone sent them jerking apart. Jonas looked at Sidney with wide eyes, and Sidney cringed so exaggeratedly that Jonas had to bite back a laugh. Jonas lowered Sidney to the ground, and Sidney stepped in front of Jonas, looking sheepish.

"Oh. Uh, no. We don't need a boat."

"And were you going to come in and let me know that before or after little Freddie coaxed me into the coat closet?"

"Sorry," Sidney said. Leo huffed, looking between the two of them with his hands on his hips.

"If you two have made up, can we go get coffee? I'm exhausted."

49

The Silver Platter was as busy as usual when Leo, Jonas and Sidney walked in. They took seats at the counter, Sidney between Leo and Jonas.

Jonas was surprised to receive what felt like fewer stares than normal. Had people always assumed he was otherworldly? Did they not recognize him? Or perhaps they just didn't care. Hector, for one, seemed entirely unperturbed, and came over to take their orders without so much as a batted eyelash. But then again, the diner did seem to be short staffed; Hector and Dom were the only ones shuttling plates in and out of the kitchen. Maybe there was no time to be shocked by Jonas's appearance.

Sidney seemed more comfortable too, which Jonas was still puzzling out. Sidney leaned his shoulder against Jonas's arm while Leo engaged enthusiastically with Hector over the extensive variety of omelets on the menu.

"So what is going to happen with the house? It's Morrow's now? Just like that?"

"Magic and ownership are funny things." Jonas kept his voice low, not that it looked as though anyone was listening. "When I bought the property, I bound myself to it, mostly for the sake of security. Banishment rights, and that sort of thing. For someone else to take ownership I'll have to unbind it, which takes magic and reagents stronger than what I have. So, I'll need to go find them. Ideally soon, because I don't know how long finding them will take."

"Five days?" Sidney frowned. Jonas shrugged.

"Hopefully not."

"On Clement's Island?" Sidney asked. Jonas nodded.

"It's a caldera, with a few thin places where composite minerals from the other worlds sometimes slip through."

"That sounds complicated," Leo said. He was cradling his coffee in both hands, leaning around Sidney to look up at Jonas. "Are unbindings really that uncommon?"

"No," Jonas admitted. "But sourcing my own materials is cheaper than buying from an alchemist."

"There's got to be a half dozen alchemists at the Ascension party," Leo said, and Jonas almost had to chuckle at his confidence. "Surely one of them will cut you a deal on reagents."

"And that is how I know you've been spending too much time with Congressman Quince," Sidney interrupted, looking askance at his brother. Leo rolled his eyes and Sidney elbowed him, and Jonas suddenly missed Karolina very, very much.

Breakfast continued on like that, and would have thought he was in some kind of a beautiful dream, if Sidney's arm hadn't stayed pressed against Jonas's, anchoring him to reality. Sidney was here. He was alive and well. He had forgiven Jonas, and now they were sitting in the diner together. Jonas almost didn't believe it.

"When do you go back to Holyworth?" Leo asked Sidney as he scraped his plate clean. Sidney shrugged.

"I don't know. I need to speak to Karolina about it. And…" Sidney glanced over his shoulder at Jonas, trailing off with a small smile. Hope fluttered again in Jonas's chest. They could work something out. Perhaps Jonas could find a place closer to Holyworth.

"Why don't you come to Bainbridge?" Leo suggested to Jonas. Sidney flushed immediately.

"Don't listen to Leo. He likes to think everyone's problems are his to fix."

"What's wrong with Bainbridge?" Leo pressed. "It's a nice town."

"I did enjoy living there before," Jonas admitted. "It's close to Karolina. And the college." *And you.* He looked at Sidney, almost afraid to say the words. Sidney met Jonas's gaze and then grinned down at his cherry muffin. Jonas couldn't help but smile. It was a relief to be understood.

"Let's get the unbinding sorted out first," Sidney said, as he slid his hand onto Jonas's thigh beneath the counter. Jonas sipped his coffee, more pleased than a man who was about to be homeless had any right to be.

Dom came by with the check a little later, sweeping a handful of curls back out of his face, as Jonas reached for his wallet.

"Any luck?" Dom asked. Jonas came up short, for a moment, and then realized what he meant.

He was supposed to have been looking into Dom's brother.

"Ah. Sorry. Not yet. Do you mind— I'll need some more information from you, I think."

"Whatever I can do," Dom said. It was information Jonas should have gotten the night before: Ares Silva, last seen October 31st, ten years ago exactly. "Like me," Dom said. "But bigger. Heavy-set with shorter hair." He glanced over his shoulder toward the register where Hector was finishing up with some other patrons, and lowered his voice. "Hector really doesn't like to talk about it, so if we could keep it between us."

"Give me a couple of days," Jonas said with a nod. "I'll ask around."

"Thank you." Dom was so sincere that Jonas felt guilty he hadn't started already. As though there hadn't been other pressing issues at hand.

"Dom," Sidney leaned forward. "Jonas tells me you have a room for rent."

"I do," Dom said, arching an eyebrow. "Are you in the market?"

When they got back into the truck, Sidney had a slip of paper with Dom's number on it.

"Just in case we decide to stay here a little longer," Sidney said. "We might need it."

"*We* might?" Jonas asked, as he pulled out onto the street. Living with Sidney was a thrilling prospect. It was a terrifying prospect. Jonas had been planning on staying on the boat until he could find something more permanent. Somewhere, he'd thought, on the other side of the known world, as far away from the memory of Sidney as he could physically get. But living together sounded infinitely nicer.

Sidney leaned against the window, his cheeks bright again.

"I won't leave until you're settled somewhere."

"I don't want you to leave at all," Jonas confessed. Sidney slid into the middle seat and kissed Jonas's cheek.

"What have you done to my brother?"

The door snapped shut behind Karolina and Sidney whipped around, nearly knocking himself off the arm of the chair where he'd perched with a stack of books.

"I don't have any idea what you mean," Sidney said, confident that denial was the best place to start.

"Yes, you do," Karolina accused, her chestnut ponytail swinging behind her head as she skirted several half-empty crates to cross the room. "He's got Claire, Asterion and Leo up in the study and I heard actual, genuine laughter up there!" Sidney smiled. He ought to finish up and go help them, he knew. He'd gotten caught up in a text about soul binding. The lines of silver in his palm itched slightly, like a scab healing over.

"I am sorry about all the trouble," Sidney offered. Karolina rolled her eyes, resting her hands atop the stack of books beside him.

"It's good for him," Karolina said. "And for you."

"Speaking of me," Sidney began, glancing down to memorize the page he was on before closing the book. "I don't think I want to go back to Holyworth until we get things sorted with the property. I don't want Jonas to have to deal with Morrow on his own." Karolina nodded approvingly.

"Claire and I have a guest room, you know. For after, I mean." Sidney shrugged, grinning.

"That's up to Jonas. I just don't want— It's my fault he's losing the cottage."

"He needed to lose the cottage, Sidney," Karolina said firmly. Sidney frowned at her.

"I don't think that's fair."

"What happened with Morrow before, it scared him." Karolina sighed. "I mean, it scared all of us. But Jonas was hiding here. Before he had projects and research and it all just sort of vanished. Like he didn't know what to do with himself without magic. It's a thing that can happen to creatures. Someone had to remind him about the world outside this wretched little cliff."

"I still think the cottage is nice," Sidney defended, ignoring the heat in his cheeks.

"You'll be able to find someplace nicer." Sidney had missed

the surety of Karolina's attitude. He took a breath, and tried to adopt some of that confidence for himself.

"I think I might take a research sabbatical," Sidney said. Karolina smiled.

"Good."

"There was something else. About the dissertation." Karolina nodded. Sidney took a breath.

One more plunge into unknown waters.

50

The sky was heavy with clouds, and the fog had lifted just enough to create a shroud over the water. Sidney leaned against Jonas in the wheelhouse, and Jonas tried not to be too obvious about how much he was enjoying Sidney's warmth. It was cold on the water, and the little heater on the navigation panel whirred away, as Jonas sipped his coffee.

"Alright," Sidney sighed, dropping his arm around Jonas's shoulders along the back of the chair. "What are we looking for exactly?" Jonas smiled.

"The thin space on Clement's Island leads to a demonic realm called the Abyssal Plane—"

"The Abyssal Plane? Where Peregrine the Traveler came from?"

"How do you know that?" Jonas asked, his hand lifting to his ribs, where Peregrine's constellation was inked into his skin. His favorite. Seeing Sidney's notes about those stars might have changed the course of both their lives forever. Still, Jonas had a hard time believing that Sidney would take any particular interest.

"You left me that book, *Parables of the Stars.*"

"Mostly as a joke. Those are ancient stories, rewritten for children."

"Nothing you've just said means they're unimportant." Sidney reached across, his hand resting on Jonas's above Jonas's ribs. Above his tattoo. Jonas swallowed down a sharp knot, rising in his throat. How had he almost let himself lose this man? "So," Sidney prompted gently. "A portal to the Abyssal Plane?" Jonas brushed Sidney's fingers with his thumb.

"It's one of the only places, outside of volcanic fumaroles, where you can acquire salichite. It's an alchemical sulfate that I'll need to bind Delilah to something new. And technically speaking—"

"Of course."

"—the Abyssal Plane is largely volcanic, so it's just a matter of luck and timing. If something has erupted recently there, it might push some salichite through. Otherwise, I'll have to buy it."

"At an alchemist's," Sidney said. "Which will be…"

"If they have any, it'll cost a fortune, which I don't want to spend because I might be moving soon." Sidney hummed, frowning as he nodded.

"I am sorry about that, by the way. Again."

"It's alright." And it was alright. Jonas would miss the cottage. But there was something about the prospect of change that was thrilling to him now. Jonas wrapped an arm around Sidney's waist and tugged him onto the seat, scooting himself halfway off the worn leather to make room. "It'll be good for me. A change of scenery." Sidney chuckled.

"That's what Karolina said."

When Sidney leaned against Jonas, something in Jonas's chest loosened, and he exhaled. He'd expected things between Sidney and himself to feel tense. Or even tenuous, but instead, just like when Sidney first arrived at the cottage, Sidney slotted into Jonas's life so easily; it was like this was an old habit of theirs. As though they were always traipsing off together, looking for something esoteric and largely unfindable. Maybe they could spend half their days researching, the other half exploring. It sounded wonderful and, more importantly, it felt like it could be real.

Jonas examined Sidney's face in profile. He watched the way Sidney's eyes flitted across the navigation console and then up and out over the miles of softly rolling waves. There was no coastline in any direction. Just the clouds threatening rain, and the grey rolling waves with leagues of darkness beneath.

They were close enough that Jonas could smell the soft, clean scent of Sidney's skin, and he kissed Sidney briefly, just below the corner of Sidney's jaw. Sidney smiled.

"What are you thinking?" Jonas asked quietly, because he couldn't begin to guess and because he'd never sat with Sidney in silence for so long before. Sidney cocked his head to the side, his gaze still out the window, exposing the tempting line of his neck, and the base of his throat and where the collar of his sweater draped open. He glanced over at Jonas, a smile curling up one corner of his mouth. Jonas chuckled and shook his head.

"I'm thinking, and maybe it's strange," Sidney mused. "But I was just thinking how nice this is. I'm excited, of course. But this feels easy, I suppose. Like it's where I ought to be."

Jonas let himself kiss Sidney's neck again. After that little speech, how could he do anything else? Sidney made a soft, pleased sound.

"I've never taken anyone with me before," Jonas confessed.

"Not even Asterion?"

"No," Jonas laughed. "If it's not an eighty-foot yacht in ninety degree weather, Asterion won't go near a boat."

"You've been going out alone all this time?" Jonas hummed

his confirmation and Sidney gave a disapproving huff before pressing a kiss to Jonas's temple. "Not anymore."

THE RAIN STARTED AS THEY ARRIVED AT THE NARROW DOCK THAT jutted out from the lowest edge of Clement's Island. To Sidney, it looked as though someone had scooped up the forest from behind Elmmond House and placed it on the water, cliffs rising up beyond the trees to the edge of the sky. Jonas tied off the boat, explaining that there were only a few inhabitants of the island, and he suspected that most of them would have come to the mainland for the Ascension.

"Pierre and Magda run the lighthouse," Jonas said, pointing up to where a tall lighthouse perched on the cliffside in the distance. "Magda's fae. Beautiful wings. But the last time I saw her she was pregnant, so I imagine they'll be traveling back through to have their baby."

"Who'll run the lighthouse in the meantime?" Sidney hoisted his rucksack onto his shoulder.

"Oh, Pierre's a sorcerer. He's got some kind of enchantment on it, I'm sure." Jonas offered Sidney a hand, and Sidney stepped up off the boat and onto the dock.

"We'll head toward the lighthouse first, and then down into the caldera. Hopefully we won't have to go far. Keep an eye out for any little outcroppings. Exposed rocks. Anything that looks out of place."

That was when the thunder started.

The narrow dirt path up from the water felt treacherous with the threat of rain. The overgrowth was dense in some places, run through recently with thin tire tracks, dirt and rocks split by a wagon or something like it.

The breeze picked up, the rumbling of the waves fading as

they moved higher. They were almost halfway up the hill when the rain began. Just a drizzle at first.

"Did you ever think about moving here?" Sidney asked.

"What, to the caldera?" Jonas asked, glancing back over his shoulder at Sidney. Sidney nodded. "I'm not sure I would have been able to stick it out. At least with Hindry close by, I wasn't alone when I was alone." He paused for a moment, his step faltering before he continued on. "I know that's nonsense—"

"No, I understand," Sidney said, thinking of how he'd hidden himself in among the twenty-three residents of Kilton House. "Alone doesn't feel the same when you can convince yourself it's a choice. When you have an option to escape it, even if it's only for a little while." Jonas nodded and pushed his windswept hair back between his horns, turning toward the bay, frowning at the oncoming storm. Sidney took two steps to come alongside him, slipping slightly as a cluster of pebbles gave way under the toe of his boot. Jonas reached down and caught him by the wrist.

"You shouldn't have been doing this by yourself," Sidney grumbled as he braced himself against Jonas's arms. Jonas chuckled.

"It's not that steep. You just don't have the right shoes for it."

"These are the only shoes I have."

"We'll have to buy you new ones," Jonas said. Sidney rolled his eyes, despite his grin.

"I suppose I'll need them, if we're going to be making a habit of these sort of trips."

"You don't have to come with me," Jonas said quickly. Sidney shook his head.

"I like it," Sidney said. Jonas arched an eyebrow and Sidney elbowed him. "I do. But you have to remember, my practical research has primarily been walking down to the beach and kissing merfolk." Jonas snorted.

"You do have a unique method for gathering evidence," Jonas said. Sidney winked at him, and then grinned as the cherry red flush returned to Jonas's cheeks.

"You'll have to teach me better ones."

"Stop kissing strange creatures."

"I think you've said that to me before."

"And I'm fairly certain you didn't listen." Jonas arched an eyebrow and Sidney laughed and kissed him. Jonas's grip on Sidney tightened just so, and Sidney pulled him closer. 'Alone' was a distant thing, fading away with every passing minute, and Sidney was amazed and relieved to feel it go.

BY THE TIME THEY REACHED THE LIGHTHOUSE, THE SKY HAD opened up. More than once, Jonas was afraid he was about to lose Sidney to a jutting root or a particularly slick patch of wet leaves. Good hiking boots marched their way right to the top of Jonas's shopping list as he grabbed Sidney's hand again, and pulled him up the washed out path.

"Do you think we can get in?" Sidney shouted to be heard over the rain, his head tilted up to look at the towering stone building.

"We can try." The odds were bad, but Jonas wasn't about to let Sidney get any more soaked than he already was, and attempting to go back to the boat was the surest way for one of them to break a leg. Jonas wasn't inclined to let Sidney sustain any further injuries, so they made their way carefully, tripping in the mud, through the short white gate, and up to the front door of the lighthouse.

They crowded together beneath the narrow overhang above the door. Jonas wiped drips off the tips of his horns as Sidney glanced around and then rang the bell. There was, predictably, no response.

"Think we can wait it out here?" Jonas stuck one hand back out into the rain and Sidney rolled his eyes.

"Just stand on the doormat for the next what? Six, eight hours?"

"It won't be that bad."

"I want to move somewhere with fewer rainstorms," Sidney sighed, resting his shoulder against the door. Jonas smirked.

"Fine with me." Sidney smiled and closed his eyes, dragging a wet hand across his forehead, pushing his hair back from his face. "Where would you like to go?" Jonas asked. Sidney sighed and opened his eyes, mouth slanted in an appealing smirk.

"Where would *you* like to go?"

Jonas thought about it for the first time in his life. It had taken years for the cottage to become his home. It had felt like a cage first, but that had only been fear and loneliness, twining themselves together, stronger than any wall. Because of Morrow's interference, home would have to shift again. Again. But with Sidney beside him, that seemed like a much more manageable thing.

"Maybe the desert. Clear night skies, at least."

"True. I like being near the water though. I'd miss the boat."

"I thought you weren't a fan of swimming."

"I'm not sure I am," Sidney laughed. "But being in the boat isn't the same as swimming."

"True," Jonas agreed, unreasonably pleased by this simple admission. He was rather partial to the boat himself.

"I don't mind the cold either." Sidney stepped closer to Jonas, and Jonas smirked.

"I've learned that about you," Jonas said. "Trying to freeze to death is a forte of yours."

"I don't have to worry about it anymore."

"No? Why's that?"

"You'll keep me warm," Sidney said, before tugging Jonas down into a kiss. Jonas would keep Sidney warm, that was true. And safe and fed. And anything else that Sidney could ever want or need.

Sidney slid his fingers into the back of Jonas's hair. He was pressed against Jonas from knees to chest, and there was something incredible and miraculous about the feeling of Sidney against him. Sidney's warmth and energy made Jonas forget all about the cold, and about how they were stuck in the rain and how their quest for the salichite would be delayed another few hours.

Truthfully, the storm could have ceased, the sun arrived, and Jonas would have been none the wiser. Every moment with Sidney was perfect weather, blue skies and a soft breeze. And he wouldn't give it up for anything in the world. Maybe he would just buy the salichite after all.

Sidney lowered himself slowly, glancing down into the space between their bodies, his cheeks beautifully flushed. Then his brow furrowed and he lifted a hand, pushing Jonas back a step, into the rain.

"What—"

"The mat." Sidney crouched down and yanked up the doormat to reveal a silver key laying on the stoop.

51

The lighthouse was dim, but homey. Dustcloths draped over the large pieces of furniture, their owners very clearly planning to be gone for some time. Jonas took a deep breath, the tang of the bay mingling in the air with the scent of rain and the warmth of Sidney's skin. There was a soft thud as Sidney put his bag down and toed off his shoes. Jonas did the same, bending down to untie his laces. They stripped off their soaked outerwear in comfortable silence. Jonas hung Sidney's coat on the hook by the door, and Sidney nudged Jonas's boots under the shoe rack.

"You're sure they won't mind?"

"I've known Magda for a long time. She's a distant cousin of Asterion's. We grew up... 'together' would be a strong word, but close enough. And, like I said, it looks like they've closed shop for the time being." Jonas leaned back to look at the lintel above the door where several runes were glowing brightly in the wood. He frowned, narrowing his eyes as he read the protection incantation. Then he grabbed up his bag. Sidney had wandered over to one of the windows on the far wall.

"This would be a great vantage for stargazing."

"Come here a moment," Jonas said. Sidney padded back over in his socks, as Jonas produced his folded workman's knife from the inside of his pack.

"What are those?" Sidney pointed up to the glowing runes, his eyebrows arching apprehensively.

"It's a warding spell, to keep out unwanted guests." Jonas sliced the tip of his thumb and pressed it to the edge of the last rune in the series. The light shimmered. Jonas pursed his lips.

"Do I need to do that too?" Sidney asked. The rune light stayed firmly blue.

"I think so. But since you haven't been marked, it might not work. We may have to leave. Try our luck on the path back to the boat."

Sidney exhaled and took the knife out of Jonas's hand before Jonas could protest, or suggest that they just try to get back to the boat. But then Sidney's blood was in the air and Jonas could smell it as clearly as though he was holding his thumb directly beneath Jonas's nose. Which was odd. It had been like that in the chapel too, but there had been so much more blood there, he'd written it off.

Sidney pressed his thumb alongside Jonas's on the final rune. The blue light shimmered and shifted, fading slowly. Sidney glanced at Jonas, and Jonas shrugged.

"There's usually some sort of sign, or a—" Beneath their thumbs the final rune glowed a deep, emerald green, pulsing twice, before falling dark alongside the others.

Jonas looked at the runes as he lowered his hand. He could feel Sidney staring at him, and knew they were thinking the same thing.

"So, I am marked?" Sidney asked. Jonas bit down gently on his bottom lip.

"I suppose." He looked at Sidney, a thousand thoughts and worries crowding in his head. Maybe it hadn't been him. Maybe it had been Morrow's demon friend, Mears, or maybe when Jonas had touched Sidney's soul in the watch.

"I don't feel—" Sidney paused and reconsidered, cocking his head to the side. "I don't think I'm any more or less drawn to you than I was before. I mean, I always have been, I suppose."

"I'm sorry." Jonas apologized. Would keep apologizing.

"No," Sidney shook his head. "Please don't be. I don't feel any different. I want to be here. And if I didn't want to be, I wouldn't be. I think I've proven that."

That was true. And compelling. Jonas frowned as he considered this for the first time.

"Marking without a contract has always worked a little differently."

"What about for a couple in love? A wedded couple. I mean, we're certainly not the first," Sidney said. Jonas nodded. How had he never considered this? He knew of several magical and human pairings, his own sister among them. He was so quick to assume there was always going to be a power imbalance, but what if there wasn't? What if it could be counteracted by intention. Or by love.

"I don't know," Jonas said. Sidney hummed, stepping closer to Jonas, his hand resting on Jonas's hip, as he looked up at Jonas through his lashes. Jonas could feel himself warm toes to horns, chasing away the lingering chill from the rain. He wrapped an arm around the small of Sidney's back, and Sidney smiled.

"Maybe we ought to find out."

THE GUEST ROOM ON THE SECOND FLOOR FACED THE WATER. A small balcony jutted over the edge of the cliffs; a wide view of the bay spread out in front of them. Or spread out in front of Sidney. Jonas still had his eyes closed, chest rising and falling slowly in sleep. Their clothes were scattered about, drying wherever they'd landed, and Sidney sighed, deeply content to be wrapped in Jonas's arms.

Their line of scientific inquiry had quickly been forgotten, as pleasure had mounted in the narrow double bed. Wherever they ended up, Jonas's large, soft mattress would have to be made room for. As it was, Sidney was half stretched out on Jonas's chest as he looked out at the clear purple sky. The sun was sinking into the distant bay, sending streaks of pink and orange across the water.

Sidney had loved the cosmos for years because they felt infinite. To a boy trapped in a life with little control over his own future, they'd captured his imagination, and he had been convinced that there was nothing so vast and incredible that he would ever be able to truly grasp. His world had seemed so horribly knowable against the ever-changing stars.

But there was more wonder to be had on earth than he'd ever allowed himself to imagine. In magic, certainly. In adjacent realms and portals and demons and fae and all kinds of creatures he hadn't encountered yet. But more than that, he understood that there was an infinite space inside himself. That he could do things he hadn't thought possible before, and it had all started with letting himself do one thing.

The first time he'd kissed Jonas had been foolish and brave. But he wondered now if he'd had some inkling even then, of what it might unlock in him if he could just do it. That Jonas was special, different from Sidney but so much alike. They understood each other from their first conversation, and Sidney knew something deep within him had been recognized. By himself and by Jonas. And there was true magic in that.

Jonas kissed Sidney's collarbone softly, and Sidney ran his fingertips down Jonas's ribs, tracing the lines of ink on Jonas's skin.

"We fell asleep," Jonas murmured. Sidney yawned, nodded. "When did you wake up?"

"Ten minutes ago." Sidney yawned again. "Do we need to get back out there? The weather's cleared up."

"I can't do the unbinding until the full moon. And I think perhaps I'll just call around to some alchemists I know. Can't risk you getting drenched again." Sidney rolled his eyes, but the gesture made him smile all the same.

"In that case, can we stay here tonight?" Sidney asked.

"I don't see why not," Jonas said. "Although, are you sure you don't want to try and get back for the Ascension party? There are bound to be some realm-based professors there who would be good to talk to about your dissertation." Sidney stared out at the evening sky, and took a deep breath.

"I wanted to talk to you about that. My dissertation."

"Oh?"

"I was thinking. I mean, I was wondering if you'd consider working with me." Sidney glanced up at Jonas, appreciating the way confusion made his brow crease in the center. "On researching the celestial skies. Determining what kind of an impact they have across the realms. Karolina thinks it's a good line of inquiry. She said you had connections at some of the universities, and we'd be a good team to—Not that— I know your research partners in the past, haven't been..." Sidney trailed off, looking down at Jonas's arm as his cheeks flushed. Come on, Quince. Come on. "Maybe he put you off the idea, which I do understand, but—"

"But you're not him." Jonas said softly.

"No." Sidney said. "Jonas, I would never—" Jonas slid his fingertips over Sidney's skin.

"I know," Jonas said. He was quiet for a long moment, and then kissed Sidney's chest, over his pounding heart. "As your research partner, it would be silly of me not to remind you that eventually we will have to try to get someone to peer review our work." Sidney beamed. He leaned in and kissed Jonas, trying to imbue it with a thousand meanings. *Thank you. I love you. I can't wait.*

"We have plenty of time to network," Sidney said, as he pulled away. "And also, I hate networking, so Karolina suggested I give my information to Asterion, who can pass it on to a couple of the academic types who'll be at the party."

"Did he say he'd do it?"

"He did, actually. Although that might've only been because Leo was in the room." Jonas laughed beautifully.

"Good luck to Leo."

"Oh, Leo can hold his own, believe me."

"I can't wait to see where the dust settles there."

"Disgusting." Sidney nuzzled his head down into Jonas's shoulder. "I can't think about it any further than that."

"I have something else you can think about," Jonas murmured. He wrapped his arms around Sidney's waist, dragging his hands across the small of Sidney's back. Sidney sighed arching into the touch, his mind immediately occupied by the compelling evidence that Jonas was presenting.

"I wish I had a telescope," Sidney said, half an hour later as he lay, once again, in Jonas's arms. The stars were twinkling in the deep purple sky, winking in at him from the balcony window. Maybe it was tedious, but Sidney couldn't help himself. It was the only thing he was missing. "I'd love to see the stars from all the way up here."

"Good thing I brought one."

"What?" Sidney demanded. Jonas eyes were still closed. Sidney poked him and Jonas grunted. "What?" Jonas batted his hand away. "You have a telescope?"

"I have your telescope," Jonas yawned.

"Were you planning this?"

"Was I planning for us to get trapped in a lighthouse by a rainstorm?" Jonas snorted. "I saw it on the bedside table, and I picked it up and put it in my bag. Just in case."

"In case we got stuck out here?"

"Did you know you can look at things besides the stars with a telescope? Like if you get lost on top of a caldera, and you need to find your way back to a boat?"

"No." Sidney shook his head, poking Jonas again. "That doesn't sound right." Jonas reached up and grabbed Sidney's wrist, flipping Sidney onto his back. Jonas straddled his thighs with a smirk. Then leaned down and kissed Sidney's throat. Then his chin and his jaw. Then his lips. When he spoke, Jonas's voice was soft.

"And maybe I thought it might be nice to have, in case we spent the night on the boat or in the woods. I have your notebook too. If you need it."

"Thank you," Sidney said. Jonas hummed, laying his head on Sidney's shoulder.

"You're welcome." Sidney took a deep breath, reveling in the joy of being fully understood. He smiled as he reached up, and ran his fingers through Jonas's hair, stroking lightly against the base of Jonas's horn. Jonas shivered and Sidney kissed his cheek.

"You'll stargaze with me tonight?" Sidney asked. Jonas nodded.

"I'd love to."

THE END

Thank you for reading *The Stars Over Bittergate Bay*.

The adventure continues in *The Prince and the Silver Platter*.

Coming Spring 2025

ACKNOWLEDGMENTS

This book, more than any other I've written, has been a labor of love. Deciding to publish meant a whole host of new fears and anxieties and I am forever grateful to everyone who helped me, and listened to me, and encouraged me along the way. Thank you all so much. And the following people, especially.

First, Scott. Editor, confidant, and dearest friend. No one has cried with me, laughed with me, or listened to me complain about this book as much as you have. Thank you for all of your time and love and support. You double-dog-dared me to do this, so here we are. I hope I've made you proud.

And Alex. A woman with more talent in her little finger than the ocean has water in its depths. My collaborator and my cheerleader. I wouldn't have even gotten to the beginning of this book, if you hadn't been with me for all the ones that came before it. Thank you for years of love and practice.

Alyssa, Emily, Christin, Nat and Kat. Thank you for taking time to go through this book. To talk to me and give me your thoughts. You are my heroes. I hope you've enjoyed the finished product.

My incredible cover artist, Abby Gavit. Your knowledge and your professionalism was invaluable and instrumental in getting here. Thank you for being so patient, generous and kind. Check out more of Abby's work at https://acgavit.com.

Marabella, thank you for the gorgeous pictures! You have such skill and were wonderful to work with. Check out more of her work at https://belladecephotography.mypixieset.com.

Finally, to my family. Mom and Pop, thank you for taking Liv. For giving me time to work, and asking me questions and being so positive and supportive. If you got this far, I hope you enjoyed it!

Mom and Dad. Thank you for never stopping me from reading any book I wanted. For always encouraging my writing and for teaching me to love stories with my whole heart. I love you.

Tristan, you've always been there to talk plots and action sequences and anything else I need. Thank you for always proposing something even wilder than what I've thought of. You're the best sibling in the whole world, bar none.

Finally, finally, Mitch and Liv. Liv, you're too little to read this, but you are by far the best thing I've ever made. I'm so proud of you every day. You are the light of my world. Thank you for being in it.

Mitch, I couldn't have done this without you. You stood next to me, and believed in me, and went above and beyond for me time and time again. You helped me make my dreams come true, and I don't know how I got so lucky. Thank you. I'm sorry Goblett didn't make it into this one.

And, finally finally finally, to you, the reader. Anyone who takes a chance on self-published or indie books is a champion. Thank you for reading. I hope you enjoyed, and that you'll come back for another one.

BIBLIOGRAPHY

Alcott, Louisa May. *Louisa May Alcott: Her Life, Letters, and Journals.* Edited by Ednah D. Cheney. Boston, MA: Little, Brown, and Company, 1898.

Austen, Jane. *Sense and Sensibility.* New York City, NY: Everyman's Library, 1992.

Shakespeare, William. *The Tempest.* From: *The Complete Pelican Shakespeare. 2nd Ed.* Edited by Stephen Orgel. London, England: Penguin Classics, 2002.